GUARDIAN

T.B. WIESE

Dev Editor: Lisa Wong

Copy Editor: Olivia Piper

Sensitivity reader: 小林 ナギ

Cover Design: Drea D Art (instagram)

Chapter art: Will Dwiggins (TikTok) & RDG (Facebook)

❀ Created with Vellum

*Because not every story has a happy ending -
and that's okay*

AUTHOR'S NOTE

Guardian does NOT have a happy ending. It also has a lot of loneliness, despair, depression, drug use, murder, death, and suicide. There is the death of a child & spouse (not on page), as well as arranged marriage to a minor (no sexual scenes with said minor), and mention of semi-infidelity where the partner knows what's going on.

There are explicit sex scenes, both male/male and male/female

1

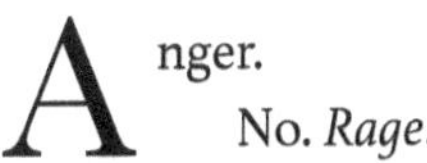

nger.

No. *Rage.*

I've never felt this before. Hate. Darkness boiling. Pressure pulling me apart. Crushing me, but at the same time, making me lighter. My magic boils and churns, shifting from its usual bright silver to an angry red—as deep and vibrant as blood.

Blood. Pain. Revenge.

Death.

They must die. With every strike, I sing. With every fallen foe, I shine brighter.

More.

Bodies all around. Still, I vibrate with rage.

More.

A soft gasp draws my blood-thirsty attention to rare green eyes framed by skin splattered with gore. Her mouth moves, but I don't hear the words, not really caring what laments she mutters. The only thing I care about is her death. But then her eyes flash with the light of her own magic.

A yokai?

Those green eyes smile, the pupils narrowing to cat-like slits. Feline ears twitch where they poke out of her wild, grey hair. I yearn to scream my fury at her, but I will settle for the taste of her blood. With her death, will this buzzing fade? Will this itching need to rend, to tear, to slash subside?

How dare she smile in the wake of my rage? Death is on display all around her, the villagers' bodies strewn where I struck them down, their dead, sightless eyes still holding the pain and terror of their final moments. Swift and silent, I strike, my magic burning a deeper red, no trace of the bright silver it once was. Her blood splatters, but still, she smiles. Her hemp dress billows around her as she drops to her knees, swaying as death comes to take her. But she pins me with her green stare, her eyes blazing. Her voice rasps, almost pulled away by the wind as she says, "Only truth will mend what ego has destroyed."

Truth? She wants truth? It's not enough. All this death, all this blood ... it's not nearly enough.

Power shoots from her body, arching her back with the explosion of it. I brace against the sting of it, but I give her a grin of my own, because she'll be dead before she can take another traitorous breath. I watch as her blood gushes from her neck, but her smile never falters as she falls, her open, sightless eyes now dull without the shine of her magic.

And then her power pushes and pulls at me, my own magic resisting as the village flips and swirls.

I'm falling.

I don't feel the impact of the ground—before I hit, agony tears through me.

Another sensation new to me. I've known pain. I've known sacrifice. But this ...

I'm blinded as the yokai's magic pulls me apart. My

power fights against it, forces clashing, warring for dominance. But the agony is too much.

Everything fades, and I tumble through nothingness.

Awareness snaps through me. A scream builds, and I'm startled at the primal sound that erupts from me. Sensitive skin scrapes against stone. Nearly deafening sound rushes in from everywhere, and I'm astounded when I realize it's just the wind.

I almost laugh, the cackle building ... my glee mixing with the sorrow and the pain. It's almost too much to hold inside.

Breathing heavily, I blink, finally focusing enough to realize I'm ... I'm on my ... back. In a ... a cave? As I take in the rough, grey stone overhead, I try to move, but my aching muscles refuse, and all I manage is the fetal position.

What is this? What happened? Where the fuck am I?

Weak light streaming in from the mouth of the cave does nothing to chase away the freezing temperature clawing at me. As I get used to the rush of sensations, I realize I'm lying on something ... my saya, my scabbard. The familiar black lacquered wood gleams dully. I'm in awe of its simplistic beauty. I reach out to stroke its smooth surface, but freeze, staring at my spread fingers. My cheeks hurt with the breadth of my grin as I wrap my hand around my saya.

The collar of the katana scrapes against the rocky ground, and I wince, my smile falling, my ears too sensitive for the harsh sound. And then I notice it ...

A flicker of rage reignites within me. There, on my left

forearm, are characters carved deep into the flesh of my skin. My name. With gentle fingers, I trace the characters, hissing at the pain of even that soft touch against the cuts. Still, I do it again, wanting to feel the pain, wanting to feel everything.

Picking up my saya, I hug it to my chest, curling into a tighter ball on my side. I grit my teeth against the freezing bite of the wind and the bone-deep ache in my muscles. Those haunting green eyes flash in my mind again as I recall her dying curse. *Only truth will mend what ego has destroyed.*

Fuck that yokai, for that must be what she was, disguising herself as human amongst the villagers.

A cold wind howls through the stone cavern, screaming down unseen tunnels. My teeth chatter, my scabbard clattering against the ground. But my thoughts boil with my rage as I think of that yokai.

Truth?

I look down at my palms and jump at the sound of my chuckle that quickly turns to a cough as the freezing air hits my lungs. I spread my fingers wide, the skin stained a faint red. Blood. I curl my hands into fists and grin.

My truth? I only wish there was more ... more flesh to slice, more screams to harvest, more blood to bathe in.

My trembles turn to violent shakes, forcing my grin into a grimace as my vulnerable skin scrapes against the stony ground. With a grunt, I force my quivering muscles to cooperate until I'm on my hands and knees, my scabbard under my left palm. Breathing hard from that simple movement, I clench my jaw, trying to slide a foot under me to stand. Sweat slicks down my arms despite the cold, and my muscles give out. Collapsing back onto my side, I hug my saya again.

The yokai's laughing eyes flash through my mind again.

Her weathered, cracked lips pulled back in a silent laugh, her grey hair swirling around her head. But mostly, I see those eyes, green and wicked.

Grinding my teeth until my jaw aches, I'm finally able to force the image of the yokai's cat-like green eyes from my mind, only to have them replaced by soft, brown ones filled with kindness and wonder. Eyes that I loved. Eyes that I witnessed fill with pain ... and then, the emptiness of death.

Father.

Sorrow mixes with my rage like the swirling snowflakes outside the cave, lifted and spun in a little cyclone by the unforgiving wind.

The truth?

I'm not sorry.

2

Pale light behind my eyelids sucks me up from the darkness of a bottomless void. As awareness seeps into my body, I realize … I can't feel anything. A gasp of alarm claws up my throat but is unable to pass my mouth. Pressing my tongue to the back of my lips, I realize they won't open. Frozen shut.

As are my eyes.

I can hear the hairs in my nose crunching as I inhale. And with that inhale, sensation flares through me. I scream behind my frozen lips. I think I'm on fire. I had no idea pain like this was possible. When I try to roll off my side onto my back, white dots of pain dance behind my closed eyelids as my skin sticks to the rock I passed out on last night. I manage to wiggle a finger, hearing the scrape of the ice crystals on my skin against the lacquer of my scabbard.

I stop moving, and the freezing air settles over me, numbing me once more.

I should be dead. Why am I not dead?

Every inhale stretches my skin against where the ice holds me to the ground, and I know if I force it, I'll flay myself. All I can do is wait and see if the sun warms the day enough to free me.

So, I wait. And I shiver. My flesh tugs with my uncontrollable shaking. There are no sounds of animals from deeper inside the cave or passing by outside. Even the wind is still. It's just me, my saya, and the cold.

The light behind my eyelids grows brighter and slightly warmer. I try to open them, but they remain stuck, still frozen together, so I relax as much as I can in my frozen state.

I wait.

And then it hits me. Like my flesh is melting off my bones. Like a swordsmith thrusting a blade into the furnace, and I'm that steel. My skin tingles and burns as feeling starts to come back to my numb limbs. A violent shiver wracks my body, and this time, when I scream, my lips tear apart, and the hoarse sound echoes around the cave. I lick my lips, trying to warm them, and I taste the copper of my blood.

Bit by agonizing bit, I shift, working small patches of skin free from the ground. Time has no meaning. There's just pain.

The back of my hand pulls away from the rock beneath me, leaving some of my flesh behind. The agony is so sharp, my eyes fly open, ripping a few lashes from my lids. Blinding white light. That's all I see. Tears streak down my cheeks, freezing before they get the chance to drip off my chin. After blinking a few times, I reorient myself, and the mouth of the cave comes into view just a few meters away. Beyond my shelter, there's an open patch of dirt, dried grass, and frost, and then ... trees. The thick forest takes up my view, the trunks of the great pines wide, their branches still and hanging low, heavy with ice. Weak sunlight casts long shadows, telling me I've spent almost all day trying to unstick myself from the floor of this cave—a cave and a forest I don't recognize.

My father and I traveled far and often, so for me not to know where I am means the yokai's magic tossed me far from home. I grin, still slowly working myself free. That's fine. I didn't want to stay in that village anyway. Not without my father.

With another couple of tugs, I free myself, rolling onto my back, breathing hard, my saya held to my chest. As I exhale, I watch the little white puffs of air float above my face, luxuriating in the warmth of my own breath. With a groan, I sit up, and after the cave stops spinning, I drag myself and my saya to the wall. Leaning back, I rest my head and catch my breath again.

I shiver, my back muscles aching, the tears in my skin leaking sludge-like blood, as if my insides are frozen as well. But at least my blood is warm.

The light of day is quickly turning orange as the sun drops towards a horizon I'm unable to see through the thick press of trees beyond this cave. Stretching my legs out, I flex my feet, getting used to the sensation. Muscle cords my lean thighs. There are fiery-red patches of frostbite bordered in burnt black skin but, overall, it's not as bad as it could have been. Even the sections of flesh I tore as I freed myself from the ground have already stopped bleeding.

I glance at my scabbard, rubbing my thumb over the guard. My heart races as I apply a little pressure to the collar, ready to release the blade within. It gives slightly, but I immediately slide my thumb away, stroking the shark skin wrapping of the hilt, keeping it sheathed. I whisper, surprised at the depth and raspiness of my voice, "This is quite the predicament we're in, but I'm glad we're together."

Gripping the comforting lacquered wood of my scabbard, I press the palm of my free hand to the stone behind me. I wobble like a toddler learning to walk as I inelegantly get to my feet, leaning heavily on the wall. The lacquer squeaks under my grip as I say to it, "Another freezing night approaches. I don't think I have time to find us any better shelter outside of this cave, so let's go deeper, yes?"

My right leg remains stiff, refusing to move properly, so I drag my foot as I shuffle into the darkness. I'm moving so slowly; my eyes have plenty of time to adjust as I continue farther into the cave. I'm forced to lean back as the downward slope of the tunnel intensifies. As I descend, my muscles loosen up, and after a few moments, I'm walking a bit steadier as the passage widens. I stick to the wall, my left hand sliding over smoother rock. A faint *drip drip drip* draws me closer.

And then the tunnel opens and I'm in a larger section of the cave. There must be a whole system of caverns down here. A large pool of water stretches before me, dim light filtering in from somewhere. I peer across it to the far wall and figure if I could walk over it, it would take me at least twenty strides or more to get to the other side. I'm sure the water is freezing, but I'm curious to know how deep it goes.

Drip, drip, drip, echoes from the far wall to the right where ice and snow must be melting from above, filtering down into this space. Holding tight to my saya so it doesn't drag on the ground, I push myself away from the wall.

Slowly, unsteadily, I make my way to the edge of the pool. I stop before my toes touch the ice crystals forming where the water meets the dry rock of the ground. I lean over to look, my breath puffing in white clouds before me. I wobble and reel back, stumbling a few steps. If I fall in, who knows if I'll be able to pull myself out? I move to kneel, biting my lip to keep from yelling in pain as my sore muscles protest. Still, I refuse to use my saya as a crutch. That's not what it's for.

Finally settling on my shins, I gently set the katana on the ground next to me. Then, pressing my palms to the frigid floor, I lean over the water. I stare wide-eyed, turning my head side-to-side. My reflection looks back at me, a man with black hair just long enough to brush my shoulders. Dark eyes rimmed with long lashes blink up at me. There are small age lines at the edges of my mouth and eyes, but no grey in my hair. I'm too old to be called a youth, but too young to be called old. Scrunching my nose, I peel my lips back, revealing straight, white teeth. I bring a hand to the smooth skin of my cheek. No stubble even after a full day in this cave. Holding my hands in front of me, I flex my fingers, feeling the strength there.

And then I see it again.

The letters carved into the skin of my forearm—surprisingly healed over into thick scar tissue. Quickly, I glance at my thighs, my stomach, my sides, my arms, my chest. Every inch of my skin is unblemished, healed from the frostbite ... healed of all my wounds except this word cut into my arm.

I growl at the marking, a red haze shining from the corner of my vision. Tilting my head to look down at my reflection in the water, I blink a few times to make sure I'm seeing what I'm seeing. My eyes look like pits of red hellfire, and as my anger builds, they burn brighter until I'm casting a red light around where I'm kneeling.

The glow of my eyes trails through the air as I shake my head, trying to calm my rage. I imagine my eyes look like someone waving a burning torch in the dark of night—like the torches the villagers wielded when they came for my father.

But I had my revenge. My only wish is that I had drawn it out a bit more.

I grin, and slowly, my heart rate calms. The red of my eyes dims to their normal black. Holding my hand before my face, I turn it over, rubbing at the scarred skin. I don't know if it's my magic or the yokai's that healed me, but I'm grateful that most of the pain is gone. I'm still fucking freezing, though it is a touch warmer in this pool chamber.

Cupping some crystal-clear water in my hands, I splash my face. Even though the water is extremely cold, it's almost warm against my frozen skin ... refreshing. With a sigh, I pick up my scabbard, but when I curl my toes under, ready to stand, I find my muscles are too tired to respond.

I look at my saya. "Can you carry me, please?"

It says nothing, and I roll my eyes. "Fine. I'll do it. Come on."

On hands and knees, I crawl my way back to the wall and curl into a tight ball, hugging my only possession to my chest.

I'll rest for a bit. Yes. Once I've rested, I'll be stronger.

I'm afraid to close my eyes, afraid they'll freeze shut again, afraid that if I fall asleep, I won't wake up again. But every blink lasts a little longer until I give in and let my eyes stay closed. I shift, squeezing my thighs around the end of the katana that's down between my legs. With a chuckle, I say to my lacquered scabbard, "At least my cock didn't freeze and fall off. Small victories," and I imagine my saya laughing with me.

Eventually, the rhythmic *drip drip drip* of the water carries me to sleep where I dream ... silent scenes of blood, of the delicious fear in the villager's eyes, of their deaths.

And in my dream, I smile.

3

How does anyone survive without magic?

Most of my soreness is gone from yesterday. I'm sure it's helping that it's not as fucking freezing as it was yesterday. The air still bites at my naked skin, but I can tolerate stepping outside the cave. With my scabbard in my hand, I walk out into the clearing. Despite the brutal weather last night, there wasn't much snowfall. The ground is hard-packed dirt with a few tufts of crunchy frozen yellow grass that tickle the soles of my feet. I pause and turn in a slow circle.

Trees all around. A hint of warmth from the weak sunlight. A cold breeze. Distant birdsong. The rustle of leaves and branches brushing together.

A new day. A new me.

When I face the entrance to the cave, I realize most of the interior must be underground. Where I expected to see a mountain or at least some looming hills, there's nothing but a few large boulders grown over with moss framing the wide entrance to the cave. It's so unassuming, I imagine unless someone were looking for this particular cave system, they'd never find it.

The other thing I notice is the quiet and how very alone I am.

I ask my scabbard, "Where the hell are we?" My gravelly voice carries across the open space only to die in the shadows of the forest. Taking a large inhale, letting my ribcage expand, I bellow, "Hello!"

A gust of wind brings with it the far-off clacking of bamboo as the only answer to my shout.

I call out again, "Hello?"

Silence.

"Well, I can't stay here, naked and exposed. Let's go."

Adjusting my grip on the katana, I pick a direction. West, so I can soak up the slight warmth of the sun on my face for as long as possible. It feels so nice, and a small smile lifts my cheeks. I wave my free hand at the cave behind me. "I appreciate the shelter, but I hope to never see you again."

As I walk, my muscles loosen, and I find a steady rhythm, only faltering a few times when a rock digs into my feet. I stop to pee, then continue on. The shelter of the trees kept the ground from freezing here in the forest, so the ground is squishy, almost springy, and the earthy scents of pine and decayed leaves soothes me.

I'm alive.

And despite the pain, I'm grateful and filled with wonder. I don't know these woods. These trees are all new to me. Even the air feels different here. I've always loved traveling, and my current predicament aside, this feels like the start of a grand adventure.

The orange light of the sun struggles to reach me through the tight press of the trees. Running my hand over the rough bark of an old pine, I pause, tilting my head back, letting that bit of warmth wash over my face. After a few deep breaths, I pat the tree and clutch my scabbard a little closer to my side as I weave through the forest.

"What am I going to say when I come across a traveler or when I find a village?" I wave at my nakedness. "I can't just walk into town completely naked. How am I going to explain this?" I grin and chuckle as I ask, "But more importantly, what is going to be our first meal when we get out of here? Gods, I'm starving."

I place my palm on my belly, and it rumbles. With a happy sigh, I pat my stomach, anticipation making me walk faster. It's going to be so nice to put on some warm clothes, cozy up to a roaring fire, and fill my belly.

Pain explodes across my face.

"Fuck!"

Stumbling back, I rub my nose, tears pooling in my eyes. Pulling my hand back, I expect to see blood, but there is none. I was so deep in my thoughts of warmth and food, I ran into ...

Nothing.

There's nothing in front of me.

I hold out my hand, nose still throbbing. My fingers brush against ... something. But there's nothing there. I press my palm to the invisible barrier. It's not cold or hot. It's not rough or smooth. It's just there.

Flexing, I press against the barrier. Nothing happens. I push harder. Digging my feet into the ground, I lean my shoulder into the invisible wall. Nothing. I step to the right, my hand trailing along the continued force.

Okaaay.

Doing my best to ignore the dread building in my chest, I bend down, grabbing a rough stone with a sharp edge. I tap it against the barrier. Nothing. As I scrape it back and forth, I realize there's no accompanying sound. Strange.

Reeling back my arm, I slam the sharp edge of the rock into the wall. Nothing. Not even a ripple.

I look to my right, then my left. If I can't go forward, I'll go ... right. Pressing the rock against the bark of a large pine, I scratch an x into the flesh of the tree. Holding the small stone in the same hand as the katana, I trail my free hand along the solid stretch of air. I come to another tree in its path and quickly mark the bark.

I stop to pee again, noticing the color is much darker.

On I go, noting the position of the sun. Hours pass and dread builds to a point I can no longer ignore. It's an ache tightening my shoulder blades and worrying my stomach into knots.

I'm walking in a circle.

Sure enough, I drop my hand and stare at the first x I carved into that tree.

The shark skin wrapping of my saya groans under my tight grip. I throw back my head, yelling at the patches of orange, pink, and purple streaked sky peeking through the pine branches. "Fuck! Fuck that yokai! Fuck everything! Godsdamn it! Fuck! Fuck! Fuck! Fuck!"

My eyes start to glow, the red so intense, I can see the glare on the skin of my nose. My magic rages, pricking and clawing at my insides. This power is not gentle like my silver used to be. No, the red is just as angry as I am. I punch the barrier. Nothing. No reverberation. No sound. Nothing. I punch it again, and again. My knuckles split. Blood coats my fingers but fails to smear the invisible wall before me. A primal shout tears from my throat as I wildly punch the barrier.

A soft thud stalls my tantrum.

Looking down, I see my scabbard on the ground. I didn't even notice I dropped it. My knees hit the ground, and I scoop up my only possession, hugging it to my chest. I rock back and forth, head bowed over my saya. "What do we do now? Fuck!"

As I fall silent, the forest seems to press in on me, the shadows growing longer, the branches reaching for me like bony fingers. I clutch my bare chest, and it feels as if a small crack fissures across my heart. It hurts. It's hard to breathe. I'm trapped in this fucking forest. My earlier gratitude is nowhere to be found. I'm cold, naked, tired, and hungry.

A calm voice in the back of my head whispers, *"Remember your training."*

Father.

I slow my breath and relax my shoulders. I wiggle my toes on the earth under the tops of my feet. *I'm alive. Be thankful.* Closing my eyes, I breathe in the scents of the forest. I swallow the lump in my throat that's trying to become a sob. Looking down at my scabbard, I say, "Back to the cave? We'll find a way out tomorrow. First light. Even if it takes all day, we'll get out. I promise."

Of course it doesn't respond, but in my head, I imagine it saying, *Don't make promises you can't keep. If this is that yokai's curse, the odds of escape are—*

I stop, holding the scabbard up in front of my face. "Never tell me the odds."

Despite the determination lacing my tone, my body resists returning to that cave, my feet feeling like they are stuck in mud. I don't want to go back. Last night it was a shelter, but what if it's actually my prison?

Forcing my feet to move, my muscles protest with every step, but finally, the mossy boulders come into view, the grey and brown stone slowly turning darker colors with the setting sun.

With a heavy sigh, I look down at my scabbard. "Well ..."

I prop my saya against the rock, unwilling to spend another night almost freezing to death. As if my thoughts conjure it, a gust of freezing wind grabs at my naked body. My skin pebbles, and I start shivering as I search the clearing and the edge of the forest around the cave. I pick a few rocks I think might work, tossing them into the mouth of the cave. The rough bark of twigs and branches dig in and scrape the flesh of my arms and chest as I carry large bundles, one after the other, into the cave. Once I have a decent pile of sticks, I make several more trips back and forth, hauling mounds of dry pine needles, moss, and leaves. Then, I carry the katana inside, sitting cross-legged on a pile of pine needles with the gathered dried leaves before me. The pine needles poke and tickle, but it's better than sitting my bare ass on the cold stone.

The wood of my saya clinks softly against the rock as I set it on the ground next to me. Leaning over, I pick up two of the rocks I threw in here earlier, noticing my knuckles are now completely healed from my earlier punching tirade. The loud *snap* of me striking the stones together bounces off the rock walls and ceiling. Again. And again. And again.

A spark floats towards the dried leaves and excitement has me leaning forward, but its red glow dies before it catches.

I look at my scabbard with an apologetic smile on my face. "That was close. I'll get it. Don't worry. You'll have a fire this night."

In my head, I imagine it saying, *I believe in you.*

Grinning with a nod, I bend back over the rocks in my hands. "Thanks."

I strike the stones again. And again. One breaks, slicing into my palm. I swear, tossing it away to quickly replace it with a fresh one. I strike them together. Again. A spark. It dies. Strike. Strike. Strike.

The small cut in my hand heals over quicker than it should, but there's no time to marvel at my healing ability because I'm shivering harder now. My hands shake so violently, I almost miss the next strike completely, glancing the rocks off each other.

Still, I continue. It's just like training with my father. Repetition. Concentrate. Strike. Spark. Strike. Spark. Strike. Smoke curls from the leaves, and I lean over, shielding it with my body. It's fully dark outside, and the cold is all-encompassing. But at least it's not windy. There's not even a slight breeze.

I nearly shout in excitement as a small flame flickers in the center of the pile of crushed leaves. Using my palms, I scoop the outer leaves towards the center, feeding the flames with gentle breaths. *Come on. Come on.* I sigh as the first lick of warmth caresses my skin. Slowly, I add twigs, then larger branches until I have a proper fire going.

I throw back my head and laugh in triumph before scooting closer, wanting to hug the flames to my chest. I'd eat them if I could. My stomach rumbles, reminding me of my hunger. That will have to wait until tomorrow. First light of day, I'll find food and a way out of this place.

But that's for tomorrow-me to worry about. Right now, I smile at the dancing flames, shifting to rotate every so often, warming my sides and back.

Staring at the fire, my eyes grow heavy. But I have to stay awake. I ...

I jerk as the sensation of falling wakes me up. I lick my lips, realizing my tongue is dry and my throat is scratchy.

Dehydration.

Reluctant to leave the hard-earned warmth of the

flames, I grumble as I push to my feet, bringing the katana with me. I walk as quickly as my dizzy head allows, eager to get back to my fire. Approaching the chamber with the pool of water, I kneel, wobbling to one side before bracing my hands on the ground, my scabbard a comforting presence under my palm. I lean over, pressing my lips to the frigid water, sucking in deep gulps. With each swallow, I feel a little better, a little steadier. Once my belly is full, I splash my face, then my underarms and my crotch.

I hurry back to the front of the cave, the flickering flames greeting me like an old friend. As I sit back down on my cushion of pine needles, I rub my thumb over the soft wrapping on the hilt of the katana. My father's dead body flashes through my mind, and I grit my teeth, anger racing through my blood like a horse freed from its pen, my eyes blazing red. But then I take a deep breath, replacing that horrible image with my father's kind eyes, the corners crinkled with his ready smile.

Slow, deep inhale. Hold. Even longer exhale, letting all my muscles relax. Slow, deep inhale ... and everything drifts away.

4

The scraping sound of rock against rock grates on my nerves as I carve yet another slash mark into the wall of my cave.

Sixty-seven days.

Grabbing the katana from where it's propped against the wall, I say, "Today's the day. We're getting out of here."

That's what you say every day.

"And one day it will be true. Why not today?"

Though I'm finding it harder and harder to believe my own words of encouragement, I can't give up. If I give up, then there's nothing but despair and darkness stretching out before me. Nothing but more of ... *this* ... forever.

No. I'll cling to the delusional hope that there is a way out of this prison.

I'd kill that yokai again, if I could. And once I'm free of this place, I'll hunt down its spirit and find a way to destroy it. There'll be no ritual to calm or redeem that spirit. No, there will be no second chance for that yokai when I find it.

Blinking away the sting of the bright sunlight, I exit my cave. A little shiver trembles down my body as a breeze wraps around me. At least the weather is milder these days —mornings still draped in chilly fog and nights bringing back the colder temperatures, but the middle of the days gets downright warm.

Weaving my way through the trees, I notice the worn path. It's fascinating how the simple imprint of my feet has slowly made a mark on this place—even the smallest of actions on my part affects the world around me.

The bark is rough as I press my fingers to the x mark in the pine, delineating the edge of my prison. Glancing down, I scowl at the hole in the earth I made trying to dig under the barrier, the fifth such hole I've dug during my time here. I flex my free hand. My fingers are no longer scraped and bleeding from yesterday's work—those wounds healed overnight—but a soreness lingers.

A taunting, clanking noise draws my attention, and I press my palms and face against the invisible wall, my mouth watering. Bamboo. So close, yet still so far away. That thicket will grow and spread quickly, and one day they will be within my reach, then I'll be able to enjoy the sweet shoots.

I lick my lips, eager for the bamboo to grow faster, but also naively hoping I won't still be here when the tender young shoots do finally make it inside my prison.

I shake my head and turn away from the tasty temptation beyond my reach. Adjusting my grip on my saya, I say, "Let's make a round."

It rolls its eyes in my head with a sigh. *Sure. I guess.*

I reach out until my fingers brush the invisible wall. Then I start walking the same path I walk every day. I glare at the narrow trail I've worn into the ground with my daily treks around this cursed place, searching and hoping for a break where I can slip through. Eighteen kilometers all the way around. Like a mantra, I count my steps. I count because it's something to do other than obsess over the hopelessness of my situation.

Eighty-three, eighty-four ...

The texture under my fingers changes from smooth nothingness to rough bark as I run my hand over a tree in the path of the barrier.

Two hundred sixty-seven, sixty-eight ...

Sweat drips down my back and between my ass cheeks. My feet have grown tougher with my daily walks, but they still ache.

A little over four hours pass before the tree I started at comes back into view with no break in the wall.

I could have told you that and saved us the time.

I chuckle, setting my scabbard against the tree with the x mark. "Saved time? For what exactly? Do you have some pressing matters I don't know about?"

I place both hands to my lower back, arching, enjoying the stretch and pop of my spine. Straightening, I swing my arms across my body, loosening up. I crack my neck side-to-side as I interlace my fingers to stretch them.

Grabbing a low branch, I haul myself up. Like my feet, my hands have toughened over my time trying to escape this place, so the scratch of the bark barely bothers me. I puff out a breath, dislodging the pine leaves that slap me in the face as I climb.

Finding a steady branch, I balance as I reach out, drawing my magic from my belly, gathering it in my palm. It tingles, burns, crackles. It feels ... red.

From the ground, my scabbard laughs. *How can something feel red?*

My fingers meet solid air. Pressing my hand flat, I shove against the barrier as I say, "I don't know. My magic used to be silver ... calm, bright, clean, shiny. Now ... it's red."

I push my magic a little harder. Nothing. Not even a ripple of response.

Damn it.

I climb, testing the barrier until the tree starts to bow with my weight. I can't climb any farther without serious threat of snapping the top of this tree and falling. I'd probably survive, but pain is a friend I'd rather not invite here today.

Curling my hand into a fist, I pound against the barrier. There's no sound, no thud, no resounding clatter. I can only imagine how ridiculous I look up here in this pine, banging on air.

"Shit."

I scrape my shin on the way down, and blood wells, dripping down my leg. By the time I touch down on solid ground, the small injury has already stopped bleeding. I grab a small rock and carve an arrow facing up into the bark of the tree, right next to my x mark. Then I slash through the arrow. Another tree checked and eliminated.

Picking up my scabbard, I tap a finger against the lacquer as I make my way towards the next tree close enough for me to test the barrier. Because if I can't go under, maybe I can go over. Doing my best to hold onto hope, I prop my scabbard against the new tree, then lean back, looking up the length of the great pine. This one is taller, another of my x marks scaring its thick trunk. I have to jump to reach the lowest branch. Swinging, I wrap my leg over and haul myself up, careful not to scrape my balls on the rough bark. Sitting in the giant pine, I lean over, pressing my palm to the barrier, sending my magic into it. Nothing.

I stand, steadying myself with a hand on the wide trunk.

"Onward and upward."

Glad it's you and not me.

"What, you don't like heights?"

I don't know, but it doesn't look like something I'd enjoy.

"How do you know until you try it?"

Well, you'd have to hold me and climb at the same time. You may heal from a great fall, but who knows if I would.

"True. True. Let's not test your durability, my friend!"

I'm yelling at this point so my scabbard can hear me. I know I'm tumbling into madness, but I fear there's no way to prevent it.

I shrug it off and climb. I'm happy to keep myself company.

I stride into the caves, saying to my saya, "We've been stuck here long enough. Let's try to make it a little more comfortable, hmm? A little homier?"

Finally.

I roll my eyes, but my mirth can't completely chase away the little kick of anger and sadness in my chest—because this feels like giving in.

We're not giving in. We're just making the best of it until we can find a way out.

"What's this *we* business? How have you been helping?"

I help by keeping you company.

The walls of the first chamber bounce the weak flicker of light back to me. Looking around, I notice this small cave seems fairly solid, but I might as well make sure ... what else do I have to do?

My saya chuckles, and I blow out the flame. The smoke curls up, and when it hits the ceiling, the grey tendrils billow outwards and hang heavy above my head.

No ventilation.

Walking back outside, I grab another stick, repeating the process again, and again. When I enter the chamber I've been sleeping in, I do it again and watch the smoke cling to the rocky ceiling.

Not here either.

Repeating the process, I sigh as I enter a small cave farther back. A week into my imprisonment, I tried sleeping in the cavern with the pool of water since it was a little warmer than the others, but the incessant *drip drip drip* kept me awake and I gave it up after one sleepless night.

Shoulders slumped, expectations low, I puff out the little flame. The smoke drifts to the ceiling, but instead of hovering overhead, it crawls over the rock before being sucked out of the room.

"Ah ha! A vent! This will be our new sleeping chamber."

Yes, yes. Now the hard part. Do you even know how to build a hearth?

"No, but I have plenty of time to learn."

5

The cold water of the pool in the back of the caves laps my ankles, my calves, my thighs. I hiss as the water licks at my cock and balls, but I push forward, gritting my teeth.

I found nothing new today. My daily trek produced no breaks or slips in the barrier. I climbed every tree even remotely close to the wall, finding no weaknesses. But my new hearth is coming along. My first attempt collapsed before I made it halfway up to the ceiling. The second one didn't vent correctly, and I ended up smoking myself out of the cave. The third one was a success ... for a week. Then it cracked and fell into a heap. But this one might be the one to make it.

With a smile, I bend my knees, holding my breath as I slide under the water.

I've heard people describe being under water as a heavy silence.

Suspended, my hair floating around me, I swish my arms and slowly exhale, bubbles popping on the surface. Being under the water isn't silent at all. There's a rushing.

There's the sound of my heartbeat in my ears. I can feel the vibration of the disturbance I've made as the ripples lap at the shore and echo off the cavern walls and ceiling. And beyond my own heart thudding, it's almost as if the water has its own pulse. It crackles around me as little bubbles snap, and the trickle of the stream from above feeds the pool. There's also the soft *glub, glub* of the underground spring pushing water into the pool from below.

No. It's not silent at all. It's alive. There's energy in the water. I let myself become one with the weightlessness before my gasp bounces off the ceiling as I break the surface, sucking down a great lungful of air. I float on my back, listening to the small sounds of the cave, the tiny reverberations echo against the cavern walls.

I fill my lungs, and as I exhale, I sink.

Heavy but light.

Down, down, down, into the depths of the darkness. My skin starts to tighten from the pressure. I can't see them, but I hear the bubbles leaving my mouth and nose, dancing to the surface, now so far away.

My back hits squishy silt, and the murk folds around me, like a watery hug, before settling. Burning, my chest aches with the need for air. But the pain is good. Adrenaline courses through me, tingling all the way to my fingers. How odd, that being closer to death makes you feel more alive.

I smile, planting my feet to push off the bottom, but my right ankle catches on something. My brain begs me to take a breath as I grab my foot, pulling, trying to free myself. A root? A rock? I can't tell. The silt is too thick, and my vision is going dark.

A few bubbles float from my mouth as I yank again. My hair swirls around me, and the red glow of my eyes reflects off the black strands. The darkness closes in, and my last thought slips through my fading mind.

My poor saya is going to be all alone now.

S puttering, I choke and vomit water as I bob on the surface of the pool. My throat feels like it's on fire, and my lungs struggle to inflate. Pulling myself onto the hard ground of the cave, I shake from fatigue and ... confusion.

I must have blacked out before floating to the surface. But I really thought I was dying ... Just like I thought I was dying that first freezing night.

Glancing at my scabbard, I ask, "Did I just ... die and come back to life?"

6

y eyes burn, and I blink away the threatening tears.
The scratch of the rock against stone feels like it's
scoring my soul. I toss the stone to the ground with a sharp
clink. Scowling at the markings on the wall, I rub a hand
over the back of my neck.

"I should really stop making these marks, they're just
depressing."

Yes, but it's something to do.

My eyes travel over the wall. It blurs, turning wavy then
sharpens as a single tear falls. That's all it takes. A sob
breaks free, and I slide to my knees, my palm dragging over
the scored stone, the marks scraping my skin.

Three years, three months, and seven days. Three. Fucking. Years.

Bowing my head, I release the sadness, the loneliness,
and the despair. Just for a moment, I let it all out. A scream
rips from me, and I beat my fist against the wall. It's as if
there are thin cracks in my heart splintering outward. Snot
drips from my nose, and I choke on my tears. I feel the
katana watching me. I feel its pity, knowing it's my subcon-

scious pitying myself. Sitting back on my heels, I take a few slow breaths and look at my scabbard that's propped against the rock wall.

The katana whispers, *I don't like it when you're like this. You try to leave me.*

I sigh, calmer now, running my fingers over the smooth skin of my wrist where I cut myself with a sharp rock a little less than a year ago, seeking a death that ignored me. A few months after that, I'd tried to hang myself only to end up passing out then dying before waking with a choking gasp. I'd kicked and struggled until 'dying' again. For two days this went on until I was finally able to swing my body with enough force to snap the branch. I didn't try that method of killing myself again. I did try drowning again. Didn't work ... obviously. Ingesting the poisonous lantern plant behind my caves didn't work, and an accidental fall from a tree didn't end my suffering either.

Shaking my head, dislodging the depressing thoughts, I say, "I know. I won't try to leave you again. Not today, at least." And that's the truth of it. I'm constantly at war with myself, hanging on to any thread of hope, only to tumble into despair. Then I remember my father, knowing he wouldn't want me to give up, so I cling back onto hope. But eventually the darkness creeps back in again. Over and over. Hope and despair.

Gripping my scabbard, I stare out of my cave as the first light of morning brushes the tops of the pines with a soft golden glow. A part of me wants to stride out to the patch of dirt I now use as my training area and just flop on the ground and watch the clouds until night falls.

But, after my good cry earlier, I feel a little better ... I want to *do* something. So, I exit the cave, breathing in the crisp air. The berries haven't fallen off the lantern bush yet, so it's been days since I've eaten anything besides the wild mushrooms that grow on the side of the dead tree in the north-west section of my prison. Those and the bamboo shoots.

I'm tired of bamboo shoots.

Don't complain. Remember those early days when you used to dream of being able to eat bamboo shoots?

"I know. But I also didn't think I'd still be here. I am grateful, I just don't think I can force another charred shoot down my throat right now."

So dramatic.

Glancing down at my scabbard, I smile. "A man needs a little variety. Let's go check the traps ... unless you have something else to do?"

Let me think ... Nope. My day is free.

I chuckle at myself as I stride across my training area. Footsteps light, I stalk through the woods, barely breathing, listening for movement. I aim a scowl at the large cluster of bushes to my right, releasing an exaggerated shiver. The deep purple berries beckon to my grumbling stomach, but I know better. I learned that lesson early on.

I shiver again as I recall the days I spent sweating and moaning on the cold floor of the cave. I literally shit myself to death, or I would have if I could die. All because of those tempting plump purple berries. I never want to go through that again. There are better ways to try to die.

Just for good measure, I smack the shiny green leaves of the bush as I walk past, sending the branches swaying violently. A few of the poisonous berries drop to the ground, rolling away as I continue on my way.

Over the years, I've memorized small game trails that crisscross through my prison. It's usually rodents and squirrels, but beggars can't be choosers. Though today, I'm really hoping for a rabbit. Why not be optimistic? My mouth waters just thinking about it.

A soft rustling stops me in my tracks. I wait. There it is again. Following the path of the small noises, I stalk my prey, unsure of what it is. It doesn't matter. It will be dinner. As I track the scurrying, I realize my prey is circling back towards my cave, and I quietly pick up my pace.

The light of the clearing comes into view through the trunks of the pines, and I spy dull grey fur hidden in the brush just a few paces ahead. I adjust the grip on the hilt of the sheathed katana. One good thump is all I need.

My magic sends a slicing sensation down my back, pricking at my calves in warning. This feels like ... My heart skips a beat as a branch snaps behind me. The rabbit darts across the clearing and out of sight.

Damn it!

I spin around and nearly drop my scabbard.

A man stands not fifteen paces from me.

I chuckle, and the sound morphs into a barked laugh. "Well, this settles it, I'm mad. I'm completely insane."

My scabbard whispers back, *I think he's real.*

I nearly jump when the man speaks. "Is that it? H-have I ... have I actually found it?"

7

My throat closes, and tears spring to my eyes. I can't seem to stop trembling, nearly falling to my knees as hope fills me. Is this man really real? Have I been found? Am I rescued?

But then I notice his eyes are not on me or my nakedness, but on the katana in my hand. He takes a step towards me, and I take a step back. He's breathing from his mouth, lips parted, revealing the iron and tannins staining his teeth black. His gaze remains on my scabbard, completely ignoring my state of undress.

The katana mutters, *Strange that he only has eyes for me. I don't like it. Say something.*

The shock is wearing off, and trepidation creeps in. Clearing my throat doesn't break the man's attention, so I say, "Hello?"

The man bows, his short black hair gleaming in the sun. As he stands, he finally meets my gaze and says, "Sorry. Hello. I am Takamoro Yuki."

After so many years of only hearing myself talk, it's both odd and exhilarating to hear another voice. But as soon as his introduction is out of his mouth, his eyes dart back to my scabbard, and I grip it a little tighter. My voice comes out higher pitched, laced with eagerness ... and hope.

"Takamoro," Glancing over his shoulder, I ask, "Have you come to help me?"

Takamoro blinks at me, his attention darting between my face and the katana. He says, "I ... um. You need help? I, um ... well ..." His gaze drops back to my scabbard. A long, awkward pause hangs between us, but I stand still, assessing this stranger—the first person I've seen in years. This man who can't seem to take his eyes off the katana in my hand. And then I realize what he's actually looking at ... the guard. Traditionally, the collar would hold the crest of a clan or feudal lord, but not this katana. The guard is plain, the only marking a beautiful and distinctive stamp of the master swordsmith who forged it. My father.

Finally, his eyes lift back to my face. "Um, why are you naked?"

I shrug, "Long story. One I'm happy to share if you—"

Takamoro shakes his head, pointing at my scabbard. His eyes darken as he swallows, and heavy anxiety worms its way through my chest as he asks, "Is that Guardian?"

My stomach drops, and I flinch at the name I haven't heard in years ... not since the village.

The forest seems darker all of a sudden. The trees seem bigger. I feel closed in. Trapped. I need space. Doing my best to act nonchalant, I turn my back to Takamoro. I stride out of the woods and into the clearing, but I keep my senses attuned to the movements of the man behind me. I try to keep my voice calm as I say, "I haven't heard that name in a very long time. Where did *you* learn it, Takamoro?"

His footsteps stop, and he says, "Please, call me Yuki."

I shake my head as I turn back around to face him, a bit

more settled now that we are out of the confines of the forest. "We are not that familiar." I paste on a fake smile to hide the sorrow making my chest ache. He's hardly looked at me. And the fact he knows that name … Guardian …

He says, "Please. I've been searching for so long. Tell me, is that Gua—"

My voice comes out with a bit of a bite. "An answer for an answer, Takamoro. Where did you hear that name?"

He sighs, finally looking me over, then quickly averting his eyes as he rubs the back of his neck. "There is a legend told in whispers and from drunken mouths. But until a few years ago, that was all it was … a legend. A tale. A fantasy. But then *he* showed up in our village."

"He?"

"Motosue."

I stop myself from reacting this time at the mention of another name I haven't heard in years. A name that tears through me like a well-honed blade through the heart.

When I remain silent, Takamoro continues, his gaze going distant as if seeing his memory. "Motosue showed up in the village in the dead of night, travel worn. He stayed to himself for a few days, taking lodgings at the small inn. We don't get many strangers in our village, so he was a bit of a curiosity, but as long as he paid his bills and didn't cause trouble, we left him alone."

Takamoro focuses back on me, and my magic crackles in warning. I realize his gaze isn't on me but once again on the katana as he says, "And then one night, Motosue got deep in his cups. His hands shook so much, his liquor sloshed over the rim. When asked what was troubling him, he dropped his head and started crying. Right there in the bar. The tale he told …"

Eyes still on the katana in my hand, Takamoro shakes

his head. "We all thought he was simply weaving a drunken tale as he murmured about a sword—a blade honed to perfection and imbued with magic. A sentient weapon. A sword that had every form, every move, every defense, and every offense literally hammered into it. A blade that could whisper to the one holding its hilt. A magical blade that made its wielder ... unbeatable."

Takamoro licks his lips, his focus solely on my scabbard gripped tightly in my hand. "And Motosue told those of us in the bar that night of how that katana, named Guardian, was used to slaughter his village."

Takamoro's eyes snap to mine, a hardness in his stare. "Motosue swore the sword was still out there. That it needed to be found and destroyed. He became angry with the telling of his tale, tossing his drink and slamming his fists on the bar. He screamed that the blade was too powerful and if it fell into the wrong hands ... even the so-called 'right' hands could be made to do terrible things with that blade. As he raged, it ended up taking four of us to restrain him."

I take a slow breath, clenching my free hand to hide my trembling. "A magical sword? That does indeed sound like a tall tale. A drunken man speaking nonsense."

His eyes flash with his rising emotions. "You know that look in a man's eye when he's seen something that's changed his life ... and not for the better? Motosue had that look. A few of us in the village were convinced enough to go out in search of the blade. But, still, I didn't really believe. Not until this moment." His eyes slip to the katana then back to my face. "I've been looking for over a year. That stamp on the collar. It's just how he described. That's it, isn't it? That is Guardian."

I shake my head. "If it were, would you destroy it as the drunken Motosue warned?"

He doesn't answer, but his intent is clear in his hungry gaze as he asks again, "Is that the magic blade?"

Kill him.

No.

"No."

"You're lying."

Raising a brow, I hold out my arms, the black lacquer of my scabbard glinting in the sunlight. "You think I'm just hanging out, naked in the woods with a magical sword?"

His eyes track the movement of the katana. "You asked if I was here to help you. If I help, will you give it to me?"

My scabbard scoffs, *This man can't help.*

I know.

I drop my arms and stroke my thumb over the slick lacquer, calming myself. Centering myself. Getting ready as my father's voice drifts through my head, *Move with purpose. No wasted energy.* And in answer to Takamoro's question, I simply say, "No."

Takamoro pats his chest, and a crinkling sound comes from under his shirt before he pulls out a folded stack of paper money displaying the mark of a clan crest, one I don't recognize.

"I'll pay you for it."

I laugh. "What would a naked man in the woods do with that?"

"That naked man could leave the woods and buy clothing and anything else he desires."

I shrug, "That money is only good within the boundaries of your clan's domain, which I have no idea where it is, nor do I particularly care." This conversation is giving me a headache. I find the thought of my scabbard in the hands of someone other than me nauseating.

Now that the hope of him being my savior lies in ashes, it's easy to turn him down.

"You cannot have Guardian."

Takamoro's eyes narrow, and he shifts, putting his money away before staggering his feet and bending slightly at his knees. His hand slides to the hilt of his sword, shifting his weight forward. "I *need* that sword."

"Is it worth your life?"

"Yes."

And here he comes.

Takamoro flexes his arms and pushes off his back foot.

He's going to lead with a cross-strike.

Shifting to my right, I easily avoid the slash of his sword, and I'm there to meet his counter, my scabbard clonking with a hit that sends vibrations through my hand. Despite the circumstances, I smile. This feels good. This clash of weapons. My strength tested against another. I recall all the many hours spent practicing with my father, and I fall into the dance of the blade.

Deflecting his strike, I spin out of the way as my magic whispers, *Upwards cross-slash.* Takamoro's breaths come faster, heavier, and I haven't even broken a sweat. My smile blooms into a broad grin as my scabbard laughs. *Seems a man who is on the hunt for a magical blade would be better trained in the art of swordsmanship. He's quite terrible.*

Takamoro's next attack is clumsy, and he stumbles past me. Not able to pass up the opportunity, I slap my scabbard against his back with a sharp *thwack*. Takamoro growls, turning back to face me, his blade raised between us as he says, "I'm not leaving without that sword."

I sigh. "Then, you're not leaving."

There's a moment of hesitation in his posture, his shoulders stiffening slightly. The red glow of my magic reflects back at me through Takamoro's wide eyes. But even the manifestation of my power doesn't deter him. Takamoro scowls, adjusting his grip on the hilt of his katana. "I will have Guardian!"

I've already mapped my moves as he takes his first running stride towards me. Letting him in close, I spin, hooking his sword arm with my elbow. My shoulder-length hair slaps him in his face, distracting him. With a quick wrench of my arm and a smack to the back of his head with my scabbard, I take possession of his weapon.

Completing my dance-like turn, I use his blade with practiced precision and ease. I have not spent almost four years in this infernal forest being idle. I've practiced. I've stayed vigilant as my father would expect of me. And, well, the art of the blade is in my blood.

The metal of Takamoro's sword sings as I use it against him, and I strike—Heel, hamstring, waist, neck.

Stumbling, Takamoro grabs the side of his throat, red blood dripping between his fingers—the same color that illuminates my eyes. He staggers three steps away before falling to his knees. Calmly, I walk around him so we're facing each other once more. He looks up at me, face already pale from blood loss.

Emotions tumble through me, but I shove them all down to look at later ... or never.

Kneeling before him, I hold my scabbard at my side. "Was it really worth *this*?"

Takamoro slumps over, coughing. "I'm not the only one searching for that blade. You will meet your match eventually."

I laugh, standing and walking away. "Good. I welcome the practice"—I gesture at my naked body—"and the clothing."

A calm resolve settles over me. Let them come. I'll face down an army if I must.

Even you aren't that good.

I'll be as good as I need to be to keep you out of the hands of men like that.

As I stare at my cave, I hear a heavy thud as Takamoro falls to the dirt.

Silence.

My magic settles, and I blink as the red luminescence drains from my eyes. Looking down at Takamoro's bloodied blade in my hand, I flick my arm, sending red splatters to the dust at my feet. I glance over my shoulder, saying to the dead man, "You know, my magic used to be silver. Bright and beautiful. But I find red suits me better."

I kneel and set my new katana on the ground, then draw my scabbard around to rest on my thighs. The lacquer glints as I stroke it. What if others do come in search of Guardian? Will they come with greed in their hearts like Takamoro? Or will someone care ... about me?

I set my scabbard against the rock wall, wondering, hoping that Mostosue Saito might come to find me himself. Is he out there now, searching? It would be nice to see my friend again ... but after what happened in the village ... what happened between us ... if he does come, will it be to help me or to end me?

Brushing aside the thoughts of my past, I stand and press my palms to my lower back, arching, speaking to my scabbard. "Let's see how Takamoro's pants fit." I laugh, the sound loud and bitter in the silence of my solitude. "After all this time, I'm not sure my cock will like being confined."

My harsh chuckles float around me, keeping me company as I stride back across the clearing. Kneeling, I push Takamoro onto his back, his open eyes staring blankly at the sky. I grit my teeth, my hands curling in the fabric of his shirt. My voice is barely a whisper, the tone raspy with emotions that are forcing their way out as I shake the dead man. "You didn't notice me. You didn't notice ... anything. I told you I needed help, and you didn't care. You didn't deserve Guardian."

My scabbard says, *Thank you. You are a good friend.*

Saito's warm brown eyes flash through my mind, the eyes of my father's friend and apprentice. A man I haven't thought about in a very long time.

"Am I?"

I shove my anger and despair down as I yank Takamoro's shirt out of the hem of his pants and start wrestling the garment over his head. A little clatter draws my attention to the ground, and I gasp, fingers diving for the small flint that must have tumbled from a pocket as I jostled him around. My hands shake with desperate excitement as I pat Takamoro down, finding the steel. I sit back, holding the treasures in my palm. No more blisters and raw skin as I try to strike the stones to create the smallest of sparks. I can practically feel the heat of the flames of the fire I will easily build tonight.

I set my new prize aside and get back to work on Takamoro's clothes. His head thumps to the dirt as I free him of his shirt. Doing my best to bury my misery at being alone again so soon after someone finally found me, I force myself to see the positive ... because what else do I have? I wave the bloodstained shirt over my head like a flag.

Grinning at my scabbard, I shout, "I have clothes!"

8

The rough fabric of my pants brushes my thighs as I crouch, stoking the fire barely crackling in the stove. As I lazily poke the charred wood, I look outside through the open doorway. My eyes travel over the tightly stacked wood planks that took me months to chop down, strip, treat with pine resin, and bind together to make the walls of my little kitchen that sits right outside the entrance to my cave.

My fingers flex as I recall the weeks I spent mixing dirt and water and burnt ash to coat these walls. I smile with pride at the fairly smooth texture, noticing a few cracks near the wide roof, the overhang keeping the rain from washing away all my hard work. I learned that lesson with my first attempt at building this structure. All it took was one heavy rain, and my hut melted into the mud. Strong, gusting winds tore down my second attempt. But this one has stood the test of time.

Grabbing a log from the stack I replenished yesterday, I toss it into the stove, made from the same mud mixture as the walls—the same mixture I used to build the hearth in my sleeping chamber.

I blow on the struggling flames in the stove until they flare. Sitting back, I nod before pressing my hands to my thighs and standing. My father would have been proud of what I've built here, and that knowledge warms me better than any fire could. As I walk outside, I tilt my head to the sky and breathe deeply, letting the warm sun beat down on my face. I press my palm to my bare chest, taking another slow inhale.

I'm alive. And today, that's a good thing.

My nose wrinkles as I think about my one and only shirt. I couldn't bear to put that thing on this morning, and luckily the warmer weather allows me to go without.

I've gone through several shirts since Takamoro all those years ago, wearing each garment until they literally fall apart. My current shirt is back in my cave. I've had this one for ... three, no, four years now, but no matter how much I sweat through it, no matter how many times I wash it in the rain or in the pool in the back cavern of my home, the stench of the man I took it from still clings to the garment. If I have to spend one more day inhaling stale smoke and chicken shit, I might go mad.

I press my palm to the hilt of the katana at my hip. "Don't say it. I know I'm already quite mad."

A sarcastic scoff is all I get in answer, and I give my saya a little pat. "I know you didn't have a choice in the matter, but thanks for sticking around and being my friend all these years."

Forty-six years.

My mind goes numb when I think about the endlessness of the time I've spent trapped here ... and the void stretching before me if I never get out. The walls of my cave look like a feral mole had a personal grudge against them with all the hash marks I've made to track my time here in my prison.

Every morning, I tell myself to stop making the marks. And every morning, I scratch another into the wall. Just like every day I walk the perimeter, daring to hope for some weakness to let me out, and every day another tiny chip scars my heart at losing that hope.

Lifting my arm, I stare at the back of my hand. The skin is brown, the veins pronounced, the nails short and trim. My forearm flexes with strength, the light dusting of hair appearing fairer in the sun. It's the same. Nothing has changed since the night I took my vengeance, since the night that green-eyed yokai cursed me, since I landed in this cave with nothing but my lacquered sheath hugged to my naked body. And if I were to wander to the back of my home and peer into the pool of water, the same face—the face of a man in his late thirties—would stare back at me. There are no new wrinkles, no grey hairs, no signs of time passed.

I rub a hand over my smooth jaw, begrudgingly appreciative for the magic that keeps my facial hair from growing. No need to shave. And though I've never taken a blade to my black hair, it remains the same length, brushing the tops of my shoulders.

I draw breath to my core as I approach the bare stretch of earth a few paces from the mouth of my cave. A handful of people have found this place, each one in search of Guardian. A few walked away disappointed and empty handed, but alive. Most did not leave this place.

I wiggle my toes in the dirt, connecting to the earth. It's nice. I like being out in nature. I like the calm it brings, the peace. It makes me feel *alive*—the only time I feel more alive is when the katana is in my hand and I'm moving through forms.

My right hand falls to the hilt of the sword at my hip,

secured by the cord to my sash. I rub my thumb over the shark skin wrapping, and it soothes me with its familiarity. A light breeze tickles my nose, bringing with it the scent of flowers. I wish I could find those blooms, caress their petals, enjoy their colors. I wonder if they're soft and pale or bright and bold? As I exhale, I toss away the wish. There are no blooms other than the orange lantern plant within my prison, and those flowers have no scent. No, it's just pines, scrub, and this infernal cave. Wherever this sweet scent is coming from, those flowers are out of my reach.

Rolling my shoulders, I pat my scabbard. "Off we go."

I walk the complete perimeter of my prison, the path so worn it's nearly a trench. Eighteen kilometers around. It used to seem expansive. Now it closes in on me a little more every day. A few hours later, I complete the round. I drop my hand from the invisible wall with a sigh. No difference today. I know my scabbard is winding up to say something sarcastic, so I bark out, "Don't say it."

It remains silent, but smirks in my head.

Back in the clearing, I brace my feet and untie the cord. With careful, practiced moves, I begin the sword form of the day. My grip on the hilt of the katana is firm and confident as I stagger my legs, bending at the knees. I picture my father doing this form, the strength in his arms, the concentration in his eyes. Intention and purpose in each strike. A longing ache presses against my ribs. I miss him. Sorrow rises, but there's also a sense of joy, because doing these forms makes me feel close to him once more.

Raising my saya over my head, I breathe in, and as I exhale, I strike it down, halting sharply when it draws in line with my front knee. I smile, resetting to go again. I love this. I go again. And again. And again. Sweat slides down my chest and back, pooling in the waist of my pants, turning the worn fabric a darker brown. I don't know how much longer this garment is going to last.

As if the fabric hears my thoughts, a sharp tearing sound breaks the rhythm of my breath. I don't bother to look. I don't need to as the breeze caresses my left knee through the new hole.

Great. Just great.

Time fades. The kirioroshi form becomes part of me. Inhale, blade overhead at the perfect angle. Tight core, strong thighs, grounded feet. Exhale, a sharp downward swing stopping level with my left knee.

Over and over, I move through the form.

Finally, I stand, appreciating the ache in my muscles as I hold my saya around the middle. I picture my father's smile at a practice well done. The sun is well past its peak, telling me I've been doing this single form for hours. Absently, my gaze runs over the section of shark skin on the hilt hiding my father's beautiful script. I can see it in my mind's eye. It's different from the stamp on the collar that has a sharpness to it, making his signature stand out boldly against the smooth metal of the guard. The sword's name in the hilt, that's more fluid, the characters seeming to dance across the section of blade that's concealed. Like it's only for me.

I miss him so much.

The joy of my practice melts away as my thoughts turn dark. It has been decades, but that familiar tingle of rage flares to life in my chest, quickening my heart rate. My father was kind. His mastery of swordcraft was unmatched. And his light, his knowledge was snuffed out.

Stupid, ignorant people!

Gripping the lacquered wood tighter, I dig my feet into

the earth as I stride towards the trees, leaving the small open area outside my cave behind. My palms start to sweat, and I find myself walking faster. A branch scratches my shoulder, and I bat it away. My stride falters, and I growl in frustration as a rock digs into my bare heel.

I'm jogging. Faster. I have to get out of here. I must. Almost fifty years! I don't deserve this. I want to live beyond this ... out there ... I have to ...

You just tested the barrier. It won't give. It won't let you through. Slow down. Stop!

That inner voice of my saya just makes me pick up my speed. My time here has pushed me into insanity. I *have* to get out of here! I glare at the tall pine tree with the x carved into its bark as it comes into view. Gritting my teeth, I bellow, my eyes blazing a furious, desperate red.

Speed. Power. I'll break through.

Lowering my head, I push into a sprint, my loose pants flap around my legs. But at the last second, some self-preservation takes over, and my shoulder drops as I slam into the invisible wall. Pain shoots up my neck and down my side. I'm weightless for a second as I fly backwards. I have just enough time to flatten my body, throwing my arms wide to avoid landing on my scabbard. I hit the ground, and my mouth drops open, trying to suck in air, but nothing happens for a long, terrifying moment. I gasp, cough, wheeze, and I'm finally able to inhale. I grip my side as my vision goes blurry with pain. I don't think I broke my ribs, but I sure bruised the hell out of them.

It doesn't matter. I'll heal in a few minutes.

Rolling over, my bare knee punches through the tear in my pants, and a sharp stick digs into my skin.

"Fuck."

My scabbard chuckles at me. *Well, that was stupid.*

"Shut up."

I can't talk to you when you're like this.

I shake the katana, screaming, "You can't talk at all!"

Then why are you talking to me?

With a deep sigh, I chuckle. "Who the hell else am I supposed to talk to?"

I spit into the dirt, then sit on my heels. Tilting back my head, I stare at the patches of blue sky peeking through the boughs of the forest. The scarlet glow fades from my eyes like a dying sunset. I don't bother to glare or curse at the barrier. There's no use. I've tried everything.

I've spent decades testing the damn thing ... blades, fire, rocks, sticks, bones, my magic, blood ... nothing.

You know if you sit here too long, you're going to get stiff.

I press my palms to my thighs and stand, no longer able to hold on to my rage. It's too exhausting.

"Yes, yes. I know. I guess we should go check the traps."

I brush off my pants with another chuckle, tying my saya to my sash. I used to think the rats, rabbits, and birds that got caught in my snares were stupid. But those *stupid* animals can come and go as they please, not even twitching a whisker as they pass through the barrier that might as well be solid iron for how well it keeps me here.

Quickly killing the small hare in my second trap, I sling it over my shoulder, recalling the first time I caught an animal. The berries on the lantern plant hadn't fallen to the ground yet, so I couldn't eat those unless I wanted to spend days writhing in pain. I'd been living on ferns and water for weeks when finally, a small rodent got caught in one of my traps. I was so hungry, I nearly tore into it while it was still alive. But my hunger for freedom was stronger. I had to try. So, I held the rodent against my chest, getting bit and scratched for the trouble. I prayed to whomever I thought would listen as I approached the barrier.

Hope is such a bastard. It was hope that made me grip the rodent tighter, and as its little paw slipped through the invisible wall, I shouted with joy, startling the creature. But the second my fingers touched the edge of my prison, I met solid air. And to make matters worse, I dropped the rodent, and it scurried away. I fell to the ground, weeping at the loss of food and the hope of freedom.

I shake off the morose thoughts as the trees thin, and my home comes into view. A soft curl of smoke twirls from the chimney of my small kitchen hut. As I step into the clearing, I pause, dropping my dinner to the dirt. I run my hands through my sweaty black hair, pulling it back and tying it at my nape with a faded red cord. After I secure it tightly, I allow myself the indulgence of rubbing the silk tie between my fingers, recalling the man who gave it to me.

Matsumae.

I sigh, and a bird startles from a tree, its wings beating furiously as it takes to the sky.

"How long will my imprisonment last? Another fifty years? Forever? How long must I suffer for a vengeance that I was rightfully due?" My thumb rubs the shark skin of the hilt at my hip. Doesn't matter. I'll pay this price.

I shake my head with a smirk as I speak to my scabbard. "You'd tell me if you knew the answer, right? The answer to the yokai's riddle ... the so-called truth that will set us free?" It raises a proverbial brow at me, and I nod. "Yeah. I know you would, my friend. Don't worry about it. It was all bull-shit. That spirit was a hypocritical cunt and a liar. Yokai are known to be cruel, but this ... Her words were obviously meant to serve as another form of torture, a false hope ...

hope that there is actually a way out. There's not. Because my truth has not changed, and it never will."

I pat the sheath, the lacquered wood resounding with a hollow sound. "But we've made a good little life here. We're making the best of things. Yes?"

Scowling down at the katana, I flick it. "But as my only friend, I find it very rude that you have yet to utter even one actual word to me out loud. The silent treatment is getting old."

You hear me fine enough.

Rolling my eyes as I walk into the cave, I nod at the wall of the wide tunnel that leads to my bedchamber. I point at the sheathed swords hung on pegs I embedded in the stone. "I should hang you up there, add you to my collection. Maybe swap you for that pretty noble son's sword. Maybe *that* fancy piece of steel will talk to me. Huh?"

The katana at my hip remains tight lipped, calling my bluff, knowing I'd never trade it for another.

The temperature drops slightly as I enter my bed chamber, the small circular 'room' echoing with my footsteps. Over the years I've amassed a decent amount of material for bedding—three padded horse blankets, a captain's thick winter coat, and a wool cloak. And using needles I carved from animal-bone, I've stitched myself a fairly luxurious futon, stuffed with pine needles.

They poke us in the middle of the night.

I shrug. "It's better than freezing."

Running my hand over the smooth wood of the table I made ... who knows how long ago now, it wobbles slightly, and I grin as my three bone needles click against each other. I pat my tiny pile of folded clothes. I treasure each and every item, appreciating how far I've come from my early days, curled naked against the rock wall, freezing to death but not dying. While I wish for more, I do admit my life isn't that bad. It's better than the alternative.

Today, I'm alive and grateful.

Turning back to my futon neatly laid out on a large bamboo mat, I swipe my small knife off the rock I rolled in here to use as another table before stalking back outside. I kneel, ready to dress the rabbit to get it ready to cook before it gets too dark.

Another lonely night awaits.

Followed by another lonely day.

And another. And another.

I finger the cord holding back my hair, and Matsumae's smile flashes through my mind again. For a time, with him, I wasn't lonely, but not for long enough. A wistful sigh leaves my lips.

When he arrived in my clearing, boasting his premature victory with a puffed-up chest, I brushed him off with a laugh. Little did I know there was a kind, passionate man underneath that bravado.

I start to get hard as I recall his strong fingers untying this cord from his black, silky hair. He'd then wrapped his arms around my neck, tying back my hair with the red silk. His chest was pressed against mine, and his breath whispered over my lips as he said, "Red suits you." I almost chuckled with how right he was, but then his mouth was on mine, and from that day on, he called me Red.

Even now, I can recall the taste of him. Our affair lasted a couple of months that summer, mending a few of the cracks and chips in my heart. The evenings were hot, the fireflies dancing around my cave, drawn in by the sweet temptation of the large poisonous lantern plant. Our sparring was intense but fun, our fucking even more so. Sometimes our passion would overtake us mid fight, and our bodies would clash right there in the training area.

The rabbit now forgotten, I slide my hand inside my pants, gripping myself. I stroke slowly as I recall my first time with Matsumae. I was all fumbling hands and nerves as I struggled to learn the moves to this new dance. But soon enough, we found our rhythm, and I realized I didn't need to think, only feel.

I grip myself a little tighter, sticking the fingers of my other hand in my mouth ... just like Matsumae did. My tongue swirls, and I collect my saliva, my hole pulsing in anticipation. I stroke and circle the head of my cock as I recall those steamy nights with Matsumae. Leaning forward, I yank my pants down and slide my hand between my cheeks, circling my hole once, shuttering at the memory of Matsumae's teasing touch. My finger pushes in, and I groan, precum coating the tip of my cock. I sink it deep, reaching for *that* place. After a few pumps, I insert a second, moaning at the stretch, recalling Matsumae leaning over me from behind, his hand wrapped around my cock, his hard length driving in and out of me.

I groan as my pleasure builds. I can almost hear him praising me like he did that night, grunting in my ear, "Yes, Red. You take me so well. Look at you, Red, gripping me so tightly."

I ride my fist, eyes closed, hearing Matsumae's grunts, his skin slapping against mine, and finally, his stuttered moan of ecstasy—his head thrown back, his fingers pulling on my hair, his lips parted, his breath panting desperately as his cum filled me until I was dripping.

I grunt as I drive my hips into my hand and come with a soft shout, pleasure taking me away from this place for a few seconds.

Slowly, my heart rate returns to normal, and I tuck myself back into my pants.

Feel better?

"Yes, in fact, I do."

My scabbard snorts, and I chuckle. Brushing my hands off on my pants, I reach for the rabbit. "And now I'm starving. Let's eat."

9

My shins are raw, and the graininess of the dirt has left pock marks on the flesh of my knees from my constant kneeling. With every breath, I release the discomfort and move through the nukitsuki form of the day.

Sweeping into the sweet dance of sword practice, I lift my butt off my heels, and in one clean move, lunge and draw my scabbard. The lacquered surface reflects the bright sun as if it's smiling at me. I like to think it's enjoying this as much as I am, and I grin as I picture my father's smile.

The time spent practicing the samurai forms—the time I spend with my body in complete harmony with the katana—is the only true peace I have in my forest prison. I feel whole, and I understand the joy my father felt for the art of the sword.

I blow a dangling drop of sweat from the tip of my nose, and a stray strand of my hair flutters with my breath. Crackling red magic snaps down my left side. Moving to take my kneeling position again, I pause, speaking through the corner of my mouth in a hushed tone. "You felt that, right?"

The katana nods in my head, and I strain to listen past the mundane sounds of the woods.

There! A snap of a twig.

Standing tall, I slide the scabbard through the sash around my waist and give it a pat. "Okay. Seems like we're getting a visitor! Be nice."

I'm always nice. They *hardly ever are.*

Little puffs of dust kick up as I cross my practice area. Bending over, my back pops as I grip the animal-skin pouch laying in a shaded patch of grass. The water cools my dry mouth as I take a big swallow, then I pour some over my chest and back to rinse away a bit of the sweat and dirt. Gooseflesh erupts across my skin for a delicious moment as the water chases away the heat of the day. But all too quickly, the sun dries me off.

"Do you think they will mind that I'm greeting them shirtless?" I shrug, waving the water skin. "Doesn't matter. Can't be helped. At least I'm not naked like the first time."

A few weeks ago, I cut up my foul-smelling garment to make new rope for snares as well as a pair of waraji to tie around my feet. I thought about repairing a small hole in my futon, but the thought of sleeping with that fabric that still carried the stench of chicken shit anywhere near me changed my mind. I hated that garment and was glad to see it go even though cutting it up left me without a shirt. But I might be getting a new one today!

That's grim. Maybe they're here to help.

Maybe. Probably not.

Brushing my hands down my thighs, I realize it's a futile effort to try and make these pants look like anything more than they are ... dirty rags on their last leg.

"Ha! Last leg! Get it?"

My scabbard barks a laugh in my head, and I chuckle

along with myself, but my smile fades when my magic sparks across the right side of my ribs, warning me of my visitors pending arrival. Movement catches my eye. Nerves build in my chest, but I force myself to stand still, hand on the hilt of the katana, my other arm relaxed at my side.

I wait.

A shadow takes form and moves closer. An arm lifts to shove a low branch out of their way. Pine needles and twigs crunch under heavy footfalls. For a second, I wonder what kind of footwear this person is wearing and if they'd fit me. I shake my head with gritted teeth.

Don't count the spoils yet. Have hope.

I turn to my right as they break through the trees and pause, staring across the clearing at me. His mouth is open, elongating his flat face. A leather band holds back dark hair glinting silver at the temples, and beautifully tooled leather armor clings to his wide frame.

He's wearing kegutsu! Riding boots!

I fail to squash the giddy excitement that bubbles in my gut at the thought of having decent footwear, but I keep my face void of my emotions.

He takes a step into the clearing and lifts his arm to shield his eyes from the blazing sun, calling, "Are you him?"

I nearly jump at the strength of his voice. It's been so long since I've heard a voice not my own. Anxious and unwisely optimistic, casting aside my yearning for his fine clothes and shoes, I send up a silent prayer to any god who might listen. *Please, let this one be different.*

Clearing my throat, I respond. "That depends on who you are looking for." I sweep a hand towards the fire pit to the right of the mouth of my cave. "I have some dried rabbit I'm happy to share if you are weary from your travels. Can I offer you some pine leaf tea?" I move across my practice area, frowning at my dirty feet, but there's nothing to be done about my appearance.

Waving at my kitchen hut, I say, "Let me grab my kettle. I only have one cup, but it's clean and you're welcome to use it. I'll be right back." I'm so excited to have a new 'guest', I nearly jog towards the hut.

Before the shadow of the roof's overhang reaches me, the man's voice calls out. "Are. You. Him? The keeper of the sword?"

I sigh, stopping and making the slow turn to face him. When I remain silent, the man takes another step, placing his hand on the hilt of his katana, his thumb pressed to the collar.

He opens his mouth, but I hold up a hand. "If it's the magical katana you seek, you have wasted your time. But I'm happy for the company. Please, come, sit. Rest for a while. I imagine you've traveled far. Why don't you tell me a little about yourself?"

Please. Just ... talk to me. Hear me. See me. Help me!

I keep my desperate thoughts inside, knowing from past experiences that coming on too strong too quickly tends to scare my visitors. Casually resting my hand on the hilt of the katana, I wait for the man to make a decision, trying to look as non-threatening as I can. Does this man realize his fate will depend on his next move? Will he accept there is nothing to be gained in pressing the matter of the magic sword and agree to enjoy a nice cup of tea with me? Will he sit and rest and trade stories with me? Will he promise to find a way to free me ...?

I snort. That's too much wishful thinking, even for me. Those who *have* left on their own two feet have never made such promises, nor have any returned.

Or ... will he demand the prize he has come for and die for his troubles?

Finally, the man says, "No tea. What do you want in exchange for the sword?"

Well, shit.

I glance over his shoulder before looking back at him, stalling. "Where is your horse?"

His back stiffens. "Why do you think I rode here on a horse?"

I tilt my head at his clothing. "Your armor is not suited for long journeys on foot. And you're wearing riding boots." I look down at my bare feet to hide my small smile. "Plus, there is an abundance of horsehair on your clothing."

Glancing back up, I watch as he looks at his pants before snapping his gaze up to meet mine. "Let me take this burden from you. You are too young to be the original keeper of Guardian, so the protection of the blade must have been passed down to you. Let me free you of this task. You can rest now. Go do whatever it is you want."

Oh, this one is good. He's definitely saying all the right things. And I must admit, I'm tempted. But his words are too honey sweet. There's a fire in his eyes I don't trust.

Besides, you'd never give me up, right?

I rub my thumb over the guard of the katana, giving it my reassurance with the touch.

The man goes on, "I will take good care of Guardian. The people of my town need the legendary blade. And yes, I *have* traveled far. My lord—"

"I am sure your journey was long and tiring." Gesturing calmly, I try again. "Why don't you take a seat? Rest for just a few moments at least, and you can tell me your story. Let me fetch my kettle."

He shakes his head and starts pacing, kicking up dust in

his wake. "Time is of the essence. I wasted too much time searching for you. Six months!" I almost scoff at that inconsequential amount of time, but I hold it in as he continues, "I almost gave up, but the gods finally led me here."

I barely manage to keep from rolling my eyes. Divine intervention? I think not. Unless the gods hate this man ... leading him to his death.

He stops, turning to face me. "My lord sent me to find the legendary blade. I cannot return without it. So tell me, what do you want?"

I sigh, still holding my arms relaxed at my sides, calm but ready to move. Keeping my voice even, I say, "I do need help, but I cannot give you what you seek."

I tap my middle finger against the hilt, the shark skin wrapping still smooth, strong, and unchanged even after all these years, stuck in time with me. Once again, I wave towards the mouth of my cave. "I have many fine swords I've 'collected' over the years. You are welcome to any of them"— I glance at the scabbard at his hip, admiring the white lacquer and silver tooling— "but if your saya is anything to go by, you have a fine piece of steel already."

The man shakes his head. "Tell me how I can help you. I need the *magic* blade. I need Guardian." His hungry eyes land on my scabbard. He's not listening. They never listen! I've seen that look so many times, yet it still makes me sad. The greed. The uncompromising drive that keeps them from seeing the truth before them ... that I won't relinquish this katana. And not only because it has been with me from the beginning and because it's my only friend. And not because it's the last piece of my father. But because I *can't*. I cannot give him Guardian.

I shrug, still hopeful for a peaceful resolution. "I'm sorry you've come all this way for nothing. You have a capable look about you, and if your blade is as well made as the sheath it is in, then surely you possess a weapon good enough to serve your lord's purposes."

The man shakes his head again.

I ask, "Why?"

"You know why."

I stand a little taller, holding my silence.

He points at my scabbard. "I need more than skill and good steel. I need magic!"

"Who is it that you ... or your lord ... are so afraid to face without a mystical blade that may or may not exist?"

One of his brows raises. "Guardian exists. And my lord's brother is coming to claim our land. He has an army. My lord has barely half his brother's numbers."

"So instead of recruiting and training, or maybe, I don't know, trying to find a way to make peace, your lord has bet his people's lives on the hope that a magical sword will save them?"

The man glares at me, easily picking up on the anger in my voice. Then his eyes fall back to my scabbard. "Yes. And we will win"—He nods at the sheathed katana at my hip—"with that."

Closing my eyes, I take a slow breath before meeting his gaze once more. "I empathize, my friend. But as I've said, I cannot give you what you seek. I *can* offer you some tea. It's bitter but it's hot and can be quite replenishing."

The man's thumb pushes the collar of his hilt, drawing my attention to the fancy crest emblazoned on the tsuba, probably the mark of his lord's house. I hold my breath, waiting for it. That sound. The sound of freedom. The sound of a musical note announcing the start of a beautiful melody. The sound of a blade slipping from the security of its home.

I shiver at the soft *snick,* my eyes tracking the smooth glide of his blade.

His voice draws my attention back to his face. "You say you can't. But what you mean is, you *won't.* And I didn't come all this way for *tea.*"

It's on the tip of my tongue to argue, but I don't bother. Instead, I look the man over from his boots to the crown of his head. He's seen battle. Scars crisscross his hands, and while his armor is finely made, it's also well worn. But as he was pacing back and forth earlier, I picked up on a slight hitch in his left hip, and his left shoulder slipped slightly every time he spun around.

Just like Takamoro all those years ago, this man licks his lips as he stares at the gleaming black of my scabbard.

You can't let him leave here alive. What if he comes back with reinforcements?

Would this man's lord waste more valuable time, money, and men on a quest to find a magical sword? Maybe. Doesn't matter. This man isn't walking away from this. We've reached an impasse. I know the signs. I've seen them too often.

I don't feel my father in this moment. I never hear his voice when this happens. He's never with me when I'm about to take a life. But I don't mind. I won't give up Guardian. I can't. I don't need my father's approval for what I'm about to do.

I let my smile creep onto my face as the man's knees bend slightly, his muscles flexing as he says, "If you will not hand it over, then I'm afraid I'll have to take it."

10

I crack my neck, looking at the dead man at my feet. I could have bested him without my magic, with my eyes closed, and one arm tied behind my back.

No challenge at all, but still, it was nice fighting someone other than myself. A chuckle passes my lips. I didn't even know this one's name. I hope his horse is able to find its way to a village or town. I'll go out later and see if it's tied up somewhere within my boundary. Hopefully I can find it and collect its dead owner's belongings. The saddle blanket alone ... Oh, just the thought makes my skin itch with anticipation.

But first ...

Kneeling, I recognize the callousness of my emotions as I rub my fingertips together in anticipation of stripping this man of every scrap of clothing and anything he carried in here with him. His head is a heavy weight in my palm as I undo the leather thong holding back his hair. I luxuriate in its suppleness, especially since thus far, I've been unsuccessful in tanning a hide pliant enough to hold my hair as tightly as I like. I have Matsumae's cord, but I'm grateful for an alternative that will extend the lifespan of my lover's precious silk tie.

Placing the thong on the ground, I maneuver the body and start to remove the outer armor. A soft caress of my magic slides down my back, so gentle, I dismiss it as a trick of the breeze. As I wrestle the body to remove the straps of the chest piece, a noise freezes me in place. I sit absolutely still, holding the dead man's arm sticking straight up, hand dangling limply in my face. The touch of my magic grows to a tickle, not in warning ... more like a whisper.

And then that noise ... there it is again.

Giggling?

The sound is so foreign to me, I don't know how to react, so I do nothing as I spy a little girl peeking around the trunk of a pine. Her dark eyes crinkle with her smile, her small mouth lifted at the corners, rounding her youthful cheeks. Her stick-straight black hair flutters like silk in the breeze, brushing just below her shoulders.

She can't be older than six, maybe eight.

What the hell is a child doing—

She steps around the tree, her movement stalling my thoughts, drawing me out of my stupor. Her hands fiddle before her, and I realize she's clutching a beautiful temari ball, shifting it from palm to palm. I drop the dead man's arm, and that musical giggle fills the air again. I know nothing of children, but this one seems ... odd.

And then a thought hits me and my heart sinks to my stomach as I sit back on my heels. I nod at the girl. "W-was this your papa?"

I shouldn't feel bad for taking this girl's father from her, because he attacked me ... and I really want these boots. Still ... I wait for her tears and screams, but instead she wrinkles her nose and approaches me with a smile, shaking her head. "No. He didn't seem very nice. My papa is nice."

As she approaches, she holds her head high, clutching the small ball in her left hand, looking around with confidence ... like she belongs. She must hail from a wealthy family—her posture speaks of training, and the embroidered fabric of her long-sleeved kimono screams money.

When she reaches the edge of the bare circle that makes up my training area, she pauses, keeping her tiny wooden geta shoes on the grass and out of the dirt I'm kneeling in. Her expensive-looking silk tabi socks make a soft swishing sound as she curls her toes. Though, on closer inspection, I notice a dark patch on the outer edge of her right sock, and dirt darkens the hem of her dress. The gold thread woven in her kimono shines in the sun as she says, "What are you doing way out here? Do you live here?" She doesn't even glance at the dead body.

"Yes, I live here. You don't. You should go home."

She goes on, as if I said nothing. "Living in a cave seems ..." She tilts her head, looking past me into the shadows of my home "... silly. Doesn't it get hot? And freezing in the winter? Is that a kitchen?" She points at the hut, but before I can answer, she goes on. "And that's a pretty big fire pit." Taking a few steps towards the large circle of rocks just outside my kitchen, she cocks her head. "That's nice. You can cook inside that hut or out here." Turning back to face me, she looks over my shoulder towards the mouth of the cave. "Do you have a futon in there or do you sleep on the ground? What else have you built here? Why here? You're out in the middle of nowhere. That really does seem silly to me."

I give up on trying to answer her stream of questions and just let her speak. I think this is the most I've heard someone talk ... ever. And it's wonderful. My own questions burn in my throat, and I swallow several times to keep myself quiet. I want to know about the outside world. I want to know where I am. I want to know how things have changed, or not changed at all.

And I want to know how this child found me.

But I don't want her to stop talking. Her voice is so light and happy.

Innocent.

I shuffle on my knees, turning away from her to grab the dead man's arm, yanking the chest armor off before lifting the undyed hemp shirt over his head. His blood has turned the entire left side of the garment a dark red, and a hole marks where I stabbed him with his blade. But the shirt is still usable. *Everything* this man owned will be put to good use—nothing will go to waste, except his life.

I'm very aware of the girl's presence behind me, but I ignore her, waiting for her to get bored and leave. Because she will. Everyone leaves, either on their own two feet, or at the end of a blade. Though I ache to ask her to stay, to keep me company for a while longer, I dare not. I don't dare feed that wretched emotion, hope. Because if this child stays here for a few minutes or a few hours, I'll hope for more. No matter what, I always end up hoping for one more hour, one more day ... please don't leave me all alone again.

But this is no place for a child. I'm not decent company for a young girl.

Trying to squash the desire to just sit and talk to her, I distract myself, brushing my fingers over the quality leather as I work to loosen the armor skirt, and thigh and shin guards. I can't believe this man trekked through the woods wearing all this.

As I start wiggling his boots off his feet, the girl asks, "Just how long have you been here?"

Without turning, I say, "A very long time." *Go away. Don't do this to me.*

"All by yourself?"

"Yes."

"Aren't you lonely?"

Extremely. But don't offer me hope. Just go, because you will eventually, and every moment you stay will make it that much more painful when you leave. Please.

My silence doesn't deter her stream of questions. "I don't think I'd like to live out here. I mean, for a while, I guess it could be fun." Her voice raises. "Like an adventure!" There's a small pause before she speaks again, softer this time. "But only for a little while. I'd miss my friends, though I suppose if I brought them with me, it wouldn't be so bad. But you're alone. You must like being on your own, huh? There's an old woman in my town that lives at the very end of the road, and she dumps pig's blood in her yard, always yelling at people to go away. She's not very nice. But you seem … nice. And you're not nearly as old as she is, so I don't know why you'd want to live out here on your own."

If you only knew.

The sound of her shuffling feet comes a little closer, and my shoulders tense. When she pauses, she says, "I don't think it's good to be on your own for too long, even if you think you like it. *I* think you should live in a village or town. Oh! Would you like to come to my town? My papa owns a fine fabric store. Everyone knows my family. It's a good place to live. You should live there!"

I would if I could. "That sounds nice."

"It is! Though I don't like the new tutor my papa hired. She's very … scrunched."

I chuckle, knowing better, but finding myself drawn into this girl's rambling conversation. As I work to loosen the ties of the dead man's pants, making sure my body is blocking her view, I ask, "Scrunched?"

There's a little *swish thump* sound, like she's tossing and catching the ball as she talks. "Yeah. Her nose and forehead always scrunch when she's telling me what to do. So, I pretend I'm sick to get out of lessons. Or sometimes I slip out through the kitchens while she talks to mama. One time, I told her I couldn't study because my friend, Isayo, needed my help to run errands for her mama." She laughs. "Isayo's mama wouldn't trust her with carrying a hairpin from one room to another."

"You're a sneaky little thing."

She giggles, and I marvel at the happy sound. "I am! It's easy to sneak away and do what I want. Papa is always busy with his business, and mama is always hurrying around, bossing the servants. She's always saying to me"—I glance over my shoulder, watching her clasp the small ball in both hands. She tilts her head, looking down her small nose at me, and her voice pitches deeper—"Running this house is an important job. You don't understand now, but someday, you will run your husband's house."

She drops her arms and shakes with a dramatic shiver. "I don't need to learn that stuff though, because I'm *never* getting married."

I don't bother to correct her as I refocus on my task of going through my new possessions. The dead man's undergarments look to be of good quality. After a thorough wash, they'll be practically new.

There's another soft shuffling sound, small feet over grass. Her voice is quieter than before as she asks, "How ... um, how did you do that?"

There's a pain in my chest, and it's expanding. The longer this girl lingers, the more her sunny chatter fills this space, the more she pushes my loneliness away, the worse it will be when she leaves. But I can't help myself, and I force a smile into my words as I ask, "How did I undress a dead man?"

She giggles again.

She really is quite odd.

"No. How did you beat him? You never drew your sword from its sheath, and he had all that armor. But you still won. How?"

The dead man's leg flops to the earth with a thud as I pull his pants off. "I was better than him." When there's no response from behind me, I hold the sole of one of his boots to the bottom of my foot. "Damn it! Too small."

Dropping the boot, I sigh. I'll find uses for them, but who knows how long it will be before someone who has the same size feet as me will come in search of Guardian? Months? Years? Damn it! I scowl at the boots. They didn't even have to fit perfectly. Too big would have been better than too small. I once spent three years wearing sandals two sizes too big, wrapping extra cloth around the bindings to keep them on.

I wiggle my toes in the dirt. Barefoot it is, until ...

Pressing my palms to my thighs, I stand in one fluid motion, then brush off my pants. My magic tickles down my back, alerting me that the girl is still watching me, so I bend over and flip the man onto his stomach. She doesn't seem bothered by the dead body, but getting an eye full of a dead man's cock, that's a bit much. Grabbing the now naked man by the wrists. I start to drag him out of my training area, away from the girl.

She calls after me. "What are you doing? Are you going

to bury him? What about his family? Will you tell them what happened?"

I shake my head. "No. And No. Burying him would be a waste of energy. The animals will just dig him up. But I don't want him stinking up my home, so ..."

What I don't tell her is that this dead body is now bait.

Years ago, after I killed the second man that came in search of Guardian, I left his body where he fell for three days. It was the middle of winter, and I spent those three days going back and forth in my thoughts. Should I flay the body? Not for meat, I'd starve to death before I cannibalized a body. But the fat ... I could make candles. Though, I had no idea how to make candles, I was sure I could figure it out. But, in the end, I just couldn't. What I did do was drag the half-frozen body deeper into the woods and set up watch downwind. That time of year, food is scarce for all animals, me included. When a boar approached, then tore into the man's flesh, I pounced. I got a tusk to the thigh and nearly bled out for my troubles, but I won and ate like an emperor for days.

The girl watches me drag the body away, her white teeth chewing on her bottom lip. Her eyes slide to the man's katana where it lays in the dirt. After the man fell, it was habit that had me executing the chiburi move, flicking the man's blood from his blade. But the chiburi seldom does the job completely, so a few smears of red still mark the bright silver of the fine blade—A sliver that shines like my magic used to ... before it changed to the rageful red it is today.

The girl stares at the sword for a long moment, and for the briefest flash, I see it in her eyes. That hunger I've seen on the face of every man that has come to this place. But in a blink, it's gone, and she turns her attention back to me.

I keep backing up, dragging the body, his heels leaving

twin trails in the dirt. The girl watches but holds her tongue. The shadows of the tree line cross my path, and I drop the man's arms. Standing, I meet her gaze. "This is no place for a little girl. Go home."

Her eyes narrow, and her small hand clenches into a fist, the other squeezing her temari ball. In anger? I guess children never like being told what to do. But her outrage seems ... more. She's almost trembling with it. With a grunt issued through gritted teeth, she throws the ball at my head. "Don't boss me!" I have the absurd urge to laugh as I duck, and the brightly colored temari sails by, bouncing a few times before rolling to a stop. I raise a brow and allow a little of the humor bubbling up in my chest to escape with a smirk.

She stares at me for a moment, her eyes wide as if she can't believe she just threw her ball at a stranger that just killed a man. Then, her gaze drops where it lands on my scabbard at my hip, and my heart plummets into my stomach so quickly, I fight to keep from rubbing my belly at the ache. Has this little thing come for the magic sword after all? How would a child even know of it? Was she sent by someone as a cunning scheme to get their hands on the katana? Her father? A brother?

She toes the dirt with her pretty wooden shoe, opening her mouth, then closing it. She opens it again, then snaps her lips shut. The girl glances around the clearing that is my training area and stares at the dead man's boots for a few seconds. She chews on her bottom lip, and when she finally lifts her head, she smiles and waves. "Okay, bye! It was nice to meet you!"

"Wait!" The plea is out of my mouth before I can stop it. She looks over her shoulder, one small brow raised. What do I say? What *can* I say? A strange man in the middle of a cursed forest can't ask a little girl to stay and talk with him. Right? No. That's crazy.

Well, you have to say something, you idiot.

My scabbard is right, so I blurt out, "What's your name?"

A cute smile lifts her lips. "Atagi Meiko. What's your—"

"It was very nice to meet you, Atagi-chan."

Her dark eyes crinkle as her smile deepens to a broad grin, and she waves again. "See you later."

If only.

She hurries off, moving as swiftly as her kimono allows, and all too soon, the shadows of the forest swallow her up as if she'd never been here. And maybe she wasn't. Maybe I conjured her into existence. Maybe my madness has risen to a whole new level.

Cracking my neck, I grab the dead man's wrists once more, determined to forget all about Atagi Meiko. Though her sweet little giggle keeps ringing through my mind. A sound too joyous for this dark, cursed forest.

A sound too good for me.

11

Today's form is doing little to distract me.

I've already walked the perimeter of my prison, as I do every day, and of course, there was no change. No breaks. No weak spots.

The lack of breeze makes the intensity of the sun all the more oppressive. The bare skin of my shoulders and chest tingles with the sting of the sun's rays. Still, I'd rather be hot than cold. My first night here, so long ago, still haunts me … of the freezing, of the burning, of waking frozen and alone.

My old, patched up pants flap around my calves as I move. I dare not wear my new clothing during my practice. I don't want to get them all dirty and sweaty. Sure, I can wash them, but I need the new clothes to last as long as possible. Who knows how long it will be before anoth—

I shake off the depressing thought, only to have Atagi's bright smile light up in my mind. It's been a fortnight since the strange girl appeared in my forest, and I haven't completely convinced myself that she wasn't in fact a figment of my imagination, but the pretty little temari ball in my cave says she was real.

Her laugh though ... sometimes I swear I hear her giggle on the wind.

Relaxing my arms at my sides, I refocus my thoughts for what feels like the hundredth time this morning. My bare feet glide three strides across the dirt. My right hand grabs the center of the scabbard at my hip. As I wrap my left arm across my body to grab the hilt, sweat slicks where the skin of my forearm brushes against my exposed stomach.

Normally, this form would require me to draw the blade straight out, keeping the scabbard close to my body. But I keep it sheathed. As always.

The smooth lacquer slides through the loose grip of my right hand as I draw it forward. Moving through the dance of the form, I turn to my right, drawing the katana around. Flexing my muscles, I smile as I stab the scabbard straight forward, imagining my foe before me hunching over my blade as it pierces their stomach. Pulling power from my shoulders, I slide the katana from my imaginary foe, spinning to my left with an overhead slice, bringing the scabbard down with a violent *swish* of air. I hold my stance for a breath before rotating the hilt, letting the wood of my sheath slide along my left thumb to find its place back at my side.

I reset, take a few breaths, then move through the form again.

And again.

The familiar burn of fatigue builds in my back and shoulders. My arms ache as the scabbard seems to get heavier. Usually, at this point in my practice, my mind goes blank, and I sink into a space made of nothing but movement and peace. Swordplay is like meditation to me.

Usually.

I stop halfway through the form, lowering the katana with a sigh. "Today's just going to be one of *those* days."

My scabbard frowns in my head. *How bad?*

"I just can't focus. Don't worry, it's not like *that*. Not today."

My free hand drifts to my wrist, absently rubbing the skin. A phantom shock of pain lances up my arm as I recall that night almost sixteen years ago ... The bite of the steel against my flesh. The knife, a prize taken from my second 'visitor'. I'd cut myself to the bone and watched dispassionately as my blood dripped with loud *splats* on the stony cave floor. I was relieved when my breaths became labored. A smile actually lifted my cheeks as dizziness took me to the ground, that cursed emotion taking hold. I *hoped* I wouldn't wake. I *hoped* this would all finally end. Cold. It was cold, and I remember gasping as my heart stuttered. I'd gathered my scabbard to my chest, hugging it much like I had that first night. A single tear dripped down my face, sliding between my lips as I'd whispered, "I'm sorry I couldn't get us out of here. I'm sorry I couldn't fix things." As dark spots took over my vision, I choked back my tears with a grin, seeing my father's face in my mind. "But I'm *not* sorry for what I did. I never will be."

But, like always, I'd woken with a gasp, the skin of my wrist already scabbed over.

My saya whispers in my head. *That other time was worse.*

Pressing my palm to my chest, I look down at the smooth skin where magic healed the wound I inflicted upon myself. I drop my hand, wishing there was a scar from that night ... the night I fell on one of the many swords I'd collected over the years. That was over a decade ago, and I haven't done it again since. One blade through the heart is enough. I recall waking with a piercing pain in my chest and the bloodied blade on the ground next to where I lay. I don't remember pulling the sword from my chest, but I must have at some point.

Shaking my head, I slide my scabbard through the sash at my waist, giving it a little pat. "Let's not spend the day going over every time I've tried to kill myself. Seems like a depressing waste of time. Besides, if a sword through the heart won't kill me, I don't think anything will."

I smile at my scabbard, the weight of my existence keeping my expression from holding any actual happiness. "But, no, I'm not there. Not today."

Curling my toes under, I roll my foot one way then the other, and my ankle pops. The hole in my pants is larger now, my entire knee and part of my shin exposed, but it's the middle of summer, and this is all the clothing I need.

I'd go naked like I was forced to when I first arrived here, but you get sunburnt on your cock one time and it makes you really, really appreciate pants.

"Let's make some tea. That might settle the mind."

My scabbard rolls its non-existent eyes. *Your tea is awful. Too bitter.*

As I stride towards my kitchen, I click my tongue. "I know it's bitter, but sometimes you need something other than just water. And before you say it, yes, yes, I am thankful for the water. Constantly 'dying' of dehydration during the dry seasons would be ... problematic."

Problematic?

I chuckle, shaking my head. "Okay. It would be horrific. So, yes, I'm thankful. But I'm still making tea."

My bare feet slap quietly on the packed ground. As I enter the hut, I head for the slightly crooked shelf where the brass of the small kettle glints in the weak light coming through the open doorway. I pick it up, rubbing my fingers lovingly over the scroll work on the handle. I've had this kettle for years, but I've taken great care of it, and it shines almost as bright as the day I got it.

The man I took this from was my favorite 'visitor' by far … besides Matsumae … and Atagi. He arrived on horse—which he rode right into my camp, stomping all over the mushrooms I had been drying out in the afternoon sun. But I easily forgave him after one look at his bulging saddle bags. His horse was so overladen, the weight practically bowed the poor beast's back. After killing the man and stripping him and the horse of all his possessions, I gave the gelding a gentle pat, hoping he found his way back home.

You were quite quick to kill that man. All it took was one look at me. You didn't even let him finish asking if I was in fact Guardian.

I chuckle again. "Yes, I'll admit, I was a bit overeager to end that fellow's life. Didn't really give him a chance to walk away." I wave the kettle around. "But look! You must admit. He had so many good things. Which made up for the fact he was too short that his pants barely fell past my knees, making it look like a child's summer jinbei. And he was so fat, his shirts looked like a little girl's kimono on me, barely skimming my navel. And I could have fit two of me in the waist of his pants. His clothing did make a good cushion and some nice rope."

With a sigh, I lower my arm, swinging the kettle from my fingertips. "Ah, remember how we ate that week? Like the emperor himself! He had so much food stashed in his bags, it was a wonder a wild animal didn't maul him before he found us." My head falls back with a sigh. "And his tin of tea … just holding a steaming cup of hot sencha in my hands, the floral aroma dancing around my face, drifting up my nose with every inhale … ahh, it was heaven."

I reach forward with my free hand, and the brass of my single cup scrapes lightly against the deep brown wood of the shelf as I pick it up. I grab the leather pouch—also taken from that same man—where I keep my dried leaves. A hollow *ting ting* rings out as I tap my cup against a little tin sitting next to where the pouch was. "If only there was just a little bit of that sencha in there."

I smile as I recall the other spoils from that day so long ago, now sitting neatly in my bedchamber. The saddle bags, the squares of cloth that held that man's biscuits and dried seaweed. A coil of actual rope. The ivory buttons from his pants.

Farther down the shelf, I grin at the dented tin plate and the chipped set of chopsticks. "He was a great visitor."

It's funny you call them visitors. They're thieves. Selfish thieves.

I cock my head. "Mmm. None of them have ever taken anything from me, so potential thieves. Intent of thievery? Is that a thing?"

My saya chuckles, and I join in as I kneel. Being a little crazy in the head isn't so bad.

Setting the kettle down, I refold and stack the rough fabric of the three burlap sacks I got from that same fat man. I can still detect a slight hint of the dried rice they once held. I made myself sick that afternoon, just an hour after killing him. I ate not one, not two, but three bowls of rice. My stomach was not used to that, but I *refused* to vomit. I wouldn't waste that meal. I just dealt with my aching belly.

"Now all this lamenting has made me hungry, and the traps were empty yesterday. So, after tea, we'll go forage, yes? Maybe a few of the berries on the lantern plant dropped last night."

Stopping at my pool in the rear of the cave, I scoop some

water into my kettle. Once I'm back outside, I kneel before my firepit, piling dry wood and leaves in the center. Drawing my prized flint and steel from my pocket, I strike once, sparks catching in the tinder with ease. As the fire begins to snap, greedily eating its fuel, I carefully place a flat rock on the partially buried taller stones I have set up to hold them in place around the fire. My ingenious version of an outdoor stove ... for when it's too hot to cook in my kitchen hut. The flames begin to heat the flat rock, and with a soft *clink*, I set the kettle on top, sprinkling a few leaves inside.

I scratch my chest, my skin itching with what feels like a gentle scrape of my magic, but it's so faint, I brush it off as the burn of the sun. I clasp my hands in my lap, counting in my head. Not too long, or the tea will go beyond bitter into undrinkable.

"YES!"

I jump, the shout startling me so badly, I nearly knock the kettle off its stone. When I look towards where the sound came from, I rub my eyes, blinking with my mouth hanging open. There, at the edge of the tree line stands a bay mare, her black mane glossy, her braided tail flicking. But it's not the horse that has me speechless.

It's her.

12

Atagi Meiko.

A tie holds back her black hair, fully revealing her smiling face. Her short legs nearly stick straight out around the wide girth of her horse, the bright arrow pattern of her silk hakama pants billowing like a flag with her little kicks. And ... I just now realize the mare is without a saddle. Atagi is riding bareback, her waraji sandaled feet bouncing with her excitement.

So that *was* my magic. But it wasn't warning me, at least not in anger. It felt more ... silver. I'd almost forgotten how that felt. Odd that I'm feeling it now ... with this child.

Throwing a leg over the neck of her mare, Atagi slides off her horse, landing at a jog. I still haven't moved, unsure that what I'm seeing is actually real. But Atagi runs across the clearing, her hair swishing behind her. She must have been riding for a while, because there are sweat stains on the insides of her pant legs with horsehair stuck to the fabric.

I'm still just blinking at her, mouth agape, as she skids to a stop, dust kicking up around her. After she catches her breath, Atagi lets loose a stream of words. "I finally found you! It took me days! I tried to come back right away. Well, not *right* away. I had to wait a day because my scrunched-up tutor didn't believe I was still sick. And then my mother's sister came to visit, and I had to do all this work around the house. But finally, I slipped out. When I got to the forest, I followed the red strings I left last time, but they only led me halfway. Then I just ended up going in circles. It was so strange. I know I marked the trees right. I'm very good at finding my way. I never get lost. My friend Isayo gets lost all the time. She once got lost between her house and the market! And this other time she ..."

As Atagi keeps talking without pause and seemingly without taking a breath, I take in what she just said. This little girl marked the way here, but when she tried to follow it back to me, it had changed. As I suspected, the magic of this place makes it hard to find me, making me even more grateful for those visits from Matsumae all those years ago.

So, how did he find his way back? And now, Atagi?

And why?

I tune back into her continued stream of sentences.

"I tried to come back here again the next day with no luck. It took me a few days to find the right time to sneak out again, but the red strings still took me nowhere. But I'm no quitter! I tried again and again." She raises a hand, waving at me. "And here you are! I found you! I won't mess up marking the way this time." She mumbles. "But I don't think I messed it up last time."

I hold up a hand. "Atagi-chan, it is good to see you again, but—"

She spins, her hair whipping around. "Are you making tea? Can I have some? I've been riding for hours through this crazy forest. Do you think it's haunted? Is that why I couldn't find you? Ooh! Are there yokai in these woods? Do spirits protect you or something?"

Or something.

I'm being greedy, hoping she'll stay and just keep talking. I need to send her away. She doesn't belong here. But I smile and say, "I'd be happy to share my tea with you, though, I'm afraid it's bitter and not all that good."

She crinkles her nose, but then quickly smooths her features, and I see her calling up the manners her mother or her tutor taught her as she stands taller. "I'd love a cup, please."

My smile broadens, and I realize ... I'm happy. It's been a long time since I've felt happiness because of another person. It feels strange. Warm. Almost dizzying. It's the way I felt whenever Matsumae would walk out of the woods into my clearing. The same feeling I used to get when practicing forms with my father, or simply listening to him tell Saito stories at night over a shared meal.

I press my lips together as I kneel before my now ruined batch of tea. Wrapping my hand in the scrap of cloth I keep near the fire pit; I pluck the kettle off the stone and dash the tea into the dirt off to the side.

Atagi gasps. "What'd you do that for?"

I shrug. "It had been steeping too long. I will make us a fresh batch, but I need to go fetch water from the pool inside. I'll be right back."

"Oh! You have water in there? A pool! Can I see?"

She skips to keep up with me. I should tell her to stay outside. Does she have no self-preservation? Who goes into a dark cave with a stranger you saw commit murder? I should send her home. I should ...

Instead, I scoop up one of the torches I keep near the entrance. Sticking the end in the fire, I wait as the fabric and dried moss wrapped around the tip quickly catches. I can easily make my way in the dark, but Atagi will need the light.

I step into the cave, the torchlight flickering against the rock that surrounds us as I say, "Yes. There is a pool in the back cave. It's fed by an underground spring and also collects rainwater."

"There's more than one cave in here? Wow! Do you wash in it too? Is it cold? I hate taking cold baths. But mama says if my bath water has gone cold, it's because I wasn't respectful of our servant's time. It's not like I do it on purpose, but sometimes I lose track of time when I'm out playing with my friends. Or I'm in a good part of a book and don't want to put it down. Or ..." She trails off, tilting her head as we walk deeper into the caves, and her voice echoes. "What else is in here? I take back what I said before, this *is* a pretty neat place to live."

Tears fill my eyes as I continue to lead the way. To hear another's voice in this place ... and not just my own insane ramblings to my saya. I'm all too familiar with how hollow these caves are going to seem after Atagi leaves.

Maybe just try to concentrate on the now. Don't worry about later.

But all I have is later. Too much later.

Swallowing the lump in my throat, I watch Atagi in the dim light as her head swivels, taking in the rough stone of the passageway. My little piece of hell must seem like a grand adventure to her.

Dropping my gaze, I clench my hand.

What am I doing? I shouldn't be indulging myself. I shouldn't be indulging her. Will she get in trouble if she's caught sneaking out? Who knows what's out in those woods. What if a wild animal attacks her? What if her horse throws her and she's hurt with no one around to help her? What if the magic of this place turns things around so much that she can't find her way home? This is bad. I can't endanger this child's life. She doesn't understand what she's stumbled into.

My thoughts keep spinning, but I keep walking, taking a few steps before I realize I'm alone. Turning back, I see little Atagi facing the wall, her head tilted back, her eyes wide. She points at the wall, then turns, her astonished face looking at me as her arm swivels to point at my chest. "Did you kill all these men?"

I manage to cover my laugh with a cough. *What an odd girl.* I stride back to her side, turning to face the wall of swords. I look over each one, some in their scabbards, some bare. Nodding my head towards one near the top, I say, "Not that one. That man gave me that blade." *Matsumae.* Pointing at a smaller blade sheathed in a plain wood scabbard, I say, "And that one. Its owner dropped it and ran when he realized he wasn't going to win against me."

I recall watching that man scramble away, his sandals slipping in the dirt as he sprinted towards his horse. I wasn't concerned with letting that one go. I felt fairly confident he wouldn't try to gather reinforcements to come back because that would require him to tell his tale and admit that he ran away empty handed—and I know a coward when I see one. But for months, my saya whispered that I could be wrong, keeping me on edge.

I wasn't wrong.

My magic tingles down my side as Atagi looks at me, but I keep my eyes on the katanas. So many lives. Seventeen to be exact. Fifteen lives lost, and only two smart enough to walk away ... All for the sake of a magic blade.

Atagi reaches out, her fingers hovering over the gold accented white lacquer of a saya before her, but she drops her hand without touching. I'm sure to her, this seems like a lot of swords, but to me, each one marks a visitor ... here then gone. Moments of reprieve from my endless existence. In almost fifty years, only seventeen men have found me. And none have offered to help. None have even asked my name. Not even Matsumae. I wasn't the reason they came here. All came for Guardian.

I rest my hand on my saya at my side as Atagi asks, "Why don't you carry any of these? Some of them are much nicer than ..." She nods at the scabbard on my hip. "Why that one? It's the same one you carried last time I saw you. The one that man wanted. What's so special about it? Is it really magic?"

I pat her head, ruffling her silky hair before continuing down the tunnel, keeping an eye on her. Atagi runs her hand over her hair, smoothing it out with a huff before rushing to keep up with my long strides as I ask, "Do you believe in magic, Atagi?"

She takes a few moments before answering. "I don't know. Maybe? What I don't understand is if all those men believed your sword is magic, then why would they bother trying to fight you for it? Who would fight against someone with a *magic sword*?"

She may be young, and she may be odd, but she's smart. I like her.

How do I explain to a little girl that desperate men will do almost anything to get what they want, consequences be damned?

I'm saved from having to tell her these harsh truths as we enter the pool chamber. Atagi looks around, her dark eyes round with wonder, her previous questions seemingly forgotten. She goes right up to the edge and kneels to dip her finger into the clear water. "Oh! It's cold!"

Shaking her hand, sending droplets flying, she stands as I say, "The water is always cold, no matter how hot the summer days get. And the edges of the water freeze in the winter." I point towards the far end of the pool. "Out there is where it's fed by an underground spring. Despite that, one winter it was so cold, the entire pool froze over."

That was a rough year. Though, I managed to stay alive that winter. No more freezing to death for me, not with my collected clothing and blankets, and the hearth I built in my sleeping chamber.

Moving to the edge of the cave, I dip the kettle into a naturally formed pocket of sorts in the side of the wall. When it rains, water from above dribbles down the wall into this reservoir.

Atagi stands on tiptoe, peering into the basin that's no bigger than her face. She gasps, "Oh! It's deep." I nod with a smile, amused at her delight in every little thing. "How deep does it go? Do you know?"

I nod. "I can touch the bottom if I stick my whole arm down in there. But just barely."

"Wow. It's like a sink. This place is amazing."

Without realizing it, my hand has moved, hovering over her back as if to pat her. My fingers flex, but I drop my arm, gesturing to the exit. "Shall we?"

Atagi lowers to her heels, and skips out of the room, her hair swinging behind her. As we pass the wall of swords, her gaze lingers, and I see the desire on her face. But what does a little girl want with a bunch of swords?

Reflexively, I touch the shark skin wrapping of the hilt at my side.

Or is it one sword in particular that she wants? Atagi may be a little girl, but I can't discount that someone may have sent her here for Guardian.

I don't want to believe that of her ... she seems like a sweet girl, if a little reckless.

She may not even be aware she's being used. I imagine there are plenty of ways to manipulate a child into doing what you want.

Is someone using her to get to Guardian?

Atagi shields her eyes as we break back out into the sunlight, her mare still standing in the tree line where she left her. I make a little detour, quickly striding into my bed chamber to grab her little ball before joining her back in the clearing. As I set the kettle to boil once more, Atagi gasps. I snap my head up, dropping her temari as I look her over. "What's wrong? Are you okay?"

A happy little laugh bubbles from her lips. "I completely forgot!" She smacks her forehead and spins around, running towards her horse.

In a panic, I stand, holding out a hand. It's there on my lips, the shout to ask her to wait, to stop, to please don't leave. But when she gets to her mare, she jumps, grabbing a string draped over the horse's neck. Once again sprinting back, her little chest rises and falls quickly with her panting breath. Her grin is so pure and happy, I'm stunned into continued silence.

She holds up her arm, her prize dangling from her clenched hand. "I brought you sandals!"

13

"Y ou ... you brought me ..."

She giggles, shaking the string in her hands, causing the sandals to bump together. "I brought you sandals. I think they'll fit. I saw you looking at those boots last time. I figured if I brought you something you wanted, then you would ..."

She trails off, dropping her arm, the toe of her waraji digging into the dirt as she stares at the ground. Is she trying to bargain with me? Does she think a pair of sandals will pay for Guardian?

I take a step back, my fingers curling around the hilt.

Shit. Shit! What do I tell her? How do I explain? Will whomever sent her be angry if she returns empty handed a second time? Will they punish her? Will they hurt her?

I can't ... I *can't* ...

"Teach me."

I blink at her. "What?"

Looking up at me, there's hesitance in her eyes, but her little hands are curled into fists. "Teach me how to use a sword. Teach me to fight and these sandals are yours."

She doesn't want Guardian. She wants to learn sword-play? Wait. What? She ... what? My brows furrow as I try to process what Atagi just said. I certainly wasn't expecting *this*.

She sweeps her gaze to the entrance of the cave behind me ... where all those katanas are on display. Atagi's voice is quiet but strong. "Girls aren't allowed to fight. We can't even *hold* a sword. Everyone is always telling me, 'Stand straighter, keep your gaze down, comb your hair, straighten your clothes, smile, keep quiet, walk, don't run.' I'm expected to cook, clean, sew, follow orders and pray to the gods that a wealthy man asks to marry me. UGH!"

She focuses her eyes back on me, nailing me with her fierce gaze. "Being a girl is ..." She scowls, her posture tight with tension. "Being a girl means you're heard but no one listens. You're looked at, but not really *seen*."

Maybe this child is older than I thought. She has intelligence beyond what I guessed to be her six years of age.

And, not seen? Atagi could go unnoticed as much as a thorn stuck in one's foot. She demands attention simply by being in your presence.

Mentally, I shake my head. I can't do this. I can't feel sorry for her. I owe this child nothing. My responsibilities start and end within my prison and hoping to find a way out. I take care of my scabbard and myself. That's it.

We end up in a stare-off, and after a long silence, I cross my arms. I really want those sandals. She hasn't asked for Guardian ... yet. I still can't dismiss the fear that someone might be pulling her strings.

"No."

Atagi looks up at me, her jaw flexing as she blinks rapidly, like she's holding back tears. Her voice comes out quieter, hushed with emotion. "Please."

I shake my head, dropping my gaze so I don't have to

look at the disappointment on her face. "I'm sorry, Atagi-chan, but—"

"I'll do whatever you say! I don't care how hard the training is, I'll do it. I won't complain." Her eyes glisten with unshed tears, but to keep them from falling, she says—maybe more to herself than to me, "I won't cry. I'll do whatever it takes, whatever you want."

Fuck. I want to say yes.

Don't. It will only end in heartbreak ... one way or another.

Hope. Fucking hope. How nice would it be to teach someone, to spend hours practicing forms and sparring, and not just with myself. I want that so bad ... but I can't. I can't do this to myself, and I can't do this to her. I can't encourage her and this careless behavior.

My voice comes out harsh with the intent of pushing her away. "You don't know me, Atagi. You're a little girl. You can't go around asking strangers to teach you to use a sword. You saw me kill someone! Did you even stop to think of why a man like me would be living out in the middle of the woods, alone? What if I'm dangerous? What if I'm a bad man, Atagi?" She opens her mouth, but I keep going. "No. You didn't. You didn't think, Atagi. You just wanted something for yourself, consequences be damned."

She flinches at my foul language, but I have to drive her away. I have to save us both. It feels like a sword to the gut as I demand, "Go home, Atagi."

Despite her promise from just a moment ago, a single tear drips down her face. She sniffles but doesn't wipe it away. Staring at me, she clenches her fists, and I wait for her to beg some more, but she draws back her arm, throwing the sandals. They land with a thud at my feet, a little puff of dust kicking up around the woven hemp as she shouts,

"Fine! I don't want to learn from a stupid man living in the stupid woods anyway!"

Atagi spins around, running to her mare. I take a step towards her before I know what I'm doing. I force myself to stand still as she gathers her horse's reins.

How is she going to get herself up there without a sadd—

Atagi shimmies onto a low branch of a tree, grunting with her effort. To her mare's credit, the horse stands still, patiently waiting for her rider to jump on her back. Atagi flops onto her horse, her little feet kicking to worm her way up before throwing one leg over her mare. Without looking back, she kicks her mount and rides into the woods. The shadows swallow her, and the *crunch, crunch* of leaves and sticks under the horse's hooves get quieter, then fade.

And then silence.

Deafening silence.

I look down at the sandals. They are finely made. They look expensive. I didn't even ask where she got them. Are they her father's or some other relatives? Will they notice they're gone? Will Atagi get in trouble? My knee cracks as I kneel, and I pick up the shoes, running my hands over the expertly woven hemp. These are fine shoes indeed.

I look at my scabbard, looking for reassurance as I ask, "I did the right thing, right?"

It doesn't answer. My head bows, and my hair falls around my face, hiding the tears as they splat to the dust, creating little spots of dark brown between my bare feet.

"I did the right thing."

I'm slow to stand, my body heavy and sore, but not from my practice earlier today. This drag isn't physical, but emotional. The weight of my loneliness is literally pressing down on me.

You could have asked her for help.

"When I finally gathered the courage to ask Mostumae for help, I never saw him again." I don't know why my lover didn't come back, and I never will. The hurt and loneliness remains, but I hold on tightly to the good memories. "No, asking for help is too dangerous. Besides, what would a little girl know of such things?"

So, are you going to wallow in self-pity all day?

I scowl at my scabbard. "Can I have a few moments to just be sad?"

When it doesn't answer, I sigh. Swiping up the pretty ball I dropped earlier, I brush the dust from the brightly colored surface, and I grab the sandals, carrying them to the mouth of the cave where I set everything down before walking to my fire pit. The little lid on the kettle dances with a soft *tink tink* sound as the water inside bubbles. I no longer feel like making tea, but I have found that the foe to boredom and depression is routine, so I crouch, removing the lid and dumping in a pinch of pine needles.

As I wait for the tea to steep, I wiggle my toes. My feet have gotten tough over the years of me being barefoot. The skin is rough and calloused. Dirt has permanently stained the bottoms and edges of my feet.

I bet those sandals are soft.

Once the tea is ready, I sit, crossing my legs and pouring myself a cup. Absently, I blow on the liquid, sending steam billowing away from my face. I bring the cup to my lips, getting a whiff of pine and earth before I take a sip. I wince at the bitterness, but a small sad smile lifts my lips.

Atagi would not have liked my tea.

14

Sweat drips from the tip of my nose as I slash my scabbard up and across the imaginary foe before me. Twenty times left-to-right. Twenty times right-to-left. And again. And again. I've done this move over a hundred times today, thousands of times over the years.

My magic tingles down my body, always facing east, and I wonder if a visitor is on the way. I ignore it. They'll find their way to me eventually, and then we'll see ...

Until then, I continue with my practice. My shoulders ache with the familiar soreness of fatigued muscles. I appreciate the strength in my thighs as they ground me. I tighten my core with every sharp exhale. Relishing the flex of muscles in my upper back and biceps, I slash upwards again. I feel my father with me, his smile bright in my mind, his calm presence breathing life into each move.

But then, an image of Atagi's dark eyes flashes through my mind, and I pause, lowering the katana. I take deep, slow breaths, allowing my heart rate to come down. It's been a month since I sent Atagi away. And every day since, her face has haunted me ... that look of disappointment and anger.

Glancing down, I stare at my dusty toes. I still haven't worn the sandals. I haven't even tried them on. I don't deserve them.

Do you deserve *any of the items you've taken over the years?*

I glare at my scabbard. "Yes. I won those in combat."

The katana gives me an imaginary eye roll. *Well, I'd wear the sandals.*

"You're a katana. You don't have feet."

No, I'm you. Stop arguing with yourself and put on the sandals.

I adjust my grip on the shark skin hilt, resisting the urge to turn towards the cave where the sandals still sit ... where I left them weeks ago. Sliding my saya through the sash around my waist, I stride barefoot towards the tree line. "I'm going to check the traps."

The shadows of the forest swallow my words as I walk silently through the dappled light shining on the narrow trails I've created over the years. The first trap is empty, so I reset it and move on. A gentle breeze makes it through the tightly woven trees, and I tilt my head back slightly. This is nice. I take a moment to just *be* ... to appreciate being alive, because it really is a gift.

My thumb taps absently on the hilt at my side, its presence comforting as I move on.

As I kneel, resetting the second empty snare, I say, "If there's something in the third trap, we'll take it home and enjoy a nice meal. If the snare is empty, we'll move on to our daily check of the barrier."

My saya sighs. *Sure. Why not? Let's ruin a perfectly nice day by reconfirming how trapped we are.*

I don't let my scabbard bring down my good mood, giving it a little pat as I chuckle. "That's the spirit."

Unfortunately, the third snare *is* empty, so after resetting it, my scabbard and I make our way to the nearest tree marked with an x. I reach out a hand, pressing my palm to the invisible barrier. Looking out past my prison, I stare into the seemingly endless forest beyond.

I've forgotten what open space looks like. Like, really open space, where a person can see for miles. Where the wind can touch your entire body full force without the filter of leaves and trees. Where the open sky stretches endlessly. Where a person can walk and walk and walk without anything in their path.

I recall the times my father and I traveled together, usually to deliver a commissioned blade. Father preferred delivering his pieces himself, never relying on a messenger, and hardly ever asking a client to come to him. He used to say travel makes a man, it expands the mind and broadens your experiences. I loved those times together, just the two of us walking down dusty roads with seemingly no end in sight. Rice paddies filled with green shoots. Mountains painted against the horizon. Travelers smiling as they passed. The tea houses we'd visit. The sites. The smells. The people.

Keeping my palm on the barrier, I slowly stride along the wall of my prison, tapping occasionally, kicking at where it meets the ground, sporadically sending a shot of my red magic into it ... not really expecting anything different to happen than all the other times I've done this before. But who knows. One day, there might be a crack. It might give. I might find a weakness.

And then I'll be a free man.

And that's why I do this ... every day. Just in case. Because I want to travel again. I want to see the world beyond this cursed forest.

Only truth will mend what ego destroyed.

I grit my teeth at the reminder of the yokai's words. My truth hasn't changed, not for even a second of my long imprisonment. Yes, I'd do it again. I'd kill them all.

My father's lifeless eyes flash through my mind.

In fact, I'd make that spirit's death slower, more painful. I'd punish her unnecessary cruelty. She had a hand in stirring the fear the villagers had for my father—my father who they all knew for most of their lives. A man they'd drunk tea with. A man they'd shared meals with. A man who was always kind, greeting everyone with a smile. A man who, when he found a single-use spell he believed would help and protect the people of his village, used that magic to create a sword ... and was murdered because of it.

Because those people we considered friends had never seen magic before. Because they didn't understand. Because they were *scared*. Because *that yokai* spread rumors. 'Abomination', 'Evil', 'Unnatural'. Those words were whispered between bent heads and glancing looks. Eventually, the fear turned to anger and ... *SNAP!*

Cowards.

Fuck them all.

Yes, I'd do it again. *That's* my truth.

My fist slams silently against the barrier as my mood plummets and the familiar rage fills me, my eyes softly glowing red, reflecting off my brown skin. I carve my nails down the invisible wall but pause as my magic concentrates down my left side. My roiling thoughts are interrupted by a soft, "Umph."

I turn my head, listening.

Another low grunt comes from my left and slightly behind. Walking on the balls of my feet, I follow the sounds. The bark of a large pine scrapes against my palms as I pause, letting the width of the trunk hide me from the person I hear on the other side.

A shuffle of feet. Another grunt. Shuffling again. Then a pause.

I peek around the tree ...

Atagi. She's here.

A red tie holds back her black hair today. Sweat glistens on her face as she clenches her jaw, holding a large stick at her side. With a quick exhale, she steps forward, slashing her 'weapon' up and across her body with a little grunt.

That is the form I was doing earlier. She's ...

Looking around, I don't see her horse. Did she walk here? How long has she been here? Was she watching me earlier, then came out here to ... what? Practice on her own?

Quit being a creep. Quit hiding. Send her home. Don't let her play you. She can't have me, so send her awa—

I step around the tree, saying, "That branch is too big for you. It's throwing off your balance." Atagi stumbles with a gasp, turning wide eyes on me. Her mouth drops open, her 'sword' held between us with shaking arms. I raise a brow, crossing my arms. "But it was a strong strike."

My saya slaps its proverbial forehead with a groan. *Nice. Perfect. Just great.*

15

The smile that lights up her face makes me feel so light, I almost glance down to see if I'm floating.

Atagi lowers her stick, the end digging into the soft ground as she says, "This was the best I could find. I thought about taking my papa's blade, but he would have noticed for sure. He's never touched it. Not that I've seen. It's always just sitting there, on its stand. I imagine it's sad. But if I take it down, papa will notice and yell at me, and if he doesn't notice, mama will for sure, and she'll tell him. Still, it's just sitting there ..."

The thought of Atagi wielding an actual blade with no training makes my heart thud painfully against my ribs. She could get hurt ... or worse. She's being too reckless. She—

She holds up her branch. "But I found this stick, and I've been practicing! And before you say anything, I'm sorry for yelling at you last time. You're not stupid. You are the best swordsman I've ever seen." She lowers her head, scraping her branch across the dirt. "Please. Teach me."

It's on the tip of my tongue to tell her that a true swordsman would never drag their blade on the ground. I grit my teeth, keeping my mouth shut, but she whips her head up, meeting my gaze head on. "Pleeeeease! Please!" She shifts. "Look, watch. See?" Atagi raises her 'blade' overhead, moving into another stance as she says, "I'm not sure how to get my grip right, and with this stick it's … it's just not right."

Before I realize what I'm doing, I place my large hand over hers, adjusting her grip, lifting her arms slightly before shaking them to get her to gather more strength to her core. She tightens her entire body, and I gently kick her calf. She stumbles a step before catching herself, and I say, "If you're too tense, you're easily toppled. Strength is patient and efficient, going only where it's needed. Like water, or like the wind. A rush of water flows around a stone, but a focused stream of water can create a hole through that stone. A breeze passes by. A concentrated gust topples."

I pat her head. "Be the gust of wind."

She blinks at me, a small smile lifting her round cheeks. "So, you'll teach me?"

Shit. I got carried away.

Crossing my arms, I shake my head. "No."

"But—"

I hold up a hand. "Atagi. Did you not listen to me last time? What you're doing, coming out here, is dangerous. You are young. You are brave, but you are small. What if you were attacked by an animal out here? Or by a person? This isn't safe. And I'm not … good."

She taps her stick to the ground, placing her other hand on her hip, she says, "Because you killed that man?"

No. Because I slaughtered my entire village and I'm. Not. Sorry. I refuse to feel remorse. I won't.

"*Pfft.*" Her lips vibrate with the funny sound, and she waves a hand. "He attacked you. And you were briiiliant." As she draws out that last word, she spreads her arms dramatically before letting them fall. "You're the best!" A little frown furrows her brow. "My mama always says, in order to 'fetch' the best husband I have to have the best tutor, the best clothes, the best hair pins, the best shoes ... and I don't even care about that stuff. I do care about *this*, so ... I need the best."

I sigh, rubbing my hand down my face. "Atagi. You don't understand. You need to stop. I'm not going to teach you. Go home, and don't come back."

She tilts her head, her eyes narrowing at me. "Why? Is it because I'm a giiiiirl? I want to learn. I can be just as good as a boy, better even! Please! No one in my town will even let me touch a sword."

"For good reason, Atagi. Let's say you do learn the art of the katana. Then what? What will a woman do with such a skill? No one will hire you. If you're seen carrying a weapon, you will be arrested, or worse."

Maybe the times have changed, but I doubt it by the uncertainty now clouding Atagi's eyes.

I press on, even though my chest is tight from denying myself the company and refusing to give this cute little girl the one thing she seems to want most in life. "You need to give this up and face the future you know is coming."

Her shoulders bunch as her free hand curls into a fist. "I won't become some stinky man's wife to be locked away. I want—"

"Atagi!" She snaps her lips closed, her eyes going wide, tears brimming. I lower my voice, trying to take the bite out of it. I don't want to hurt her, but she can't keep coming here. "This is a child's dream. One you will grow out of, I promise. You will find your purpose in something else. Just give yourself time to grow up."

Her cheeks flex as she grinds her teeth. "I found you. This forest tried to keep me away, but I never gave up. You are *supposed* to be my Sensei. I knooow it." She throws her entire body into that last part, clenching her fists and thrusting her chest forward with the kind of dramatics only a child can pull off. It's cute. She's cute.

And stubborn. And determined. She would make an excellent student.

I force the smile away from my lips, drawing some false anger into my voice and hating myself for it as I sneer, "You *knooow* it? Like you knooow that you'll never get married? Like you knooow that learning to handle a sword is some noble thing? It's not. It's a bloody and violent pursuit. Never pick up a blade unless you're willing to use it." I grab Atagi's hand, lifting her arm and pressing the end of her branch into my gut. "Would you use it, Atagi? Could you stab me? Could you take a life? Because that is what you are signing up for if you pick up a blade."

She tries to pull back, but I keep her where she is. She shakes her head. "I won't hurt you. I don't want to hurt anyone. *That's* why I want to learn, so I can protect myself and keep the people I love safe."

I snort, gently shoving her back, ripping the stick from her hand and throwing it to the ground. "You are a naive little girl." I draw my scabbard, holding it out. "This sword. Do you remember what the dead man called it?"

Her voice is barely a whisper now. "Guardian."

I nod, hating myself more with each harsh word. "That's right. Guardian. My father forged this blade for exactly that purpose, Atagi. To protect. To *guard*. But it's seen blood, Atagi. So much blood. And not all of it was spilled out of honor. No, most of the blood Guardian has tasted was from rage and revenge ... the blood of my entire village."

She stares at my saya for a long moment, but I can't take it anymore. My heart is breaking. I'm pushing away a chance at companionship all because I'm too much of a coward to face the pain of loneliness when she leaves me … because everyone leaves. But my sorrow isn't *all* self-centered. My chest aches because I'm crushing this girl's dreams, her spirit. But what I told her is true. Women don't wield swords. Training her will only make her life harder, it will give her a skill that could get her killed.

Spinning on my bare heels, I stride away, unable to look at her sad eyes for another moment. "Go home, Atagi. Forget about this place. Forget about me."

I know she doesn't leave, but she also doesn't follow because the silence drags behind me like a barbed rope, cutting me deeper with each step. I feel her eyes on my back like a hot poker.

I leave her behind and stomp through the woods, heading towards my caves.

Why does she have to be so stubborn? Why did she have to be so cute with that branch? Why is she so determined to chase this impossible dream in a world that will crush that fierce nature out of her … just like I did?

I'm not angry at her though. I'm angry with myself. Always with myself.

My strides lengthen with desperation as I enter my caves. My eyes barely have time to adjust as I walk down the tunnels, but I don't need to see, I know the way. I strip as I go, leaving a trail of clothing in my wake. Entering the pool chamber, I gently place my saya on the ground, but as soon as I reach the edge of the pool, I jog out, the water splashing around my thighs until I'm chest deep. With a deep breath, I dive, kicking my legs and exhaling. Bubbles pop and crackle around me. The silty bottom greets me, and I stay there in the darkness until my lungs burn, begging me for air. I know I can't drown, so I won't try.

But it's tempting.

Atagi has actual promise. She had decent form, and only from watching me a handful of times. With a little guidance, she could really ....

No.

But ...

I break the surface, sucking in air as I lean back, floating along the chilly surface, my arms and legs swishing lazily through the water.

I was very harsh with her. She won't return.

I hope she does.

16

I push through the final move in my form, knowing it wasn't my best day of practice. I'm distracted … happily so.

For days—eighteen to be exact—I've waited and hoped for my magic to give me that distinctive tingle, the one that says Atagi is nearby. A fool's hope. But one that's paid off.

As I finish the eight-wheel pattern with a strong slice across the midline, I stand, sliding my scabbard into my sash at my hip. I wipe the sweat from my forehead, keeping my back to the western tree line. My magic prickles down my spine like sparks escaping a crackling fire. It's been doing this for over an hour, alerting me to Atagi's presence a couple meters back in the shadows of the forest. And for the past hour, I've gone about my practice, moving through the eight-wheel form over and over. I've waited with building dread for the moment Atagi got bored and my magic calmed with her departure.

But she hasn't. My magic continues to dance across my skin, always shifting to point to her location. With a sigh, I turn in her direction and head into the woods.

My scabbard chuckles. *You just can't help yourself.*

I poke the hilt, whispering, "I'm just going to warn her away ... again."

The katana scoffs. *Okay. Sure.*

My magic fizzes along the front of my body as I get closer, like bubbles in a hot spring. I walk slowly and silently, keeping to the shadows, hiding behind wide tree trunks until I see her.

I can't keep a small smile from lifting my lips as I watch. She's doing the eight-wheel pattern. Well, she's trying to. It's sloppy. Her footwork is all wrong, and the constricting fabric of her kimono isn't helping. With a huff, she stumbles, and the end of her stick digs into the ground. A grimace pulls at my face. Wrong. It's all wrong.

Atagi whips around as I stride towards her. She drops her branch and clasps her hands, wringing them nervously. She looks around, chewing on her bottom lip, avoiding my gaze. "I was just ..." She glances at the stick at her feet. "I mean, I just thought if I ..."

My voice comes out with more bark than I intend. "If you're going to watch, you should pay better attention." Bending over, I grab her branch. With quick slashes, I move through the form in record time—the best round I've done all day. Starting over, I go slower this time, explaining, "See my feet here?"

Atagi's eyes are wide, and she nods, staring at me with riveted attention.

"And you see where my elbow is here and how I move with my waist first?"

From my periphery, I see her nod again.

"And here, your hip was too far rotated. You were very off balance. That's why you stumbled."

When I finish the pattern, I pause. Atagi's smile sparkles

in her dark eyes as she holds out her hand, presumably wanting her stick back, as she says, "Yes, Sensei."

Shit. I did it again.

Well, she's obviously going to try to keep coming, so you might as well give in and give the girl a proper lesson or two.

Ignoring my scabbard, I toss the branch to the side, away from Atagi's outstretched arm. "Never mind. Forget all this." I turn, heading back to my cave, to my solitude. To my punishment. Surprisingly, there's no response, no stream of rushed words or whining pleas. My neck aches with the desire to turn around, but I keep going. And slowly, painfully, the tingling of my magic fades as Atagi leaves.

Think she'll stay away this time?

"I hope so."

No, you don't.

"No. I don't. But she should."

She really should.

Just ... be quiet.

Thirty-six days.

Thirty-six long days since Atagi's last visit. And each day, I've let go a little more, I've let the hope drain out of me. Three days ago, I gave up on ever seeing her again, or at least that's what I tell myself.

My knife hovers over the small piece of wood in my hand as I pause carving. I stare at it, and after a moment, I toss it to the side, and it clunks against the others I've made. Why am I even doing this?

It's something to do.

"Yeah, but it's not useful."

It's keeping you busy. That's useful.

"I guess."

I'm hungry.

"No. *I'm* hungry. You're a katana."

Still ...

With a sigh, I set my small knife down and press my palms to my thighs. Standing, I rub my hand over my grumbling stomach. The mushrooms aren't an option, they need time to replenish and grow, and there has been no game in my traps for weeks.

My fingers still ache from cutting and peeling my latest harvest of bamboo, so I guess I'll slice and boil that batch today.

I push aside the small handful of berries I picked up off the ground under the lantern plant yesterday. Over the years, that bush has doubled in size, then doubled again. And while the entire plant is extremely poisonous, once the pretty berries fall off, they're okay to eat.

I pop one into my mouth, and a burst of tart juice hits my tongue followed by a little sweetness. Swallowing the treat, I then grab one of the ginkgo leaves from the small pile I picked a few days ago. I chew on it, cleaning my teeth as I walk into the forest. I'm far from excited about yet another meal of bamboo shoots, but it's better than starving —my curse keeping me from wasting away while the hunger hollows me out.

I spit out the ginkgo pulp as I approach my first trap, already seeing that it's empty. The next trap is nearly four kilometers away, and I find I just don't have the energy to check it. But I also know lethargy is a warning sign, so I go anyway.

Empty.

I trudge on, my feet dragging.

Stop! Look!

Focusing on the forest floor, I nearly weep as I drop to my knees. My fingers tremble as I I carefully pluck the warabi stalks. I don't know how I missed this large patch of bracken, but I'm beyond thankful for them now. It's a struggle not to take them all, but I leave the newer shoots to grow and spread. I make a mental note of where this is before heading towards my next snare.

Now I have a little more energy as I munch on the stem of a warabi, trying to chew slowly. I don't even mind the bitterness as I finish the stalk and roll up the leaf and take a bite. A moan vibrates from my throat at the earthy, grassy taste. There's even a slight sweetness that lingers on my tongue. Such a simple thing, but it fills me with gratitude. I smile, savoring each bite. If I can keep myself from eating this entire bunch, these leaves would make a very nice tea.

My magic zips down my spine a split second before something jabs me in the back. I don't turn, recognizing this tingling thrum.

Atagi's confident voice comes from behind me. "I got you!"

My lips quirk into a smile, but I wipe it away as I spin. Still clutching the bunch of bracken, I smack the backside of my other hand against her stick. Her 'blade' goes flying, landing in a bush with a rustle of leaves.

Raising a brow, I scowl down at the little girl. "What did I tell you about wielding a weapon?" When she remains tight-lipped, I say, "Don't even pick it up if you don't intend to use it. There was no follow-through, Atagi. If I were truly your enemy, you should have struck me in the back of the head with that stick, or if that was an actual blade, you should have driven it right through me."

She bites her bottom lip. "But that's not very noble."

"Nobility has nothing to do with it. You see an opening, you take it. Always look out for yourself."

Her lips tilt downward. "That's not what a samurai would do."

I tsk. "You never said anything about learning to be a samurai. You said you wanted to learn how to sword fight. That's two different things."

She rolls her eyes. "Aren't you a samurai?"

Narrowing my eyes, I say, "What gave you that impression?"

Silence wraps around us, and I can practically see her thoughts sprinting behind her eyes as she looks at me for a few long moments. Then, as if snapping out of a daze, Atagi suddenly bows. "Thank you for the lesson, Sensei." And before I have a chance to formulate a response, she runs off, disappearing into the shadows.

Ha! She got you again.

I smile, turning to head home. Birds chirp and critters scurry. The wind whispers through the trees, and the leaves laugh as they dance. I let the music of the forest surround me. I'm alive to experience this beautiful day, and I'm thankful.

Atagi will be back. I'm sure of it.

17

Dappled light paints the forest floor, but the beauty is wasted on me. I can't find the joy, the wonder, or the gratitude. The sun is shining, but there's a cloud hanging over my soul. It's just one of those days.

I shift, trying to make myself more comfortable where I sit cross legged in the dirt and scattered pine needles ... but it's no use. The ground is too hard, the pine leaves poking me at every opportunity. I scowl at the bare strip of earth before me, stretching out in either direction, marking the path I take every day as I walk the perimeter to check for weaknesses. I pick up another small rock from the pile to my left. Rolling the smooth surface around my palm, I sink deeper into my depression, angry that I can't find the happiness that was so abundant just a few weeks ago. But with each passing day, the gloom has spread like spilt blood. I know the signs. I've been here many times before, but I'd hoped ...

And there it is. I let myself hope, and this is the result.

You're in a mood today.

I don't answer my scabbard, tossing the stone, watching

it sail right through the invisible barrier. Oh, to be that stone.

Is it because Atagi hasn't—

"It has nothing to do with her."

But you do admit, you're in a mood.

"Sure. Fine."

Sliding my left leg out from under my right, I press my toes against the barrier. My foot flexes with the motion, and I push a little harder.

Nothing. No give.

Absently, I grab another stone and throw it. The rock hits a tree, creating a soft cracking noise before it thuds almost silently to the carpet of moss resting at the base of the giant pine. It's just a few meters away, but my fingers ache with the need to touch that moss. I know every tree, every bush, every stone in my prison, but that little patch of moss right there ... I don't know that. Does it feel the same as the moss that covers the small patch of boulders to the north of my cave or is it cooler? Softer?

With my foot still pressed to the barrier, I toss another stone, watching as it bounces twice before coming to rest where I will never tread.

How long are we going to sit here and throw stones?

"You have somewhere to be?"

We didn't even do our normal practice this morning. We've been sitting here for hours. Let's move. Let's do something. I'm bored.

"Oh, soooo sorry. I do exist for your entertainment. But this is it." I grab three stones and throw them. *Thud. Thud. Thud.* "I have nothing else to give right now."

The smooth, perfect lacquer slides against my hand as I grab my saya by the middle. Holding it out, I poke the barrier. Just like always, it doesn't go through. The barrier is so solid I always expect some kind of sound when I come in contact with it. Even after all these years, I anticipate hearing a *clink clink* as I tap the katana against the invisible wall. But there's nothing. No shimmer of air, no sound.

Setting my scabbard back on the ground by my hip, I exchange it for yet another stone. I toss it, watching it go where I cannot.

So, she hasn't been back in a while. That's no reason to pout like this.

"Forty-three days."

That's a single leaf in a forest compared to the days we've spent here together. I'm still with you. Always.

"I know. And I'm grateful. I would have truly gone mad without you. I mean, I am mad, but ... you know what I mean."

My hand meets dirt as I reach for another stone. I've depleted the pile I made this morning. I fall back, flopping to the forest floor, tucking my hands behind my head. The negative space between the branches and leaves overhead reveals little jagged shapes of blue sky.

As a single puffy cloud makes its way across my field of vision, I mumble, "What do you suppose that yokai meant?"

Oh, this again? Didn't we decide she was crazy and cruel, and that her cryptic words meant nothing?

"Yeah, but what if ... There must be a way. This can't be it."

My saya sighs its frustration with me, and that makes me smile. I'm frustrated with myself, projecting through the katana. I've been talking to it for so long, sometimes I forget it's not really talking back—that every word is in my head.

Truth. What fucking truth? Repentance I would understand. It'll never happen, but at least that would make sense

... repent and be set free. But truth? I've always been honest about that night. And I'm not sorry.

I don't move, keeping my foot pressed to the barrier while I stare at the sky. More clouds move in, and the sun slowly paints them orange, then pink. The blue of the sky deepens, and the bright green of the trees begins to darken, the branches swaying to a melody I can't hear.

And still, I don't move.

My scabbard stays silent, leaving me to my thoughts.

I may be in a bad mood today, but at least it's not *bad* bad. No. I'm in the kind of mood where even the thought of trying to end my life ... again ... feels like too much work. Besides, what if ...

Atagi.

What if she comes back and finds me dying ... or dead and I haven't come back yet. Or it actually works and I do die.

Well then, you'll be dead, and Atagi will no longer matter. Nothing will. Because you'll be dead.

No. I'll keep going. I'll keep existing. Just in case she comes back.

I take a deep breath that presses my upper back into the ground. My lungs expand. My chest deflates as I slowly exhale. A little ray of contentment warms my insides, gently pushing a sliver of my depression away.

Yes. I'll keep going.

18

My back muscles flex as I slice my saya through the air, moving fluidly through my form of the day. I feel better ... stronger and steadier than I have in a long time. The soft *swish* of my feet moving over the dusty ground of my practice area accompanies my breaths.

Though, my attention is split between what I'm doing and the girl trying to stay hidden in the woods to the west. From the corner of my eye, I watch Atagi. She has steadily moved closer over the past hour, attempting to mimic my moves. Her swings are wild, and she's lacking the sharpness this form requires, but she's trying.

I've been careful not to give her any indication that I know she's here. Instead, I've let my magic tingle across my skin, always letting me know where she is as I turn and shift through my practice. Bracing my thighs, I prepare for the next sequence of moves. They are quite complicated, and while I'm able to execute them with speed and accuracy, I slow down to allow Atagi the time to follow along.

She stumbles on the downswing, a twig snapping under her shoe. She freezes like a bunny that's caught the scent of a predator, but I keep moving as if I didn't hear her. Atagi remains still and silent for several long moments, and it's not until I finish the complete form and reset to start over that she finally moves.

This time, as she tries to follow me, there's a hesitance in her strokes and thrusts. The words burn in the back of my throat—to tell her to tighten her belly, to slice from her core first, to loosen her grip slightly, to move her feet a little farther apart ...

But I ignore her.

My saya rolls its proverbial eyes. *Just invite the girl over and teach her, for fuck's sake.*

The thought has crossed my mind at least a dozen times since my magic first flared sharp and excited, alerting me that Atagi was here. Her presence feels different than all the others who have come to this place. My magic is ... calm with her. Like bubbles. Or dandelion fuzz. Like when I was with my father.

With everyone else it's harsh. Like the scrape of bark against flesh. And when the threat is very high, it almost hurts, like the charge in the air right before a lightning strike.

Still, I hesitate to engage with Atagi. For so many reasons.

Yeah, like, if someone has sent her here for me, how long will it take before you give into those dark puppy-dog eyes of hers? Or worse, what if they threaten to hurt her ... to use her against you. Would you give me up to save her?

Would I? I don't want to find out.

Taking a break, I stride to the mouth of my cave, retrieving my water skin. As I swallow down the cool liquid, I keep part of my attention on Atagi where she still thinks she's hidden in the shadows. She should rest too, but in my periphery, I see her practicing the last slice and stand of the movement we were just doing. She does it again and again, her brow furrowed, her bottom lip between her teeth. It's not quite right, but it's better than it was an hour ago.

Did she bring water with her? Food? What if she works herself too hard and passes out?

My anxious thoughts dissipate as she huffs and tosses her branch to the ground. I curl my fingers into the water skin with the urge to berate her. You never treat your blade like that, even if it's only a 'practice sword'. I find myself turning to face her fully, crossing my arms. My voice barks with admonishment as I say, "Atagi."

My voice spurs her into action. Her hair sways as she darts off into the woods, calling over her shoulder with joy in her voice, "Thank you for the lesson, Sensei!"

Dropping my arms to my side, I follow her but keep my distance. I want to see her pass through the barrier. My long strides allow me to easily keep up, making sure she doesn't hear me. We've barely covered a kilometer before she slows, her breathing heavy.

That's no good. She needs more stamina if she's going to be any good with a sword.

I don't answer my scabbard, because I have no intention of teaching her.

Yeah, right.

I watch as Atagi passes right through the invisible wall— no hesitation, no reflex, no indication she felt anything at all. My attention bores into the area she just went through. I mark the spot in my mind as I stay in the shadows. Atagi's mare huffs out a big breath and swishes her tail in greeting when she sees her owner. The little girl pats the horse on the neck, whispering something before standing on her tiptoes to reach into a small bag attached to her saddle.

Bringing the water pouch to her lips, she tilts her head back and empties it with a few big gulps. Her gasp of satisfaction scares a bird from a branch, and Atagi wipes her lips with her sleeve. "Well, Hori, it was another good lesson."

She pats her horse once more before taking the lead to pull the mare closer to a pair of trees that have grown so close together, their trunks form a V. Atagi sticks her hand into the folds of her dress, and a little red string comes out in her grip. She ties it to a branch then scrambles up one of the leaning trees, bark scattering to the forest floor under her. With a grunt, she flops onto the saddle on Hori's back, righting herself quickly. With a soft kick of her feet, the little girl and her horse trot away ... to a world I can only dream of.

My steps are nearly silent as I walk to the place in the barrier where Atagi passed through. Reaching out, I hate the flicker of hope that jumps in my chest. But, of course my fingers meet solid air. I press my palm against the wall of my prison, leaning my forehead next to my hand, staring at the trees beyond.

And once again, I'm alone.

She'll be back.

I hope so. But no matter who stumbles into my life and for how long, I'll always be alone.

19

The wet tearing sound rips across the clearing as I skin the rabbit. My mouth waters in anticipation. I've already planned how to prepare and cook it to stretch it over a few days. I may even smoke some ... though this animal is pretty small, it will be a challenge not to just eat the whole thing today.

My knife slips, slicing into my thumb. I barely flinch, ignoring the sharp pain, knowing all traces of the small injury will be gone in a few hours. Still, I watch my blood well into a little drop. After all these years, I still bleed, I hurt, I heal, I live. The cycle of hope and despair continues.

But today I'm hopeful. I'm thankful for each experience.

Keeping my head down, looking at what I'm doing, I ignore the little girl trying to hide in the woods. Only eight days have passed since her last visit, and as I continue to skin the rabbit, I tell myself to be careful, to not get used to having someone around, to not get attached—I know better.

But I also know I won't be able to help myself.

Like she's done for the past twenty minutes, Atagi creeps

a little closer to my training area, hiding herself in the shadows. And doing a good job of it. Seems she's quite stealthy when she wants to be.

I hide my smile by dropping my head. My eyes are on the now skinned rabbit, but my attention is on Atagi as she shifts, peering around the wide trunk of the pine she's hiding behind. No doubt, she's waiting for me to start my form of the day so she can observe and get her lesson. Well, joke's on her. I'm not practicing today. Today's plans consist of prepping and cooking this meat, sewing up some holes in my clothes and making some repairs to the walls of my kitchen hut. I also have to gather some mushrooms and sweep out my bedchamber ... the mice have really been making themselves at home in there. I've even started naming them. It's getting out of hand.

You should just eat them.

I've thought about it. And I have in the past—grabbing the little rodents that scurried into my cave in the winter to get out of the cold. But right now, I'm not starving, so the effort to catch the little mice is more trouble than it's worth. Plus, they're kinda cute.

I set the rabbit pelt aside to tan later. As I go about cutting the flesh into pieces, I shoot discreet glances to the forest. Atagi darts behind the tree, and I smile, shaking my head.

It seems you have a student whether you want one or not.

Excitement builds at the thought. I can't give her Guardian. I can't give Guardian to anyone. But it seems Atagi really doesn't want the magic sword. She wants knowledge, training, to be stronger. *That*, I can give her.

My magic scratches at me, feeling Atagi's impatience. But I take my time with the rabbit, placing its thighs on my flat cooking rock, the meat sizzling on contact. I slice the breast into long strips that I then place on the large piece of bark propped up to the side for smoking. As I wait for the thighs to finish, I pick the tiny bits of muscle off the small front legs, popping the raw meat into my mouth, chewing slowly. The taste is coppery and gamey, but I relish every bite.

From the corner of my eye, I see Atagi peering around the trunk of her tree, her little hand curling against the bark. Well, if she's going to be my student, let this be her first lesson.

Patience.

The thighs are almost done, so I toss a few mushrooms on the hot stone, poking them every so often with my chipped chopsticks to let them brown on all sides. The smell of fat, meat, and earthy mushrooms dances in the air, and my mouth waters. Glancing at the little pouch on the ground next me, I nod. This small feast is worth the splurge.

Sticking my fingers in the bag, I grab a pinch of crushed wild ginger. A few years ago, I found the small plant growing just at the edge of my prison wall, half in, half out. I've tended those shoots with the care of a parent towards a child. Now, the crop is quite large, but I hoard the ginger, grateful but cautious ... knowing one harsh frost could take this small joy from me.

Tossing some of the ginger on the meat and mushrooms, I wait another few minutes before carefully sliding my meal off the stone onto my tin plate. Pinching a small piece of meat with my chopsticks, I raise the morsel to my lips and pause. My eyes dart to the trees, and Atagi ducks behind the trunk.

I sigh with a smile. "Come on, Atagi. There's enough to share."

A few seconds pass before she pokes her head around the tree. I wave her over, and she walks towards me, her fingers interlaced and fidgeting. Flopping to her knees, tucking her kimono under her shins, she asks, "How long have you known I was here?"

I hold out the plate towards her. "Since you got here."

Her eyes widen, then she squints, biting her lip. "But I was sooo quiet."

I shrug, and Atagi curls her lips to the side, then her gaze falls to my offered plate. "You don't have to share that with me. I ate before I left home."

I keep the plate raised, knowing my next words will be life-changing for us both. "Are you telling your sensei the truth, Atagi?"

She nods, then freezes, her eyes snapping to my face, her mouth open, her eyes nearly bugging out of her face. Slowly, like the petals of a flower unfurling in the morning light, a grin spreads across her face, and her eyes sparkle.

"Sensei? You'll do it? You'll teach me?"

I nod, still holding the plate up between us. "I have a feeling you'll keep showing up, so I might as well make sure you don't hurt yourself. You'll need your energy. Eat."

Atagi wiggles on her shins, her arms bent at her sides in a happy little dance. "I promise, I ate before I came." She hops up, shifting to the balls of her feet. "I'm ready, Sensei!"

With a chuckle, I set the plate in my lap and pinch another small piece of rabbit, collecting a mushroom as well between my chopsticks. As I bring the perfect bite towards my mouth, I say, "Well, I'm not. Your sensei needs his energy too. Sit. Wait."

I chew slowly, watching her. Atagi remains standing, fidgeting slightly. I dart my eyes to the ground then back to her. Atagi shifts back and forth for another minute, her small body nearly vibrating with impatience that my magic picks up with a tingling sensation against my skin. But eventually, she loosens her shoulders and sits down.

I swallow, reaching into my sleeve. Grabbing her temari ball, I hold it out to her. "You left this here."

A bright grin lights up her face as she holds out both hands, gently taking it from me. She turns it over, running her fingers over the bright colors before tucking it into her sleeve. "Thank you, and um, sorry for throwing it at you."

I chuckle, taking another small bite before asking, "Did the red strings lead you back this time?"

She chews her lip, shaking her head. "Well, for the first little while, yes, I was on the right track, but then I realized I kept seeing the same string. Hori, that's my horse, kept making funny huffing noises. I think she was getting tired of walking in circles, but I told her it wasn't my fault. The strings should have led us right here." Her nose wrinkles as she looks towards the tree line. "Stupid forest. It really must be cursed or something because I KNOW I was going the right way."

"So, what did you do?"

I take another bite as she answers with a smile, "I stopped following the strings."

I nearly choke, patting my chest to get the piece of mushroom to go down. "So, you what? ... you just wandered around the woods?"

Atagi rolls her eyes, dropping her shoulders dramatically. "Noooo. I had a plan."

"And that was ...?"

"Any time I saw one of my red strings, I turned and went the other way."

I shake my head. "You were wandering. It was sheer luck you found me."

"Well, it worked. I think that once the forest realized I wasn't going to give up, it let me through."

I pause with my chopsticks halfway to my mouth. "Through? Through what? Did you see or feel something?"

She purses her lips, emitting a *pfft* sound. "No. You're silly. I just meant it seemed easier to find you when I didn't try so hard."

Falling silent, I eat, wondering why the magic is letting this little girl find me again and again. Does it mean something? Does *she* mean something? Or is this all just crazy luck? I'll probably never know, so I try to put the mystery of Atagi and the forest out of my mind and focus on my decadent meal. I haven't eaten this well in a while, and I'm going to enjoy every bite.

Atagi watches me eat for a minute, then I guess she finds me boring because she looks around, taking in my cooking stone, the cracking fire, the mouth of my cave, my little kitchen, and the tree line beyond. Pride fills me as I look around with her. I've learned a lot. I've taught myself so many things. I'm resourceful and smart and have made a good little existence for myself.

Father would be pleased. He would be proud.

Atagi looks at the patch of dirt I use as my training area, and I notice her gaze tracking the impressions of my footprints. Looking back at me, she glances at my lap, and briefly looks at Guardian before raising her gaze back to my face. For a moment, I think she's going to ask for some food after all, but when she opens her mouth, she says, "You aren't wearing the sandals. Did they not fit?"

I pause chewing, wiggling my toes. Are her feelings hurt? When I look back at her face, there's no sadness in her eyes, just honest curiosity. Do I lie and tell her they didn't fit?

No, she'd probably bring you a new pair.

I shrug, settling on the truth. "They were given to me in payment for a service I had not yet delivered, so I couldn't wear them."

She tilts her head, considering, then another bright smile lifts her round cheeks as she nods. Her eyes slip to my plate, then back to my face. "Now?"

I look down, realizing my plate is empty. Damn it. I barely tasted that, and now it's gone. But ... I find I don't mind. My expression is impassive, but I'm just as excited as Atagi to start her training, even though I know she's not going to be thrilled with her first few lessons.

But, it is the way.

Indecision wars within me for a moment. Will she grow impatient with my teaching? Will she stop coming? A heavy pit of anxiety drops into my stomach, almost ruining my delicious meal. But I push that dread away, uncrossing my legs and standing. If I'm going to teach her, I'm going to do it right.

I keep my smile hidden as I say, "I have to wash up— whenever possible, hold your sword with clean hands to maintain the integrity of your hilt. Then, I need to flip the meat I'm smoking before we start."

Atagi shuffles her feet together, standing tall and straight before bowing. Her curtain of hair falls to either side of her face, muffling her words slightly as she says, "Let me clean your plate, Sensei."

Gods, she's cute.

"Thank you, Atagi-chan, but I made the mess. I'll clean it. What I want you to do is go into the woods, not too far, and find a proper branch—not the one you were using last time." She blushes, toeing the dirt as I continue, "Pick one you think will make the perfect practice sword for you."

Her eyes flit to the mouth of my cave, no doubt recalling all the swords I have hung on the wall inside. She opens her mouth, but I hold up a hand, stalling her words.

"You're not ready for a real blade."

"Oh, come on! I can do it. I'm ready! I've been practicing!"

I raise a brow. "I'll decide if you're ready. You promised to do as I say, remember?"

She looks up at me, and I see the frustration in her eyes, reminding me how young she is—with the ever-fluctuating emotions of a child. But Atagi keeps her cool and nods, turning and walking towards the tree line. Her steps are short but fast, her light-weight kimono stunting her stride.

That's a terrible garment for sword fighting. It's restrictive ... and I realize clothing is just another aspect of women's lives that holds them back, that contains them, that keeps them 'controllable.' I've never had a reason to think about it, but Atagi was right. Being a girl must be ... difficult.

I find myself walking a little faster than usual as I head into my cave, quickly washing up in the little natural sink before putting my plate, knife, and chopsticks away. I may not have much, but I take good care of what I do have.

As I come back into the clearing, chewing on a few ginkgo leaves to clean my teeth, Atagi almost jogs from the woods, her little feet moving in a blur of motion. She stops in front of me, holding out a stick. It's the right diameter, but too long, and the slight bend at the end won't do.

I shake my head, crossing my arms. "No. Try again."

She looks at her branch, her nose scrunched. "What's wrong with this one?"

I raise a brow. "You tell me."

She studies the stick, biting her lip in the way I'm starting to learn means she's thinking hard on something.

"It's ... crooked?" I nod, but keep my brow raised, and she assesses her branch again before asking, "Too big?"

I shake my head. "Too long."

She points at the katana threaded through the sash on my hip. "But your sword is longer."

"Lift your arm." She obeys, and I move to her side, kneeling. I hold my arm next to hers. "We are not the same. You cannot compare yourself to me, or anyone, only to yourself, Atagi-chan."

She looks at our arms, side-by-side, for a long moment before nodding her head with determination. She tosses her stick on my pile of wood next to the firepit and strides back towards the tree line.

With a smile, I stand, turn, and cross my arms. Propping my shoulder against the rock of the mouth of my cave, I take a moment to enjoy the slightly cooler temperature in the shade. After a while, Atagi comes back, but before she makes it halfway across the clearing, I shake my head. She pauses, looking at her new stick, head tilted. She looks back at me, and I shake my head again. With a huff, she throws her branch on the wood pile, and stomps back into the woods.

That stick actually would have worked fine, but *this* is also a lesson for her. Follow orders, no matter how frustrated you get.

I reject six more sticks, and Atagi's face gets redder with each branch thrown on the wood pile. Her kimono is a little darker around her neck and under her arms from her sweat, but she hasn't uttered a single word of complaint.

The next stick she brings, I approve with a nod. She jumps in the air, holding her prize over her head with a whoop. Crossing the clearing, I hold out my hand, and she passes me her branch. It's a good size, and heavy enough to challenge her strength.

My palm lands on the top of her head, and I marvel at the softness of her hair as I tousle it. "Well done."

She giggles, ducking out from under my touch.

Still holding her stick, I say, "Leave this with me. That is all for today. Time for you to go home."

A deep frown pulls at her lips, and her mouth pops open, but I stop her with a lifted finger. "Do as your sensei says, Atagi-chan."

She opens her mouth again, and I raise a brow. She snaps her lips shut, visibly fighting with herself as she clenches her fists and shifts on her feet. But eventually she nods and bows. "Thank you for the lesson, Sensei."

I set her stick down, walking with her into the forest. Looking down at the top of her head, I ask, "Did you ride here?"

She nods. "I always ride. It's too far to walk."

The barrier gets closer, guilt creeps in, and I place my hand on her shoulder, stopping her. She looks up at me as I say, "I don't want you to get in trouble. I don't like that you're having to sneak and lie to your family." Doubts swarm through my chest, making it hard to breathe. I shouldn't have given in to my greedy desire for companionship. What am I doing? I can't teach her. She's a child. She—

"I'm careful. I promise. I won't get in trouble. But I don't know how often I can come. Maybe you can come to my house and teach me? I'm sure I can convince my papa to pay you for lessons"—She chews on her lip—"somehow."

How I wish I could.

I search for an excuse as to why I can't leave this place, but all I come up with is, "I can't."

She frowns, but shrugs, accepting my words with a child's faith.

Atagi must see some emotion on my face, because she wipes away her frown, and smiles, patting my hand like *I'm* the child. "Don't worry, Sensei. I'm sneaky, remember. I'll be careful. I don't know when I'll be able to come back, but I will."

I nod, and we walk side-by-side, the barrier getting closer. My palms start to sweat. Maybe? Maybe this will work? Maybe this is why the magic of the forest is letting her in ... to lead me out? I imagine freedom from this place and nearly stumble at the thought. What will I do? Where will I go?

I'll eat. I'll eat all the things. I'll have hot rice with baked chicken, or maybe autumn harvested mackerel. I'll have broth with soba noodles and soy sauce with miso and ginger. I'll have mochi with red bean paste. And tea. I'll have hot tea to my heart's content.

And I'll sleep. On a real bed with a fluffy pillow. Oh! And a bath. A hot bath.

Snap out of it. None of that is happening.

I scowl at my scabbard as Atagi passes right through the invisible wall, and all my hopes and dreams scatter like dead leaves in a strong wind. The barrier pushes my hand from her shoulder, and when she looks back at me, I wave, hopefully hiding the despair from my face.

I'm stupid for hoping. I know better.

She waves back with a grin before walking a few paces to her mare. This time, there's a convenient stump that Atagi uses to help her jump onto her horse's back. And off she goes. As soon as she's out of sight, I press my palm to the barrier. It doesn't give. I feel all around the space where Atagi went through, but nothing.

Fuck.

At least you have something new to look forward to now, Seeenseiiii.

I force away the tears that want to fall, because I know if I start crying, I might not stop. So, I smile at my scabbard at my hip, ignoring the sarcasm as it called me teacher.

"Indeed, I do."

20

Clouds hang low across the sky, their bellies grey and heavy with the threat of rain. Still, the gloomy weather does nothing to keep a small smile from twitching my lips as Atagi sprints into the clearing, her wide-legged pants making it easier for her to run. As she gets closer, I notice a smear of dirt on her forehead and a scratch on her cheek. There's also dirt under her nails, and the knee of her left pant leg has a dark stain.

She skids to a stop in front of me, and a little cloud of dust kicks up.

I nod at her. "What happened?"

A confused frown flashes over her face as she lifts her hand, brushing at the small scratch. Then, as if remembering, her eyes lighten as she waves her hand. "Oh, yeah. Nothing. Hori stumbled and well ... I wasn't paying attention and fell off. She's usually so sure-footed." Atagi looks over her shoulder where her mare calmly stands at the edge of the tree line. "She's a good horse. It wasn't her fault."

Crossing my arms, I ask, "You're okay?"

She nods her head enthusiastically, her hair swishing around her face. "Mhmm."

It's been twelve days since I last saw my new student, and while that is an insignificant amount of time … it was long enough to have concern clawing at my stomach, keeping me from solid sleep. I didn't even make my usual rounds along the barrier; too afraid I'd miss her if I was away from the cave for too long. But idle hands make a busy mind, and these past few days have been filled with my spinning thoughts … Am I doing the right thing, agreeing to teach Atagi? What if she doesn't come back? What if she *can't* come back? What if the magic keeps her from me? What if she's followed? What if she's caught? What if …?

But here she is, all bouncing energy and bright eyes, and I'm determined to appreciate each moment. Even if this is the last time—and I hope it isn't—I will cherish it.

Hope, the worst of all the emotions.

I jerk my chin over my shoulder. With a little skip, she jogs over to where her carefully selected branch from last time leans against the wall of my cave entrance. She wraps her hand around the wood, turning back to me with wide, slightly shimmery eyes.

Her voice has an almost reverential tone. "It's a real bokken. I have my own bokken."

She grips the hilt of her practice sword I carved and sanded as best I could the night of her last visit. Her bokken is not as polished as a traditional practice sword, and the length is a little shorter than a traditional katana but is more suited to her size.

I wave her over, and she joins me in the dusty training area. Once she's before me, I say, "Point it at me."

Atagi raises her practice sword, a little too high, but I don't say anything. And when I remain silent, she starts to lower her arm, but I shake my head. With a little grunt, she raises the bokken, asking, "Now what?"

"Now, you hold it."

Atagi frowns, shifting her shoulder to keep the practice sword raised. "Just hold it?"

I nod. "This is your first official lesson. The weight of your blade determines how well you will be able to move, to maneuver. But even the lightest blade will feel like the heaviest stone if your body is not strong and used to the weight."

Her arm lowers slightly as I talk, and I nod at her bokken. She grits her teeth and raises her arm without complaint.

I nod again. "Good."

After only a minute, the sword in Atagi's hand starts to shake. I grip the hilt of the katana at my waist, and raise it, still sheathed. "You're doing well, Atagi-chan. Hold it with me for a little longer."

Her wrist bends as the weight of the bokken pulls at her straining muscles. But she spreads her feet and forces it back up as she says, "I can hold it as long as you can."

I smile. "No. You can't. But one day, if you keep practicing, you will."

I keep a close watch on her eyes. As soon as I see pain, I wait five more seconds before dropping my arm with a nod. Atagi lowers her branch with a sigh and says, "That was hard, and all I was doing was holding it. My arm doesn't get that tired when I'm moving through the forms." She smiles up at me, a little bit of mischief behind her eyes. "Let's do forms!"

"No. We're starting with the basics."

Her lips turn down. "But—"

"Are you questioning your sensei, Atagi-chan?"

She looks at me, her frown of frustration melting into a

grin of determination. "No! I can do this. I'm going to be the best swordsman in my town. In the world!"

I believe her. I believe *in* her. And that damned cursed emotion spreads through me.

Hope.

I find myself hoping that I'll be able to keep training Atagi. That I'll see her struggle and then conquer those hurdles. That I'll witness her greatness one day.

But I know better.

Besides, hope is about the future, and I don't need to worry about tomorrow or the days ahead. I need to concentrate on right now, on this moment. So, like kicking sand over the embers of a dying fire, I smother that hope inside me and focus as if the future doesn't exist.

I raise my scabbard. "Again." Atagi rolls her shoulder before lifting her bokken. I tap the tip. "A little higher. Good. Like that. Now put more strength here." I tap her forearm, pleased when I see her little muscles flex, and the wooden sword becomes steadier in her hand.

After another full minute, I let her lower her arm, and she rubs her biceps, her gaze once again drifting to the mouth of my cave. I smile, lightly swatting her arm with my scabbard. "If you think that practice sword is heavy, you certainly aren't ready for a real sword."

Atagi swipes her bokken through the air. "It's not *that* heavy."

Raising a brow, I say, "Trust your sensei."

Stopping her slashing movement, she looks up at me and asks, "What's your name?"

"Sensei."

Atagi purses her lips but doesn't push back. As she moves to lift her bokken, I hold my scabbard above it, keeping her from lifting it too high. "Don't overdo it. This time hold it here." I direct her arm to a downward angle so her sword points to the ground ahead of her. "We'll go through a few different positions, just to get you used to the weight. But you don't want to do too much or you'll strain yourself which could lead to an injury, and then you won't be able to practice."

"Injure myself? Just by holding my bokken?"

She giggles, but I nod. "Your muscles aren't used to this. You are teaching them the weight of your sword. If you push too hard, before they're ready, your muscles will snap. I've seen it before."

"Has it ever happened to you?"

While we've been talking, her arm has lowered, so I tap her bokken, and she stiffens her arm. I shake my head in answer to her question. "No."

The entire left side of her body hitches, and her neck flexes with the strain. Moving behind her, I gently tap her shoulder then her elbow with my scabbard. "Soften here." I touch my saya to her stomach. "Stronger here." She grunts as she flexes her core, and I press my lips together to keep from chuckling. She's really doing a great job, and I don't want her to think I'm laughing at her. She's just so determined. Adorable.

The tip of my scabbard points at her feet as I say, "Spread your toes and bend your knees."

When she almost squats with her effort to follow my direction, I can't keep the soft laugh from passing my lips. "Not that low, Atagi." I press a hand to her upper back, directing her to stand a little taller.

As my hand slides away, I find myself fighting my emotions as I circle my new student. Swordsmanship is in my blood. It is what I live for, it's who I am, and being able to share my knowledge ... It's a gift.

And I'm not alone. For the first time in decades, I'm not weighed down by my oppressive isolation. I have a purpose. I can share my love of the katana with someone who genuinely loves it too.

But my ever oppressive thoughts linger at the edges of my mind ... because Atagi will leave after this lesson, and it might not be next time or the next, but *eventually* there will be a last time. Maybe the magic keeps her from finding her way back. Maybe she grows out of this phase and moves on to other things. Maybe she gets married and abandons me for her new family. And maybe years from now, she will become too old to come see me. It doesn't matter when. Days or years. I know that one day I'll be all alone once more.

Focus on today, on right now.

The internal voice of my scabbard is right. I won't let my gloomy thoughts steal away these happy moments.

As the sun travels across the sky, pulling the shadows one way before pushing them back the other, I center my attention on Atagi. We hold our swords in different positions, taking small breaks when I notice her muscles reaching their limit. Hori's soft knicker draws my focus from our lesson, and I look across the clearing at the mare, realizing the day is almost gone.

"You've done well today, Atagi. You should head home. I didn't mean to keep you so long. I'm sure your family is worried about you."

Atagi rolls her shoulders with a smile. "It's alright. Old woman Futsu has supposedly come down with some *illness*, so mama went to her house to help her." When I raise a brow at her sarcastic tone, she rolls her eyes. "I think Futsu-san just likes the attention. Sure, she's like a thousand years old, but she's still strong enough to smack me with her cane when she catches me running through her garden. I use it as a shortcut to Isayo's house. Futsu-san doesn't catch me all that often, but when she does ..." Atagi rubs the back of her arm, I suspect in some remembered pain of Futsu's strike. "I'm sure that old woman is faking being sick just so people will come and make a fuss over her."

Shrugging, she smiles at me. "Doesn't matter. My mama will probably stay the night at Futsu-san's house, and papa will still be at the shop even by the time I get home." She chews on her lip, dropping her gaze. "I was supposed to practice my tea ceremony today ..." Again, she shrugs off her worries, this time with a wave of her hand. "I'll just practice extra tomorrow. This was waaaay more fun than steeping and pouring tea all day."

She grips the center of her bokken, mimicking my hold on my scabbard. Bowing, she says, "Thank you for the lesson, Sensei."

I grit my teeth, willing my tears to remain where they're lodged in my throat, a mix of emotions swirling through me. I don't want her to go. I enjoyed today, more than I have in a very, very long time. But while I'm sad to see her leave, the depressive mood I expect doesn't invade my thoughts. Instead, the delight of the day clings to me, fills me ... because today I shared a piece of myself, and Atagi was happy to accept it.

I bow to her, letting the curtain of my hair hide the emotions I'm not sure I'm hiding on my face. When I straighten, Atagi stands tall before me, her hand gripping her sword. Then with a whirl, she spins and jogs to her horse. She looks around, biting her lip, and I assume she's looking for a low branch or rock to help boost her onto her mare. I stride across the clearing and bend down, holding out my free hand. "Up you go."

She turns, palms pressed to Hori's side as she bends her knee to place her foot in my palm. With an easy flex, I help lift Atagi onto Hori's back. Gathering the reins, she adjusts her hold several times, trying to work around her grip on her bokken. Shaking my head, I reach up, curling my fingers in a gesture for her to hand it over before opening my palm. "I'll keep it safe for you."

She chews on her lip, and I wait to see if she'll argue, but after a moment, her shoulders slump and she hands me her practice sword. It's small enough to clasp in the same hand that holds my scabbard, and I lower my arm to rest by my side.

Atagi's gaze lingers on her bokken.

Or is she looking at me?

She doesn't want Guardian. Right? She has shown no interest in it. No. She's just reluctant to give up her first 'sword.' And I don't blame her. She's going to make a great swordsman ... woman ... person.

Atagi lifts her gaze to meet mine, and she smiles. "This was the best day of my life."

Mine too.

She continues. "I'll be back. I promise."

I nod, not trusting my voice not to break if I speak as she steers Hori away and kicks the mare into an easy walk. As she melts into the shadows of the forest, the deep melancholy I was afraid of finally makes an appearance, pressing heavily on my shoulders. Now that she's actually gone, I slump over, running my palm over my face. Each time she leaves, the loneliness is going to wrap around me a little tighter, suffocating in its hold. The bit of joy and companionship Atagi brings with her will make my prison that much darker with her absence. I know ... from experience.

Matsumae and our passionate affair flits through my mind.

Everyone leaves eventually.

Yes, but it will be so much fun while it lasts.

I smile as I walk back to my fire pit, straightening my back. Yes. She'll be back, and it will be great fun.

I start planning her next lesson, adding and discarding ideas with building excitement.

Hope is cruel, but I let it in anyway.

21

I can't sleep. The sky shifts from velvet black to midnight blue as the morning approaches. It's been a fortnight, and Atagi has not returned.

Rolling onto my back, I stare at the few sprinkles of stars I'm able to see through the opening of the clearing outside my cave. The enclosure of my bedchamber seemed stifling tonight, so I came outside to enjoy the light breeze and hopefully find some rest.

My scabbard, laying on the ground at my side, scoffs. *No, you came out here, like you have every night, to listen for her ... waiting for your magic to prickle with the awareness that she has come back.*

"She would know better than to wander these woods at night."

I wouldn't be so sure ... if that's the only time she can find to sneak away, she'd do it. Just another way you're a danger to her.

I sigh, resting the katana on my chest, stroking the smooth wood, still glossy and perfect after all these years. "I know."

Little flashes of soft light dance around me as the fireflies put on their final show before morning. A bird flies overhead, its wings a dark shape against the languidly lightening sky. How I wish I could fly away ... far, far from this place.

Where would we go?

"I don't know. Who knows? I don't think it would matter. Away. Just ... away from here."

Breathing slowly, I let myself fall into a meditative state. The earth is both hard and soft under my back. The smell of dirt mixes with the fresh scent of pine and grass wet with morning dew. Branches rustle softly with the barely-there breeze. The sky bleeds from midnight, to sapphire, to a purplish-blue as the sun prepares to make its appearance.

It's moments like this that make me love being alive. I love the textures, the smells, the sounds, the experiences of life all around me. There's nothing flashy or brazen about life in this forest. Sometimes it's brutal and harsh. Sometimes it's soft and gentle.

The black of the forest lightens to a dark green, and little skitters and scratches come from the woods as small creatures wake up and start moving. I should start moving as well.

Why? It's nice here. Your breathing is relaxing.

I glance at the katana on my chest, my scabbard rising and falling with each of my gentle breaths. It's right. Just laying here and breathing *is* relaxing. I'm tempted to just stare at the sky all day and mark its changes. Maybe today we'll just do this ... do nothing.

Yes, nothing sounds nice.

. . .

My body jerks, and I grip my scabbard tightly to my chest as my magic prods me awake. I blink, realizing I'm warm from the bright sun and that morning is already pushing towards afternoon. I don't recall falling asleep, but I know I needed the rest, so …

Wait, what woke me?

Like a hand gently shaking my shoulder, my magic tells me she's here. I roll onto my side, bringing the katana with me as I stand and turn to face southeast. Atagi hasn't come from that direction before, but that doesn't mean anything. All I care about is that this cursed forest let her in.

With every scrap of patience I have, I wait. As I stare into the tree line, I narrow my eyes. Do the pines seem to be closer together, their branches woven tighter, the shadows deeper?

A huff of frustration meets my ears a moment before a small hand pushes through the branches, shoving them aside to reveal a haggard looking Atagi. A few scratches create raised red lines on her face as well as her hands. She winces, reaching up to untangle her hair from a branch, and sap sticks to her, creating a nest of her usually straight locks.

Practically tumbling into the clearing, she meets my eyes with a grin. "I did it! This stupid, stupid forest! It really didn't want me to find you this time. I mean, at first, early this morning, it was easy enough to find the way, but the closer I got, the more the trees just"—She spreads her arms, then closes them in towards each other—"pressed in on me. But I kept going even though I had to leave Hori back there. The trees were too tight for her. So, I walked. I did it!" Atagi looks back at the trees she just fought to get through. "Stupid forest."

My lips twitch with a smile, but I don't let it break

through as I step towards her. "Atagi, maybe this isn't such a good idea. This place ... I don't want you to get hurt."

Her eyes go round. "But, Sensei, you promised! I'm here! I made it." She digs her sandal into the dirt, twisting it, her gaze down. "Though, I can't stay for long today. I have to cook dinner and bring it to papa at the shop. Mama says I have to learn all these different dishes to impress the important families who will be looking for a bride for their sons ..." Atagi screws up her nose and sticks out her tongue, making a *blech* sound. But then a bright smile lights up her face, and she pats her tunic before sticking her hand in a pocket. "That reminds me, I brought you a rice ball from breakfast." She holds it out, biting her lip. "It's a little squished but should still taste fine. I—"

Closing the space between us, I take the rice with both hands as a sign of respect. I bow. "Thank you, Atagi. That was very kind of you to think of me, but you don't have to bring me things. I'll teach you because I want to." A chunk of rice falls off the deformed triangle, but I catch it, bringing it to my mouth. It's hard to swallow past the tears in my throat. It's so simple, rice, vinegar, sugar, salt, and flaky seaweed, but it's often the simple things that matter the most. Pinching off another piece, I bring it to my lips, eating slowly, determined to make this treat last.

While I take small bites of the sticky rice, Atagi walks to the mouth of my cave, wrapping her small hand around the hilt of her bokken. Several sleepless nights ago, I passed the time by carving a scrolling cloud design into the hilt of her little practice sword, and she runs her fingers over the shapes before gripping the hilt.

Atagi stands before me, and I can tell she's trying to be patient, but she keeps flexing and relaxing her grip around the sword, her knuckles turning white. She follows the movement of my hand as I bring the last of my treat to my lips. I swallow the last bite, and Atagi's eyes widen with hope.

I nod. "Let's get started."

Dirt clings to the hems of Atagi's silk pants, and I wonder how she'll explain her dirty appearance to her mother. The question sits on my tongue, unasked as she slows from her jog, stopping to rest her hands on her knees. Damp strands of her hair stick to her face, and she brushes them away as she gasps for breath. We have only had three lessons, but it has quickly become apparent that she has absolutely no endurance. Hence the running.

I tsk, "I didn't say you could stop, Atagi."

Her hands remain on her thighs, but she glares at me, the angry expression making me want to chuckle as she says, "I've been r-running for hours. I n-need to r-rest."

Raising a brow, I reply. "You've been *jogging* for three minutes, Atagi."

She takes two big breaths before standing. "Nuh uh. No way. It's been at least an hour!"

I bite my cheek to keep from laughing. "Three. Minutes."

Atagi shakes her head, wiping sweat from her neck. "No. No. No way." Her cheeks are red, and the cream fabric of her tunic is darker around the neckline, under her arms, and across her middle. She throws her head back with a frustrated, "Ugh!"

Waving a hand towards the firepit, I say, "Okay. Sit down. You can have a small break."

With a dramatic sigh, she lets her head fall back. "Finally!"

I manage to swallow my chuckle as she flops onto the flat rock. She crosses her legs, planting her hands behind her to lean back, trying to catch her breath.

"So," My voice draws her attention from the clouds. "Where does your mother think you are today?"

I hate that she lies to her family to come see me, but I'm too selfish to tell her to stop. I console myself by remembering I did try and warn her away, several times. And, I'll admit, I enjoy hearing the creative stories Atagi comes up with to explain her absences to her mother.

Twirling a piece of her black hair around her finger, she smiles. "I told her Uncle Hotta was taking me to the next town over to shop for a new hair pin. He's papa's brother. He hasn't found a wife yet, and mama says it's because he's lazy and doesn't make as much money as papa does."

I frown, uneasiness stirring in my gut. "And what happens when your mother asks your uncle about this trip, or when she asks to see the hairpin?"

Atagi purses her lips and blows out an exaggerated, *pffft*. "Mama doesn't like Uncle Hotta. He took me fishing *one time* and I got fish guts on my dress. The stain wouldn't come out and mama has never forgiven him. I don't know why she was so upset. She complained to papa for days, telling him that fishing isn't something a lady should be doing and that his brother's bad influ ants was going to 'ruin' me." I think she was trying to say influence, and I cough to hide my chuckle.

Atagi rolls her eyes. "It was only a little stain, and it's not like I don't have other dresses. Anyway, papa said it was good for me to spend time with Uncle Hotta, and that only made mama madder, but when papa gets that look in his eyes, it means he's done arguing. I heard mama mumbling that she 'washed her hands of Uncle Hotta', whatever that means. I just know that she doesn't talk to him anymore, so she won't ask him about taking me shopping."

She drops her gaze, but not before I catch a sly smile. "Plus, I was a bit ... naughty yesterday, so mama was happy to get me out of the house today, even if she thinks I'm with Uncle Hotta." The smirk she sends me is so diabolical, I almost burst out laughing. Such a sweet and innocent face trying to pull off a conniving look ... it's somehow cute and terrifying at the same time.

You shouldn't be encouraging this, but it is adorable.

She waves a hand, letting her dark hair fall back into place. "And if she asks me, I'll just tell mama I didn't find a pin I liked."

She's going to get caught one of these days.

I don't want to think about that, so I turn, striding towards my cave, but her voice stops me. "Where are you going?"

"Don't worry about it. I'll be right back. Rest. You'll need it because when I come back, you're getting back to work."

As I return, I keep my hands in my pockets to conceal the item I retrieved. Atagi is still sitting on the rock, her breathing back to normal, and the redness has faded from her face. She looks up at me and starts to stand, but I shake my head.

"You get another few minutes. Stay here."

She blinks at me, her eyes trying to find the answer to what I'm up to, but I remain silent as I stride into the woods. My magic tickles down my spine with her gaze on my back. My bare feet are so tough and calloused, I hardly notice the crunch of pine needles or even the small twigs and rocks as I move into a fast jog.

From my hip, my scabbard asks, *Why aren't you wearing the sandals?*

"I don't need them right now. I'd rather save them for the first cold snap. They should help me from getting frostbite this year. Maybe."

You could ask Atagi to bring you socks.

"That would be nice, but I meant what I said. I don't need or want her to bring me gifts. Teaching her is gift enough."

You're such a softy.

As the carved x in the bark of a tree comes into view, I stop, scowling at the invisible barrier. Before my mood sours, I take the string from my pocket, tying the red cord I removed from one of the katanas in my cave to the low hanging branch of a tree to my right.

Picking back up into a run, I head back. Atagi stands when she sees me. Brushing off her pants, which does nothing to clean the dirty material, she faces me and waits.

I point into the woods. "I've tied a red cord to the branch of a tree. It's a little less than three kilometers that way. Now, we're going to race to that tree. I've already run there and back, and you're rested, so you have the advantage, Atagi. Are you ready?"

Her eyes dart to the woods before snapping back to my face. "Three kilometers?"

"A little less than."

"What does this have to do with sword fighting? I want to work on forms! Can't we just—"

"Atagi."

Snapping her lips shut, she glances back to the tree line. I wait for more complaints, but with a sigh, she braces her feet. I grin, shifting my weight, prepared to give her a little head start as I say, "Ready? Go!"

With a burst of speed, she sprints across the clearing, dashing into the woods as she shouts, "I'm going to beat you!"

She quickly moves out of sight, and I let loose the little chuckle that's been building in my chest as I jog after her. There's no way she'll beat me, but I like her confidence.

22

Atagi giggles as I poke her side with my scabbard, halting the form she's working on today. She grabs her waist, her laughter building, tears of happiness rimming her dark eyes. "Sensei, stop!"

My smile is not only on my face, but in my words as I say, "Make me, Atagi-chan. What movement would deflect this?"

I gently slice the edge of my scabbard across her ribs again, sending her into another fit of giggles. "Sensei, that tickles!"

I draw back, shaking my head with a grin. "It doesn't tickle when it's real."

Her laughter dies off, but her smile remains, "I know, but I can't help it. I'm so ticklish."

Taking my stance, I ask, "What movement am I about to make?"

She tilts her head, looking at me from head to toe before saying, "Kesagiri?"

I nod, pride swelling my chest. "Correct." I wave a hand at her. "Show me." When she takes a big step forward, squatting deep, I shake my head. "No. From the beginning." With her seemingly endless eagerness, Atagi resets.

She's been coming sporadically for six months. Once, I was lucky enough to see her twice in one week. But usually, there are stretches between her visits, the longest one being twenty-three days. A very long, nearly endless twenty-three days. I now think of my life in these cursed woods in two phases ... before Atagi and after. It doesn't matter that there are more days without her than with. Each morning, I wake up with excitement, eager to plan for her lessons. And even those many days when she doesn't come, I still go to sleep with the hope she'll come the next day.

Even the pleasure-filled visits from Matsumae didn't have me this driven, this enthusiastic ... this hopeful. I'm passing on my knowledge, and Atagi soaks it up, eager for each lesson. She challenges me to challenge her. And I find more appreciation in the small things ... the soft sting of sunlight on my skin, of a cool breeze, of water pouring down my throat, of a good night's sleep after a lesson with my student ...

We've been practicing for almost an hour today, and I can't believe how fast the time has gone. She'll need to go soon, having told me upon her arrival that she had to leave before noon because she had extra dance lessons after lunch, her nose scrunched in exaggerated disgust. I told her that dancing would help with her sword practice, and that her sword practice would help with her dancing. Both help you become more aware of what you are doing and how you are moving through the world. Sword art is its own dance. She smiled at that, and I thought to myself, *I hope I'm being a good teacher. My father would have been better at this. More patient. Kinder. But I think he'd be proud of me passing on my knowledge.*

Atagi staggers her feet, gripping her trusty wooden sword at her side. With a smooth draw, she brings her bokken over her shoulder, pointing it forward before lifting it overhead.

I raise my hand, a gesture she has learned means I want her to hold her position. I tap her shoulder, and she obediently lowers it. With a gentle press of my fingers, she adjusts the angle of her sword. With a nod, I back up, and she continues. Stepping forward, she slices downward, then quickly steps back, switching her lead leg as she sideswipes her blade.

I raise my hand again, and she pauses. I ask, "What's wrong?"

Without moving her body, she eyes her arms, and strains to look down at her feet. Slowly her gaze travels back up, looking at her sword. When she bites her lip, I know she hasn't figured it out, so I tap the outer edge of her blade with my scabbard. Her eyes soften as she realizes what she's done, and Atagi pulls the blade back a few inches closer to her body.

When I nod, she sweeps into the next part of the movement. From her deep squat, she raises her left arm over her head in the perfect right angle, her other elbow pointed straight up ... just like I taught her. But ...

I cross my arms, my saya tucked under my bicep. "Atagi."

She freezes, looking at me with the first fringe of annoyance in her eyes, but she doesn't verbally complain at my constant interruptions. Atagi grits her teeth and adjusts her stance so her blade covers her from behind from shoulder to knee.

She's a fast learner, eager to soak up anything I throw at her as long as it has something to do with swordplay. I can't believe how far she's come in just a few months. Luckily, there's still much for her to learn because the way of the katana is a life-long pursuit of training. Not something you ever perfect. Even the best swordsmen in the world practice every day, which is why they are the best.

My father practiced almost every day.

My scabbard scoffs, *You know she'll grow out of this one day. She'll get distracted by the pretty things females love. She'll come less and less. She'll get married, start a family ... She'll forget you.*

Crack. I practically hear something inside me break at the thought. I know one day she'll leave and it will be the last time, and that terrifies me. I'm trying to live in the moment as my father always liked to say, but the thought of being tossed back into the dark pit of my loneliness ...

I grit my teeth, doing my best to banish those thoughts, focusing as Atagi steps forward, swiveling her hips just right to bring her blade back overhead followed by a quick slash down and across. She reverses the move, with only one small bobble, finishing the Kesagiri.

She holds her final position for a long second before standing, posture tall, her wooden sword tucked back into the sash at her waist.

Keeping my arms crossed, I say, "Again."

With the fire of determination in her eyes, Atagi does the entire movement again, a little more smoothly this time. I make her go through it twice more.

Knowing our time today is drawing to a close, I decide to send her off with a little sparring match. She loves those best. When I take my stance, my sheathed sword at the ready, her round cheeks lift with a giant grin. She steps forward to meet my position, and together we move through the same forms she just practiced, our 'blades' tapping every now and then. As we sweep through the change in position,

I tilt my head at the space between us and say, "See, Atagi-chan, this is a dance. It's beautiful, isn't it?"

She matches my steps as we rotate to face off again, moving faster this time, our swords clashing a little harder. And with that grin still lighting up her face, she nods. "Yes, Sensei."

23

"Atagi, why have you stopped? Raise your blade. A little more bend in your knees. Don't make me tell you again." When she doesn't move to follow my direction, I lower my scabbard and shrug. "Okay. Then I guess we're done for the day."

As I go to turn around, she says, "You're really not going to say anything? Do you really not remember?"

Raising a brow, I cross my arms, the lacquer of my saya thudding against my hip. "Say what? What have I forgotten that's sent my student into such distress?" She rolls her eyes, dropping her arm until the rounded end of her practice sword scrapes the dirt. I tsk. "I don't care what you think I've done, Atagi-chan, there's no excuse for letting your blade touch the ground."

With a scowl, her eyes narrow, and she drags her stick across the dirt, digging a sharp line between us. "I'm tired of this old practice sword anyway. I want to use a real blade today."

My eyes widen, and then I throw back my head with a

barking laugh. When I look back at my student, it's to find her cheeks red and her jaw flexed with her irritation. My magic flickers red across my chest, but the warning is hardly warranted since I can see Atagi's intent in her eyes.

I know my student well and have plenty of time to dodge as she draws back her arm and flings her bokken at me. "You don't care at all!" The wood sword sails past me, flipping end over end before clattering to the ground with a soft thud. I look at the small bokken, noticing where the hilt is darker, almost shiny from the oils of Atagi's hand over these past ...

Wait.

Ohhh.

I count backwards in my head. Time means little to me, but I imagine to a regular human, and especially a child, time passes with agonizing awareness.

Keeping my expression passive, I turn back to where Atagi stands with hands clenched, and I ask, "Are you done, or are you going to throw something else at me?"

She stomps her foot, which does nothing but make her look adorable, which I know is certainly not her intent.

I must not laugh at her again. I must not laugh.

My scabbard chuckles. *That little spitfire looks like she wants to cut you to ribbons.*

Before I crack a smile and risk sending her rage into tears, I hold up a hand. "Atagi-chan, I'm sorry."

With my half-apology floating in the air between us, some of her anger melts away, loosening her fingers from their fists. But there's still a tightness to her posture.

My saya says, *Don't let her off too easy. Samurai don't let their emotions rule them.*

I'm not teaching her to be a samurai. I'm teaching her to use a sword. Not necessarily the same thing. But I don't plan to let her behavior go unpunished, even if it was slightly warranted. Every moment is teachable. That's what she wanted when she first came to me, so I'll keep teaching until she's done with me.

Atagi's gaze flicks between her wooden sword lying on the ground behind me and the mouth of my cave ... where she knows all those katanas hang on the stone wall.

"Atagi." My voice draws her attention back to me. "You've been with me for a full year now." Her eyes widen. I should have made a fuss over this anniversary of ours, but honestly, I overlooked the passage of time with my student. I took our time together for granted. And I can't afford to do that. Not when her time passes so quickly ... and mine stays at a standstill.

But I can't let her tantrum stand, so I nod at her discarded bokken as I ask, "Is that any way for my student of one year to act? Were those the actions of a student ready to wield a real blade?"

Her expression falls, and the sadness in her eyes nearly guts me. I must stay strong and resist giving in to those dark, weepy eyes. Dropping her gaze, she digs the toe of her waraji sandal into the ground, dirtying her sock. "I'm sorry, Sensei. Can I have my bokken back?"

"Answer the question, Atagi-chan."

She flattens her foot with a huff, her little fingers curling back into fists, but she keeps her gaze down. "No."

"No, what?"

Her head snaps up, revealing her eyes, filled with so much emotion ... frustration, sadness, disappointment, anger ...

Remind you of anyone?

Ignoring my scabbard, I wait for her answer. After a moment, she seems to collect herself, softening her gaze before dropping her head once more. "No, I shouldn't have thrown my sword at you, and no ... I don't deserve to use a real blade yet."

She looks so dejected, shoulders slumped, her hair hanging over one shoulder from where it's tied back. Her arms are now limp at her sides as she waits for me to tell her what to do next. She really has come a long way in this past year. She's stronger and sure on her feet. Her endurance still has a way to go, but ...

Don't give in. Stay strong. Where's the lesson if you give her what she wants? Don't do it. Don't ... you're going to do it, aren't you?

Inwardly, I smile at my scabbard as I wave towards my cave. "Go on then."

This time, when her head snaps up, a smile lifts her cheeks and her eyes sparkle. "Really, Sensei?"

I nod, and she kicks into a sprint, but I hold up a hand, and she skids to a stop. "But, if you pick the wrong one, you have to go back to your bokken."

Her smile falters, and she chews on her bottom lip before asking, "How will I know which one is the right one?"

"You've been training with me for a year. You should know. And if you don't, you're not ready. It's as simple as that."

Her weight shifts as she dances side to side with obvious excitement and nerves. There are actually a few swords on my wall that would be suitable for her current size and skill level, but I'm curious to see if she goes for the prettier, flashier ones, or if she chooses appropriately.

I wave towards my cave again, and with a little whoop, she takes off, the thuds of her sandals fading as she runs down the passageway.

Can you believe it's been an entire year?

I pat the katana on my hip. "I get that saying now."

Which one?

"Happiness makes times move faster."

24

The knife in my hand pauses mid cut. I look down and smile at the intricate carvings I've made on this final piece. "Finished. And just in time."

I slip it inside the leather pouch on my lap, and it clatters as it joins the others I've made. I set the pouch aside as my magic prickles down the front of my body, telling me Atagi is approaching from the south today. A few weeks ago, Atagi told me that it's been easier to find her way, even if the path is slightly different each time.

Hori's hooves clip-clop softly on the fallen pine needles as the mare breaks through the trees at a steady walk. Atagi waves excitedly, sliding off her side saddle before Hori even comes to a complete stop. I wince as she slips before catching herself against her mare. The harshest parts of winter have passed, but freezing temperatures still blow in overnight, making the patches of yellow grass slippery until the sun has time to thaw the ground. Atagi straightens her kimono before quickly crossing the clearing, her stunted steps making her slower.

Sometimes, I think she wears these dresses to keep me from making her run laps.

You should make her do them anyway.

Maybe. Not today though.

Atagi walks past me. I wait to see if she notices her sword is not on the rock by the firepit where I usually set it for her. Sure enough, her eyes flick to the flat stone, and seeing it empty, she heads towards my cave.

I hold up a hand. "Atagi. Sit."

She looks at me then at the cave. When her gaze comes back to me, she chews her lip, but sits across from me, kneeling gracefully. I shift, pulling the carved wood board out from under my legs where the fabric of my loose pants was hiding it.

I set it down on the hard-packed dirt between us, and Atagi looks at it. My carving skill is decent, but it still takes her a few minutes to figure out what it is.

Looking up at me, she asks, "You want to play shogi?"

I nod.

Scooting a little closer, she says. "There are no tiles."

"Come now, Atagi. You should know by now that your sensei is always prepared." Grabbing the small pouch, I turn it over. It's a happy sound, the small wood pieces clattering against the board as they settle.

I can't wait to play.

As I set the pieces up in their starting positions, Atagi bites her lip again before glancing behind me towards the cave. I know she wants her sword. I know she wants to practice and spar. That's why she comes here. But today, I want to see how much of a mind for strategy she has. I already know from our lessons that she's able to quickly memorize patterns and mimic forms. But is she able to actually think through her moves? Can she anticipate what her opponent will do next? Can she adjust?

You just want to play this game.

Well, that too. It was father's favorite.

Once the pieces are set, I ask, "You know the rules?"

She nods, and we begin.

Atagi picks up one of her pawns and slaps it on the board. Whoever taught her this game is an aggressive player. I move a pawn, and she moves a lance. Just a few moves later, I've got her in checkmate. Atagi shifts on her shins, looking over my shoulder once more.

Her desire to practice with her sword is distracting her from the game.

Another teachable moment?

Of course.

Maybe she's just bad at shogi.

Maybe. We'll see.

As she resets the board, I ask, "How about some tea while we play?"

Wrinkling her nose, she shakes her head with a grin. "Not that gross pine tea. *Blech.*"

"I can make dried mushroom tea."

Finishing setting the board, she giggles. "That's not much better."

Her fingers reach for one of her pawns, but I hold up a hand. "Wait. Think. What moves will you make to win, and how will you adjust if I get in your way?" She tilts her head, looking down at the board. Her brow furrows, and as I stand, I say, "Think it through. I'll be right back. *I* want tea."

In my kitchen, I collect my kettle that I filled with water earlier today, and the dried leaves from my stash. Atagi still stares at the board as I start a fire in the outdoor pit and set the kettle to boil.

"Do you have a plan?"

Her finger taps a steady rhythm on her lap as she says, "I think so."

I wave a hand, indicating for her to make the first move. A pawn.

As I stoke the fire, I reach with my free hand to slide one of my pawns forward.

Eight moves later, my knight reaches her end of the board, allowing me to promote it to a more powerful piece. And five minutes later, I've got her in checkmate again.

Atagi's shoulders slump. "You're too good. I'll never win."

I tsk at her. "Two games and you're ready to admit defeat? You did better this time."

"But you kept"—She waves her hand over the board in frustration—"getting in the way of everything I wanted to do."

I chuckle. "That's the point, Atagi. To keep your opponent from winning."

"I thought the point was to win."

Ah, good. She recognizes that those are two different things.

Slowly, I reset the board. "I know the rules of this game. I know where my pieces can go and when. I don't have to worry about myself. I have to worry about you, Atagi. I need to pay attention to your moves, to what I think will be your next attack. Focusing on you, learning your strategy is what will best protect my king."

She looks up at me with an adorable smirk, like she has figured me out. "Like sword fighting."

I grin with a nod. "Like sword fighting."

The sound of her tile slapping against the board brings me back to the game, and I move my piece. All those frustrating hours carving these small pieces were worth it. With a grin, I watch Atagi as she bites her lip.

I'm going to win in four more moves.

25

I sidestep as Atagi comes at me with a strong thrust of her sword ... the same one she picked three years ago on our one-year anniversary. The construction of the katana is sturdy and it's the right size for her smaller frame. But the blade is blunt from years of not being used prior to her selection, and because I won't let her sharpen it ... for her safety and mine.

You'd heal just fine.

I roll my eyes at my scabbard, answering in my head. *Yes, but the cut of a blade still hurts like a bitch. And also, the questions ... Atagi would have a string of them, endless and never ending. I'd just rather not.*

Flexing my core, I lean to my left as her blade passes my face in an upward slash. She gets so close, the whoosh of air created by her attack blows against my cheek. Absently, I block her next strike with my scabbard, realizing how much she's grown ... and not just physically. Atagi is several inches taller now, and while she still holds some of the softness of childhood, she's gained a lean strength from her training.

It's been four years since she first showed up, giggling at

me as I undressed a dead man. These have been the best four years of my existence.

But there's an edge to Atagi today. There seemed to be a dark cloud over the usually bubbly girl when she walked into my clearing a few hours ago. And every time she strikes and misses me, her eyes get more intense, her jaw flexes as she grits her teeth, and the grip on her sword turns her knuckles white. The hard-packed dirt crunches under her boots, the frost clinging to the ground even though it's nearly midday. As I step into her space, forcing her to back up, I wiggle my toes in the soft boots Atagi brought me a little over a year ago. She told me she sold a few of her hair pins and a silk scarf to buy them, but the way she averted her gaze made me think there was more to the story of how she got these boots.

A sharp *clink* echoes in the clearing as I tap her blade with my scabbard, deflecting her strike. She huffs, and her eyes glisten with frustration, but she sniffs away her tears. Atagi seems to get annoyed with *everything* these days. Gone is the constantly sweet and cheerful child, replaced with a more temperamental ten-year-old. Or at least I think she's ten. Ten-ish. She's never said, and I've never asked, because it really doesn't matter. And because I don't want her to ask me how old I am.

As I watch Atagi grunt with her next swing, I smile to myself because I always look forward to teaching her, emotional outbursts and all.

But who knows how long this will last. What if she's starting to outgrow this?

I want to shout at my saya to be quiet, but instead I press my attack on Atagi. Pushing her a little more, I lunge and slash, running my saya across her middle. I step back, and she glares at me as I say, "Fatal strike, Atagi. You're not focused."

A little growl comes from her throat as she steps forward, striking, and missing. "I'm focused!"

I raise a brow, and with a quick spin, I tap her upper back with the tip of my scabbard. "Really?"

Atagi stumbles forward, catches herself, and spins, blade raised. There's fire in her eyes, both hands gripping her hilt too hard. "Yes!"

Shaking my head, I lower my saya to my side. "That is all for today."

Her fingers flex around the ray skin hilt of her katana. A cold gust of winter wind whistles through the clearing, billowing the wide sleeves of her kimono even though they are tied back. There's a little crunch of dirt as her front foot shifts so she can put more weight into it.

I shake my head again. "Don't, Atagi. We're done."

I see it in her eyes. The anger. The frustration. There's more going on here than losing to me. With a little cry, she charges. I sigh and let her get close, stepping to the side at the last moment. I grab her blade at the guard, and even though the steel is dull, it still cuts. I ignore the slice of pain as Atagi gasps, her eyes going wide. I use her distress against her, twisting her sword from her grip before shoving her past me.

She stumbles, her head bowed, her black hair swaying where it's tied back at her nape with a blue cord. I slip my saya through the sash at my waist and grip the hilt of her blade in that hand so I can lower my injured one. As I flex my palm, blood drips to the dirt. It's not too deep. It'll be healed soon.

Atagi hasn't turned to face me, her shoulders tight, her head still bowed. Rotating my hand to hide the closing wound, I take a step towards her, but her body tenses even more so I stop. Keeping my voice low and calm, I ask, "Atagi-chan, what's wrong? You are not yourself today." She huffs with a little shake of her head, but doesn't answer so I ask, "Where is my student?"

She spins, her hair slapping her in the face. Her cheeks are red, and not just from the cold as she slaps her chest with a trembling hand. "*I* am your student! It's been *years*. I'm better. I'm stronger. I know I am, but I still can't even touch you! This is all ..." She drops her arm, clenching her fists. "This is a waste of time."

Panic squeezes my chest. "Atagi-chan, I—"

A tear drips down her cheek, and she slaps it away with such force, she leaves behind a mark. "They've been coming to the house."

"Who?"

"Men." Oh. *Ohhhh.* "They look at me like I'm some trinket they are considering buying at the market. And to them, I guess I am."

Fuck, she's still just a child.

Before I can think of anything to say, she shakes her body from shoulders to toes. She holds out her hand, her eyes darting to her sword in my grip.

I shake my head. "You are not in the right mind to hold a weapon right now."

Her body tenses again as she narrows her eyes. "I'm in the exact right state of mind to hold that weapon. Let's go, Sensei. I need to get better. Now!"

"No."

She looks at me with such rage, I almost give in to let her work through some of her anger. But this is not the way of the katana.

You do it all the time.

Just because I fight through my emotions doesn't mean it's right. It's hard to be patient, to know when it's time to step back. She will learn from this.

If she had magic like mine, I think her eyes would be blazing with it right now as she grits her teeth. "You don't understand. Who knows when I'll be bought and married off? Once that happens, I doubt I'll be able to sneak away and come here anymore. I need to be great now!"

"Atagi-chan, the art of the katana is a lifetime practice. There is no finish line to greatness."

Some of the fire dies in her eyes, but her knuckles are white where they're clenched at her sides. "I don't *have* a lifetime. You just don't understand. You're a man."

Atagi storms off a few paces to her right, her boots crunching on the frozen earth with every stomp. As she approaches the nearest pine, Atagi draws back her arm, and with a little grunt of anger, her fist slams against the rough bark of the tree.

"Atagi!"

My shout does nothing to stop her strikes. Her sword drops from my hand, and I'm at her side within seconds, but not quick enough. Her small fists pound against the trunk, her knuckles coming away scraped and a little bloody. Grabbing her wrists, I hold her still as she struggles in my grip. So much sadness. So much anger. I want to hug her and tell her everything will be alright.

But will it?

After a moment, she calms down enough, and I loosen my hold. Ripping her wrists from my grip, she rubs her knuckles, sending little pieces of bark sprinkling to the ground. Her gaze drops to my injured hand. My fingers are curled into my palm so she can't see that it's already scabbed over. A flash of concern crosses her eyes, but after a moment it's gone. She stomps her foot, spinning and walking away. "Fine. You're right. We're done."

I watch her go, dread holding me in place as if I'm stuck in deep mud. With slow breaths, I tell myself she just needs time to cool down.

My scabbard whispers, *Yeah, but what if she doesn't? What if she stays mad and never comes back?"*

As it often does, the threat of being thrown back into my endless loneliness comes out of nowhere and hits me like a punch to the gut, stealing my breath. I watch as Atagi stretches to shove her foot in the stirrup of her ever-patient mare. She swings onto Hori's back, and trots into the woods, never looking back.

"Please don't stay mad. Please, come back." The wind blows my whispered words back in my face.

26

T he red rush of my magic gently tingles down the outer edge of my left arm and pulls at my left hip. Turning my head, I stare into the woods.

Oh, thank the gods. She's here. She came back.

It's only been nine days since Atagi left in anger, but each day has weighed heavier, my thoughts roiling as I considered her situation. How could I help her? *Could* I even help her? I haven't come up with an answer, but now that she's here, I take my first full breath in days.

My scabbard narrows its proverbial eyes at me. *You're too attached. I get it. I am too, but prepare yourself, because we both know how this eventually ends.*

I flick Guardian's hilt. "Quit reminding me!"

"You sound like a lunatic, talking to that katana. You know that, right?" Atagi's voice is light and happy, sounding like her old self. I smile as I look up at her from where I'm sitting near the crackling fire within the circle of stones to my right.

"What kind of friend would I be if I never talked to him?"

She looks down at the lacquered wood of my saya sitting on the ground next to me. When she lifts her gaze back to my face, she scrunches her whole face. "Is it really magic? Can it ... can it understand you?"

Atagi has only asked about the katana a handful of times in the four years she's been coming here, and I've always evaded her questions. She's never pushed. But I know the day will come when I'll have to talk about it.

Grabbing my scabbard in the middle, I stand before sliding it through the sash around my waist. "What do you think, Atagi?"

Shaking her head, Atagi's hair swishes around her face, brushing her shoulders, the black strands glossy and straight as always. "I think you're a crazy man who lives in the woods and thinks a sword is his only friend."

Placing my hands on my hips, I raise a brow at her. "Not my *only* friend, surely?"

She giggles but doesn't respond. I want to comment on her better mood today, but I'm afraid that will trigger a change in her current happy state. Atagi's smile falls, and she toes the ground, biting her lip. "Sensei, about the other day—"

I hold up a hand. "We can't be at our best every moment of every day. I don't expect that of you, Atagi. What I do expect is for you to give me your best today ... whatever that looks like. And next time, your best will look different than it does today. Okay?"

She still hasn't raised her head, her boot scraping at the ice crystals sparkling in the dirt. "But ... still ... I shouldn't have ... I mean ... I was so ..."

"Atagi."

Slowly, she looks up. Her dark eyes shimmer with held-back tears. She's so young, and it seems the world is already placing a lot on her small shoulders. Maybe, in some way, these lessons with me will help her be able to bear that weight ... because I have a feeling it will just get heavier. Or will my lessons make things worse? Am I feeding her a false hope of what her future could be?

I need a moment to center myself and my thoughts, and I think she does too.

Taking a step to my left, I sit back down, crossing my legs, setting my scabbard back on the ground at my side. I place one hand on my belly and the other on my chest. Atagi knows what I'm doing, but she hesitates. At least her eyes are dry now. I wait another second before nodding my head at the space across the fire. She sighs, coming over with short shuffling steps. She's moving like that more and more these days, even when wearing her less restrictive kimonos or pants.

I think back to life in the village and of all the times I traveled with my father. It's only now, with Atagi in my life, that I realize how much women always remained in the background ... quiet, seemingly only there when something was needed of them. And now, seeing that in Atagi, I want to break her of these habits, to teach her to be free, that she doesn't have to make herself slower, smaller, quieter. But the practical part of my brain knows I shouldn't undermine whatever 'training' she's receiving at home. Securing a good husband is the only way to ensure an easier life for herself.

That's unfortunate. Given the freedom, Atagi could be glorious.

I know, and that breaks my heart.

With grace taught, I assume by one of her tutors or her mother, Atagi kneels, tucking her fur-lined kimono under her, sitting on her heels. One of her small hands presses to her middle, and the other lays flat on her chest. She stares at me across the fire, the flames reflecting in her dark eyes.

As I take a deep breath, my ribs expand, and my upper back stretches. Atagi follows my breath, and we exhale together. Before we take our next inhale, she smiles. "Thank you for the lesson, Sensei."

I duck my head, leading her through the first couple of breaths. After a few minutes, once we are both focused, I stand, and she follows. We've done this before, so she knows to stay where she is as I circle the fire, coming closer to her. Closing her eyes, she drops her arms at her sides, standing a little taller, bracing her feet as wide as her dress allows. Heel-toe, I approach. Silent. I come in close to her right side, then back away. As I move to flank her, she turns, following the sound of my movements. I stop. She halts, eyes still closed, breath steady. I take one step back the way I came, and she pushes her breath out with a huff of sound, dropping into a short lunge, thrusting her arms out. Holding her position, she opens her eyes. When she sees I'm just slightly to her left, her jaw flexes as she grinds her teeth. She closes her eyes, sliding her boot back so she's once more standing tall, breathing slow, trying to follow my movements just by listening. By feeling.

I move, the fire warming me as I get closer. This time, when Atagi lunges, she's right on. Opening her eyes, she smiles, seeing her outstretched arms pointing right at my chest.

I nod. "Good. Again."

She resets, closing her eyes, and now confidence bolsters her posture. Good. This is what she needed. What we both needed.

.   .   .

Atagi raises her small ceramic cup to her lips, taking a sip of her matcha that she brought from home. The fire died down to flickering flames while we trained, so I toss on a log before picking up my own dented cup. Atagi's cup is also one she brought from home—one her mother ordered be thrown out because of the small chip on the rim. It's such a lovely, delicate thing. And when Atagi's not here, the cup sits in my kitchen hut, waiting for her to return. Just like me.

Atagi sighs, looking at the sky. "I have to go."

So soon? I keep the question inside, saying instead, "You did well today, Atagi."

She shrugs a shoulder, peering into her cup. I thought I had built some of her confidence back up today, but it seems the weight of her worries is too heavy. I'm all too familiar with how constricting some days can feel and not have a way to pull yourself out. Does Atagi have anyone to talk to? I may be alone, but at least I have my scabbard to unburden myself to.

That's because you are crazy.

Does Atagi talk to her friend, Isayo? She hasn't mentioned the girl in a while. Does she have other friends?

"Atagi." She lifts her gaze, the steam from her cup curling around her face. "Do you want to talk?"

Her eyes shimmer, and her teeth worry at her lip. I don't want her to cry, but if that's what she needs, I'm happy to give her the space to just let her emotions go. We all need that from time to time.

You've wept your fair share over the years.

I ignore my scabbard's quip, waiting for Atagi's response. Lifting her cup to her lips, she takes another sip before lowering her hands to her lap. The movement is so demure and gentle. Polished. Trained.

When she smiles at me, it lacks any of the joy from earlier in the day. "I'm fine, Sensei. It's nothing." She shakes her head, sweeping her hair behind her shoulders, again in what seems like a practiced move. "Did I tell you that Hori almost kicked papa last week? Oh, he was so mad. But it was really his fault. He came up right behind her. I guess he didn't realize she was sleeping, but she was so startled, she just kicked out. Luckily, she missed, but her tail whacked him in the face. It left a mark!" She giggles, some warmth creeping into her expression.

I know this is a diversion from whatever is really bothering her, but I let her ramble. Atagi goes on, telling me stories of her family and of her town. Some I've heard before, and some are new. She even brings up Isayo, who it seems was sent to her aunt's house for the winter, explaining why Atagi hadn't spoken about her friend.

As she talks, I hold my warm cup of tea, reflecting on how much more comfortable my life has become since Atagi stumbled into my clearing. Over the years, this girl has brought me little odds and ends, things discarded by her mama or papa or neighbors. Blankets, old biscuits gone hard, sacks empty of their dried rice, a shirt with a hole in the side, a spoon with a bent handle ...

I think of the socks she brought me a year ago, and the serious question she dropped on me. *"Sensei, are you in trouble? Are people after you for what you ... you know ... about what you told me about your village? Is that why you stay out here and never go into town?"*

I'd nearly dropped the socks as I scrambled for an answer, only coming up with, *"It's complicated, but no, Atagi. No one is after me."*

Not counting those hunting Guardian. And maybe

Motosue Saito, my father's apprentice. Is he still ranting with drunken stories about the magical katana? Is he searching for me? Is he even still alive?

But I didn't say any of that, and she'd held my gaze for a long moment before shrugging her shoulders and saying, *"Well, I guess it's fine if you want to live out here all on your own. Besides, I wouldn't have been able to learn swordplay if you lived in town."* And with that, she'd dropped it.

Beyond the things Atagi has brought me, more importantly, she has given me companionship. She reignited my love of life. She has given me a hope that hasn't stabbed me in the back. I owe so much to this little girl.

But even after she's gone, you'll always have me.

I nearly growl at my scabbard for shoving that thought into my head, but I keep it buried, smiling and nodding as Atagi keeps talking.

And then she's gone home for the day, having said so much, but in the end, told me nothing. I throw another log on the fire, and the burnt ones at the bottom collapse, sending sparks dancing into the sky. There's still several hours of daylight left, even with these shorter winter days. Atagi was here for barely three hours this time.

It's starting. She's pulling away.

"No. It's just a phase. Don't children go through these *moods* as they mature?"

Ha! Just wait until she's a little older and those hormones really kick in ... if she keeps coming that long.

"You're not being helpful."

No, but I'm being practical.

"I don't want to be practical. I want to be happy."

And Atagi? Don't you want her to be happy?

"Of course I do! But whatever is going on at her home doesn't seem to be making her very happy."

And what you're doing ... continuing to feed her false dreams, teaching her swordplay, an art that is useless, not to mention dangerous to a woman ... that's going to make her happy?

I clench my fists. "Even if what I'm teaching her ends up not making her happy ... It will make her stronger."

27

"Sensei, it's my birthday!" Atagi sings the announcement as she jogs out of the forest, her wooden geta kicking up dust, her wide-leg silk pants flapping around her legs. There's a thin strap over her shoulder, and she grabs it, slinging it over her arm, revealing a small bag that she drops to the ground as she yells, "I'm thirteen years old!" Stopping before me, she stands tall, lifting her chin as she swishes her hair back over her shoulder. "I'm a woman now."

I press my lips together to keep my bark of laughter from escaping, but my lips quirk slightly despite my best effort. She notices, shooting me her darkest glare, which is adorable. I hold up a hand to stall any angry words from leaving her mouth. "I'm sorry, Atagi. You caught me off guard. Happy birthday." My smile slips as I ask, "Why come here on your special day? Don't you want to celebrate with your family and friends?"

She shakes her head, sending her hair swaying, and I realize it's gotten much longer, almost to her middle back now.

"Papa had a big order to fill for an important client, so he'll be at the shop all day, and probably all night. Mama is having one of her headache spells. She won't leave her bed for hours, if at all today. Mama's servant will have to sit in that dark room with her waiting for her to need something. Poor Akimii-san. The incense she uses to help with the pain stinks. I hate it. I needed to get out of the house."

I feel bad that Atagi's parents have abandoned their daughter on her birthday, but a larger part of me is glad, because she came to spend time with me.

Atagi goes on. "And Isayo is still with her aunt." Her lips quirk to the side, not quite a frown. "I'm beginning to think she won't come back."

"What about other friends?"

She shrugs. "Haru is traveling with her family for the summer. Ino is always so busy with her dance lessons, I hardly see her anymore. Kou wanted to go riding today, but his father made him go help in their shop. Their family makes paper, and Kou's papa wants him to take over when he's old enough."

I chuckle. "So, I was your last choice."

Her eyes go round, and she holds up both hands. "No! If I could, I would spend *everyday* training with you, Sensei. I'm going to be the best swordsman in the world, remember?"

"I remember. And I'm sorry, Atagi. I don't have anything to give you for your birthday."

She grins. "Sure you do." Her eyes drop to my scabbard, and my heart stops. I nearly take a step back at the excitement in her eyes. But then she says, "A lesson. I want a lesson for my birthday."

It's a struggle to keep from gasping as relief washes through me.

She giggles. "The look on your face! Sensei! Did you think I was going to ask for Guardian for my birthday? Like I'd want that old sword. You've never even drawn the blade. For all I know it's all rusty and dull."

My palms are sweaty, and my heartbeat still races from the momentary scare, but she keeps on talking, her excitement building. "No. All I want is a lesson. I want to spar, and I don't want you to hold back."

I chuckle, relief settling my frayed nerves. "I think I'll hold back just a little." Her lips push out in a pout as she kneels, sliding out of her wooden geta and begins to tie on her well-worn fabric sandals.

I head towards my cave, saying over my shoulder. "Hold on. I'll be right back."

The bright summer sunlight reaches far into my cave this time of year, making it easy to navigate even if I didn't know this place better than I know the feel of my cock in my hand. And I know that *very* well.

I stop at my wall of markings. The scratches cover every reachable surface and continue far down this passageway. I trace my finger over the mark I made this morning. Bending down, I take a sharp stone between my fingers. It's a bit sloppy, but I manage to scrape the symbols for Atagi's name into the wall under today's mark—to remember for next year.

I toss the stone to the ground, and the echoing *clink* follows me to my wall of katanas. A tingle of happy anticipation dances through my chest as I wrap my hand around the black scabbard of the one just right of center. I carry it out of my cave to my waiting student, and her eyes land on the saya at once, her mouth dropping open. She's so shocked, she scrambles to catch the katana as I toss it to her. Atagi strokes the lacquer, tears pooling in her dark eyes as she whispers, "Really? A new sword? Really!"

I nod, even though she's still staring at the saya. "You've outgrown yours. Happy birthday."

Gripping her new katana in her left hand, she sprints across the clearing towards me. I remember the days when even this small burst of speed would have winded her. I grin as she throws her arms around my waist, hugging me tightly as she says, "Thank you, Sensei." My shirt muffles her words, and I pat her back, accepting the gratitude in her embrace.

I draw my hand away from her back to ruffle the hair on the top of her head. "Okay, Atagi-chan, are you ready to test your new blade?" Pulling out of our hug, she nods enthusiastically, backing up to grip the hilt. But before she takes her stance, I shake my head. "Draw your blade, Atagi. Get to know it. Learn its name."

As she holds the saya before her, I eagerly watch as she presses her thumb to the guard. I know what's coming, and I hold my breath, waiting.

Snick.

I love that sound.

Her new katana slips free of the fittings, and with ease, Atagi draws her blade. The sun glints off the metal, winking brightly. The sword is happy. It's free. It's ready to fulfill its purpose.

Atagi brings the blade closer to her face, reading the characters near the hilt. Her whisper is like a prayer. "Mikazuki. Crescent Moon."

When she looks up at me, there's such joy on her face, my heart melts. Clearing my throat, I say, "Tonight just happens to be a crescent moon. Maybe there was one on the night of its creation. Do you know, Atagi, if *you* were born under a crescent moon?"

She smiles, shaking her head. "I don't know, but I'm going to believe that I was."

Tying her empty scabbard to the sash around her waist, she grips the hilt of her new sword and holds it before her. Her eyes travel the length of the blade, and it seems she's picked up some of my habits, because she speaks softly to her katana. "Do you mind if I call you Moon? No? Good. I think we will be the best of friends. My name is Atagi Meiko, but you can call me Mei-chan."

My scabbard laughs in my head. *Your crazy has passed on to her.*

Maybe. But I like that she's talking to her blade. It's an intimate relationship, the one between wielder and wielded.

With a deep breath, I draw my saya, holding the sheathed weapon before me. "Okay, Atagi. Are you ready for your second birthday present?"

She presses her lips together and nods, trying to look serious but unable to completely wipe her smile away.

I know what you're about to say, but don't do it. This isn't a good idea. Don't do it. It'll end up ruining her special day. Don't—

"Today, we don't stop until you've drawn blood."

Atagi blinks at me, her stance wavering slightly. Moon dips towards the ground, and I see the uncertainty in her eyes. But this is important. She knows, but she needs to *understand* what she's holding in her hands. And I want to see how far she'll actually go. *She* needs to know how far she'll go.

"Sensei?"

I don't answer. I don't explain further. I don't even give her time to raise her blade. With movements I've made thousands of times, I attack. Atagi barely manages to block my scabbard from crushing her wrist. My strike is so hard, her arms shake from the impact. She retreats, and in that moment, determination flares in her narrowed eyes. When I strike again, she's ready.

I don't make it easy on her. I'm not eager to feel the bite of Moon slicing into my skin, but I press Atagi to her limit. We dance to the *clang* and *thwack* of her katana's steel and my scabbard. It's a beautiful push-pull. She's good. I'd preen at my skills as an instructor, but it's mostly her. She has a love for the katana. She's put in the work.

Her face is fierce, her lips pressed together, her brow furrowed, her bound hair flying behind her as she widens her stance, bringing Moon up to shield her right side as I press an attack. As I shift, sweeping my saya across my body, Atagi dips and slips under my arm, her blade nearly slicing across my ribs. I smile, jumping out of her reach just in time, and she comes at me again.

An hour passes, and I realize fatigue is starting to drag at my muscles. It's been a while since I've fought this hard for this long. It's wonderful. My student is good. Being alive to enjoy this moment is a gift.

Another thirty minutes go by. Atagi's moves are becoming messy, but she's still determined, pressing her attacks, not giving up. She lunges, and by the angle of her left elbow, I know the direction her blade will follow, and I prepare to block.

"Ah!" Her little cry of pain halts my movements as she stumbles. Her head bows as she hunches over. She takes a step, but limps with a hiss.

"Atagi, what's—" Fast as a snake strike, Atagi slashes, catching the back of my arm. Luckily, the sleeves of my shirt are tied back, sparing my precious clothing from being cut by her blade. Blood wells on my arm, and I grin. "You little cheat."

She smiles up at me, her breathing fast, her cheeks red, sweat sticking her hair to her neck. Shaking her head, she says, "Nuh uh. I knew I couldn't go on much longer, so I had to keep you from winning."

Hahaha. Clever girl.

I throw back my head, letting my laughter burst from my chest. "Well done, Atagi-chan. You have won the day. Now go tend to your new blade."

As she wipes down and oils Moon, I undo the tie at my side, letting my sleeves fall to my wrists, covering the cut she gave me. Atagi sheaths her sword, the soft *snick* indicating it's secure in its saya. Rocking back on her heels, she stands from where she was kneeling and retrieves her bag. When she sits back down, she reaches into the pretty embroidered fabric and extracts ...

I just stare at her hand as she holds out the treat towards me.

Is that Portuguese pan? I've only seen it a handful of times while traveling with my father. Such a rare treat. And she's ... She's giving it to me?

"Atagi, I can't."

She smiles. "It's my birthday, and I say you can." Her eyes dart to my arm, my sleeve covering the fact that the cut is already scabbed over. She says, "I'm sorry about that."

"Atagi."

She drops her arm, the pan squishing slightly where she's gripping it. "I know. I must be ready to use my blade if I'm going to carry it. I have to be ready to hurt, to ... kill."

Her smile has completely fallen away, and guilt squeezes my chest at taking away her joy, especially today.

I nod. "That's true, Atagi, but that wasn't what I was

going to say. Today, the lesson was to see how far you could go. You didn't give up. You stayed focused even when you grew tired. And you found a way to win. I'm proud of you."

There it is. That smile. She holds the pan up again, and I take it, the slightly sweet aroma wafting up my nose. Tearing it in two, I give her the bigger piece, and we eat in silence. I couldn't talk if I wanted to. I chew and swallow as slowly as I can, understanding why this treat is so popular even with its high price. At least, it was expensive fifty years ago. Maybe it's more affordable now.

It's so good. Fluffy. Slightly sweet with a sourness that balances the flavor.

Delightful.

I take another bite as Atagi licks her fingers, already done with her piece.

What would I have done without her these past few years?

You would have existed.

Barely.

28

The clash of our blades is like music carried on the breeze, dancing with fallen leaves, swirling through the branches, echoing into my caves. Atagi's moves are sharp, her strikes strong. There's no hesitation in her today. Even when dressed in her restrictive kimono, she's learned to maximize efficiency in each step.

Atagi's mare, Hori, watches us from the shade of the tree line as Atagi thrusts her sword at my chest. I lean away from the tip of her blade, impressed at her near-perfect form.

But I'm still better.

You'll always be better.

Be that as it may, I'm proud of my student and how hard she's worked over the years. I smile at Atagi as I thrust forward, twist, then slice upwards. My scabbard watches me from my hip where it's tucked securely in my sash. Today, the blade in my hand is one from my wall. Old. Blunted. But still sharp enough to draw blood if I hit hard enough. Which I won't.

Atagi deflects my advance and grins. The look on her

face is more feral than gleeful as she says, "Do you find this funny? Am I entertaining you?"

My chuckle turns her grin into a scowl, her teeth still barred, and I say, "Can't your sensei enjoy himself?"

She shifts, slicing her blade through the air, but I counter as she huffs. "You're supposed to be fighting for your life, not laughing like you're about to eat at your favorite noodle shop."

My grin grows as I force her into a retreat. This is nowhere near a life-or-death fight, but I like that she thinks it is.

Clink. Clink. Thud. Clink.

Faster and faster, she tries to gain the upper hand. I know it's coming, because I know my student. I know how good she is, but I also know that she can't control her form while trying to move this quickly.

And there it is. A slight dip of her left shoulder. I see it in her eyes, the tightening at the edges. She knows she messed up. My blade is at her neck, and we stare at each other, our breaths panting loudly in the now silent forest. A long, tense moment stretches until it fills the entirety of my prison.

Her lips press together, her cheeks puffing out just a bit.

The corner of my mouth quirks.

We burst out laughing and lower our blades. Swiping her sword to her side, she slowly lifts it before her, the blade angled back so she can slide it home into its saya. With a soft *snick*, she secures her katana.

Atagi wipes the sweat from her forehead before reaching back, untying her hair. It falls straight down her back as she says, "I almost had you on that spin."

I chuckle. "If you think so."

She rolls her eyes, gathering her hair back up, neatly retying it. Side-by-side, we walk to the cold firepit where our water skins sit on one of the large rocks. She bends over, scooping both skins up, tossing me mine before tilting back her head to drink hers down with loud gulps.

Very unlady-like, and I'm glad to see it.

Over the years, she's slowly lost the wildness of her youth. Her mother and her tutors have polished most of her harsh edges. But here, after our practice, she's just Atagi. Still just a little girl having fun playing swords.

As I sip at my water, I start to think of different lessons for her next few visits. What should I teach her next?

How to kill.

That thought has me spitting out my water, coughing and doubling over.

"Sensei, are you okay?"

I nod, holding up a hand as I try to suck air into my lungs. Keeping my head bowed, my other hand on my knee, I wonder where that thought came from. I don't want to see blood on Atagi's hands. I don't want her to have to take a life unless it's absolutely necessary. And hopefully, with her family's wealth and good standing, she won't have need of such violence.

And when she marries?

If her husband is honorable, it will be his duty to protect and defend her.

And if he's not.

That thought nearly has my red bleeding into my eyes. I almost hope I never find out—because If I knew Atagi was bound to such a man, and that I wouldn't be able to help her

...

Atagi stretches, lacing her fingers behind her back, completely unaware of my dark thoughts. Her spine cracks as she tilts her head back. Standing upright, she swings her arms across her chest and smiles at me.

"Race you to the tree."

It's been several years now since I tied that red cord around the branch of that tree not quite three kilometers from this spot. Since then, we've raced there often.

I flash my teeth in a grin. "Swords or no swords?"

"Swords."

Her fingers grasp the tie of her kimono, loosening the belt. With a dramatic sweep of fabric, Atagi discards her dress, leaving her in a light under shirt and cropped pants. These last few lessons, she has worn her kimono over her simpler clothes to practice in the more restrictive dress. She wants to be great—in any circumstance, in any attire. And I admire that in my student.

I nod at her. "You seemed to move better today in the dress. How did it feel?"

She frowns at the expensive garment laying on the ground in a splash of red and yellow. "Better, but it's still hard to get enough power behind my forward thrusts."

"It'll come with more practice."

She nods, still glaring at the kimono. To break her out of her glower, I say, "Ready?"

Gripping our saya's in the middle, we stagger our feet, and she says, "Ready."

"Go!"

A trill of laughter bursts from Atagi as she darts into the woods. She's fast. So much faster than those early days. But she always pushes too much too soon. She gets excited and starts out with a wild burst of energy, leaving little for the finish. It's the same with her sword fighting, and I know it's a compulsion I'll probably never break her from.

You wouldn't want to. You like Atagi's enthusiasm.

I do, and I smile as she already begins slowing down. Just

to rile her up, I ruffle her hair as I pass. She swats at my hand but misses. I laugh over my shoulder, and she emits the cutest little growl, leaning into her sprint, trying to catch me. But it's too late. I tap the tree and turn with a grin. She huffs as slaps the tree before planting her hands on her knees, the cord on Moon's hilt clinking softly as she sucks in air.

"Atagi, you shouldn't be *that* tired."

Between gasps, she says, "I haaate r-running."

I pat her head again, and she smacks me away. I know it irritates her when I do that, but I think it's funny how exasperated it makes her.

"You *have* gotten better, Atagi. You remember the first time you tried to run to this tree?"

I point to the carved markings near the base of the trunk. Time has faded the numbers, but I can still make out the scratches.

67:54

Atagi laughs. "I can't believe it took me sixty-seven minutes to get here that first time."

"I can walk it faster than that. I thought you'd gotten lost."

Our laughter fills the forest, and once it dies down, I run my hand over the markings above those numbers, and the ones above those. On and on, this tree holds the ledger of Atagi's progress. The top numbers are fresh and rough under my fingers, carved there only last month.

45:20

She purses her lips. "Any faster today?"

She knows I always count in my head when we race. With a smile, I nod. "A little bit, Atagi. Well done."

I kick at the pine needles until I find a sharp enough rock. Little scraping sounds accompany the flaking bark falling to the forest floor as I carve her new time into the tree.

45:17

When I look at Atagi, it's to find her scowling at the new numbers. "Still not as fast as you."

I cross my arms, puffing out my chest. "Well, I *am* your sensei." My palm slaps against my thighs. "And look at how much longer my legs are than yours." I reach for the top of her head, aiming to tousle her hair again, but she ducks and backs up as I tease. "How does my little student expect to outrun her much taller sensei?"

I'm still chuckling, but when I look at her, my laughter cuts off. She's chewing her lip, her eyes averted, her cheeks stained red.

What did I say?

Atagi's fingers clench around her scabbard. "I'm always going to be smaller, weaker, slower. Even when I'm grown. It's not fair."

Kneeling, I put myself in Atagi's line of view. "Yes, you will always have a physical disadvantage. But compared to other girls, you're probably the strongest in your town, right?"

Her face softens slightly as she nods.

"The strongest in the country?"

Her lips quiver as she tries not to laugh.

"But you know what advantage you have over the boys?" Now her attention lands fully on me. Reaching up, I tap her temple. "This. You're smart. You watch. You learn. You're quick to understand. That, more than anything"—I hold up a finger to silence her when she opens her mouth—"yes, even more than wielding a sword, will be your greatest advantage."

I let my words soak in for a moment. I'm not sure if she

believes me. Atagi thinks the might of the sword is the answer to everything. It's what makes her such a good student.

I flick her scabbard, the lacquer thudding softly against my nail as I say, "Race you back?"

Her eyes dart to the numbers carved into the tree, then she looks at me with a smile and nods. "Go!" She screams the word, once again darting off at a dead sprint.

She'll never learn.

I chuckle as I take off after her.

Probably not, and that's okay.

29

Atagi flops to the ground, spreading her arms and legs wide as she dramatically groans. "Sensei, it's too hot to practice. Can we just play shogi today?"

Hori whinnies over by the trees where she's tethered, swishing her tail as if agreeing with her master. Atagi never doesn't want to practice, so I'm a little startled, but internally I agree. It is stiflingly hot today.

Still, I tsk. "Atagi, you're going to get your clothes dirty."

Upon her arrival today, she'd quickly ditched her summer kimono, leaving her in her linen shirt and the cropped pants she prefers during the hotter months.

"I don't care. I'll wear my kimono home. Mama won't see. And I do all the washing now anyway. I don't know why. We have servants. But *mama* says I need to get in the habit of doing the washing in case my husband doesn't have servants." She chuckles softly. "Papa actually argued with her about it. He said making me do the wash would ruin my nails and make my skin rough. Of course he's never noticed my calluses, cause papa hardly ever pays attention. But he told mama ..."

I let her ramble, surprised how easily she's talking about her prospective husband. I don't know how long she has before her father starts seriously considering marriage contracts, but usually she avoids this topic at all costs, and when she does bring it up, it's typically with anger or despair hanging on her words like poison.

I tune back in.

" ... why would we let our daughter marry into a household without at least one servant?" Atagi frowns, tapping a finger to the dirt. "They argued for a while, but mama won. Of course. And now I have to do not only my wash, but papa's too. Mama says I have to be used to handling a man's garments. *Pfft.* I bet Isayo doesn't have to wash her uncle's clothes."

Bending over, I place my scabbard on the ground, giving it a little pat before swiping up the katana next to it. Sliding the new scabbard though my sash, I frown as a few flakes of lacquer peel off, sticking to my clothes. The katanas in my collection are starting to show their age. At least my saya remains pristine, unchanged by time.

Like me.

Grasping the hilt, I let the unfamiliar ray skin wrapping mold to my hand, which doesn't take long in this sweltering heat. Atagi still lays on the ground, no longer talking, eyes closed as she tries to find some measure of coolness from the ground. I know nagging her will get me nowhere, so I decide to try and tempt her into practice.

My body goes still as I press my thumb against the collar of the katana. It's quiet. There's Atagi's breathing ... and that's it. No birds hopping through the branches. No critters scurrying. Not even the hint of a breeze. It's almost as if the heat of the day has sucked all movement and sound from the air. Sweat trickles down my back, and the tickling sensation almost distracts me from my purpose.

Almost.

With a slow exhale, I press against the guard until I hear it.

Snick.

I flex across my shoulder and down into my core as I slide the blade free, the steel winking at me as if to say, *Thanks, I'm excited to play.*

Me too. Even though it feels like I'm standing on the surface of the sun.

Fuck. It's hot.

I start simple. With a strong strike of my blade from overhead to right in front of me, I execute the perfect kiri-oroshi. And then ... and then I dance. I let my blade tell me where it wants to go, how it wants to move. I'm free. I'm alive. The metal sings as I slice through air, not bothering to picture an opponent. I just dance.

I glance at Atagi, and while she hasn't moved from her sprawled position, she has one eye cracked open, watching me. But it seems I haven't convinced my student to join me yet, so I move faster, grunts pushing from my chest as I exhale with each strike. Every deep inhale fills my lungs with the hot, sticky air of the summer afternoon.

A flash of the bright red stain on my father's shirt punches through my mind, and I nearly stumble. It's been a while since these painful memories have come to haunt me, but when they do, they're always sharp with a clarity I'll never forget.

I try to shake off the image. On and on, I lunge, spin, slice, step back, stab, overhead swing, cross body slash ... Raised voices. Angry eyes. Blood. So much blood ... I'll *never* forgive ... them or myself.

As if I've gone back to that night, I see the villagers. I hear them coming down the dirt road to our house. I see the flickering of their torches. And I hear the concern in my father's voice as he whispers to Saito, his apprentice.

I grunt, thrusting with a lightning-quick lunge. I see my father's broad back jerk as the villager stabs him. A growl vibrates in my chest as I spin and swipe through the air, my blade whistling with my speed. I blink, seeing that moment again. And again. Over and over, I see my father's muscles tense and hold for a long moment before he falls. The storm cloud of my thoughts thunders with my rage, pouring out through my sword. In my mind's eye, I see my father's eyes dim as he dies.

Faster. Sharper. Stronger. I move across my practice area, but I don't see the forest. I don't see my cave. I don't see my prison. I don't even see Atagi. All I see are the villagers, weapons in hand, rage in their eyes. Even the children were there, clinging to their parent's pant legs, their eyes wide with fear.

I see my father's blood, and the light dying from his kind eyes. A bellow tears from my throat as I spin and slash, lunge and thrust.

"Sensei."

They all fall before me. Blood. So much blood. They will all pay for what they've done.

"Sensei!"

Resistance reverberates up my arms. I blink, calming the red from my eyes once I realize they're glowing. When I finally focus, my entire body freezes. Atagi stands before me, her legs spread and braced, her knees bent, her arms up. Her blade shakes under the pressure of mine.

She stopped me. Atagi doesn't understand what an

amazing feat she just accomplished, but I can't even be proud of her—because I am horrified.

Atagi looks *afraid*. Of me.

Her eyes are so wide, they look ready to pop from her head. Her mouth is slightly open, and when I feel her trembling through our connected blades, I immediately drop my katana. The sword clatters to the dirt, and I reach out for Atagi. She backs up, tripping in her haste to get away from me. I grip my chest to keep my heart from shattering. But it's too late. I've scared her. Well and truly terrified her. Because I lost my focus. Rubbing a hand down my face, my palm comes away slick with sweat. How long was I lost in my memories?

"Atagi-chan, I—"

"I have to go."

No. No. No. No.

"Atagi—"

Spinning around, she tosses Moon away from her as if it burned her skin. I've never seen her treat her sword so carelessly.

Oh, gods.

She scoops up her discarded kimono and runs. Her long black hair swishes behind her as she heads for Hori.

I go after her, shouting, "Atagi!"

With the strength that I taught her, she grabs Hori's mane and swings onto her mare's back. She doesn't even spare me a glance as she whips Hori's head around and kicks her into a fast trot. Atagi hunches over Hori's neck and urges her to go faster. She's running as if a monster is chasing her.

And I guess, I am.

I stop and watch Atagi get farther away. And as if this cursed forest is protecting her ... protecting her from me ...

the trees seem to close in, and the shadows grow unnaturally dark even though it's midday.

I gasp, falling to my knees. I can't breathe. I can't swallow. I blink, trying to focus through my tears. But I can't see her.

She's gone.

What have I done?

30

*I*t's been two months. She's not coming back.

"Be quiet. She just needs time. She'll be back."

Why do you bother lying to me? You're just lying to yourself. You know Atagi isn't—

"No!"

I can't let myself believe that she's gone, that I'm alone once more.

Forever.

It was going to happen eventually.

Pain shoots across my knuckles and up my arm, reflecting the pain of my heart cracking and bleeding with my sorrow. I punch the barrier again, and my scabbard scoffs at me from its place at my hip.

You're just filling your day with one delusion after another. She's not coming back and no amount of punching is going to get us out of here.

My fist slams into the invisible wall again, and hot blood drips between my fingers. There's not even a satisfying smear of dark red on the barrier. Left. Right. Left. Left. I scream as I punch the wall until agony races up my arm like someone pressed a hot poker to my skin. The sound of three of my fingers breaking scares off an animal outside my prison. I fall back, landing on my ass as I watch the small marten run off.

My scabbard sighs. *That would have made a delicious meal.*

I wince as I rest my broken hand in my lap, and I grimace as my bones start to realign and knit back together. Sometimes, the healing hurts worse than the breaking.

I stare into the forest beyond my reach.

"I just want to tell her I'm sorry."

As the sun sets, a chill fills the entrance to my cave. The dying light of the day paints the stone walls a dark aubergine. Autumn will come early this year. Seems appropriate. A long, cold, bitter winter to match my mood. As I scratch the characters for Atagi's name under the score mark for today, I try to ignore the hollow pit in my stomach.

Tossing the rock onto the ground, I stare at Atagi's name. Her terrified eyes flash through my mind, and I nearly fold over from the pain of the memory. I can't believe I did that. I can't believe I was that careless. With trembling fingers, I reach into my pocket and wrap them around the small carving, running my thumb over the smooth grooves and curves.

Slowly, I pull out the tiny wood katana. It's shorter than my pinky, and it took me days to carefully carve the details that make it recognizable as Atagi's sword, Moon. I loop the piece of string that runs through the hilt over my finger and let the necklace dangle before me. It's not shiny or even that pretty, but I think Atagi would have liked it.

"Happy Birthday, Atagi-chan."

I t hasn't snowed like this in thirteen years. Giant drifts encroach on the entrance to my cave, nearly enclosing me in here like a tomb. Jagged icicles hang down from the ceiling like daggers threatening to crush my skull if I dare attempt to leave my freezing home.

Despite the snow piling up and threatening to trap me, the wind still manages to howl through my home. It's deafening, moaning and screaming. The despair in the wind mimics the emotions in my soul, and the sound oddly makes me feel less alone—like there's another tortured prisoner hidden somewhere in these caverns lamenting their lot in life.

You-u-u're n-n-not alone. You hav-v-ve me. You always w-w-w-will.

My scabbard chatters with the quickly dropping temperatures, and I hug it closer to my body, tucking every last piece of fabric I have around us as I whisper, "I kn-n-now. I know, my friend."

I groan as the small fire in my bedchamber hearth shrinks to a meager single dancing light.

The v-v-vent must be blocked ... ag-gain.

A shiver shakes my spine as I think about having to go back outside to dig the deep snow away from the hole that vents from this cave. I really don't want to.

If you don't, y-you'll freeze to d-d-death in here.

I know. Freezing to death is no fun. Well, the dying part isn't too bad. Just like falling asleep. It's when I come back that it's agonizingly painful. Like all my flesh has been ripped from my bones.

The tiny flame shimmies, then poofs out, sending a thin curl of smoke into the air where it pools against the ceiling.

Now comes the hard choice. Stay here, shivering in your blankets and every piece of clothing you own? Or go fix the vent?

My mind rebels at the idea of sticking even one finger outside the meager warmth I've built inside this bundle of fabric. But ...

I grit my teeth, and as I shrug off the blankets, another violent shiver shakes me from head to toe.

"F-f-fuck. My fingersss are already g-going numb. It's too c-cold."

Then you'll have t-t-t-to work fast.

I try to stand but end up on my ass. Looking down, I poke my thigh, then punch it. Shit. My legs are numb. I didn't notice, even wrapped in my blankets and with two pairs of pants on. Rubbing my thighs, I wince, noticing the tips of my fingers are blue. This is bad. I need a fire. My teeth rattle in my skull. I tremble until my bones ache. I shiver until my back hurts so bad I'm forced to lie down. I fumble as I draw the blankets back around me.

I'm so alone.

I can practically hear my heart breaking a little more, like the sound of putting too much pressure on a thin layer of ice. I just need to rest. I need a break ... from everything.

Don't. Please don't. What if you don't come back this time?

I curl into a tight ball, my teeth clattering. "I'm not that lucky." I pause, my thoughts drifting until I slowly come back. "I'll come back. I always do ... I always fucking do ..."

But ...

The shivering stops.

The warm scent of lingering smoke fills my nose as I

close my eyes, only to have Atagi's fear-filled eyes flash through my mind.

"I'm sorry I scared you, Atagi-chan."

I hope she is safe and warm.

I hope ...

I arch my back, interlacing my fingers behind me, stretching. With a deep breath, I force a smile to my face. I'm still alone, and it still hurts. It always will. But winter is almost over. It's been a month since I froze to death when the snow blocked the vent. A month since I came back to life, every nerve ending on fire, ripping a scream from my raw throat. I shiver at the memory but brush it off. If I'm going to continue on, knowing I don't have a choice in the matter, I will muster the will to smile.

With another deep breath, my smile becomes a little more real. There is just something about spring ... Puddles sparkle in my training area from the hard rain last night. The scent of petrichor still hangs in the air as the morning sun rises and peeks through the dark trunks of the trees.

So, what form shall we do today?

I draw my saya, my smile expanding. I stagger my feet and hold my scabbard before me. It's as beautiful as ever, and the shark skin hilt fits my hand to perfection. I draw my front leg up, ready to step forward and slash, but I stumble and freeze.

Did I just ...?

There it is again. My magic tickles down my right side.

My heart rate jumps, but I wait to see if I feel it again. I need to be sure, and that it's not just my mind playing awful tricks on me again.

My magic flickers gently over my skin, and I know ... this isn't an intruder coming for Guardian.

My heart rate kicks into a gallop. After so many months of trying not to hope, Atagi is back.

31

That's a new kimono. It's pretty.

What a stupid thought to have upon seeing Atagi for the first time in almost an entire year.

She steps into the clearing, darting a glance behind her, and it's then I realize Hori is not with her. As Atagi gets closer, I notice her nostrils flaring. She's trying to hide the fact that she's out of breath. Why?

"Atagi, it's so good to see you." She nods, glancing over her shoulder then dropping her head, her long curtain of black hair hiding her face. I clear my throat, but she doesn't look up at me, so I ask, "Where's Hori?"

She finally lifts her head. "Oh, she's uh, she's lame. Needs time to heal." Her breathing has slowed, but her cheeks are red, and the hair near her temples is damp.

"Atagi, did you ... did you walk here?"

She shrugs, but doesn't answer, looking over her shoulder once more. What is she looking for? Did someone follow her, or ...

Oh no. Has she brought someone with her? Did she tell someone about me?

Internally, I shake my head at my scabbard. 'Don't start. Atagi has never wanted Guardian. She would never betray us.'

Who knows. A lot can happen in a year.

'Not Atagi.'

I take a step towards her, but she backs up, chewing her bottom lip. The small step may as well have been a stab to my chest with how much it hurts, but I stop and hold up a hand, saying, "About the last time you were here—"

She waves me off, her words quick with impatience. "It's fine, Sensei. It was nothing."

My shoulders slump, heavy with guilt. I still see her fear-filled eyes in my nightmares.

"No. It wasn't nothing. I'm so very sorry for sca—"

Atagi takes a sudden step towards me, lifting her head, raising her chin, eyes as serious as I've ever seen them. She reaches across her waist, grabbing the silk tie. The soft swish of her sash loosening seems overly loud. The collar of her kimono slides down one thin shoulder, and I grit my teeth.

Skin. She's not wearing her usual undershirt.

With a shrug of her other shoulder, her dress starts to slide down towards her elbows. With a desperate determination, she keeps her eyes on me as she takes a step forward.

"Sensei, I need you."

Wait. What? I blink at her, not sure what she means. "Atagi? Do you want to practice?" I point behind me towards my cave. "I have your katana. Moon has been waiting for y—"

She takes another step forward, shimmying the top of her kimono lower as she says, "No, Sensei, I *need* you."

Before the folds of the fabric drape low enough to expose her small breasts, I rush forward, grabbing the edges and crossing them back over her body. Her arms limply fall to her sides, and I frown down at her as I tighten her sash.

"Atagi, what's going on?"

She sniffles. "Am I not pretty enough?"

I pat her shoulder, then drop my hand and step back. "Of course you're pretty, Atagi, but—"

"No! If you think I'm pretty, there's no problem. I want to lay with you. I'm sure you've thought about it."

"Excuse me? Atagi, I have NEVER! You're a child for fuck's sake!"

She shakes her head. "I'm not a child!" Atagi stomps her foot, her temper flaring like a, well, like a child. She raises her chin. "I'm a woman. You're a man."

Atagi moves so fast, and I'm so confounded by this entire conversation, I'm unable to stop her in time. Her sash falls to the ground, and she whips her kimono off. Thankfully, all I catch is a flash of flesh before I squeeze my eyes closed. Shrugging off my haori outer robe, I drop my head, opening my eyes but keeping my gaze on the ground as I step towards the small girl before me. With a soft fluttering of fabric, I settle my robe around her shoulders. Her small hand grips the edges, holding them closed against her chest.

It's then I notice the slight tremble of her shoulders, and when I look up, tears silently track down her cheeks. I lift my arm, wanting to pat her head or rub her back ... to give her some form of comfort, but I let my arm drop back to my side as I whisper, "Atagi. Talk to me. What's going on?"

She hiccups and wipes her nose with the sleeve of my robe. Gone is the confidence she tried to wear earlier. In its place is a little girl who seems so small and lost. "I-I shouldn't have ... I mean, I know you don't want ... I'm just ..."

She takes a big breath, the inhale stuttering with

emotion. Lowering her gaze, she shifts as she whispers, "If I'm not pure anymore, then maybe he won't ... I won't have to ..."

Oh. Oh, fuck. No. The fact that she's this desperate ... my blood runs cold.

I reach out again, this time resting my hand on the top of her head, hoping she takes it as the gesture of comfort I mean it as. "Atagi. I hope by now, you know I will help you however I can, whenever you need me. But this, I cannot do. I will not."

She sniffles again. "I know."

I let my hand fall away, and she backs up, wiping at her nose and eyes again as she says, "I'm sorry. This was ... gods, I'm so stupid."

My short robe billows around her thighs as she spins and sprints away, dashing into the thick tree line. I'm still so in shock from her actions, that all I do is stare at her embroidered kimono laying discarded on the ground. Long moments go by as I try to process what just happened. I blink at her kimono, the bright colors blurring with my churning thoughts. Has her father accepted an offer of marriage? Is this it? No. It can't be. Atagi is ...

Go after her!

Jumping from my frozen state, I grab Atagi's dress as I run into the woods, my magic pointing me in the direction she ran. Every branch seems determined to slow me down, scratching at my skin, grabbing at my clothes. It's as if I trip and stumble over every small dip or stone.

Where is she?

There!

The swish of her glossy hair and the light fabric of my haori peeks through the trees. I call out, "Atagi, wait!"

She slows, looking over her shoulder, tears still pooled

in her dark eyes. I stumble, coming to a quick halt. She huffs, catching her breath where she stands … several meters beyond the barrier.

I open my mouth to apologize again and ask her to come back, but I snap my lips shut.

Snapping, scratching, pinching. Red. My magic is angry. Someone else is here.

Fuck!

Holding out a hand, I say, "Atagi, get behind me."

She half turns, her gaze swiveling to the woods where the crunching of undergrowth precedes whoever is approaching. Bracing my feet, I reach across my body, gripping the familiar hilt of Guardian. It's a move I've done so many times, I wouldn't be surprised if I did it in my sleep. I draw my scabbard with my left hand and hold it at my side, tip of the shiny lacquered saya pointed down and slightly away from me. Ready.

Atagi's quiet, shaky voice fills the air. "No. No. He … he followed me?"

A booming male voice cuts through the shadows. "This damned forest! There was a path here just a moment ago!"

Atagi gasps, but she doesn't move. I stay focused on where my magic points towards the newcomer's voice with angry biting sparks across my skin, but I make sure my voice is calm as I say, "Atagi?" She's trembling, eyes fixed on the dark forest beyond. My voice has a desperate bark to it this time. "Atagi, get behind me!"

She doesn't answer, and a second later, a tall man leading a sleek black horse steps into view. He yanks on the lead as it gets snagged on a branch, and his horse throws its head. The man swears, pulling the horse forward. A pristine white cord holds back the man's black hair, revealing a face with rounded cheeks and a sharp nose. Silver colors the hair at his temples, and as he comes a little closer, he stumbles, pitching forward to expose a small bald spot on the back of his head.

When he rights himself, he grins, not at me, but at the girl frozen between us. "So, you thought you'd get out of our arrangement by running to another man? Come now, Meiko. Enough. I've come to take you home. This little act of rebellion won't stand, and it won't stop the wedding. The papers are signed."

Meiko? He speaks so informally to her? What the fuck? That man can't be a day younger than forty.

Atagi is no longer trembling, but she still hasn't moved. She's past the barrier. I don't know what to do. I know what I *want* to do. But what *can* I do?

Why are you even asking? Atagi needs your help. She can't marry this man. Get her back over here. Now!

"Atagi—"

The man whips his gaze to mine, a sneer on his face as he asks, "And you are?"

Keeping my stance relaxed, I lower my voice, letting the threat ring in my words. "Who I am doesn't matter. *Atagi* obviously doesn't want to go with you."

His sneer pulls back into a grotesque snarl. "My *wife* doesn't have a say. Her parents and I have signed the contract. She's my property." His gaze lands on Atagi. Holding out his hand, a gold ring with a large piece of jade winking on his middle finger, he frowns. "Come, wife. Don't make me ask again."

There's a long moment of tension-filled silence, and then Atagi finally moves, taking a step back.

Yes, come back. Keep coming.

She glances at me over her shoulder, and I hold out my hand, forgetting I'm still clutching her kimono. Facing the man once again, she takes another step back, stumbling but catching herself as she murmurs, "The contract doesn't matter anymore. I'm no longer ... untouched."

Everything in me freezes, and my arm falls to my side.

Desperate times, I guess.

The man glares at her, noticing my haori draped around her.

That doesn't look good for you.

Then his eyes fall to her expensive kimono in my grip.

And this looks even worse.

My fingers curl tighter around her dress as I raise my saya a mere centimeter, keeping his focus on me and off the trembling girl between us. Let him come and defend her honor then. I'll happily end him here and now.

And when people come looking for him? What if Atagi gets blamed?

Atagi jumps, halting her backwards movement as the man barks a laugh, waving a hand at her. "So desperate to get out of our contract? Why, my love? I'm a wealthy man. You will spend the rest of your days in comfort, raising my sons and taking care of my household." Keeping his eyes on her, he nods his chin towards me. "And besides, he's fully clothed, if you can even call those rags clothes. And he certainly doesn't have the look of a man who just found his pleasure in a virgin."

She balks, her shoulders bunching. She curls her hands into fists, taking another backwards step towards me ... but her strides are too small and not fast enough. She's scared, but not scared enough because I'm here. Because her sensei, the best swordsman she's ever known, will look after her. But she doesn't know I can't help her unless she comes back to me.

Shit. Shit. Shit.

My wrist twitches with the desire to cut this man down. The cord around the hilt clinks softly, drawing Atagi's attention back to me, and I nod, encouraging her to hurry back to me. Atagi stands tall taking another tiny shuffling step back as she says, "Well, it's true. My sensei had me."

A soft groan climbs my throat. Oh, Atagi, no. Stop. Please. Don't instigate him. Just come here. Please.

Hurry!

A shuffling sound snaps my attention to the man. In a flash of bared teeth, and reaching hands, the man closes the distance between him and Atagi. He grabs her by the robe, yanking on it as she struggles, and he yells, "Show me then. Show me your virtue's blood on your thighs. Show me you're his whore."

I leap forward, smacking into the barrier, but neither of them notice me stumbling backwards as Atagi whimpers. "No. Stop it. Sensei!"

My magic burns, almost as brightly as it did *that* night, the red light of my eyes reflecting off my nose and cheeks. I breathe, blinking away the glow of my magic—I don't want to scare Atagi again.

I raise my saya. This man doesn't know I can't touch him, but maybe if I can provoke him to move towards me ... I shout, "Hey! That's no way to treat a lady. Unhand her."

I take a step forward, hoping to draw him into my trap. But then there's a blade to Atagi's throat, and the man grips her hair, tugging her head back. He starts to back away, dragging her with him where I can't follow.

No. No. No. NO!

My voice rises with my fear and anger. "I challenge your claim and contract!" I have no idea if this will work, but I have to try something.

He snarls, "I don't think so. My *wife* and I will be leaving now."

Crack! My heart bleeds with my inability to help her. Still, I take a step forward, knowing there is only a single meter left before I hit the invisible wall again. I take another menacing step, then another before the man digs the edge of his blade into Atagi's skin, sending a trickle of blood down her neck. I stop, his threat sticking my feet to the ground. If I could see it, my breath would fog against the barrier as it tickles the tip of my nose.

I'm not sure if Atagi is being brave or if shock has set in, because she doesn't make a sound. She doesn't even wince at the bite of his steel.

The man continues to back up. "As I said, her father's signature is on the marriage papers, right above mine. Meiko-san is mine, and no concern of yours." With his next step, he tugs on her hair as he leans over her. "So, is this where you used to disappear to? Meeting this person out in the middle of nowhere to play with swords? Not a pursuit befitting a lady, and certainly not of my wife." He sneers at me as he whispers to Atagi, "But, if you've spent this much time with him and he hasn't had you, he must be one of *those* ..."

He continues to pull Atagi towards his horse as he says to me, "You like cock?" Atagi gasps, and the man laughs. "Why else would he have been able to resist having at least a little taste? Hmm?"

Atagi bucks against his hold, and blood drips down her neck as she shouts, "No! Stop it. Sensei wouldn't ... he's honorable. More honorable than y—"

He yanks on her hair, pulling her head back so her neck arches into his blade. "Don't even think about finishing that sentence. You obviously need some lessons on how to obey your husband."

I flinch, surging into action without thought, my forehead slamming into the barrier. But again, neither of them notices as Atagi goes still, her eyes closed in fear. The man hums, flicking his gaze to me before bending over her to say, "He must not be a very good teacher if this is your best effort at fighting me off … or maybe you just don't *actually* want to get away from me. Hmm? A little show of defiance to get my blood racing? You know I enjoy hunting. Are you pretending to be my prey, Meiko?"

This bastard.

Again, my body moves on its own. My saya silently hits the barrier, my muscles burning as I desperately attempt to push through.

Atagi grits her teeth, grabbing his forearm with both hands. She kicks out, but that only causes the man to press the blade harder against her skin. She goes still once more, but continues to drag her feet, doing what she can to resist as he drags her towards his horse.

There must be something I can do. Panic claws my chest, making it hard to breathe while my magic burns with the desire to cut this man to pieces, to carve his heart out, roast it over the fire, and enjoy it for dinner tonight.

Atagi's eyes land on me, silently pleading, shimmering with tears.

Resignation starts to weave its way into my thoughts, and to protect myself from the pain of failing her, I begin to rationalize … This was always going to happen. She's of age. She's been of age since she turned twelve.

Gross.

I know. But if what the man said is true, she is legally his. She only ran away because she was afraid. Aren't most brides afraid on their wedding night? Or at least, a little nervous? She's strong. She'll adapt. She'll have a family. She'll find a new purpose. She'll ...

Bullshit! She's fucking fourteen!

They are at his horse's side, and he fumbles with the blade at her throat, trying to maneuver the struggling Atagi into the saddle. I drop her kimono and scoop up a large rock.

"Hey!"

His head whips around as I reel back, throwing as hard as I can. The stone hurtles through the air before smashing into the man's face right between his eyes.

"Fuck!" He stumbles back with a cry, thudding into the horse's flank. The man grabs his nose, his blade clattering to the ground. Pride fills me as Atagi rushes to grab the fallen sword, but it seems the man has a very hard skull.

Figures.

He grabs back onto Atagi's hair, collecting his katana at the same time. The man, his eyes already starting to darken with bruises, glares at me as he presses the tip of the blade back to her neck. "Try anything like that again, she's dead. I can always buy another wife, but there's no need for you to create a problem for yourself. If you come after us, I will make your life very difficult. I have money and influence. You do not want to test me. I *will* kill her."

Make our life difficult? We're already in hell. He'd be dead right now if not for this fucking barrier! But his threat against Atagi ... he'll do it. It's in his eyes.

He wraps an arm around her waist, and Atagi grunts, trying to twist away without cutting herself any deeper. I scrape my scabbard against the invisible wall, begging in my head. *Please. Let me through. Please. Please. Please.*

Desperate and now heedless of the sword at her neck,

Atagi slaps and claws at the back of his hand as she shouts, "Let me go!" I punch at the barrier as Atagi lifts her knee, and with a vicious stomp, she aims for his foot, but misses. Atagi makes a fist and punches down and back, going for his dick. I'd applaud her efforts if I wasn't so sick to my stomach. He curls away from her, avoiding her strike. He lets go of her waist only to grip her shoulder, shaking her so hard her head snaps back. I hear her teeth clatter from here. Leaning down, he says something that drains the color from her face, then jerks his head towards the horse.

Atagi's shoulders slump.

What did he say to her?

She turns her back to me, grabbing the horse's mane, slowly lifting her leg to slide her foot in the stirrup which exposes a long stretch of bare skin up to her hip. I snap my gaze away, but the man's eyes are on her, his expression now laced with hunger. He keeps the blade pointed at her, close to her ribs, as she swings onto the saddle.

I punch the barrier again and again, my silent strikes doing nothing.

We need to cut that bastard down! We need to keep Atagi safe. We just need to find a way to buy her time. We can figure out the rest later.

Atagi's head stays bowed. The man chuckles at her, licking his lips. With surprising strength, he swings up behind Atagi, quick to set his katana at her throat again. He pulls his horse around to face me and glares over Atagi's head. "Remember, I will kill her if I even suspect you've followed us."

His gaze tracks down my dirty and worn pants. "Besides, you obviously have nothing to offer her. She's better off with me." With a smirk, he gathers some of her hair, bringing it to his face, sniffing the dark strands. Then, he whips the horse's head back around.

I slam my saya into the invisible wall, edge, side, tip, hilt. It doesn't work. Of course it doesn't.

Shame. Despair. Anger. Loathing. All aimed solely at me. I'm useless. I'm a failure. I'm … nothing. *Chink*. A piece of my heart breaks off and stabs my soul.

I lower my arm, the katana hanging in my loose, defeated grip.

Atagi leans to the side looking back at me as the horse picks up a careful trot through the forest. Her face is pale, her brows furrowed in confusion, then a moment later, a tear slips down her cheek when she sees me just standing here, not moving, not coming after her.

She doesn't understand why I'm not chasing after her, why I'm not fighting for her. Because I never told her.

I can't follow you, Atagi. I can't help. I'm sorry.

Emotion drains from her eyes. There's no more anger, no sadness, no hurt. It's like her face goes blank and cold. Softly, but loud enough for me to hear, she says, "Thank you for the *lesson*, Sensei."

The bite of sarcasm and betrayal in her words slices to my core, leaving a deep wound on my heart that will never, ever heal. I sink to my knees as she turns around and sits tall in the saddle, leaning back into her husband. He chuckles as he says, "That's a good girl."

Oh Atagi. I'm so sorry. This was inevitable. We both knew this was coming, but kept our eyes closed to it. I'm sorry.

Hairline fractures splinter across my heart, covering every inch until it feels like it's barely holding itself together.

We'll never see her again, will we?

No. We won't.

32

The sun is bright, but there's a cold bite to the wind. The exposed skin of my torso prickles with the chill of the approaching winter. Raising my scabbard overhead, I'm easily able to ignore the cold as I slash downward, lunging with a forceful exhale. I release my right hand, bringing the katana outward in an arch before grabbing back on with both hands and slicing it all the way down.

After my morning round of checking the barrier and then the traps, I started practicing, and I've been at it all afternoon. The repetition becomes a meditation. Like the old days. Back when I needed this deep meditative state to take my mind away from this place.

Before *her*.

Two years. It's been two years since I last saw her. Since I broke her trust and my own heart. I hope she's okay.

I'm sure she's fine. Atagi is smart. I'm sure she adjusted.

"But is she happy?"

We have to believe so, because the alternative is ...

I reset, starting from the beginning. Forcing a smile to

my face, I drive my saya down so swiftly, it whistles through the air. "At least I'll always have you."

Indeed.

My stomach rumbles, but I ignore it. At least, I try to. My saya won't let me.

Let's eat the mushrooms with the last of the smoked bird meat.

I chuckle with my side swing. "Eat both? Ha. No. Pick one. We're not lords, able to eat our fill with every meal."

Fiiiiine. Mushrooms. They're going to go bad soon anyway.

"Okay. Just a few more times through. Then we'll eat."

You're going to go all day, aren't you?

"It's the best distraction."

I know. So, let's go, old man.

My laugh comes out unbidden but ... genuine.

It's good that you're still able to amuse yourself, otherwise this whole situation would be unbearable.

Shifting my stance, I move through the form, twirling my saya in a complete circle at my side before raising the katana all the way over my head, blocking an 'attack' coming from behind. I move faster, imagining another opponent joining the fight, then another, seeing the dark forms of my enemies in my mind as I fight them off. The long shadows of the forest creep across the training area, but I keep going. I can't stop. Stopping means thinking. Stopping means remembering.

Remembering how I failed her.

It would have happened regardless.

Night falls, and the temperature drops, cooling the sweat from my skin. It feels good. Harsh and biting. Crickets chirp, and I know soon it will be too cold for the insects to come out and sing their song, so, I enjoy it while I can. Spinning and slashing, I dance to their coarse melody.

Hopefully, I'll be too tired to dream tonight.

F uck. I can't sleep. But I guess it is better than the nightmares.

I'd still rather sleep. I'm exhausted.

I roll over, glaring at my scabbard. My brain seems determined to torture me tonight. Every time I closed my eyes, my mind plagued me with visions of all my worst moments in this prison. And there are a lot, not least among them the look on Atagi's face when she thought I'd given up on her as her husband took her away. And every time I open my eyes ...

My gaze wanders to the narrow table next to the hearth. The back of my throat burns as I stare at Atagi's kimono, the one she left behind that day. The small wooden katana necklace rests on top of her folded dress. I never got the chance to give her the small gift. And now I never will. I should burn them both and save myself from this continued agony. But I don't. I don't think I ever will, because I'd rather have these painful memories of her than forget.

My scabbard interrupts my morose thoughts. *Are you going lay here and toss and turn till morning, or are you going to get u—*

"I'm going to lay here. No use in getting up. Like I need *more* time in my endless days?" I curl my fingers into a fist, punching the edge of my hand to the ground. "I just ... I just want to sleep. No, I want to pass out, to be unconscious. I ... I need a break."

Not this again.

"No. I don't want to die. That doesn't last long enough."

You could always eat those orange mushrooms in the back of the cave. Remember how you hallucinated for three days when you decided to test to see if they were edible?

I chuckle, scratching my chin. "That's not a bad thought. At the very least, my mind won't be here for a while."

I roll onto my side, standing slowly before heading to the small cavern at the rear of my cave system. Though, it can barely be called a cavern. It's more like a tiny tunnel with a pocket of space in the back. I crawl on my belly, my shoulders scraping the rock as I reach for the bright orange mushrooms.

As soon as I'm free of the tight space, I pop a tiny fungus in my mouth and chew. It's earthy and slightly sweet. I swallow and click my tongue on the roof of my mouth. It's fuzzy. Good. It's already working.

Back in my bedchamber, I lay down, chewing on a second little mushroom. The fire in my hearth crackles. It sounds like laughter. The stone ceiling turns into the fur of a great beast, its belly enclosing me in my bedchamber. I watch as it expands with its breath.

I ask the monster, "Aren't you hot with the heat of the fire rising to your stomach up there?"

The beast doesn't answer, so I pop the remaining three mushrooms in my mouth, chewing with a smile before swallowing. My eyes widen as the belly of the beast splits open. But it's not guts and blood that rain down on me. Instead, little white flowers dance and spin on their descent, landing all around me. None land on me though, as if I'm untouchable. As if there's an invisible barrier around me, keeping the beautiful flowers from touching me. The cave heaves, and while somewhere in my mind I know this isn't real, I clutch at the ground as my cave bucks like it's trying to expel me from its stomach.

"Fine. Okay. I'll leave!"

Somehow, I find my feet, though they're not my feet, they're blocks of wood. I stomp down the long passageway, the katanas on the wall melting as I pass. The swords dissolve into a silver puddle on the ground—all except Moon. Atagi's sword remains whole, but the hilt splits, sticking its tongue out at me. I laugh and continue, my wooden feet carrying me outside into the night.

Overhead, the stars pulsate, a few falling out of the sky, leaving a rainbow trail in their wake. The dirt under my bare feet, once again flesh and bone, turns to lush grass. The blades tickle my skin, growing taller to circle my ankles as if to hold me in place. I sit, letting the grass grow up and over me, leaving only my nose and eyes exposed. I blink at the forest as the trees reach out and hold hands before dancing in a circle.

How nice.

I smile, thinking about joining them, but the grass hugs me, so I stay where I am. I watch the trees skip and play as vines creep from the forest to wrap me even tighter in the embrace of this wild place. I know this is all in my head, but I also know this forest loves me. It loves me so much; it will never let me go. The trees dance, their twirling getting faster as they laugh. "Never. We'll never let you go. We love you. You'll stay with us. Forever. Forever. Forever."

I grin, falling onto my back, my arms spread. "Yes. Forever. I know."

I blink as the trees continue to giggle and sing all around me. The sky pulses with light, like a heartbeat, and I let myself sink deeper into my drugged haze.

Where am I? How many days have passed? Who am I?

Doesn't matter.

33

I grin, sheer glee racing through me, the dead rabbit in my hand all but forgotten. The sharp and angry needle prick of my magic scrapes down the left side of my back.

My voice is so deep it's almost a growl. "Yes! Finally!"

I drop the dead rabbit in my excitement, but quickly scoop it back up. Can't leave it here in the middle of the woods or else another animal might come and snatch my dinner away. Quickly, I tie it to my sash before arching back, flexing my arms with a primal scream that sends a few birds into flight.

You'll scare our guest away before we even get to have our fun.

"You're right." I grip the center of my scabbard and break into a run, the dead animal flopping against my thigh as I say, "Let's go and welcome our *guest*."

Twigs snap and leaves crunch as I storm through the woods, my magic directing me towards the newcomer. Excitement tingles through me as I get closer.

Not so tight, you're going to crack me.

"I don't think that's possible." But I lighten my grip slightly.

Ahead, the person comes into view. I dig my heels into the earth, leaning back as I skid to a stop. The blood drains from my head, making me dizzy, and I nearly drop my saya. Is that …? No, my magic feels too violent for it to be …

It has been eight years. She might be …

I can't keep my voice from shaking, as I start to ask, "Ata—"

The person turns, their long black hair swaying with the movement. Dark eyes meet mine, then drop to the scabbard in my hand. The hole in my chest widens, the edges cracking.

It's not her.

The man before me stands a full head shorter than me, and when he steps forward, it's with grace and beauty.

He's quite pretty.

He … is.

His gaze sweeps my body, landing on my face, and he smirks. "Well, I'm certainly *very* sorry I'm not who you thought I was." The man's eyes drop back to my scabbard, and when he opens his mouth, I hold up a hand, stopping the next question I'm sure is about to come from those luscious lips.

Luscious lips? My scabbard smirks at me.

I don't care. I can't seem to stop staring at the beautiful man before me. Clearing my throat, I say, "Yes, this is Guardian. No, you can't have it."

The man quirks a brow, and his smile makes my heart beat a little faster.

Been a while?

Other than with my hand? You know it has. Not since Matsumae.

I keep my reply to my scabbard in my head, because the man standing before me doesn't need to know just how crazy I am.

He crosses his arms, and I can't help but notice the muscle definition in his chest through his loose juban kimono. He says, "Well, that's … disappointing. Are you sure there's nothing I can give you in exchange for Guardian?"

My mind goes to places it shouldn't … sweaty bodies … grunts and moans.

You're not going to give me up in exchange for sex.

I'm not, but my dick doesn't completely agree with my conviction. I lean my weight to my left leg, kicking out my hip. "Who sent you?"

"No one."

"So, you're here for yourself."

He shakes his head, his kind smile still in place. "No. I'm here for my family. My village."

I straighten, my mood souring because it really doesn't matter why he's come here … because he's come for the sword, not for me. Never for me.

I ask, "What's your name?"

He cocks his head, and his long hair falls over his shoulder. I want to run my fingers through it. The man speaks, forcing me to pay attention. "Tomouji Ishida." His eyes travel down my body to my bare feet and back up again, not even pausing on my scabbard. He does halt his gaze right below my waist where I've started to grow hard. A small smirk lifts his lips before his eyes meet mine again. "But you can call me Ida."

My cock twitches. He not only discarded formality, giving me permission to use his given name, but a nickname at that.

Seems Ida might like you too.

I grin, standing taller. "Well, Ida, other than killing me, there's no way for you to leave here with Guardian." I spread my arms with confidence. "And I'm very hard to kill."

My scabbard barks a laugh in my head. *If only he knew how true that is.*

Ida's smile falls slightly, but then he sweeps his arm out, indicating the forest around us before placing his palm on the hilt of his katana. "The playing ground is a bit ... confining, but I'm curious enough to give it a go."

I drop my arms, tilting my head. "You think you can best me?"

He shrugs, pressing his thumb to the guard of his blade. "Maybe? Whether you are the original keeper of the blade, or a descendant, I suspect magic is in play." He nods at my saya. "Magic even beyond the power of that sword."

"So, if you believe that, why even try?"

He laughs, the sound so bright and cheerful, it nearly makes me laugh with him as he says, "Why test my skill against a legendary magical samurai?"

The humor drains out of me, pulling a frown to my face. "I'm no samurai."

His smile falls as well, but his brow raises again in what appears to be interest. "Do you only lie to strangers? Or do you lie to yourself as well?"

My eyes widen in shock, and my scabbard chuckles. *I like him.*

I move so quickly, my arm is a blur, as I raise Guardian and hold it before me. Ida does the same, just not nearly as fast. His dark eyes are more intense now, but I don't give him the time to think through a strategy. With a flex of my thighs, I burst forward. He manages to block, and my saya thuds against the outer edge of his blade.

He glances at where his naked sword presses against my

shiny scabbard, then his gaze focuses on my face. We're so close, I can smell him ... horse, grass, and ... is that jasmine tea on his breath?

Ida asks, "Come on. You're not even going to unsheathe your blade?"

I smirk, shaking my head. "No."

Ida's eyes sparkle in apparent delight. "Oh! I love it!"

He pushes against my scabbard, disengaging, but comes right back.

Here comes the eight-point wheel. Gutsy move so early in the fight.

He doesn't get past the first point as I meet him, redirecting his moves, but he keeps up. Our katanas clash and ring through the forest as we move and dance around the trees.

You're dragging this out. You could have had him at least three times by now. When I don't bother answering my scabbard, it tsks. *You're having fun.*

So, what if I am?

As if hearing my insane thoughts, Ida asks, "Are you enjoying this?"

I grin, side-stepping his next slash. "I am. Aren't you?"

He throws back his head, laughing to the sky. "I am. I've never faced an opponent like you."

I grin, slicing the edge of my saya across his ribs in what would have been a fatal attack. "And you never will again."

Ida pauses, breathing hard, and I realize we've danced our way to my clearing. He lowers his blade, keeping eye contact with me. "You had me just now. And a few other times."

Pretty, smart, talented with a blade, and honest.

I try to hide my smile as I nod. "I did." Twisting my wrist

to angle my saya to reflect the sun, I add, "We could do this for hours, for days. No matter how many times we cross swords, I'll always win."

"Hmm." Ida smirks, his gaze darting down my body before he looks around. "This your home?"

I glance at the blackened fire pit and my kitchen, noticing some parts of the roof that need repair. I shrug. "It's where I live."

With well-practiced grace, Ida sheaths his blade in the saya secured to the sash around his trim waist. "I'd like another crack at you."

I bet he does.

He goes on. "But I'm hungry."

I frown, dropping my gaze. Am I ... am I embarrassed? I think so. "I'm sorry. I don't have much, but I'm happy to share what I have with such a worthy opponent."

Ida smiles, waving away my words. "No need. I have plenty of provisions. I left them with my horse." He looks behind him before turning back to me. "Damned trees didn't seem to want to let us through, so I had to leave poor Kagi back a ways."

I don't like the thought of Ida going off on his own to retrieve his things. What if this is just an excuse for him to leave now that he knows he can't beat me and Guardian is out of his reach? Am I doomed to be alone again so soon?

My thoughts must be written on my face, because again, it seems Ida reads my mind as he says, "Care to join me for a little walk? It's good to let the muscles cool down slowly after a vigorous fight, yes?"

Vigorous.

I nod, unable to keep the smile from my face, and Ida and I head back into the woods. We walk side by side in silence, the back of his hand grazing mine every so often, making my heart race as if we were still crossing swords.

And there it is again, that frustrating emotion.

Hope.

34

Kagi knickers from the tree line, almost exactly where Hori used to wait while Atagi and I ...

No. I won't think of her now. Right now, I have a delicious opponent before me.

After we led Ida's horse back here, we shared a small meal of rice, bamboo shoots, and ripe lantern berries from my stash, as well as fish that Ida had caught the day before. As I ate the flaky trout, I couldn't help but wish a stream or pond existed within my prison. How often would I have been saved, physically and mentally, simply by having access to fresh fish?

But there was no point dwelling on the impossible, and I shook off my wayward thoughts, focusing on Ida as he ate his meal. His lips closing around his chopsticks. His throat bobbing with each swallow. His eyes smiling at me with building heat. I watched his last bite pass between his lips, as I swallowed the final pieces of rice on my plate. Without a word spoken between us, we cleaned our hands, threw off our robes, and grabbed our weapons.

We've been sparring for over an hour since, and while

it's been intense, his eyes don't have *that* look. He's not trying to kill me. I think he's honestly just testing his skill against mine.

And I love it!

Sweat drips into my eyes, and I puff out a sharp breath to blow it away. As I do, my magic rips down my side in warning, and I move out of the way of Ida's blade before he's able to draw blood. But it was close.

Very close.

He saw my slight distraction and took the advantage. Ida is good. Maybe one of the best I've come up against. But he's still not better than me.

You do have a slight advantage.

Yes, yes. I have magic.

My gaze travels down Ida's muscled torso, and I want to lick the sweat from every hard ridge.

Focus.

I am ... focused on how pretty he is.

Yes, yes. Hey. Left. Hey! Lunge left!

Ida's blade hums past my shoulder as I barely duck out of the way in time. He chuckles, lowering his sword. "You're distracted." I lick my lips, and while his smile stays in place, his eyes darken. He takes a step towards me, and my gut clenches as my cock starts to harden again. His voice is quiet and a bit deeper as he asks, "I'm not misreading this, am I?"

When he stops before me, I shake my head. "No."

Reaching out, he places a hand on my bare chest and asks, "Do you want me, keeper of Guardian? Because I want you."

I manage not to flinch at the mention of the magic sword as I nod. "I do, yes. But just to be clear, Guardian is still not part of this. This isn't in exchange f—"

"I know." Ida's fingers flex against my skin before trailing down, down, down until he grazes the waist of my pants. His voice is low and raspy. "If I thought sex would have worked, I would have offered that in trade immediately. No, it's just you I want right now."

Right now.

Good enough.

Our mouths collide with such force, our teeth click together. He licks me, and I open, dueling him with my tongue. I press my hand to his lower back, the curve fitting my palm beautifully, and when he sinks against me, our cocks rub together through our pants.

Fuck. I forgot how good this feels. I think I might like this kind of crossing swords more than the actual thing. And that's saying a lot because sword fighting is my life.

A groan slips from my mouth into his as he works his hand between us, gripping me through my pants. With a little growl, I grab his waistband and shove his pants down. Gods, I need this. He steps out of them and kicks them away, his pants fluttering to the ground like a fallen flower petal.

Ida stands before me, naked and breathtaking. His narrow hips frame his hard erection, and as I look my fill, I slide my hand inside my pants and wrap my fingers around my cock. A bead of precum escapes the aching head of my length.

He smiles, the gesture turning his face from gorgeous to downright radiant as he asks, "Are you just going to stand there and look?"

"You are just so lovely." Stay with me, please. I'm so lonely.

I lock those words inside as he reaches down and grips his cock, giving himself a slow tug as he says, "I know. Now come here."

I bark a laugh, kicking off my pants. I lunge at him,

wrapping my arms around his waist, kissing down his neck. His hand lands on my shoulder and pushes as he whispers, "On your knees." I don't even have time to think about it. My knees buckle at his sultry tone, and his cock taps my chin. He strokes his length once and says, "Open."

My lips spread wide, but before I swallow him, I say, "After this, I'm going to fuck you, Ida."

His grip on his cock stalls, and he squeezes himself ... hard. He moans. "Fuck. I would hope so."

A smirk plays at my lips as I wrap them around his head. When I suck, I roll my tongue and open my throat. I take him all the way until his black hairs tickle my nose. I swallow, and Ida's hips buck, shoving his cock even deeper. It's hard to breathe, but I don't mind, doing my best to inhale through my nose.

Death by cock would be a new one.

I choke, not because of the thick cock in my mouth, but from my own insane thoughts. Still, Ida pulls back, cupping my face as he looks down at me. "Are you okay?"

I nod, grabbing both of his ass cheeks to pull him back to me. I slurp and suck, listening and paying attention to what drives him higher towards his ecstasy. His muscles flex under my hands, and I know he's getting close. I release one of his cheeks to wrap my hand around the foreskin at the base of his cock. I pump my hand with the movement of my mouth, and two thrusts later, Ida shouts and grunts with his orgasm.

I nearly come from the sounds of pleasure I'm ripping from his body, but I hold back. I let his cum fill my mouth until he's done. With a sigh, he slips from me, and when he looks down, he notices my tightly closed lips.

His eyes darken as he purrs, "Swallow."

I shake my head and grip his wrist, giving him a little

tug. He drops to one knee, then the other. Pressing my hand to his chest, I shove, and he falls back, catching himself on an elbow. He smirks at me, spreading his legs, planting his feet wide.

Fuck me.

Still kneeling, I rise over him. Holding his gaze, I lift my palm up under my face. I open my mouth, sticking out my tongue. His cum mixed with my spit pours into my waiting hand. Ida's eyes go wide. "And what are you going to do with that?"

I don't answer. I can't. It's taking all my concentration to keep my orgasm from exploding. But I like the teasing. I like taking myself to the edge and denying myself the fall. The anticipation is painfully delightful.

Falling over him, I brace myself with my free hand and shove my other hand between his legs, smearing his cum between his cheeks and over his hole. When I slide a finger inside him, we both groan. Watching his stomach flex makes my cock jerk. I draw my finger out slowly, only to thrust it back in all the way to my last knuckle. He moans, his hips rolling, his ass squeezing my single finger so hard, I wonder if he'll be able to take me. He's so tight. My precum leaks onto Ida's sculpted body. He thrusts his hips onto my pumping finger, and I add a second.

So, so tight.

I slip in a third finger, my body tightening and tingling, pleasure coursing through me. I take my time. I get lost watching him. How his long lashes fall against his cheeks when he closes his eyes and grinds on my hand. How his throat bobs when he swallows between gasps. How his lips glisten after he bites them, looking at me through heat-filled eyes. I memorize everything, not knowing how much time I have with him.

I work Ida until his hole is sloppy with his cum and my saliva. Before long, my fingers slide easily with each thrust. Placing my hand on his inner thigh, I spread him wider. His head falls back, his hair spreading in the dirt.

He's so beautiful.

Removing my fingers from his tight ass, I grip myself. Lining up, I slam into him with one brutal punch of my hips. Ida shouts, and I grunt, holding myself still, deep inside him. So good. If only I could live in this moment forever. No, I don't even need forever, but I want more. Longer. Last just a little longer.

My voice comes out raspy. "So. Tight!" When I open my eyes, I panic. Tears leak from the scrunched corners of Ida's closed eyes. Shit. Was I too rough? Have I hurt him?

I press my palm to his chest. "Ida. Are you okay? I—"

He rolls his hips, opening his eyes, and he smiles. "Tears of pleasure. You feel so good."

Slowly, he flexes, his inner muscles pulling me even deeper inside him, and I lose control. I snap, all restraint gone. My body moves on its own, seeking pleasure, more, more, more. I'm not able to keep up with my thoughts. I can't. I'm just this building ball of need, of desire, of pressure ready to blow ...

I *need* him. I *need* this ... connection. I need to not feel so *alone*.

Shoving his thighs wide, I drive into him, pulling delicious grunts and moans from him every time I bottom out. It's so good. Every inch of my skin tingles and snaps like my magic. But this isn't red or silver. This is more. This is better. Pressure continues to build, but I somehow hold it back. I'm not ready for this to end. Not yet. Just a little longer. More. I need more.

Ida's hands trace up my arms, and when he curls his

fingers around my biceps and pulls, I fall to him. Our lips crash together once more, and I smile against his mouth as his cock starts to harden again where it's pressed between us.

I slow my pace, sliding into him with little circles of my hips. I grind his cock between our bodies, and he moans into my mouth. I pull back to see his face. His lips are red and swollen, his cheeks flushed, his eyes sparkling.

The sound that comes out of me is somewhere between a sigh and a grunt of pleasure as I say, "You are so beautiful."

Ida smiles, digging his heels into the dirt to thrust up, fucking himself on me. "I *know*."

Our passion drives higher, and our pace picks back up. The sound of our bodies slapping together is loud in the clearing. But it's just us. Only the forest creatures and Ida's horse, Kagi, are witnesses to this moment.

Ida's head thrashes in the dirt, his hands gripping my thighs. The pinch of his fingers digging into my flesh anchors me, allowing me to fully experience the bliss of sliding in and out of his tight, wet hole. I need to remember everything, because once he's gone ...

No. Stay here in this moment.

He moans with each of my thrusts, and I know I'll hear his cries of passion in my head for years to come ... and I'll play this moment in my mind as I bring myself to climax.

My fingers scrape across Ida's scalp, and he tilts back his head for more, so I grip his hair and yank, using the leverage to drive into him harder. His scream of pleasure undoes me. Bliss erupts inside me, and I let go. Ecstasy spreads like hungry flames, hitting every nerve ending as I come. My orgasm pulls a hoarse bellow from my lips. I'm so lost in the moment, I barely hear Ida's softer shout, and when I look down, his cum coats his sweaty chest.

I swallow, trying to catch my breath. "That was ..."

Ida smiles up at me, his arms going limp as his cock softens. "That was *really* good."

I laugh, falling onto my side, my wet cock sliding out of his dripping hole. I prop myself up on my forearm. As if of their own volition, my fingers comb through his long hair, and he sighs. "You keep doing that, and I'm going to fall asleep."

"Okay."

His smile softens as he closes his eyes, and I extend my arm, resting my head on my bicep. Even his profile is elegant. Ida's breaths slow and even out.

My eyes pop open. I didn't realize I'd closed them. I swallow the shot of fear racing through me. He's still here. Only a moment passed. My fingers curl where they're tangled in his hair. His hand twitches where it's splayed on my stomach, and his lips have parted slightly with sleep.

It's fine. Everything's fine ... for now.

I watch his chest rise and fall. I blow on his stomach, brushing some of the dried cum off his skin with soft strokes of my fingers. He shifts, his cock twitching from my touch, and I freeze, afraid I woke him. After a moment, he turns into me with a muffled sigh, wrapping his arm fully around my waist as he continues to sleep with his head snuggled against my chest.

Awww. How cute.

He is. I want to keep him.

You know better.

I close my eyes. I do know better. I just can't seem to help myself.

35

H ey. *Wake up. WAKE UP!*

I jerk, clutching my kimono that's draped over my body. Sitting up, I frantically look around the clearing. Kagi is still here, his tail swishing lazily, trying to keep the flies off his hide. But where's Ida ...

His voice rumbles behind me. "Look who's awake."

I turn, and my heart drops to my feet so fast, I lose the ability to inhale for a moment. Clutching my clothes to my chest, I stand, slipping one arm then the other through the wide sleeves and ask, "What are you doing?"

Ida smiles as he inspects Guardian ... in his hands. He turns it this way and that, the moonlight glinting off the shiny black lacquer. "I'm just looking."

I tie my sash with a harsh *swish*, then hold out my hand. "Give it back."

His grin grows, but he doesn't hand over my saya. "Honestly, I thought it would be more ... I don't know ... flashy. It's so ... simple. So plain."

How dare he! I'm not plain. I'm elegant. Understated.

Ignoring the indignation in my head, I keep my hand

outstretched, and my gaze hardens. "Give it back. I won't ask again, Tomouji."

He pouts, playfully slicing my saya through the air, and my silent plea scrapes the inside of my head. *Please, Ida, don't make me...*

He holds Guardian against his chest as he whines, "Tomouji? So formal. And after what we just shared together? What happened to—"

"Ishida!"

He laughs, waving a hand. "Okay. Okay. Here." As soon as I wrap my fingers around the lacquered surface of Guardian, the tightness in my chest loosens slightly. Ishida's palm lands on my shoulder, but I flinch away. He holds up his hand. "Woah. Woah. I'm sorry, okay. I was just playing around. You were fast asleep, and I was curious."

Through gritted teeth, I say, "And you weren't thinking of taking it before I woke?

As spoils of your conquest?"

Ishida rushes into my space, gripping my chin. "Hey. I'm sorry. I wasn't going to take it. I promise. You said I couldn't have it. I'm not a thief."

There's dejection in his pinched eyes, and I soften.

My saya murmurs, *You're a fool.*

I know.

When he leans into me, I give in and kiss him. When we pull away, his fingers trace my jaw, and some of his smile comes back. My palm lands on the top of his head, and I stroke his hair as I say, "Sorry."

He kisses the tip of my nose. "It's okay. I shouldn't have played around like that. Our connection was so natural and intense, I forgot we really don't know each other."

I frown. "You can get to know me. And I'd like to get to know you ... If you come back?"

His bottom lip sticks out in another sassy pout. "I don't think so, my dear. You see, I came here on a quest for a magical sword. But I've discovered that such a sword is only a legend and doesn't actually exist."

He winks at me, and I chuckle, pressing my forehead to his. "Thank you, Ida."

"Ah, it's Ida again."

"Yes, sorry."

This time he kisses my cheek. "I get it. You have an unusually strong codependent attachment to your sword. No judgment."

I grin, shaking my head. "Sounds kind of judgmental to me. But, wait." My smile falls. "So ... So, you're leaving?" I'm very proud of myself for keeping my voice even and calm, hiding the swelling pain that's building with every passing second.

He nods. "I should get back to my family. Though, I really do hate going home empty handed." He glances at my scabbard where I'm still gripping it too tightly, but when he looks back at me, he winks again.

Then his words catch up in my brain. "Your family?"

He did say that before. It was one of the first things he said to us, you dummy. You were too busy eye fucking him to pay attention.

"Yes. While my wife enjoys running the house without me getting in her way, she will be missing me by now. Even with the servant's help, my boys have the tendency to run the entire household ragged. They can be quite the little terrors. My wife will be glad to have me back if for no other reason than to help wrangle the boys. I have been gone for a while in my search for Guardian." He scratches his chin. "Too long perhaps. I think I took this little quest of mine too far. It's time I return home."

"Your wife? Kids?"

He laughs. "Yes. Are you okay? Has sex with me addled your brain? I mean, I'm flattered, but you must try to keep up."

I just fucked someone's husband. Someone's father. Wait, was Matsumae married? He never said.

You never asked either.

I shake my head. "Ida, I—"

Waving a hand, he slides on his sandals. "Don't worry about it. My wife knows I prefer men." I don't know what expression my face is making, but Ida laughs at me again. "Don't get me wrong, I enjoy my wife, very much. But I also enjoy a select few males in my village."

"A select few?"

He stands, stretching with another sexy wink. He's so playful and full of himself, I can't help but chuckle. Striding towards his horse, he gathers the reins and swings onto Kagi's back. Reaching into one of his saddle bags, he withdraws a large sack. It flies through the air when he tosses it, and I catch it, surprised at its weight.

I work the string open, and gasp. "Rice?"

He shrugs. "When I first arrived, you said you didn't have much, but you shared your food with me." Rooting around in his bag once more, he keeps his attention on what he's doing. "I can easily buy more. Consider this payment for the magnificent *sparring*."

I'm not sure if he means with our swords or cocks.

Both?

He pulls out another bag and tosses that one as well. I manage to catch it while clutching the precious rice to my chest. When I open the new bag, I blink several times to keep the burn in my throat from turning into tears.

Matcha tea. So much of it. The bright green powder is

so precious, it might as well be gold coins. I'm so engrossed with the treasure in my hands, the next sack hits me in the face before thudding to the ground at my feet. The rough landing loosens the tie, allowing me to see the contents.

Dried seaweed.

I think I might pass out.

Ida turns Kagi towards the woods as he says, "I'm not usually this clumsy ... oops."

Another small bundle falls from his saddle, landing softly in the grass that rings my practice area. With a wave over his shoulder, he says, "It's a shame that I never found Guardian."

My voice rings out. "Ida!" With a gentle pull on the reins, he stops his horse and looks back at me. "Thank you."

His grin lights up the forest as he waves again, nodding at the tea in my arms. "Think of me every time you enjoy a cup."

And with that, Ida melts into the shadows, the moonlight glimmering off his swaying black hair. I glance at that last discarded bundle across the clearing, wondering what else Ida has left me.

When my gaze falls to the bright green matcha powder in my arms, I groan, my head falling back as I say to the stars, "Great. Now I won't be able to drink this tea without getting hard."

My laughter fills the clearing, and when it dies down, I stare into the space where Ida rode off. I press a hand to my aching chest. Over the years, the anger from my past, the betrayal of the greedy men who came to take Guardian, Atagi ... especially Atagi ... My loneliness and my despair have all chipped away at me, scarring my heart with little cracks and fissures. And while Ida's kindness healed a few of those cracks, new ones spider web across my heart with the pain of his absence.

But still, I'm grateful. I got to spar with a skilled opponent. I enjoyed his company. We shared our pleasure. I laughed. And for a little while, I wasn't alone. Life is good ... the ups and downs, the hurts and the pleasures.

I whisper into the forest, "Goodbye, Tomouji Ishida. Thank you. I'll always remember you."

36

My knuckles turn white from squeezing the rock in my hand too hard. I relax my fingers, letting it slip from my grip. It clatters to the cave floor, echoing softly as if to emphasize my loneliness.

I try to dredge up the memory of the joy that I found in Ida's arms a few years ago, but even that does little to wipe away the fact that I'm alone. Very very alone. But I'm alive, and as confined as I am, I'm free ... I'm free to move and practice and swim and eat and drink and sleep ... I know I should be grateful, and I am. I am.

But I'm at war with myself, and I'm losing today's battle. There's a pit in my stomach that no amount of positive thinking will dissolve.

The cave wall is rough under my touch as I run my fingers over Atagi's name scratched under the slash that marks another day. But not just any day. "Happy birthday, Atagi." My voice goes nowhere, heard by no one.

Twenty-eight years old. What do you suppose she's doing right now?

297

I don't want to think about it, because whatever it is, I'll never know, so why speculate? I just hope she's happy.

I snatch my saya from my sash as I stride into the clearing. My muscles tense with so many emotions, anger leading the charge. Anger that I couldn't help Atagi. Anger that I failed to save my father. But anger is good. It's much better than sorrow. I can do something with anger.

Didn't you once tell Atagi not to hold a weapon when angry?

"Who's going to stop me?"

All right, then. Let's go, hypocrite.

I don't even pause to set up correctly. I don't collect my breath. I don't focus on form or technique. The faces of the villagers flare to life in my mind. Even after over sixty years, I still recall the exact looks in their eyes. I still see the angry lines etched at the edges of their mouths as they spewed hateful, untrue words at my father. I see the torches and the swords, the clutched kitchen knives and hammers. In my memory, they no longer look human. They are animals ... stupid, ignorant animals, lashing out at something they don't understand, not even bothering to try.

My eyes glow, leaving a red trail in the air with my movement.

I blame them. I blame the yokai. And I hate that a small part of me blames my father. If only he had ... No. He did what he thought was right. He was kind up until the very end. Why did he have to be *so* selfless?

My anger slips towards despair, and that won't do, so I picture each man that has come to these cursed woods, looking to barter or steal Guardian from me. Most hell-bent on taking, taking, taking ...

I slash my imagined foes before me. Faster, I move across the clearing, not feeling the ground under my bare feet. I don't notice the wind on my skin. I don't care about the lack of birdsong in the forest. I let myself get lost in the rage. Rage is good. It fills me until there's no room for loneliness or despair.

My muscles burn as I lunge, stab, slash, slice, turn, swing ...

On and on, I fight. Over and over, I kill them.

Time means nothing, but I know the shadows grow long. I dance in the moonlight, cutting down my enemies in my mind. The warmth of the morning sun hits my quivering muscles, but still, I don't stop. I can't. I—

A grunt punches out of my chest as my knee buckles and I fall to the ground, catching myself with my free hand. The heat of midday bears down on me. Sweat drips off my nose, splattering in the dirt, turning it a darker brown. Another drop, then another joins it, and I watch the ground soak it up.

"I can't do this anymore."

My fingers relax.

No!

My scabbard thuds to the ground, and I brace both palms to the dirt, flexing every exhausted muscle in my body. "I'm so tired."

No!

I ignore the katana, leaving it behind as I stand. My body sways as I shuffle to my kitchen. There's a crack running from the edge of the open doorway to the brace under the roof.

Doesn't matter.

The darker interior of the hut greets me, and the warmth of the oven slams against my already heated skin. I grab the small knife from the narrow table pushed against the far wall. I don't know why I bother to go back outside, but I do.

You want me to see. You want a witness. You don't want to die alone.

I'm always alone.

Please, don't.

"I just need a few moments of peace. Just a moment."

Please don—

The pain is sharp, but then it fades. I look down where my fingers still grip the wood handle of the knife sticking out of my chest. I chuckle, but the burst of sound ends in a cough. Blood spurts from my mouth. Without my permission, my legs crumble, and I fall to my knees. The pain roars back. Agony. My fingers tingle and my head spins as my heart tries to beat around the hole I just punched into it.

Finally, as if my body is just now catching up, blood starts to drip around the hilt and down my body, leaving hot red streaks on my skin. I fall forward, catching myself on my hands before falling to my side. The jolt of my landing sends another slash of searing pain through my entire body.

This is taking too long.

Slowly, with heavy limbs, I grip the handle of the knife.

This is idiocy. Stop!

With a grunt, I twist the blade and yank upwards. With a loud squelching sound, I rip the knife from my chest, pleased with the strong stream of blood that pours from me onto the ground. My heart kicks in my ribcage, resisting this end. I cough again. Sparking black dots dance in my vision, so I close my eyes and watch the kaleidoscope of colors behind my lids. My next breath is so heavy, it's almost impossible to take in.

Darkness.

Nothing. Finally. Blessed nothing.

. . .

I glare at the bloody blade lying next to me where I'm curled up on my side. Rolling onto my back, I stare at the painted sky, the oranges and pinks mocking me with their happy colors. The air is a bit cooler now with the setting sun, and I sigh at ... everything.

I feel my scabbard staring at me. "Don't say it."

I wasn't going to say anything.

"Yes, you were. And I know. I know."

They say that's the sign of the truly insane.

"What is?"

Doing the same thing over and over and expecting different results.

"I didn't expect ..."

Didn't you?

"Okay. I ... hoped that I wouldn't come back. I hoped for all this to be over. Happy?"

I can't believe you still have the capacity to feel that emotion. And I can't believe you hoped to leave me here, well and truly alone!

"I'm sorry."

So, are you done throwing your little fit?

With a grunt, I roll over. "Yeah, yeah. I'm done."

Good. Don't do that again.

"No promises. Forever is a long time."

You've given up on getting out?

"Haven't you?"

No?

"So convincing." I sigh, crawling over to my saya. Holding it against my chest, I flip onto my back, rubbing my thumb over the hilt. Still after all these years and after ... everything, the simple act of holding my scabbard comforts me.

Watching the sky darken, I breathe, trying to find peace

as my lungs fill and my ribs expand. My body melts with each exhale as I let go of a little piece of the tension within. A single star winks overhead, and a small smile lifts my lips. As the last of the faded light leaves the edges of the sky, more stars come out to play. Before long, the small window of sky, framed by the towering trees, sparkles with glittering specks.

If you hadn't come back, you'd have missed this.

"I know."

I sigh, the sound content. Lifting a hand, I spread my fingers, the silhouette dark against the midnight sky. Sometimes the shift from despair to hope is slow and gradual, like the rising of the sun. Other times, like today, it's almost dizzying with how quickly the hope overtakes and shoves down the despair.

But I guess, to be human is to hope ... especially when you know you shouldn't.

I stare at my palm and smile.

37

Wiping the sweat from my face, I inhale the scent of wood shavings. It's a nice smell, a calming scent, and I take a moment to appreciate my craftsmanship.

You've really improved over the years.

"I'd hope so!"

I chuckle, running my hand over the small three-tiered shelf. Some of the joints aren't as tight as they could be, but I'm proud of it. I blow on the top shelf I just added, sending little curls of wood dancing to the ground. Carrying it through my kitchen and into the little room I added on to the back, I set it on the narrow table along the back wall. With a smile, I rearrange a few things ... the small stack of bamboo I still have to peel for their shoots, my sack of dried rice which is getting depressingly low, my scraps of old clothing I use for cleaning and handling the hot kettle and warming stones. As I move the bag of matcha powder, I can't help but loosen the string and take a deep inhale of the earthy, grassy scent. I've made this last for years, only allowing myself to indulge in this treat on very special occasions.

Like Atagi's birthday.

My smile slips as the unwanted thought of my former student intrudes on my good mood. She turned thirty-six a few months ago. I wonder …

No.

Shaking my head, trying to dislodge Atagi from my thoughts, I step back with hands on hips to survey my new shelf. I nod. "Yes. That's nice. Much more organized."

Turning around, I kneel. The rough texture of the log scrapes my palm as I throw it in the oven. The flames burst and crackle before settling. Grabbing my kettle, I lift the wood lid off the small hole in the floor. Dipping the kettle in the water reservoir I dug out a few years ago, I note it'll need a refill in the next day or two if it doesn't rain. I set the kettle on the oven to boil. Turning, I gather the bamboo, setting three pieces side-by-side. Next to those, I pile a small bunch of bracken as well as a few stalks of ginger. I chop up the plants and herbs first, setting them aside before reaching for the first piece of bamboo. The process of peeling away the outer layer is tedious, the hard shell resistant to give way. I always end up with a few cuts. Then I have to trim the ends and slice the exposed core so they'll fit in the kettle.

I finish with the first stalk and roll my shoulders as I set aside the small pieces of the inner shoot. So much work for so little, but I smile. This is hard, honest work. Simple work. Satisfying.

I set the other two stalks aside for later, then turn to the happy *clink clink* of the lid dancing over the boiling water. I drop the shoot slices in, giving them a quick stir before nudging the kettle to a spot on the stove that's a little less hot. These shoots will need a few hours to simmer away the toxins and bitterness.

Grabbing one of the rags from my newly organized

stack, I clean my hands and the table, wiping the bamboo shells into a basket so I can strip them later to use to repair my tatami mats. I might have enough to start a new mat as well.

I take another big inhale as I step back outside, taking in the scent of wood smoke, pine, and ... a hint of rain. That would be nice. The vegetation in the forest is starting to wilt and could use a good downpour. But if rain is coming ...

I assess my kitchen hut, looking for repairs that need to be made before—

A gasp punches from my lips. I grab my chest, nearly doubling over. My fingers dig into my shirt as sweat breaks out all over my body. My magic flares down my back, scraping and clawing at my skin.

Someone is here.

The edges of my vision close in as every sound sharpens with a kick of adrenaline. I straighten my robe and run my fingers through my hair. I should pull it back to try to look as presentable as possible.

What treasures will we win today?

I flick the hilt of the katana. "Don't be like that. Maybe this time will be different."

You and your endless capacity to hope. It's baffling.

I snort, stepping out of the kitchen hut to hurry to the large, cold fire pit. I kneel, wiping off the two small tatami mats I made a few years ago ... in case she came back— something for us to sit on while playing shogi.

A twig snaps behind me, but I don't straighten. I don't turn.

Red. My magic grips my spine and burns in my eyes, demanding I face whoever is approaching. I clench my fists on my thighs, remaining bent over.

"Hello, Sensei."

38

My fingers tremble against my thighs. Tension threads through my shoulders, bunching so tightly, my neck starts to ache. It can't be.

Turn around.

I can't. What if this is it? What if I've finally snapped, like all the way? What if I turn around and she's not actually there? And what if she is? What do I say? What do—

Turn around!

Red snaps down my back, bunching at my lower spine, demanding I turn around. Shuffling footsteps get closer, and though I try to stop it, I flinch. The footsteps stop.

"Sensei, I understand if you don't want me here ..."

So many words tumble and fill my mouth, but none come out. Atagi sighs, and her shuffling footsteps move away.

You fucking bastard son of a bitch. Turn around and stop her. Say something!

I straighten my spine and grit my teeth, preparing myself to face the empty clearing, to face the bitter truth of my insanity.

I stand and turn.

Long black hair, hanging to her lower back, stands in stark contrast to her cream and light-blue kimono. She's taller now, but not by much, still petite. The silk of her expensive looking tabi socks glistens as she takes tiny, polished steps away from me, her wooden geta clicking softly on the ground. She approaches a bay mare standing at the edge of the clearing. It's not Hori. I guess Hori has long since passed. It has been twenty-two years since I last saw my student.

The horse flicks her ear, staring at me, and I realize I've yet to say something.

"Atagi."

She stops, and I realize her name is no longer Atagi, it hasn't been for a long time. But I never got her husband's name, and I don't feel right calling her Meiko. She doesn't correct me, though, as she stands taller, and slowly begins to turn.

I blink, and a woman who looks like she could be Atagi's mother stands before me. And then I realize this *is* Atagi. She looks the same, but so different. Her dark eyes hold a maturity, a knowledge she lacked before. She holds out her arms, palms up with a shrug and a smile that fills me with joy and breaks my heart at the same time. Her voice stretches between the space separating us. "Hello Sensei. It's been a while."

"It has. You look well."

She eyes me up and down with a smirk so familiar, it brings a flash of that little girl back to my mind. "You too."

She eyes Guardian for a long moment, and I softly chuckle at her expression, saying, "Yes, I still carry this old thing around."

Atagi smiles, shaking her head with a wistful expression.

"It's nice to know that some things never change. Do you still talk to it?"

I pat the hilt. "Of course."

She sweeps her hand towards the firepit and the large stone she used to sit on while drinking her tea after a lesson. "Well, can we talk?"

I nod, forcing my heavy feet to move. "Sure."

You're really giving her the warmest of welcomes.

I clear my throat, waving to the tatami mat on the far side of the firepit. "Would you care for some tea?"

She chuckles, the sound deeper and not as carefree as it used to be, but she says, "Yes, thank you."

As I pass through the doorway of my kitchen, I roll my shoulders, trying to dispel my crackling magic as I call over my shoulder, "Don't worry. It's not the bitter pine tea. I have actual matcha now." I don't mention that I'm down to my last few cups. I will always share what I have with my student.

Silence answers me, and my palms sweat as I reach for my kettle only to remember I'm using it to boil the bamboo shoots. Frantically, I look around the small hut as if expecting a second kettle to appear. Do I toss them? I worked so hard for those damn shoots, but I can always—

"You added on to it." Atagi's voice startles me from where she stands in the open doorway. I spin, not sure what to do with my hands, so I clasp them behind my back. Looking around the hut, I can't help but notice every crack, every crumbling piece of plaster. She looks around, quietly assessing the small space and the new room behind me. Her eyes land on her old, chipped tea cup. She stares at it for a long moment, but I can't read her expression. After another few seconds, she blinks and turns around, walking back into the clearing. "On second thought, I'm not really in the mood for tea. It's too hot."

It's not, the day is pleasantly warm, but I follow my former student back to the firepit. Bending her knees, she slides her hands down her shins, tucking her dress neatly under her as she kneels on her mat. I take the spot across from her and kneel as well. I've pictured her sitting there across from me so many times, but in my mind's eye, it was always the little girl that smiled at me from that mat. This woman before me ... She's an adult now. So beautiful. There's a softness to her. But she's also rigid, her spine straight, her hands folded in her lap, her head slightly bowed.

We sat just like this so many times, but now, it feels like the first time ... because I'm not sure who Atagi has grown up to be. She sits quietly with a small smile on her face as she discreetly looks around.

With a sigh, I release the tension from my neck, letting it melt down my back, sending it into the earth. For some reason, my magic still sparks red down the front of my body, a little less intense, but still there.

That may be Atagi sitting there, but it's been over twenty years. She's practically a stranger. The magic is right to be wary of her.

I want to flick my saya and tell it to be quiet, but I sit still, watching as Atagi tilts her head, biting her bottom lip. Her gaze travels over me before coming back to my face. She shakes her head with a soft chuckle. "You and I used to joke about that old sword of yours being magic." Her eyes slip to Guardian but quickly come back to me. "But you never mentioned *you* were magic."

I raise a brow, and she sweeps out a hand, the gesture encompassing me while somehow looking extremely elegant as she says, "You've hardly changed at all, Sensei. Maybe you're on to something, living out here, at one with the land, away from all the pressures and expectations and stresses that come with a life in a busy town or city." Her long fingers press to the corners of her dark eyes, pulling back slightly. "Growing old represents wisdom in men, but aging for a woman ..."

She drops her hands, and a small smile lifts her lips, but it's a long way from reaching her eyes. "Anyway." Her gaze lowers back to Guardian. "So, is that your secret? Magic?"

I think my heart might punch right out of my ribcage, but I try to keep my face blank. My scabbard is right. I don't know this woman. The Atagi I once knew barely cared about Guardian or its rumored legends. And now, after twenty-two years, here she is, almost immediately asking after Guardian.

I keep my secrets close, hating the distrust that's building towards my former student as I deflect, asking, "What do you believe, Atagi?"

She rolls her eyes.

"Evasive as always. I don't think I noticed as a child, but now, I realize how very little of yourself you actually shared with me."

"Is that why you came back?" My hand wraps around the hilt of my saya. "Is *this* why you're here now, after all these years, Atagi?"

She raises her head, somehow looking down at me even though she's still a head shorter than me. "I came back, *Sensei*, against my better judgment to ... I ..." She glances down, hiding her face, clutching her hands together. But then, as if finding some inner strength, or anger, she whips her head back up, glaring at me. "I came back to ask for your help."

Against her better judgment.

You didn't save her all those years ago when her husband came for her. She obviously has doubts that you'll help her now. She must be desperate indeed.

My shoulders slump as a small frown pulls at my lips. "Atagi. I once told you that I'd help you however I could. I meant it. What do you need?"

She flinches, and I realize that probably wasn't the best thing to say, because I didn't help her then. I couldn't. But of course, she doesn't know that.

She chews her bottom lip before saying, "There's trouble coming, and we need help. We've exhausted our other options. So ..."

We. Did her husband send her?

Fuck.

Shaking her head, she curls her fingers into her thighs, her dress bunching. "I won't ask questions. You can keep your secrets. I don't need to know. I just know you were the best swordsman I'd ever seen, and if you still are as good with a blade as you were back then, I need your services. I need your skill."

I realize my grip around the hilt is nearly crushing, so I relax slightly, saying, "Atagi—"

"Please, Sensei. Please. Help us." Her eyes narrow. "You owe me."

Ouch.

Angry, barbed words sit on my tongue, but I hold them back. She's right. I do owe her. But her husband? I owe him absolutely nothing. My magic flares with my temper as I stand and stalk towards her. To her credit, she doesn't back away, even though I see fear in her eyes. I wrap my hand around her wrist, careful not to grip too tightly in my anger and anxiety. I tug on her arm, not-so-gently pulling her to her feet.

"Come with me."

She stumbles after me, her wooden sandals clopping heavily as I force her to walk faster than her attire would usually allow. A grunt puffs from her lips as she stumbles again, but she doesn't say anything. As we pass her horse, I jerk my chin towards it.

"Bring it."

She tugs against my hold as she twists to grab the lead, and a second later, the soft *clop clop* of her horse's hooves follows us. Atagi's silence calms my irritation, but my magic continues to scratch down my back in warning of the woman behind me, as if I'm not acutely aware of her presence, of the skin of her wrist in my hand, of her panting breaths, of the swish of her kimono, of the soft floral scent of her hair ...

Her arm jerks in my grip as she stumbles again, and I slow down. Still, we both remain silent. Even the forest is oddly quiet, my mood affecting everyone and everything around me. The barrier looms ahead. The faded x marked into the bark of the pine mocks me as we get closer. My hands start to sweat, but I don't let go of Atagi. If I let go, I might lose my nerve. I need to do this. I can't bear her hatred for another second. She has to know.

I stop. Atagi's breaths wheeze behind me, and I almost smile. Her endurance is still shit. After a few long moments of silence, Atagi says, "Sensei?"

With a deep breath, I shift my hold on her, wrapping my hand around hers. Her palm is warm in mine, and it's ... nice. For one single second, I imagine what it would be like to hold her hand like this, walking down a street in her town

... any town. What it would be like to chat idly as she smiles up at me.

With my free hand, I wave ahead, knowing I'm being cruel with my intentional words. "Lead the way."

Her eyes go wide in surprise, and a slow smile lights up her face. "Really? Oh, Sensei, thank you."

You're a real bastard sometimes.

I swallow back the tears that want to fall, my throat burning, keeping me from speaking. Atagi walks past me, her fingers wrapped securely around my hand. What would her husband say if he saw us right now? Would he care? Did he tell her to do whatever was necessary to gain my assistance?

I shake off my bitter thoughts as Atagi walks right through the barrier, her arm stretched back where our hands are joined. She jolts, the impact nearly tearing her grip from mine, but I hold on, making my point. Atagi frowns at me, tugging on my hand. "Sensei?"

I know the sadness, loneliness, despair, and regret show in my eyes. I let her see it all ... I let her see me.

She yanks a little harder, my fingers pressed tight to the barrier that she can't see or feel. She leans back, digging her heels in, pulling me. Still, I don't move. I can't. She drops her horse's lead, freeing up her other hand to wrap around mine, and she tugs. Hard. I almost wince at the pain of my bones grinding against the invisible wall.

Atagi straightens for a second before giving me another yank. Her eyes darken with anger as she pulls again. "Sensei, this isn't funny. You said you'd help."

I place my free hand over hers, patting her as I clarify. "I said I'd help however I could. I can't do this. I can't leave."

"What?" Her fingers tighten on mine, and she begins to pull on me again, her voice rising in panic. "Sensei!"

With a sigh, I flex my arm, pulling her to me. She huffs as she slams into my chest. My arm wraps around her, and we both freeze. She is so small in my arms where she's pressed against me. So soft. All these years, Atagi has remained a child in my mind, my eager student with a bright smile and an infectious laugh. But this woman in my arms ... who is she?

Clearing my throat, I spin her next to me. I press my left palm to the barrier. She looks at my fingers, splayed like I'm waving at someone, then she looks at my face, her brows furrowed. Reaching over, I take her hand and place it over mine where it presses to the invisible wall of my prison. When she continues to look at me with confusion, I push on our stacked hands.

As I drop my top hand, I say, "I can't leave, Atagi."

She blinks at me, her eyes shining with what might be tears, but she shakes her head, grimacing as she leans her weight into my hand under hers. She waves her other hand through the barrier, frowning before coming back to push both her hands against mine. Her sandals scrape against the ground with her effort. I let her struggle. I let her come to the realization. I let her see the truth for herself.

The pressure of her hand relaxes, and her fingers caress my skin as her touch falls away.

"You ... you can't ..."

I shake my head, untying my scabbard. Grabbing the hilt, I tap the tip of Guardian against the barrier. Then I draw back my arm and swing it down. The force of hitting the wall reverberates up my arm, but there's no sound, no ripple of air. I lean down, swiping up a stick. I do the same thing, only the stick goes through as I swing. With a sigh, I toss it, and it sails away, turning end-over-end before landing with a little crunch.

"What you referred to as magic, Atagi, is actually a curse." I tie my saya back to my sash. "This katana and I are cursed. We can't leave this place."

Her gaze is still on the small stick I threw, but slowly her head turns back to me. "This is ... this is crazy! You're telling me magic is really real? I mean, really, actually real? Magic. Like *magic*, magic. Magic?"

I laugh at her rambling, tapping the barrier with my finger before lowering my arm. "Yup."

Her mouth hangs open as she looks from me to the invisible wall and back to me. Back and forth.

She's going to pull a neck muscle.

Atagi stares ahead before holding out her hand. She takes two steps forward, meeting no resistance. Turning around, she shuffles to me, grabs my arm and backs up. Once again, my hand stops at the barrier. She walks around to my side, holding my hand. I can tell her thoughts are racing, but mine are oddly calm. My attention is focused on where her light touch caresses my hand. She's warm, and my skin pebbles as her fingers trace back and forth over the back of my hand while she thinks. Slowly, she lifts my hand again and taps my finger against the invisible wall.

She lowers our hands, and I'm not sure if she's aware she's still holding me, but I don't say anything. Atagi looks out at the forest, then turning back to me, she whispers, "I can't believe ..." Her eyes go wide, and her lip sucks between her teeth as she worries at it. "So, wait. Back then, when my husband ... you didn't ... you couldn't ...?"

My body isn't big enough to hold all these emotions. Regret. Relief. Sorrow. Loneliness. Anger. Fear. I think I might crack and fall to pieces at any moment, but I lift my free arm, and the moment my hand rests on Atagi's head, I'm able to take a slow breath. Her silky hair grounds me as I say, "Atagi, I would have fought for you. I wanted to. I'm sorry. I'm so very sorry."

She dashes a few tears off her cheeks, but doesn't shove off my hand, doesn't step away as she says, "I've hated you for a very long time because of that day. Why didn't you say something?"

I let my hand slip down her hair before stepping back. "Would you have believed me?"

Her head whips up, a flash of anger in her eyes as she says, "I practiced with you for years! At any time, you could have told me." She points at the invisible wall. "You could have shown me."

"Could have. Should have. Would have. In the end, things might have changed, but they wouldn't be different."

"You don't know that."

I shrug, tired of this conversation. Just ... tired.

I turn, and with slow steps I head back the way we came, saying over my shoulder. "I'm sorry I can't help, Atagi. You can tell your husband you tried. You can tell him the truth or make something up. I don't care."

I think I hear a soft gasp from her, but I'm not sure as I continue to walk away. I've wanted Atagi to come back for so long. I've yearned to have the chance to explain and apologize, but now ... it's just all too painful. My life is too long to keep building these agonizing experiences on top of each other. At this point, I just want to be left alone.

Lier.

"Sensei?" Like a fool, I stop at the sound of her voice calling after me. I don't turn back around, but she asks, "Do you still have Moon?"

My fingers twitch as I try to keep the excitement from building. My saya was right. I lied. I don't want her to leave. I keep the eagerness from my voice as I answer, "Yes."

Soft shuffling sounds precede her voice, now a little closer as she asks, "Will you practice forms with me?"

Keeping my back to her to hide my smile, I hold out my arm, indicating the way back to my home. "As you wish, Atagi."

The quick clopping sound of her sandals gets louder as she joins me, leading her horse.

Why are you doing this to yourself?

Who knows why I do any of the things I do?

You missed her.

Every day.

You can't trust her.

I know.

When my cave comes into view, I force a bright smile onto my face. "Go on. Moon is where you left her. I've taken good care of her. She's been waiting." We've both been waiting for you, Atagi.

She hesitates for a single moment, and I start to panic. Did I say that out loud? But then a big, happy grin lights up her face, the first genuine smile I've seen from her since she arrived. She drops her horse's lead and grips her dress, lifting it to allow her to kick into a shuffling jog.

Tears build in the back of my throat as for once, time seems to slow down. As Atagi runs by, her hair sways and her eyes shine, and all I see is that little girl begging me to teach her. I see the child who used to race me to the tree. I see the frustrated girl who only wanted to beat me, just once.

She disappears into the cave and the moment passes, the shadows swallowing my vision of that little, cheerful girl.

Atagi takes longer than necessary to return, and I wonder if she's snooping. I grin. That would be something she'd do. Eventually, Atagi strides out of the cave, her katana gripped tightly in her hand. Her head is raised, determination in her eyes. I'm startled again by how different she looks. Even the shape of her face has changed from when she was a child, her cheeks and jaw somehow both hard and soft ... mature. I look, almost to the point of staring, but I don't see my little Atagi-chan in this woman before me.

Bracing my feet, I wait for her to get closer.

You're going to have to start from the beginning. She probably hasn't even held a sword in years. I bet she overextends her first swing.

I guess we'll see. I bark out, "Kirioroshi."

With a grin, Atagi sets, draws, and slices Moon with precise form. She holds her katana before her for a long moment before sheathing it smoothly.

It was perfect. Beautiful.

I raise a brow. "You've been practicing."

She lifts one painted brow to match my expression, but before she gets too cocky, I draw my scabbard and lunge at her.

39

MEIKO

This is so much fun! I'm sweating buckets, and I think I might pass out, but I'll pass out happy. How I've missed this!

But of course, I'm breathing hard, and that annoys me, because I know my sensei is going to say something. My hair, now pulled back and secured at my nape, is damp at my temples. I think I'm keeping up pretty well though.

Easily moving out of the way of my slash, he says, "Your endurance is still shit, Atagi."

I block his strike, my eyes wide as I fight to keep the grin off my face while I back up to avoid his next hit. "Sensei!"

He chuckles. "What? You're an adult now. Or have you become so polished and refined that a little word like shit offends you?"

I falter my next step, distracted by my teacher's words. I guess I have changed a lot. I'm certainly no longer that little girl he once knew. But does he really see me as a refined lady? I was sure, coming back here after so many years, that my sensei would still be able to see … me. That he'd be able to see beyond the mask I wear every day. But maybe I have become the woman I've been pretending to be … while he has barely changed. His eyes are older, yet he's somehow still the same as I remember him. Though, granted, I'm looking at him through the memory of when I was a child. I saw him differently then.

With my thoughts churning, Sensei gets past my guard and taps my shoulder with the edge of his scabbard.

Damn it.

I stare at Guardian, careful to keep my gaze neutral as I lower Moon, hating how my breaths escape with desperate little puffs of air. My head falls back as I shout, "Fuck!"

His lips twitch at my outburst, and he admonishes, "Atagi!"

Slowly, I get my breaths under control as I smile up at him. "What? You can swear and I can't? Is it because I'm a *woman*?"

My teacher lowers Guardian, pointing the tip of the shiny black scabbard down and to the side. My smile slips into a glower. All my life I've had my gender thrown in my face. Over and over, I've been reminded of my so-called 'limitations', reminded of my place in the world … below the men. Always less than.

Not that I've had a particularly hard life. No, I can't say that, especially compared to some others. But I've always, always wanted more; my dreams often drifting to these woods, to the man standing before me, to the sword in my hand, to the freedom I found here so many years ago.

Sensei's gaze darts to Moon where I've lowered it, the steel glinting orange in the light of the slowly setting sun. I rub my thumb over the soft wrapping of the hilt. I really have missed the feel of *my* katana in my hand.

My teacher nods at my lowered blade. "Why did you stop? You never used to give up so easily."

With a little sigh, I sheath Moon in the saya tied to the sash of my kimono as I say, "We've been sparring for over an hour. I need a break ... *Sensei.*"

We both smile at my teasing word, and I pause because when he smiles ...

I drop my gaze and walk to the cold fire pit. When I was younger, Sensei was this god-like person. The way he moved with a blade—I was captivated by him. I wanted to be him.

Flopping down on the large rock I've sat on so many times, I lean back, bracing my hands on the rough stone. Sneaking little peeks at Sensei from the corner of my eye, the woman I am now appreciates how he moves, even just doing mundane things. There's a fluidity to his movements, and his muscles flex and bunch even while doing something simple like crouching to start a fire—which he's doing now.

His thighs are strong, and those fingers ... who knew fluffing kindling could be so manly?

Pushing off my hands, I sit up, shaking off my thoughts, only to recall the magical barrier around this place. My mood falls as I look around, and for the first time, I really *see* this place. It's quiet, comfortable. He's made a nice home for himself here, but it feels so ... confined. How has he lived like this for so long? How does he still have the capacity to smile, to share what little he has with me, to be ... kind?

In his place, I'd be bitter and angry and ... I don't think I would have survived for long out here on my own, so desperately alone for so long. How has he found the strength to keep going?

Guilt presses against my chest, and I don't realize I'm

frowning until he stops fluffing the kindling under the logs and cocks his head at me. I smile at him, and after a moment, he goes back to setting the fire. I watch his hands as they strike flint to steel. They're strong, calloused, capable ...

What am I going to do? I *need* help, but he can't leave ... and neither can Guardian. I'm relieved to know my Sensei didn't willingly abandon me all those years ago, but ...

A breeze ruffles the ends of my hair and flutters the sleeve of his robe. There's a hint of crispness in the wind, and as the fire starts to crackle between us, I say, "You've made a lot of improvements. I could almost call your cave homey."

I smirk as he narrows his eyes at me. I don't say anything more, but I know he knows I poked around when I went to retrieve Moon. The caves are much the same as I remember, but also different. I was fascinated by it all until I saw my old kimono folded on the crude shelf in his sleeping chamber, dredging up memories of *that* day. I was so angry with him. I can't believe I've held onto that hate for so long just to find out the truth now.

I chew my lip; the crackling flames the only sound in this small clearing. Why did he keep my kimono?

Because he was waiting for you to come back.

That thought makes me sad. I may not be able to sympathize with his level of loneliness, but I can empathize. I've known my share of solitude—even while surrounded by the constant presence of family and servants.

My teacher holds his palms before the flames. I doubt he needs the warmth. It seems like he's just keeping his hands busy. There's a tension in him, even while we were sparring. I think he's wary of me, and I understand that. Still, it hurts.

With his eyes on the fire, he says, "Calling that cave homey might be a stretch, but this place is a constant work in progress. It keeps me busy." He rubs his hands together, finally lifting his gaze to meet mine, a soft smile on his face. "You were good today, Atagi."

I return his smile but can't quite make it reach my eyes. Does he notice?

Sensei sits back, crossing his legs. I drop my head, breaking his gaze. I'm much better at hiding my emotions from my face than I was as a child, but still, I worry. Sensei knows me better than anyone, or he used to. And I want to be that version of me that he remembers—I want to be that girl who was quick to smile, who playfully pouted to get her way, and considered a day of swordplay and a meal of rice balls and tea to be the perfect day. But I'm not her anymore. I can't be.

I'm thankful for the strong woman I've built myself up to be, but I don't necessarily like her.

I nod at Moon where she rests in her saya on the ground next to me as I say, "I've practiced over the years. As much and as often as I could. At night or early in the mornings before the household woke up. Sometimes I'd find time in the middle of the day to slip away to our walled garden ..." My fingers weave together in my lap, fidgeting, as I recall all those quiet hours of just me and a blade. Moments where I didn't have to worry about how I was presenting myself to the world. Moments where I didn't have to worry if my boys were behaving. Moments where I didn't have to stress about what dishes to have prepared, what tea to serve, if my face powder was evenly applied, if my lips were red enough ... Moments that were just mine.

Keeping my eyes averted, I realize my lips are still curved upwards. I don't even realize when I'm making this expression anymore. It's like it's pasted on, presenting this demure, pleasant woman I'm supposed to be.

I shrug off my thoughts because it doesn't matter.

I stare at the fire as I say, "Once my oldest son started taking lessons at the age of five, I would ask him to show me what he learned every day. I could tell sword fighting was not in his blood, but he obeyed his father and endured the lessons. And he humored me, showing me the forms he learned."

A bit of actual happiness seeps into my smile as I recall my son rolling his eyes, trying to act annoyed by my questions. But I saw the pride in his smile as he showed me his forms. My lips twitch with the beginnings of a chuckle at the memory. He was really quite awful.

Lifting my gaze, I glance at Sensei, noticing his tightly pressed lips at the mention of my son. I drop my gaze, chewing on my lip again.

Yes, that's right, so much has changed. I'm not the little girl you watched ride away with her new husband all those years ago. You may not have changed much, but I have.

I'm no longer smiling. Sensei doesn't need that placating expression from me anyway, so why bother.

I continue my story. "My husband had many blades. He collected them. It was an obsession." I scowl, shaking my head. "No, it was a taunt, filling our house with swords I was not allowed to touch." I don't mean to, but my gaze lands on Guardian, the black lacquer flickering gold from the firelight. Peeling my eyes away from the saya, I settle my unfocused gaze back on the fire as I say, "It worked to my advantage, though. He collected so many katanas, he never noticed if one was not put back exactly the way it was before." I smirk. "All those blades. All I had to do was reach out and take one." Lifting my head, my gaze lands on his across the fire. "And I did. Over and over, I took up a blade and practiced."

My teacher smiles, but stays silent, as patient as ever.

Suddenly, I'm tired. While I knew I'd have to share some pieces of my life and who I've become, that's not why I came back here. I slip on my smile, realizing how sad it is without any joy behind it. I wave a hand, the gesture delicate, its intention to distract. And it works as I say, "Enough about me. I'm just glad I was able to keep up with you today. Practicing on my own isn't the same as getting instruction from my sensei, and I know my form and technique have slipped over the years."

He shrugs as if in agreement, and while it riles, I keep my mask in place as he says, "Still, you did well, Atagi." I preen at his praise. "And even though I can't leave here with you, I'm glad you came to see me." After a pause, I curl my bottom lip between my teeth, worrying at it. He must see the concern on my face because he asks, "I am sorry, Atagi. If you tell me what's wrong, maybe I can help another way?"

Maybe ... Possibly, but the threat that drove me here is still just rumors and whispers. I like to be prepared. I'm not one to leave my fate in another's hands if I can help it. But who knows if anything will come of the gossip? Still, I wake every morning, my heart racing, wondering if a letter will come that day with the news ...

Casually, I wave my hand again, wearing the smile that says everything is fine, even if it isn't. "Don't worry about it, Sensei. There's nothing you can do." He frowns, and I know he's about to push back, so I quickly add, "May I come back? I'd like to brush up on my skills."

"I would like that very much, Atagi."

The affection in his eyes nearly undoes me. I came here,

still hating him for something that wasn't his fault, and here he is being ... kind.

I nod, standing and straightening my kimono. As I pick up Moon, he says, "You moved very well today. The kimono no longer holds you back."

That sad smile slips over my face again, bringing to sharp focus just how often I wear this expression. I'm starting to hate it. I pass Moon to my teacher, and with a harsh *swish*, I tighten my sash as I say, "No, my *clothes* don't hold me back."

Being a woman does that.

I gather the reins of my horse, the leather soft in my grip. My fingers clench around a handful of glossy mane as Sensei steps next to me, bending down and holding out a hand for me to step into. With a flex of my muscles, I pull myself up, Sensei's strong hand making the mount easy. As I settle into the sidesaddle, he pats my horse's neck, and I get the sense he's searching for something to say. And I find myself wanting to linger. Just a little longer.

I brush my fingers over the top of his hand before curling them to give him a little squeeze. His muscles tense for a moment before he relaxes and looks up at me. My sad smile is ready for him as I say, "Thank you for the lesson, Sensei."

40

The dappled light paints Atagi in shades of green and yellow as we stroll through the woods. Every so often, her hand brushes against the bark of a tree as we pass. This is the third time she's come to see me in as many days. I feel spoiled by her presence, but I wonder how it is that she's able to get away to see me each day ... and for hours at a time. She's been here all day today, having arrived with the first rays of the morning sun.

Instead of sparring, she asked to go back to basics, and we spent half-an-hour going through a few simple forms. Her movements were sharp and steady, and I only had to correct her a few times. After, we enjoyed tea and baked bamboo shoots, along with some rice balls she brought from home, each of us nibbling our small meal in silence.

I scratch my outer arm where my magic scrapes against my skin. I miss the way it used to tickle in her presence. Now, my magic is reacting to Atagi as if she's just another adversary. But she's not. She told me why she came, and I explained my situation—well part of it—so, why ...?

Maybe she's gotten better at shogi?

What is that supposed to mean?

Maybe she's setting her board, adjusting her strategy, moving towards checkmate.

No.

As the edge of the barriers gets closer, I shift direction, and Atagi moves with me. She frowns at the tree with the x mark but doesn't comment. After a few more minutes, I gather courage in my gut and let one of my many brewing questions loose. "Are you finding your way here well enough?"

She nods, her gaze moving around the forest. "Yesterday, there was a well-worn path that surprisingly led me right here. Today was a little harder, but I managed. It's still hard to believe this place is actually magic. So wild."

I smile at the wonder in her voice. I suppose from the outside, it is pretty fantastical.

After a short silence, I ask, "You mentioned your son. Is he with his father or do your servants watch him while you're gone?" What I'm really asking is how she manages to spend so much time with me when she obviously has responsibilities back home.

A few flakes of bark crumble to the forest floor as she runs her palm over a tree. Her gaze is far away as she shakes her head. "No, they don't. *I* raised my boys. I tried to be involved in every aspect of their lives. They'd probably say I was too involved. But ... the oldest is away up north attending school. A young man now, though I still see him as my baby." She chuckles, the sound wistful. "Though any time I find myself pining for the days when my boys were small and still clinging to my skirts, one of my nieces or nephews seems to intuitively choose that moment to get up to some kind of mischief."

I smile as I ask, "What are their names, your sons'?"

Gripping the tree, Atagi swings around to the right before moving on. I follow as she says, "The oldest is Harada, named after his father. He's twenty-one now."

It's hard to imagine a fifteen-year-old Atagi large with child. Guilt swarms through my stomach like a nest of angry bees. Was she scared? Was she excited? Was someone there to help her?

Her voice softens. "The younger one was Sen. He would have been twenty this year. He was an old soul. So calm. So smart. Tender."

Was. Oh, my poor Atagi. Her words don't waiver, but my throat burns with sympathy for her as I ask, "When did he pass?"

"Two years ago. Both him and his father. Tuberculosis."

I should be ashamed at the zip of joy that kicks through my heart. That awful man, her husband, is dead. I wince as I recall the bitter words I threw at her, thinking her husband was the one who sent her here. But if he's dead, then ... did she really come here on her own? My magic crackles down my left side, aimed at Atagi, and I can't help but wonder if someone else is pulling her strings?

I shake my head, focusing. Atagi not only lost her husband, but her son, and while there are no tears in her eyes, there's pain in her voice. Reaching out, I rest my palm on her shoulder, giving her my support through the simple touch. "I'm sorry, Atagi."

She smiles at me, patting my hand before walking away. My hand falls to my side as she says, "It's alright. It's a horrible sickness. In the end, Sen welcomed the peace of death. I did too, if I'm honest. It was agonizing to see the pain in my child's eyes and be able to do nothing."

I wince. I know she's not talking about me. This isn't even remotely about me or the fact that I was forced to watch and do nothing when her husband came and took her away. But my guilt eats at me anyway.

Needing to steer our conversation in another direction, I ask, "How many nieces and nephews do you have?"

"My late husband's sister has seven children and is about to have her eighth. They're a lot. They're cute, but they're a lot. My husband's family has been ... kind, allowing me to stay even after my mourning period ended. My husband's younger brother is the head of the household now. He's a few years older than me yet can't seem to make a single decision without consulting his mother. But, all things considered, he's doing alright."

I tilt my head, asking, "So, does your brother-in-law not wonder where you go every day?"

She doesn't break stride, but her head hangs a little lower as she shakes it. "No. He's away, in the north with my sister-in-law's husband and a few of the other men in our town. Has been for months. The feudal lord called him and others from all over our region."

I don't know much of the outside world, but I do know what I learned at my father's side in our village and during our travels, and a feudal lord doesn't call up his fighting-age men for no reason.

She sighs, "Honestly, I've become a bit of an afterthought in the house. Which is fine. As long as I do my duties and stay out of the way, I have a decent amount of freedom." She spreads her arms. "Hence my long visits here."

Her gaze is still distant, but a small smile plays at the edge of her lips as we continue to stroll through the woods. I'm starting to realize this is Atagi's new smile, the one that doesn't reach her eyes, the one that holds a hint of sadness. I miss her bright bubbly smiles and laughter, but she's very obviously not that little girl anymore.

I ask, "And Isayo? How is she?"

Atagi's hands slide into the sleeves of her kimono, her expression falling. "She died giving birth. Six years ago, now."

Fuck. I keep slamming into Atagi's painful past with every word out of my mouth, so I don't know why I ask, "Your parents?"

"Mama died eight ... no, nine years ago now. Papa still gets around and runs his shop. He's a bit slower these days and often takes the afternoons off to nap. He has a reliable apprentice, but he hardly lets the man do anything. And when he does, he follows him around, watching him like a mother hen."

I think I would have liked her father. I wish we could have met.

She chuckles to herself. "I don't see papa ever completely handing over the business and doing nothing. He'll stop working when he dies." Her chuckle turns into a full laugh, and I smile. There she is.

We walk in silence, and eventually, the cave comes into view. Atagi stops next to her mare, patting her deep brown rump. "It's getting dark. I should go."

I hadn't realized how long the shadows had grown while we walked. Bending down, I cup her foot and help her onto her horse, passing her the reins.

"Thank you for coming to see me, Atagi."

A soft chuckle passes her lips, and she shakes her head. "I haven't been Atagi for a long time now."

I know. I just didn't want to call her by *his* name. Still, it's only proper ...

"Sorry, habit. And ... I never asked. What *is* your new name?"

She looks down at me, her gaze slipping to Guardian before rising back to my face with an expression I can't quite read as she says, "No. Atagi is fine. With you, that is who I am."

She rides off without another word, and I watch her go until I can no longer see her ... my magic scraping and sparking until she's gone. It doesn't trust her.

She's not telling us everything.

Well, I'm not telling her everything either.

My hand wraps around the hilt of Guardian as I whisper, "Please don't be who my magic thinks you are. Please, prove me wrong, Atagi."

41

MEIKO

A week goes by, and then a month. I've scoured scrolls and texts, those that I can read anyway, looking for lore on Guardian ... for a way to help my sensei. I've listened in tea houses and to the drunk males stumbling out of the pleasure house. I've discreetly asked the other wives in town, causally requesting them to let me know if they hear any mention of the famous sword. I don't bring up magic or curses, knowing that's a quick way to get a visit from the doctor then finding yourself drifting in a haze of drugged incense. No, I won't give my neighbors any reason to think I'm crazy.

But I need to know more about Guardian. It was fairly easy to track down the name of the village that Sensei mentioned all those years ago. And sure enough, anytime I spoke the name, gazes would shift, spit would land in the dirt, and I'd be warned to forget that village and the violence enacted upon it. One old woman in a neighboring town started performing a cleansing ritual before I'd finished asking my question, shaking bells and mumbling about curses and yokai. I'd given her a coin and my thanks, walking away with her worried mumbles trailing behind me.

I've even started having dreams about Guardian. Nightmares filled with flashes of steel, red blazing light, and blood. So much blood.

Still, I can't stop. I need to know. I've sent a letter to a man who might be a descendant of a survivor of that night, Motosue Saito. I'm not holding out much hope that I'll hear anything back, but I had to try.

I haven't told Sensei anything about my search, because if I fail to find anything that can help him, I don't think I could bear the weight of his disappointment. At least some of my anxiety has eased since there's been no news from the north, and the whispers of conflict have trickled away, overshadowed by the rumors of a possible pregnancy within the emperor's court. Maybe a peace was brokered, and everything will be okay. My brother-in-law will return home soon, and life will resume as it was.

I'll miss Sensei.

My Sensei.

I'm enjoying my time with him. Every day, I've made the trek through these woods, spending hours, if not the entire day, with him. And every day, I know more of my mask slips away as I rediscover the joyful little girl inside me that I thought I'd buried a long time ago. Sensei and I practice, we spar, we sip tea, and we walk around the forest. When we move through our forms, I find I'm able to quickly sync with his moves, and I feel myself improving.

I've missed this so much. Unlike my son, swordplay is in

my blood. It makes me truly happy. It fills me with joy and contentment until there's no room for anything else. And that exhilaration shows in my grin as Sensei paces around me now, his scabbard gripped behind his back.

I lunge, thrust, stand, and twist. The tap of Guardian to my hip brings a scowl to my mouth as I grunt, "Damn it. I know."

"If you know, then tell me."

I roll my eyes, an expression I'd never dare at home, as I reset and say, "I'm leading with my hip instead of my core."

"Good. So, if you know, fix it."

I glare at him, blowing a strand of loose hair from my face. "I'm trying! My hip just … moves."

His lips twitch with a smile as he calmly stands before me, hands reclasped behind his back. "Slower this time."

I'm surprised as a small growl of frustration escapes from my throat. I'm letting my emotions show, letting my guard down bit by bit with my teacher. If I'm not careful, this side of me will bleed into my home life, and I can't let that happen.

Slowing my movements, Sensei shakes his head, saying, "Slower."

My jaw flexes. "If I move any slower, I'll stop all together."

"Atagi."

"What?" I bark the word at him, but he remains calm, dropping his gaze to my left leg.

Ugh! I throw back my head, noticing my left hip is pushed forward again. "Damn it!"

"Want to take a break?"

I shake my head as I reach back, undoing the tie in my hair before gathering it back up and retying it tightly as I say, "No! I want my body to cooperate."

He chuckles which earns him another glare from me, but he seems to shrug off my sour mood, which is just as well because I'm not mad at him, I'm frustrated with myself. I should be better than this. I am better. Aren't I? In the absence of instruction from my sensei, have I been teaching myself bad habits without knowing it?

Shit.

With a huff of determination, I reset, moving through the form a few more times. Each pass, I improve a little, but I never quite nail it down. My anger is growing, so before it turns into a very unladylike tantrum, I lower Moon and sheath it with a smooth snick. The silk cord whispers against my fingers as I tie my saya to my sash before placing my hands on my hips, explaining, "I need to stop. I'm just getting more frustrated. I'm not going to get it today."

He nods, his knowing expression seemingly proud of me for acknowledging my limits and knowing when to stop ... but I'm sure I'm just seeing what I want to see on my Sensei's face.

He asks, "Are you too tired to race to the tree?"

Adrenaline kicks my heartrate up. Can I beat him? I chew my bottom lip as I wave a hand down my dress. "I won't beat my last time in this kimono. Which means I certainly won't beat you."

He laughs, placing his hand on the top of my head like he used to, ruffling my hair. The gesture is so familiar, it brings tears to my eyes, and I realize how deep my feelings for this man go.

He says, "You'll never beat me, Atagi."

I slap his hand away, along with my uncomfortable emotions as I say, "Not wearing this, I won't."

Crossing his arms, he looks down at me, and I want to

fidget under his gaze as he asks, "You think you can beat me in different clothes?"

I smile, letting a little mischief show in my eyes. "Maybe. You don't know what I've been up to all these years. Maybe I've run kilometers every day?" I haven't, but teasing and joking around is nice. This freedom to be myself is ... dangerous, but I can't seem to help myself.

But I need to remember that as good as it feels to rediscover who I was, I need to keep hold of who I am, of who I've become. Because I'll always have to go back. I need to. I *want* to. I love my family, and I won't walk away from my responsibilities.

I need to remember who I *really* am.

I am the woman who birthed two sons before her eighteenth birthday. I'm the woman who had to learn how to cover the bruises when I displeased my husband or his mother. I'm the woman who had to pretend I was fine any time I was sick. I'm the woman who dared to sneak away in the night to practice my sword forms. I'm the woman who whispered in my husband's bed, directing him to make certain investments, to sign certain contracts, to let our son attend a more expensive school ... I'm the woman who made my husband fall in love with me. And I'm the woman who survived losing that husband and her son in the same year.

I'm strong, despite—or maybe because of—the woman who, as a child, watched as my teacher, the one adult I trusted above all others, did nothing to stop a cruel man from taking me away and changing my life forever.

Knowing what I know now, I hate the bitterness I harbored for my Sensei, but I'm also thankful for that hate, because it helped me grow up. It helped me see the world for how it really is.

As Sensei sweeps a hand towards his cave, I'm pulled

from my contemplation, remembering that we were talking about racing to the tree. Wow, I really got lost in my thoughts there.

He says, "There's a spare pair of pants in my chamber. You can borrow them, but I swear, Atagi, if you rip them, you'll repair them."

My body goes still, my eyes blinking rapidly. Finally, I ask, "You ... you want me to wear your pants?"

His shoulders tense, and his jaw clenches. I don't think he thought before he spoke, inviting me to wear his clothing. So inappropriate. But ... slightly exciting with the forbidden nature of it.

He waves a hand, his cheeks turning pink with what I assume to be embarrassment as he says, "I meant just to race. I—"

To dispel the unwanted emotions gathering in my chest, I laugh, cutting off his words. I press a palm to my belly with my exaggerated laughter. "The look on your face, Sensei! You were really panicked there."

I double over with my loud laughter to hide my sudden nervousness, because I really like the idea of wearing his clothes. And I love the idea of him seeing me in his clothes. Thankfully, he doesn't seem to notice my edginess and gives my shoulder a little shove. "You are terrible."

Getting myself under control I stand, grinning at him. "Maybe, but today is the day you lose to me, Sensei."

I slap his arm as I jog past him, ignoring the flutter in my gut at the flex of the lean muscle of his bicep under my hand. As the shadow of the cave drapes around me, and the cooler air greets me, my mood sobers. I pass into my teacher's bedchamber, averting my gaze from the crudely stitched futon sitting on a large tatami mat. The smooth hearth is cold and unlit, but I imagine this room gets quite warm when the fire is going. I look around. This has been his existence for ... I don't know how long.

I chew on my lip as my gaze lands on my faded kimono, still neatly folded on that table. There's something on top of the garment, but I don't move closer to find out what it is. Suddenly, me being in here seems like an intrusion.

It doesn't take long to thumb through the small pile of folded clothes to find a pair of pants. I shrug out of my kimono and shimmy into Sensei's pants. This feels very intimate, and my cheeks heat as I wonder what his reaction will be when he sees me in his clothes.

Bending over, I roll up the hems to keep them from dragging before I drape my kimono over my arm. I head back outside into the bright sunlight, my head bowed as I tighten the string around the waistband. I realize that while he's tall and muscled, Sensei is lean and trim, because these pants are only slightly baggy. I kick out a leg as I walk, grinning. Oh, I've missed wearing pants. It's so ... freeing. I do another little kick and skip out of the cave. When I lift my gaze, it's to find Sensei staring at me. I can't quite read his expression as his gaze travels down, down, down my legs clad in his pants. My face gets hot as I suddenly imagine him peeling his pants down my legs.

I shake off my wayward thoughts, setting my kimono on the flat rock by the firepit. Then, without warning, I spin and shout, "Go!"

I take off at a dead sprint, determination blazing through me. I'm going to win, damn it!

Sensei laughs behind me, his footfalls thudding softly as he comes after me. I almost slow down, wanting him to catch me, but then I bite my lip and go faster as he yells, "Cheater! I wasn't ready!"

I giggle, the sound surprising, one I haven't made since I was a child. I say, "Not *my* fault."

In less than a kilometer, he catches up to me but doesn't pass. I hear him keeping pace behind me, and my mind conjures more unwanted questions ... is he watching my hair sway across my back, wondering what it would feel like around his fist? Is he watching my ass in his pants?

I'm breathing hard as I skirt around a tree, my struggling breaths not all from exertion as I imagine Sensei watching me from behind.

And then his footsteps get closer, and my heart rate climbs even more. He taps my shoulder, and I look over at his smiling face. He's not even breathing hard. The bastard. But then his eyes fall to my lips, then lower to my chest, which I'm sure is heaving with my struggling breaths.

I mentally slap myself, then I slap at his hand, but miss. He passes me with ease, and I call after him, "Damn you!"

He kicks into a sprint, leaving me in his dust, and I throw a few more curses at his back, doing my best not to notice his firm ass. Our tree comes into view, my teacher already there, hand pressed to the bark, the many numbers of my running times carved into the trunk. He grins, and my heart stutters with ... longing. But I brush it away and complete the final sprint to the tree.

I'd laugh if I could breathe, because this is fun. I'm so glad I came back. I never want this to end. I know it has to, but not yet.

Just a little while longer.

42

I stand back where the weak cloud-filtered light of the sun fades into shadow. Atagi stands ahead at the mouth of the cave, her silhouette dark against the steady fall of rain outside.

Lifting my arm, I rub my chest. I'm enjoying life, more than I have in a long time. And with that enjoyment comes the hope ... I can't help but hope for more. I want this to last ... having Atagi in my life every day. If this were to be my existence until she grows too old to make the journey here, I think I might be content for the rest of my days. I covet every one of Atagi's smiles, even the sad ones. I want her to stay with me instead of going home each night. I want to hold her.

I'm well aware how fleeting time is with her, so I imprint as much as I can on my memory for something to hold and cherish ... for later.

Like the memory from the other day that turned into a fantasy ... of her perfect ass in my pants as she ran through the woods. As I chased after her, I had the urge to wrap my arms around her from behind, taking her to the ground, pressing my lips to the back of her neck to see if she'd arch into me ...

I grit my teeth, banishing that image before it takes root and I get hard ... again. I stride forward, coming to stand on her right. I allow myself one moment to glance down at her face as she turns to look up at me. The soft sound of the falling rain fades. My world narrows to her. I don't know when it started happening, but now, I often end up having to catch my breath and slow my racing heart when our gazes lock.

I find myself moving closer, but my magic scrapes down my body, and I fight to keep the scowl off my face. It's still reacting like this, like it doesn't want me getting close to her, physically or emotionally.

Protecting yourself from inevitable heartbreak.

Not inevitable. I could ask her. I could finally find the courage to ask the question that's been burning inside since that first day she came back. I could ask her to stay. I can keep her safe as long as she's with me. I can protect her from anything. I know I can.

She won't leave her home for you.

And that's why the question sits unasked as I turn my attention to the rain and say, "Monsoon season is upon us."

With a bright giggle, she runs a few steps outside, holding her arms wide, tilting her head back, mouth open to catch the water falling from the sky. She swallows a few times, and I'm entranced at the sight of her. There is no past. No future. Just now. This moment. It's perfect. There's joy and life and companionship.

With her head still upturned, she says, "Isn't it wonderful? I love the start of the rainy season. Everything was parched, and now the rains are here to soak into the ground, to fill our wells, to give life." She chuckles as she drops her arms, her drenched hair hanging heavy around her shoulders, little beads of water spilling down her face and off her chin. "But I'll be bitching in a month when everything is soggy and nothing ever seems to completely dry out."

I laugh, walking out to join her in the downpour. "You're right. We need this. The earth needs this."

I let my head fall back, and I blink at the thick clouds as rain pelts my face. It's nice. Free. And I'm grateful. For every breath. For every movement. For every experience. I don't recall the last time I just stood out in the rain, but because of her, I'm out here, head back, cataloguing every drop that lands on my skin. I marvel at how even though the rain is warm, my skin pebbles. I puff out a breath, smiling as water sprays from my lips.

Glorious. Being alive is glorious.

My gaze drops to her as she asks, "Does that feed your water reservoir in there?"

I turn my attention to my kitchen where she's pointing. I smile as I watch the rain slide down the roof, collecting in the bamboo gutter along the wide overhang before funneling down through another hollow piece of bamboo I cut into the wall.

I nod. "Yes. It's tedious hauling water from the pools in the cave, so I came up with that system to collect rainwater. Another reason to love monsoon season."

She grins. "Very smart, but what if your reservoir overflows?"

I lift a brow, crossing my arms. "You think your sensei didn't account for that?"

Her gaze lowers to my chest, and I realize the rain has soaked through my shirt. Atagi has seen me shirtless countless times, but there's something else in her gaze, something that reminds me of Ida.

I shake my head. "There's an overflow drain that moves excess water back outside to that trench around the kitchen."

Atagi licks rain from her lips before lifting her gaze, turning away to look at the hut. "Smart."

I close the space between us, placing a hand on her shoulder. "You're soaked through. I don't want you to get sick, Atagi. You should go inside and change into dry clothes."

She frowns up at me, slapping my hand away before cocking out a hip. "I'm not that delicate, Sensei. I can handle a little rain. Besides, it's warm."

It is warm. Too warm. I think ... I think I'm flushed. Maybe I'm getting sick, though I've never had so much as a sniffle in all the time I've been here.

You know you're not sick.

I know, but I ignore the truth as I ask, "So, what? You want to just stand out here in the rain?"

Straightening, she grins. "No. Let's spar!"

Her words light me up, and I smile with a nod. "Okay."

Atagi runs her hands down her hair, squeezing out some of the water. When she leans over and to the side, twisting her hair, her wet shirt hangs heavily from her body. I get a flash of skin. Wet skin. It's definitely not some ailment making me hot. Atagi grips the hem of her shirt, and still bent over, wrings out the wet fabric. Her shirt pulls tight across her body, revealing every curve.

I blink at the tempting sight of her before turning away and striding towards my cave. "I'll go get Moon for you."

"Thanks!" She calls from behind me.

Images of Atagi parade through my thoughts, each one involving fewer clothes. But despite the desire coursing through me, I'm not sure what to do with my wayward feelings, if anything. I shouldn't complicate things. She has a life outside of this forest, apart from me. I can't forget that.

I grab Moon and stride back outside, but I nearly stumble as I fight to hold back a groan at the sight of a soaking wet Atagi. With a flex of my arm, I toss Moon, and Atagi catches it, swiftly tying it to her sash and taking a staggered stance.

I smile, a little steadier now that our swords are involved. Blowing rain from the tip of my nose, I ask, "Ready?"

She charges, going full out, just like when we race. That's who she is, and I lov—admire that about her.

Seriously? Did you almost just say you love he—

No.

43

MEIKO

The *scrape* and *clack* of my shogi piece echoes across the clearing. Sensei shakes his head with a smile, gently lifting his knight between his fingers, pretending to consider where to place it as he says, "You still slam your tiles, Atagi."

I grin with a shrug. "It's how I play."

My husband hated how I slammed my pieces down, never wanting to play with me. Neither of my sons enjoyed this game, so I've fallen back on old habits, never needing to create new ones—at least where this game is concerned.

I wince when Sensei wins, collecting the pieces to reset the board. The years of me not playing are showing. As Sensei moves his pawn, I find I don't care. It's nice just to have the freedom to sit here and play ... however I want to.

Sensei's knight has barely touched down before I reach for my piece, eager to make my next move. Gods! He doesn't see it yet. I might win this one! Adrenaline kicks through me as he sets down his next tile. I move mine, a smile threatening to pull at my lips, but I keep my cool. As he reaches for his next piece, my entire plan unravels. A frown spreads across my face, and my eyes dart over the board as I frantically search for a way out of the trap my teacher has obviously set for me.

Damn it!

He moves with intentional slowness, his piece hovering over the board on its way to victory. He's taunting me. Fuck. Come on. There must be a way to win. I shake my head, still looking at the pieces, looking for a way out.

The inevitable registers, and I groan, "No. No. No. No! I had you!"

He sets his piece down. "Checkmate. And no, you didn't. I had the win five moves ago."

My hands thread through my hair as I stare at the board. "What?" I chew on my lip, recalling my plays before dropping my arms and leaning back. "Damn it! I really thought I was going to win this time."

He chuckles as he resets the board again. I glare at him, shifting on my shins. I'm annoyed at how easily he beats me, at this and at swordplay, but still, I'm having fun for the first time in years.

He sets the last piece down, and I grab my pawn.

Scrape. Clack!

Sensei shakes his head again. I know I'm too aggressive, but I don't care, because he doesn't care. My teacher lets me be me. As we play another two rounds, Sensei winning both, I lament what could have been. It's a child's fantasy, because I know that even if he had somehow saved me that day over twenty years ago, my life would have probably turned out the same, or maybe even worse. I need to let this go. I didn't need rescuing from real life, I needed rescuing from the fantasy I'd built up in my head—the fantasy that I'd travel the country with Sensei at my side, taking contracts, fighting evil, saving villages ...

It was a beautiful dream, but a dream that I had to wake up from.

The cicadas sing to us as the warm breeze carries the scent of dust and pine, and I smother the anxiety that tries to take over, because every passing day, I find myself hoping for more ... more time ... more time with him.

But just in this past week, the whispers in town have started back up, the gossip holding hints of panic. There are no more smiling murmurs about the emperor's new baby. The other wives no longer hide the worry from their eyes as the threat of conflict looms. I'm running out of time, and I still haven't heard from Motosue's relative ... if I even found the right man. And I fear if I keep asking about Guardian, I'll bring trouble down on my family. Not a lot of people have heard of the legendary sword, but those who do react in one of two ways; with greed in their eyes, desperate to know what I know of the magic blade, or with fear, hissing warnings to forget I ever heard the name Guardian.

It's so frustrating, because I'm getting nowhere. And we're running out of time.

My teacher scoops up the tiles after our final game, dropping them in the worn sack. They click and clatter against each other, reminding me of the sound of fat rain-drops on the tiled roof of my home back in town.

Home.

What will I do if I can't free Sensei from this place? I've tried sending letters to my brother-in-law, but I have yet to receive a response. My mother-in-law just tsks at me, telling me I shouldn't concern myself with such things, that my anxiety will give me wrinkles. She's always waving her spotted hand, the fingers bent with age as she says her son will come home soon and everything will be alright.

But I can't just sit and wait, because what if ...

As Sensei wipes down the shogi board, I stand and head towards my mare. He calls after me, "Are you leaving?"

I don't turn, warring with the emotions that beg me to stay, and not just for another hour, or for another day. How easy would it be to just leave all my worries behind and stay here with Sensei?

I shake my head, bending down to grab the thick loops of the large bundle that I brought with me this morning. I'm surprised Sensei hasn't asked about it, but then again, he's rarely ever been one to pry.

With a little huff, I swing the bundle over my back. Sensei presses his palm into the ground, shifting as if he's going to stand, and asks, "Can I help you?"

Again, I shake my head. I stop next to him and drop my shoulder, letting the bundle flop to the ground. Without saying a word, I stride into his kitchen and pick up his kettle. The handle is worn from his fingers wrapping around it over and over. I imagine I can feel the warmth of his skin in the metal. Scooping some water from the reservoir into the kettle, I wonder if my teacher has opened the sack yet. Probably not.

I smile, shaking my head. He's too polite.

Pausing, a little frown pulls at my lips. Who taught him those manners? Who helped shape him into the man he is? I chew on my lip, realizing again just how very little I know about him.

Stepping to the doorway, I lean my shoulder against the frame. Sure enough, the sack sits right where I dropped it, untouched. I raise my chin at it with a smile. "Open it. It's for you."

"Atagi, you don't have to bring me things. I'm fine."

I wave my free hand as I turn back into the kitchen, calling over my shoulder, "I know. Just open it, Sensei."

The water quickly comes to a boil, and I carefully measure out a bit of matcha into each of our cups. Even though I brought more from home to replenish his dwindling supply, I'm still cautious with how much of the deep green powder I scoop out, knowing my teacher is precious with all his possessions.

I say I know him, but do I? Who is he really?

For a moment, I let my finger trace the delicate edge of my ceramic cup, the chip catching against my skin. He kept it. Tears blur my vision, and for just a moment, I let myself mourn the girl I used to be, so happy, so carefree, determined to become the best swordsman no matter what.

Blinking away my tears, I pour a little hot water into each cup, finding a small bamboo chasen to whisk the tea into a rich froth before filling them the rest of the way. The cups are hot in my hands, but I'm used to it. Once again, I pause in the doorway to watch as Sensei stares at the contents of the bundle I brought him. His eyes are wide, his fingers flexing against where they're pressed to his thighs. I step out into the clearing, setting his cup on the ground next to him, then I sit across from him on the small mat, holding my steaming cup in both hands.

Sensei looks over the items I brought ... Robes. Pants. Kimonos. Linen shirts. Socks. Even a thick futon blanket. I try to see the pile of fabrics through his eyes, trying to understand the awe I see in his gaze. But all I see is my son's shirt, wondering if it still smells like him. I see my husband's favorite winter blanket, the one he'd wrap around us, nuzzling into my neck. I see his socks, the ones I've washed so many times, not trusting our servant to do it exactly the way my husband prefers. Or preferred.

I frown at the black and yellow kimono, the one my husband wore to our bed when I was barely healed from birthing our first son. The one that lay on the floor by my head as he took me roughly, telling me to give him another son.

And I did. I did my duty. I created a home, and I won't lose it.

Sensei sweeps a hand at all the beautiful fabrics. "What is all this?"

I raise a brow, my lips lifting in a smile as steam swirls around my face. "Clothes."

He frowns. "Yes. I see that, Atagi. How much did this cost?"

Shaking my head, I bring my cup to my lips, taking a cautious sip of the rich, earthy tea before saying. "Nothing. They were ... some are Sen's. Most were my husband's."

My teacher tries and fails to keep the scowl from his face, and something in me warms at the fact that he still doesn't like my husband. He wasn't a gentle man or even kind. But he learned to love me in his way.

I nod at the pile of clothes and blankets. "Just take them, Sensei. I could try to sell them, but it would be more trouble than it's worth."

"Atagi." Slowly, I look up, wary of his tone. "Were you happy? Are you happy?"

Happy? I take a moment to think about his question before letting my sad smile slide into place. "Now ...? I don't know if I can call it happiness, but I'm proud of my life." I chew my lip, considering before saying, "As for the past twenty years? There were ... moments. Yes. Moments where I was truly happy."

My gaze goes distant with my memories as I lose myself in those moments ... The first time my husband kissed me with love in his eyes. The first time I held each of my sons. The first time I worked up the courage to swipe one of my husband's swords and steal away to the garden to practice—and every time after that, dancing with a katana in my hand with the night sky above. The few times Isayo came to visit, our soft laughter filling my house. The first time my mother-in-law smiled at me as she held my first-born son. The many times my sons made me laugh with their antics. Hearing their loud giggles from the next room as they played together. Being there with my husband's sister as my nieces and nephews were born. Making cautious friendships with a few of the other wives in town. The time my husband held me in our garden, the scent of my prized flowers heavy in the air as he whispered that he loved me. Even though those tender moments were few between us, I treasure them and the happiness they brought me.

Focusing back on my teacher, I notice his hands clenched once more, and he says, "Atagi, I—"

I hold up a hand, stalling his words. "Sensei, I am okay."

He looks at me as if he can see to my soul, and after a moment he says, "What about the trouble back home? The reason you came back?"

Anxiety spears through me ... there's been no official news from the north, and my brother-in-law would send word if the threat was imminent, right?

I wave off Sensei's words. "Please don't worry about it. I fear I might have been overdramatic." He doesn't believe me, I can see it in his eyes, so I laugh. "I know, *me*, being overdramatic. Can you imagine?"

He chuckles, and some of my tension unwinds. We fall into companionable silence, sipping our tea, ignoring the bundle of my dead husband and son's clothes on the ground. By the time I take the last sip of my matcha, it's almost cold, but the slight sweet flavor is still like silk on my tongue.

Without thinking about it, I stand, sliding my long strip of fabric around my neck, tying back the sleeves of my kimono. Taking my ceramic cup in my right hand, I hold out my left to take Sensei's. He gives it to me, and I go into the kitchen, cleaning up, my years of running my house kicking in. I smile as I gently wipe down the cups. Even to this day, there are things I don't let our servants do, and washing the dishes and cups is one of them. I like doing it. There's something about the *splunk* of water, the *swish* of the cloth over the ceramic, the *squeak* of a clean cup ... it's soothing.

As I step back outside, I grin as I watch my teacher pick up and set aside each piece of clothing. He inspects the seams, fingers the fine fabrics, even lifts the blanket to his face, taking a small inhale. Is he trying to smell me on the fabric? Or is he checking for a man's scent, wondering if my husband's smell still lingers. Does it? I couldn't smell him on the fabric when I wrapped it up, but maybe that's because I was too used to his scent.

My gaze lands on the shiny black lacquer of Guardian, and my bottom lip slides between my teeth. That blade wielded by that man. We could stand against any threat.

Before he notices me staring at his saya, I ask him, "Run through some forms with me before I go?"

He stands, gripping Guardian. "As you wish, Atagi."

44

Another week has flown by, and every day we practice. It reminds me of my time with my father, and I'm filled with gratitude that I can cross swords with such a worthy opponent as Atagi.

She grunts with her attack, and I ignore the unnecessary warning sting of my magic as I counter. We dance and spin as we spar. I'm letting her lead, assessing how she moves from one form to another, how she adjusts when I block her. She's still not great at anticipating me when I change mid-form, but she's keeping up. She's good. And I'm proud of her.

All these years, she could have given it up. It would have been the easier path. But she found a way. She found the time and kept practicing. She tried to keep learning wherever and however she could. Atagi loves swordplay, and I'm so impressed that she never gave up on her passion.

Using the edge of my scabbard, I slap her next swing aside, and she grits her teeth in frustration. My magic singes down my left side, and I ignore it. As I execute an arch aimed for her right shoulder, I say, "You're projecting your next move with your feet."

She huffs, taking three quick steps back to avoid my swift thrust. "Well, I have to move my feet, Sensei!"

I chuckle, stepping to my left so she has to follow. "Yes, but you're moving before you're ready. Concentrate on what you're doing, not what you're going to do. What if I do this ..." I lunge and duck to the right, sweeping across her path, keeping her from moving into the overhead strike of the yohomme. The edge of my saya slices over the backs of her legs with a quick swipe, then I jab the point of my scabbard into the center of her back. "And, you're dead."

She drops her head, breathing fast. Atagi slides her blade into its sheath secured on her sash. "I'm never going to be good enough to beat you, am I?"

I pat her head. "No. Probably not."

She smacks my hand away, turning to face me. I laugh at the anger on her face, holding up my hands in peace. "But I never expected you to beat me, Atagi." The red flush of anger still stains her cheeks, so I say, "Remember when you first begged me to teach you?"

Her eyes soften slightly with a smirk. "I didn't beg. I persistently asked."

I chuckle. "You begged. You told me you needed the best. Do you still think I'm the best?"

She nods. "You know you are. I just believed that once I beat you, that's when I'd know."

"You want to be the best, and that means beating the best."

She nods again. I grip my saya in the center, the smooth lacquer warm against the skin of my palm. I can't help but worry about her and what might be going on at her home. She hasn't brought it up again after brushing off my concerns, but what if she's trying to protect my feelings? Atagi knows I can't leave this place, that I can't help her with whatever threat drove her to me a few months ago.

She stares at where my fingers wrap confidently around the black lacquer of my scabbard as I say, "Atagi. I've never lost. I've fought some of the best swordsmen and have *always* come out the winner. I am the best."

She smirks, shaking her head, but when she sees the serious glint in my eyes, she sobers, and I say, "I know you told me not to worry, and I trust you. But that doesn't stop me from wishing I could help"—I nod beyond her—"out there." When I meet her gaze again, I take a step towards her, hoping to show her my sincerity. "'But do you know what helps me sleep at night? What keeps me from scraping my fingers to the bone to try and get out of here to help you even though I know escape is impossible?"

Her eyes are wide as she shakes her head.

"Because I am the best, and I taught you. You are good. You are very good, Atagi. I pray you never need it, but I trust your skill with a blade. You need to trust yourself."

She remains silent, hopefully fully absorbing my words, but after a few moments I grin, digging my hand into my pocket as I say, "Also, don't think I forgot what today is." She snaps her attention to my face, her dark eyes blinking in confusion. I gently wrap my fingers around the tiny wood carving, drawing the necklace out of my pocket. I hold it up by the string, the delicate sword swinging between us. "Happy birthday, Atagi."

Her eyes go wider, skipping between the necklace and my face. Still holding my arm out, I wait for her to take it. Her long, delicate fingers close around the carved katana, and I let the string slide out of my hand. She ducks her head, looping it over her neck before holding the wood piece in front of her face.

She whispers, "It looks like Moon."

I smile. "It is."

She runs her fingers over the curve of the sword, staring at it for a long moment before lifting her gaze to me. "I ... You remembered my birthday? After all this time?"

Always.

I turn around, sticking a torch in the firepit, waiting for it to light before striding towards my cave. "Follow me."

Her soft footsteps trail behind me. We walk down the main tunnel, past the decades of slash marks, past the wall of katanas, and past even more slash marks. I stop, pressing my fingers to the characters of Atagi's name. I hold the torch up so she can see where I marked her birth date. "This was your thirteenth birthday." I keep walking before turning down a side chamber and pointing to another mark with her name. "That was your fourteenth birthday."

She remains silent as I lead her on. Deeper and deeper, and I catch her noticing where her name appears on the wall every so often, her eyes growing wider. We reach the end of the marks with today's slash and Atagi's name. "And here's today." I turn to face her. "So, yes, Atagi. I remembered."

She holds my gaze as she tucks the necklace into her undershirt, tightening her kimono over it. I'm not sure if it's the light of the torch that's making her eyes shimmer, or maybe it's some emotion brought about by my revelation. Or does she pity me, her crazy Sensei living in a cave, marking the days and keeping track of her birthdays?

Atagi reaches out, placing her small hand on my forearm. Her skin is warm. Her touch is light, but there are definitely tears in her eyes. "How long have you been here?"

I sigh. "A long time. That doesn't matter."

She blinks, and a single tear spills down her cheek. I dare to reach out, and my fingertip brushes her face, wiping away her tear as if I can wipe away all her sorrows. "It's your birthday. Please don't be sad."

She smiles up at me, saying, "Thank you, Sensei." Her hand presses over her shirt, over where the wood charm rests between her breasts. "I love it."

I drop my hand from her face, and without another word, she turns and strides back the way we came. Fiery sunlight highlights Atagi as she exits the cave, and I follow, raising my hand against the sharp light of the setting sun. I shove the end of the burning torch into the dirt, smothering the flames before tossing it aside to use later when needed. Atagi pats her mare, and without turning, says, "It's getting late. I should go."

I stand still, arms at my sides, my saya heavy on my hip. She climbs onto her horse, pulling the reins to face me. She smiles, but it doesn't quite reach her eyes as she says, "Thank you for the lesson, Sensei. And thank you again for the gift."

Atagi kicks her mare into a walk, leaving the clearing. Leaving me alone once more.

But I think she's lonely too ... Atagi lives in the house where her husband and son died. She has to face their ghosts every day. She feels her mother's absence. She misses her friend, Isayo. She has to endure with their memories in her heart.

Our lives have been so different, but we are both lonely.

45

"Ugh, this damn dress!" Atagi lowers her blade and grips her sash with her free hand. With a quick swish, she undoes the tie and shrugs out of her kimono, leaving her in only a sleeveless linen shirt and cropped pants. Even with the bite of the quickly approaching winter in the air, sweat darkens the underarms and neckline of her shirt. The string of the necklace I gave her disappears under her collar.

It's been two months since her birthday and she's still wearing it.

Little flutters kick in my belly, and I'm suddenly too warm, but I shake off the inappropriate sensation, focusing on my student. "You were moving fine, Atagi. Don't use your clothes as an excuse."

She's breathing hard, and as she grips her hilt with both hands, my gaze lands on her chest, noticing how her breasts push together under her shirt. I snap my eyes back to her face, mentally slapping myself, wondering if she noticed the heat flooding my cheeks.

Focus!

I'm trying.

Atagi's movements are more aggressive today, not quite desperate, but heading in that direction. She pushes her attack, never letting up, moving swiftly from one form to another. She's glorious. Arms flexing with each strike. Strong legs lunging with ease. Her long, braided hair whips behind her, and the fierce look on her face takes my breath away.

Atagi is beautiful.

Watch it!

I arch, leaning back, Atagi's blade whispering past my neck. I twist painfully to get out from under her slash, but I manage to evade and come back with an attack of my own.

You need to pay attention. Seems she's out for blood today.

I chuckle at my saya as I press Atagi into a retreat. She side-steps, and I leave my right side open, just to see what she'll do. She doesn't notice because she's become over-confident.

Ha. She's going to spin.

Sure enough, Atagi twirls unnecessarily. With a roll of my eyes, I poke her arm as she comes around, and in the next moment, my saya presses to her neck. She eyes Guardian before flashing her gaze to my face, her expression spitting fire at me as she draws up her forearm, smashing her blade against my scabbard, knocking it away from her neck. I simply shift and jab the point into her ribs. Again, she knocks it away.

She's going to back up to try to press her own attack.

I stay close, slicing the edge of my saya across her upper thigh.

Here comes her upward cross-slash.

I block it, then tap her other arm.

Haha. She's going to punch you.

No, she wouldn't ...

My magic stings across my left cheek, and sure enough, Atagi grips Moon in her left hand, balls up her right fist and swings. I raise my palm, catching her punch. She pulls, trying to yank free, but I hold tight. Her struggles tug her closer, bringing along the scent of sweat and jasmine.

How does she smell so good after hours of sparring?

I shake my head, and a few strands of damp hair escape my tie, falling around my face. I blow them back as I grip Atagi's fist a little harder. "Hey. Stop. What's going on?"

Her gaze lands and stays on my chest, like she's trying to count the individual threads of my shirt. I look down at the top of her head, her black hair shining in the sun. I drop her fist, bringing my palm to the top of her head. "Atagi, talk to me."

She stiffens, and I drop my hand. She licks her lips, backing up, keeping her eyes on the ground. "Nothing. It's nothing. I just ..." She smiles, chuckling to the ground. "It doesn't matter."

I'm right back in front of her before I realize I've moved. My palm cups her cheek, raising her gaze to meet mine. "Atagi. Don't do that. It matters. *You* matter."

Our eyes stay locked. The sounds of the forest fade. There is nothing but Atagi's soft cheek under my palm and the pinks of the sky reflecting in her dark eyes. And I realize ... it's true. Above all else, Atagi matters.

Oh, you fool.

I know.

My eyes search hers while they rover over mine. We're so close. Her skin is warm under my palm. My gaze lowers to her lips, my mouth watering with the sudden desire to taste her, to run my thumb over her bottom lip, to collar her throat with my hand and hold her gaze to mine as I kiss her slowly and thoroughly.

She steps back, breaking the connection, and my hand falls to my side as she says, "I should go."

No.

"Okay."

She walks over to where she threw off her kimono, and when she bends down to pick it up, I swallow at the sight of her ass in her thin pants. Slipping her arms through the wide sleeves of her dress, she snugs the fabric around her before pulling her sash tight. She stands a little taller, her smile in place like it's what's expected of her. Her stunted steps fall lightly as she approaches her horse, her hands tucked into her sleeves. With each step, it seems as if she's slipping on a mask, becoming the woman she is at home. A different woman than she is with me.

What if the woman she is when she's at home is the real her, and this version of herself is something she's presenting to me ... a version she thinks I want ... At the very least, I know she's holding back pieces of herself. She's not telling me something. I see it in the way she chews her lip when she thinks I'm not watching. I see it in the side glances she doesn't think I notice. I feel it in my magic.

But I'm hiding plenty from her too.

I watch her as if seeing her for the first time. She's graceful, but ridged, like she might crack if pushed too hard. Atagi looks like something pretty you'd look at, knowing you're not allowed to touch.

You're objectifying her.

My saya is right, and I want to scrub those thoughts from my mind. Atagi deserves better, especially from me. I walk over to where she's slipping the bridle over her horse's head, and with my hand under her foot, I help her into the saddle.

She nods in thanks, and because I can't think of anything clever to say, I simply say, "Be safe on your way home."

Her smile is kind, her eyes soft as she places her palm over mine where it rests on her horse's neck. "Thank you, Sensei." Her thumb brushes over the back of my hand. "I'll see you tomorrow."

I want to linger under her touch. Not only am I eager for tomorrow to arrive so I can see her again, but I'm on the verge of begging her to stay. For so many reasons. She hasn't brought up the danger that initially drove her here, but still, I worry. I could keep her safe if she were here. But, I know Atagi has responsibilities at home. Responsibilities she is neglecting to spend time with me. I shouldn't want her to stay, to abandon her home and all she's built there. I shouldn't be this selfish. I should want her to live her life. She may be in her thirties, but despite her age, it's hard to imagine someone not wanting her as his wife. She's beautiful. And strong. And funny. And smart. And beautiful.

You said that already.

I slide my hand out from under hers, and I catch the small frown she tries to hide behind an impassive smile. She nods down at me, clicking to her mare, and off they go. I stare at the spot between the two trees where she left. I need to stop. I need to banish these feelings. For her sake, I can't want her like this.

Why not? Moments of happiness, remember?

I recall what Atagi told me of her life, and I realize that as different as the last twenty-two years have been for us, we share in this ... moments of happiness scattered throughout our time apart. Like crumbs, we've gathered those moments and stored them somewhere safe where we can remember and smile, if just for a little while.

I shake my head. "I can't. Not her. She deserves better than me."

She'd be safe and loved. And who says she wouldn't find happiness with you too?

I laugh, the sound cruel as I spread my arms and turn in a slow circle. "Happiness? Here? In this place? With me? In a cave in the middle of a cursed forest?" I drop my arms, hanging my head. "No. I can't do that to her. I'll simply put all this out of my mind. It will be fine. I'll shove these feelings deep down, and tomorrow everything will be back to as it was."

Yeah? And how are you going to achieve that?

I flop to the ground, laying back and pillowing my head in my hands. The first few stars wink weakly in the dark blue sky, an orange haze holding onto the horizon. The image of Atagi pops into my mind, her shirt damp with sweat, the outline of the wood necklace visible through the fabric, her breasts ...

Screwing my eyes closed, I grip my hair, pulling hard. "I'm her sensei. I'm her sensei. I'm her sensei." I let go of my hair, but the burn remains, stinging my scalp. Placing one palm to my stomach, I rest the other on my chest. I breathe. I count my inhales and exhales, concentrating on the sensation of my lungs filling and emptying, of my hands rising and falling.

Atagi's ass looked really good in those pants.

Damn it!

Breathe. In and out. In and out.

Her arms are quite toned, and they didn't tremble even a little after our sparring.

I shake my head and resettle, coming back to my breath.

Atagi's hair looked nice in that braid, but I like it better when it's loose, hanging down her back and over her shoulders.

I sigh, sitting up. Crickets chirp. The moon has yet to rise, so the stars shine that much brighter. I get up and stretch, my back popping. Then, with another sigh, I push off the balls of my feet into a jog. I follow one of the many well-worn paths through my territory, and when I reach the barrier, I turn. I run along the perimeter of my prison. One lap, then another. The air has cooled with the deepening of night, but my body is warm, sweat beading on my face. I pick up my pace and make another lap. Then another. I'm slowing down, but I don't stop. I suck in air through my burning lungs. My legs ache, but still I run.

You think you can outrun your desire for Atagi?

"I can try." My breath puffs out in a little white cloud before me, and I run through it, but my thoughts race faster. I will not ruin things with her. Not again. We're fine. We're good as we are. We're fine.

I just need to wear myself out so I can sleep.

You know what else helps you sleep? An orgasm. It wouldn't take much. Just think about how great Atagi's ass looked in your pants and how much better she'd look without them—

I run faster, my heart racing, determined to keep going until I collapse, until I'm too tired to act on my raging desires.

46

"I am your sensei, and you will do as you're told."

Atagi laughs at my barked command, placing her free hand on her hip, gently gripping Moon in her other hand at her side. "Really? You're going to pull that shit on me now?"

I scowl at her, doing my best to ignore how cute she looks with her hip kicked out like that. "Your endurance is still trash. Ten laps, Atagi."

She raises a brow. "And if I say no?"

I swallow at the challenge in her voice, resisting the urge to make her do as I say with teasing words and edging touches. Instead, I cross my arms, wiping those thoughts away. "Twelve laps, Atagi." Her eyes narrow, but she doesn't move. "Thirteen."

We stare at each other for another long moment. I'm about to up her owed laps to fifteen, but she shifts, and I know I've won. Rebalancing her weight to both feet, she says, "Okay, okay. Fine!"

When she goes to put Moon down, I shake my head. "Take Moon with you."

She glares at me from where she's leaning over, her katana a few inches from the ground. Fuck. I can't handle her bent over like that. Clearing my throat, I turn and walk towards my kitchen, waving my hand over my shoulder. "Get going. And no cutting corners or I'll make you start over."

She grumbles something under her breath, but a second later, her jogging footsteps head in the opposite direction and quickly fade. My magic tracks her, scraping across my skin, keeping me aware of where she is at all times.

You know what this means, why your magic is reacting to her like this ... Why are you ignoring the fact that she's keeping something from you?

I shake my head, whispering, "She'll tell me when she's ready."

Will she? You. Don't. Know. Her.

"Please, just ..."

Fine, live in your delusion. I'll rub it in your face later.

My attention focuses on the small ceramic cup with the chip. I recall the shape of her lips as they pressed to the rim. Of how her throat bobbed with each delicate swallow. Of how her skin glowed as the steam of her tea floated around her face ...

"One!" Atagi's shout comes from outside, and her thudding footsteps fade again as she makes her second lap. I drop my head and swear, adjusting myself. I know better than to hope for these things with her. I know better than to hope for anything at all.

Striding outside, I kneel, poking at the flames in the firepit before throwing on another two logs. The burnt ones split and crackle, sparks erupting in a quick blaze before it settles. I watch the flames dance. The rhythmic pounding of

Atagi's feet draws closer, completing another lap around the clearing as she glares at me and shouts, "Two!"

I smile and wave as she runs off. She mumbles a few curses at me, and I laugh at her retreating back. By the sixth lap, Atagi is slowing down. By the eighth, her breaths are puffing out so hard, I can hear them from all the way across the clearing. She trudges past me, her shout more of a wheeze this time. "Nine!"

I get up and jog to her side. "Come on. You're nearly done. Don't give up now."

She sucks in a few deep breaths. Her face is red and sweat drips down her neck, her damp hair clinging to her skin. The cord on Moon's hilt clinks against her saya as her feet fall heavily with each stride. "R-r-running is t-the worst."

I laugh, patting the top of her head. "I know."

She swats my hand away with a growl and picks up her pace. I shake my head, knowing my student, and sure enough, not even five paces later, she slows back down. I stay even with her in silent encouragement as we complete another lap, then another. By the time we're finishing her final lap, I think she might pass out. She staggers, gasping, "Thirteen!" And with that, she tumbles to the ground and rolls onto her back, sucking down deep breaths, Moon hugged to her chest.

I chuckle as I sit next to her. "You really are bad at running."

She flops her arms wide, letting her katana slip from her grip. "Tell me something I don't know."

I let loose a full belly laugh, but when she turns her head to glare at me, I hold up a placating hand. "It's because you're bad at it, that's why you need to do it."

She rolls her eyes, turning her gaze back to the sky. "I know."

A comfortable silence wraps around us as Atagi slowly brings her breathing back under control. With her arms still spread wide in the dirt, she closes her eyes, and I allow myself one minute. One minute to look at her. To wish. To dream.

And then I nudge her leg. She cracks open an eye, and I say, "Get up. Let's walk a lap. If you stay like that for much longer, you're going to cramp." She groans, but I take her hand and stand, pulling her up with me. My gaze drops to her mouth. Her pink lips part, much too inviting. I drop her hand and back up. Atagi takes a deep, full breath, and together, we start walking.

Half a lap in, keeping my gaze forward, I ask, "Does your family not ask where you go every day?"

A soft smirk lifts her lips, and she says, "My late husband's sister just had her baby and is so distracted with the newborn and all her other children, I don't think she knows what day it is most of the time. And her husband is still away in the north with my brother-in-law. And my mother-in-law ... she's so old. None of us know how old she is exactly, but there are entire days when she doesn't know who she is, and most days she has no recollection of who I am. Her servant takes good care of her, when my mother-in-law lets her. She was never easy to be around, but now with her confused mind and her ailing body ... I don't envy her servant."

Atagi takes a deep breath, smiling with her exhale. "So, for the first time since I was a child, I have relative freedom to do what I want." She starts walking again, but her hands curl into fists before releasing. "But that freedom has a time limit."

"What do you mean?"

"A letter arrived ... My brother-in-law comes back in four months. I was still in my mourning period when he left. But, when he returns, he means to ask me to marry him." Atagi stops and looks up at me, her eyes clear and determined. "So, we have four months, Sensei." She steps closer, her fingers gripping my hand, lifting my arm. Wrapping her other hand around mine, she holds me tightly as she stares into my eyes. "Four months until this ends ... again." Her words speed up, but time seems to slow down around me, and I struggle to take in what she's saying. "... once we're married, he will waste no time in trying to get me pregnant. I'm not a young girl anymore, and if he's going to get a son or two out of me, he'll need to do so quickly. And if ..."

Her words fade as the forest starts to go black around me.

Four months. Atagi is going to be taken from me again, in four months.

No. No. Please. This is too soon. I need more time.

The warmth of her hands drops away, and my arm falls limply back to my side. I'm not sure what else she said, but she seems to be done talking now as she frowns at my saya before walking away and striding into the clearing.

Jogging after Atagi, I help her up on her horse and watch with rapturous attention as she tucks her hair behind her ear. She is ... oh gods ... I think ....

I stare up at her, my chest aching with how full it is, but it's a good ache somehow. Like I'm filled with ... love. For her. Is *this* what love feels like? If so, it's both the most wonderful thing I've ever felt, and the most terrifying.

With a smile that she seems to force into her eyes, she says, "I'll see you tomorrow, Sensei."

47

I blink, and a month has gone by. Atagi has come every day, sometimes all day, sometimes only for an hour or two. I cherish each moment, but they seem to pass quicker and quicker. The weather is turning cold, stealing minutes then hours of daylight from the day.

I pause, lowering my saya as Atagi misses another opening I've given her. She steps back, lowering her own katana, brushing back her hair with her free hand. I watch her fingers thread through the glossy black strands. My saya creeks under my grip, and I realize I've clenched my hands with the desire to run them through her hair like that.

You are hopeless.

I know.

Atagi angles her head up towards the weak sunlight doing its best to banish at least some of the cold clinging to the air. There are shadows under her eyes.

Before you open your mouth, no woman wants to hear that she looks tired, so find something else to say, you idiot.

"Let's take a break."

She shakes her head, staggering her feet, gripping her hilt at her side. "No. No. I'm good. Let's keep going."

I nod, positioning my scabbard, setting up for the simple nana-homme. I watch her movements and intentionally slow down, but even then, her block glances off my saya instead of the forceful shove it should have been. Atagi stumbles through her next step and stops.

With a sigh, she sheathes Moon and bows to me. "I'm sorry, Sensei. I haven't brought you my best today."

Taking a step forward, I reach out, ready to pat her head teasingly, but I pause. I don't think she's in the mood for my teasing. I drop my hand, my fingers tingling with the missed opportunity to touch her soft hair. But then I notice her blinks are slowing, like she's about to fall asleep on her feet. Adrenaline tingles through me as I press my palm to her back. Why is she so tired? I gently direct her towards the crackling fire within the circle of stones to our left.

She shakes her head. "I should go." But she sits, tucking her legs to the side and folding her hands in her lap. Atagi's eyes gloss over as she stares at the dancing flames. I grab the fur-lined coat she wore here today, and I crouch to drape it over her shoulders. My hands linger for a moment, and I give her a little squeeze, indulging in this small contact with her.

From my position behind her, I see her cheek lift with a smile, but it seems distant as she sways slightly. I'm about to let my palms slip from her shoulders when she reaches across her body and places her hand over mine and says, "Thank you. I ... haven't slept well the past few nights. I ..."

I wait for her to continue, remaining still, crouched behind her. Atagi's thumb moves, whispering back and forth over the back of my hand sending shivers over my entire body. My focus narrows to the motion of her finger grazing across my skin.

Fuck. I want more. So much more. But I know better.

Still, it's getting harder to keep my breath steady, and every brush of her thumb tightens my insides, pooling desire between my thighs. My hand on her other shoulder slides down, wisping over the thick fabric of her coat, cupping her outer arm, then her elbow. My fingers begin to lightly trace over her sleeve, moving back and forth across her forearm.

She releases a little hum that nearly topples me to my ass, but then, Atagi starts to lean back. She doesn't fall or collapse, it's more like she's surrendering into me. Her back connects with my chest. The weight of her head leaning against the front of my shoulder is perfect, like she belongs, like she fits.

I focus on Atagi, holding her, barely daring to breathe, and then her hand slips off mine, flopping to her lap. Lightly gripping her arms to keep her steady, I angle my head to look at her face. Her eyes are closed, and her lips are parted with her steady breaths.

She's asleep. In my arms. Gods, the feel of her ...

But why is she so exhausted? Is she sick?

Slowly and carefully, I shift so I'm sitting, pulling Atagi fully into my lap. She doesn't even stir. I look down at her, studying her face. I press the back of my hand to her cheek, then her forehead. She's not overly hot. The faintest of lines edge her eyes. Her long lashes press into the shadows under her eyes, making her look tired even in sleep. She has changed so much. There are still pieces of her I recognize from when she was little, but I know there's so much of who she is now that she's holding back from me ... and me from her.

I'm painfully aware of how small she is with her body curled into mine. I tuck her coat tighter around her, and her brows furrow as she burrows closer and mumbles unintelligibly. I hold my breath for a few long seconds, but she doesn't wake.

Bending over her, I whisper, "Just for a moment ... I'm going to be selfish for one moment."

The smooth skin of her cheek is like silk under my fingertips. I trail my touch up her face, around her eyes, smoothing over her forehead. She sleeps on. I comb my fingers through her hair, tucking it behind her ear. Like a whispered prayer, I place a single, barely-there kiss to her temple before forcing myself to stop. With every ounce of willpower I have, I gently scoot out from under Atagi. I grab my heavy robe—one of Sen's—that I took off once we started our lesson. Balling up the material, I set it under her head, adjusting her coat to cover her better.

The fire could use a few more logs.

I shift to a crouch, and her hand curls around the fabric of my pants, grazing my ankle. Her eyes remain closed, and her voice is far away and drowsy as she says, "Don't go."

Staring down at her, I freeze. My heart thuds painfully against my ribs. What if she's dreaming and she thinks I'm her husband? Is it him she's asking to stay? Does she miss him?

They were married for twenty years. Of course she misses him.

I bury my heartache, letting it simmer with my loneliness and all my dead wants and desires. I carefully uncurl her fingers from my pant leg before patting her shoulder and standing. She curls into herself, the flames heating her face, bringing a pretty flush to her cheeks. And I allow myself to say her name ...

"I'm right here, Meiko."

48

MEIKO

The cloying scent of incense burns the inside of my nose. I hate this smell. It reminds me of when my husband was on his deathbed. It reminds me of those last days with my son, Sen. Of his wet coughs. Of his labored breathing. Of his pale skin and the shadows under his eyes. Of Harada trying to hide his tears from me, trying to be strong for me, his mother. Of the servants casting pitying glances my way. Of the shroud pulled over Sen's face.

It's the smell of death.

The room is so dark, I stare and wait for my eyes to adjust before I'm able to make out the sleeping form of my mother-in-law. Her servant sits so still at her side, I mistake her for a piece of furniture before she meets my gaze and nods, her lips pressed tightly, neither of us saying anything because we both know.

Time's up.

As I turn to leave my mother-in-law's room, my gaze snags on the two scrolls sitting partially unfurled on the low table—one that sent my mother-in-law into this state, and the other that arrived a few hours ago and changed everything. I don't have to open either of them to know what they say. I've read them enough times to have the words etched into my memory. I haven't slept much since the first letter's arrival. In fact, I think the most rest I've gotten was that day I passed out in my teacher's arms, and that was two weeks ago.

I toss away the warm feelings trying to flood my heart as I recall how safe and warm I felt there with him.

Freezing wind whips at my hair as I step outside. The wood plank walkway to my quarters is slightly slick with the freezing rain, but my shuffling steps are quick. The quiet voices of my two oldest nieces' drifts to me on the wind, one consoling the other, sniffling interspersed between their words. Another servant approaches, a bucket of hot water hanging heavily in his grip as he heads towards my mother-in-law's rooms. He pauses before me, bowing, and I place a hand on his shoulder, asking, "Any new news?" He shakes his head, and I give him a comforting pat as he stands. "Once you're done here, go home. Get some rest."

He bows again. "Thank you, okugata-sama."

I tighten my fingers on his shoulder, leaning in to whisper, "If you have somewhere safe to go, get your family out. You will always have a place here ... if we are still here once the dust settles."

He blinks away the sheen in his eyes, shaking his head. "We won't leave. You have been kind to us, okugata-sama. I know we have no right to, but we think of you as family. My wife and I already discussed it. We're staying."

The water in the bucket sloshes as I lean in, pulling him

into a hug. His wife was with me during the birth of both my sons. She saved me from bleeding out with Harada. I've watched her own children grow, slipping them little sweets in the garden while their father tended the flowers and pruned the trees.

I pull away, holding his shoulders as I say, "You *are* family, and come what may, I'll do what I must to keep you all safe."

He sniffles, bowing again. "Thank you, okugata-sama. Thank you."

I smile, realizing it's a different one than I use with Sensei, but just because it's different doesn't mean there's no warmth to it. Because there is. I love my family.

I pat his shoulder. "Go on. I've kept you long enough."

With another quick bow, he rushes off, navigating the slippery planks with ease.

I'm about to move on but I stop, shivering as I stare at a bright temari ball sitting in the frozen grass to my right. My youngest nephew loves that little ball. He must have left it there after his play time this afternoon. The bright blue, yellow, and green pattern is glossy with the sheen of ice that's covering it. Memories of me throwing a similar ball at Sensei flits through my mind, and a sad smile passes over my face.

I need to go. Now. Hopefully the weather will hold off the approaching invaders, but there's not much time. This is it. I need to say goodbye.

Clenching my fists, I steel my heart, determination driving me forward.

Sensei and I are out of time.

49

Anger. Fear. Excitement. Relief. I'm experiencing them all at the same time, and it makes me dizzy as I sprint through the forest. My magic sparks and tingles, leading me to Atagi.

It's been two weeks since I've seen her. That day when she practically passed out from exhaustion, she slept for an hour but still seemed tired when she blinked open her eyes and quickly scrambled to her horse, saying she needed to get home.

I've missed seeing her every day, but I wasn't surprised when she didn't show up the next day, or the next. Freezing rain has moved in, coating everything in a shiny, crackling layer of ice. And today the weather has just gotten worse, but Atagi is here. What possessed her to come out in this weather? Is she in trouble?

Although I'm already running full-out, I find the strength to speed up. I sprint around a large tree, the branches cracking dangerously overhead with the added weight of the ice. My boots thud across the forest floor, the soles gripping even over the occasional slick spot. These were Atagi's husband's boots, and I hate that they fit so well, but I'm not about to endure frostbite out of spite. They are really nice boots.

There!

The dark shape of Atagi's horse comes into view. It's as if the ground underneath me gives way. I stumble but catch myself and keep running. Atagi's body is slumped over the neck of her horse, her wet hair hanging over her face so I can't tell if she's even conscious or not. I skid on the wet icy ground, nearly slamming into the horse's side as the mare comes to a stop.

The horse's hot breath snorts over my face as I pat her neck. "You're such a good girl. You found me. You did so well."

The mare huffs again, swishing her tail, and I reach for Atagi. As I wrap my hands around her waist, I notice her curled fingers frozen around the reins, and I pry them free. Her hooded gaze drifts towards me, her teeth chattering so loudly, I wonder how she hasn't chipped them. She slips into my arms, and I hold her close to my chest. She's so cold, even through my own layers of clothing and her thick coat.

Walking quickly back towards my cave, I click my tongue and the mare follows. I look down at Atagi's face, noticing the little crystals on her lashes and the tips of her hair.

"Fuck, Atagi. What the fuck are you doing? You could have died!"

"I-I-I n-n-n-needed to s-s-s—"

I shake my head. "Don't try to talk right now. I don't want your excuses anyway. This was stupid, Atagi." Her body trembles in my arms, and I soften my voice. "We need to get you warm. Fast."

Never has my prison felt so expansive. Why is it taking so long to get back to the cave?

"Ow, S-S-Sensei."

I look down with a frown, realizing I'm holding her too tight. I relax my grip just slightly, but bark out, "At least you still have feeling."

She doesn't answer, probably hearing the anger in my voice. I don't mean to be so harsh, but all my anxiety is pressing at me from the inside. If I don't get her warm and out of danger quickly, I'm going to explode. She can't die. I won't let her. It feels as if it's *my* heart that's frozen. It hurts. Why did she do this? She put her life in danger ... to come to *me*.

Fuck. Fuck me and the tiny emotion inside my chest that's happy she's here.

Fuck. Me.

I barely see the clearing around me as I carry Atagi into my caves. The loud echo of her horse's hooves startles the mare, and she stops, throwing her head, her reins jingling. I shift Atagi's weight to my left so I can wrap a hand around the lead. I give the mare a gentle tug. "Come on. The first chamber is big enough for you. It's too cold outside." The horse shifts back, resisting my pull, but after a moment, a freezing wind whips past us, encouraging the mare to step forward. I lead her into the large chamber, dropping the lead and pulling the bridle off. "I'll be back to make you more comfortable, but I have to save your stupid owner's life first."

"I-I-I heard t-t-t-that."

I wrap both arms back around her, jostling her slightly. "Good."

A chattering sigh puffs from Atagi's blue lips as I stride into my bedchamber, the heat of my blazing hearth hitting us like a wall. As I bend over to grab my futon, her hair falls over her shoulder, and the ends crunch with the ice clinging to the black strands.

I sit her down and start to wrap the futon around her, but realize her coat is soaked. She trembles and shivers as I work her arms out of the sleeves, throwing the garment to the side. I run my hands over her shoulders and swear. Her kimono is wet too.

My fingers fumble at her sash as I say, "Atagi, I have to get these wet clothes off you, okay?" She nods, but her head falls forward and her eyes close. I grip her shoulders, shaking her until her eyes slowly blink back open. "Stay awake!"

Some color seeps into her lips, the blue tint fading. I shove her dress down her arms, yanking it out from where she's sitting on it. I throw it to the side where it lands in a heap on top of her coat. Patting her down, I groan at the damp fabric of the long sleeves of her tunic. Quickly untying the string, I work the shirt off her trembling body, doing my best to keep my eyes averted as my fingers skim over the bare, frozen skin of her arms and sides, pulling my futon around her.

When I touch the fabric of her wool pants, I swear again. Drenched. The gods are testing me.

As I yank off her boots and soaked socks before peeling her pants down her legs, I fight my inner battles. She's in danger of hypothermia. My stomach coils in knots with worry for her, but at the same time, my cock twitches at the sight of her bare legs.

I crawl over to my small pile of folded clothes, digging through them, uncaring of the mess I'm making. I grab a pair of socks and slide them on her feet. They are way too big, but at least they'll warm her toes. I sit behind her, wrapping the futon all the way around her. As I rub her shoulders over the blanket, her head lolls from side to side. I rub down her arms, leaning over to whisper in her ear. "Don't go to sleep."

"Okay."

Atagi turns her head to look at me. Our eyes meet. She licks her lips, thankfully now a little less blue. When I look back up from her lips, she's staring at my mouth. Slowly, her eyes crawl up my face until she's holding my gaze once more.

The moment stretches, and all I see is her.

I'm too hot. Our faces are so close, but ... Just a little closer. I lean in and her lips part. Her eyes drop back to my mouth, and fuck me if she doesn't lick her lips again and release a heavy breath. Just a fraction of space. All I'd have to do is ... I realize I can feel the chill coming off her lips without us even touching.

A violent shiver shakes her body from head to toe, breaking the spell. Fuck. I need to get her warmed up. I sit back and adjust my aching cock before I wrap my arms around her from behind, hugging the futon tight to her shaking body. I scoot us closer to the hearth until the edge of the blanket is nearly in the fire. I tuck it under her socked feet before laying us down, letting the heat of my body warm her from behind and the fireplace heat her from the front.

I'm somehow sweating and shivering at the same time. My hair is wet and my outer robe, while not completely soaked through, is damp. But despite the chill, I'm hot. Not only is the room very warm, but just the thought of kissing her ... my blood is racing, and I'm not sure that Atagi can't feel my beating heart even through my clothes and the blankets.

Reaching over my head, I grab one of my shirts and rub it over her head. She's still trembling, and as I squeeze the freezing water from her hair, I say, "Do your best to relax. Use the breathing technique I taught you." She tries to take a deep inhale, but coughs. I pat her back through the futon before setting my damp shirt to the side. "It's okay, Atagi. I've got you. You're okay. You're okay."

I'm saying the words more for myself than to her, but some of the coiled tension drains from her shivering limbs. I comb my fingers through her hair, working out some of the knots, then I wrap my arm around her, hugging her tighter to my body. I curl my left arm under her head, letting her use my bicep as a pillow. She snuggles back into me, and though she's still shivering, it's not as violent as before.

Reaching inside the futon, I run my fingers down her bare arm, over her wrist to her fingers. They're still freezing, so I lift them out of the blanket. The tips are no longer blue, but the skin under her nails is white, tinged with purple. I lean over her as I bring her fingers to my mouth and breathe hot air on each one before tucking her hand back into the blankets. I do the same thing with her other hand, all while resisting the desire to place soft kisses to her fingertips. I manage to keep myself from licking her palm, from pressing my lips to the inside of her wrist.

Sitting up to quickly shrug off my damp robe and pat my hair dry, I then lay back down and wrap my arm around her, trying to give her as much warmth as possible. I stare over her head at the flames. Never have I been so thankful that I built this hearth. It may have taken me a full six months of trial and error and several temper tantrums, but it was all worth it to save Atagi's life tonight.

Unlike with the deep snow drifts, ice storms like we're having now usually don't block the hearth vent as long as I keep the fire hot enough. So I don't have to worry about having to leave Atagi to go outside to dig out the vent. And I have plenty of wood stacked up.

Her teeth chatter, her small body shivering before relaxing, then shivering again. I curl around her, holding her.

The question still burns ... Why? Why did she take such a risk to come here?

50

MEIKO

I drift slowly towards awareness from my dreamless sleep, keeping my eyes closed. I'm comfortable but a bit too warm. Yes, I'm warm and no longer shivering, though I'm sore from my violent tremors last night. The heat of the fire blazes through the cavern ...

My eyes pop open as the events of last night rush back. When I shift, I find Sensei curled around me, his chest pressed tightly to my back. At some point during the night, he ended up under the futon with me.

And I'm fully aware of how little clothing separates us right now. I'm naked, and my teacher is only wearing pants. Sensei's even breathing floats warm air over my neck, and his body pressed to mine is a temptation that's coursing through my blood. I bite my cheek to keep from groaning. His hard erection nudges against my ass, but I'm pretty sure he's still asleep. My husband often woke in this state, so I won't assume this is because of me.

But still ...

A few peaceful minutes pass. I'm warm and safe in his arms, but at the same time, my heart rate picks up with the feel of him pressed against me. Nerves. Uncertainty. Desire. I squeeze my thighs together, and Sensei shifts. His breathing changes, letting me know he's waking up. I didn't think my heart could race any faster, but there it goes. I hold absolutely still as his chilly fingers press to my neck. Is he checking my pulse?

I swallow, and whisper, "I'm alive. Thanks to you."

His hand jerks from my skin, and he scoots back, moving his body away from mine. I immediately miss his heat. He clears his throat and says, "Oh. Good. I ... you had me really worried."

Nervous energy dances through me, and I smile to myself. It's been a while since I've felt this little flutter of anticipation. Slowly, I roll over to face him, ducking my head into his chest so I don't have to look into his eyes. My palm lands on his abs, and I just breathe for a few moments. His heart races under my touch.

This isn't why I came. I can't do this. I shouldn't do this.

I want to do this.

I can have this, can't I? Just a little bit more time?

Tilting my head back, I blink up at my teacher. His breath is warm on my face, a little sour, but all him. I realize I may not know a lot about him and his past, but I know *him*. I know his moods. I know how he moves silently through the forest. I know how he dances with joy when he practices his swordplay. I know his smiles. I know his scent.

And now I know the feel of his muscled chest under my

fingers. I lean forward, pressing my lips to his. It's a soft kiss but it sinks heavily into my heart.

I think ... I think I love him.

I wrap my arm around him, pressing my palm to his back, holding us together as I deepen the kiss, trying to hold back my tears as my love for him bursts through me, as if all it was waiting for was for me to notice.

A little growl vibrates through his chest, and his hand slides up my neck, his fingers tangling in the string of the necklace he gave me. He pulls away from our kiss, his eyes meeting mine, his breaths coming fast. His gaze drops between my breasts, and his tongue flicks out to lick his lips as he stares at the little carving of Moon. Slowly, his eyes crawl back to my face, and he asks, "Atagi, are you sure?"

I smile, because there's no doubt, not in this moment. I press my lips to his again before whispering against his mouth, "Call me Meiko."

He waits a single beat of our hearts before slamming his mouth back to mine. He licks me, and I eagerly open to allow our tongues to duel and dance. He angles his head, taking our kisses that much deeper, and I can't keep the moan from escaping my lips. I hitch my leg over his hip, needing to be closer.

He rips his lips from mine with a groan, and my pussy flutters as his cock notches against me through his pants. He grinds against me as he kisses down my neck. "Meiko."

He says my name like a prayer. He's worshiping me like no other ever has. A sound between a gasp and moan slips from me as I tilt my head back. "Say it again."

He kisses across my collarbone, down towards my breasts, and breathes out my name against the little necklace. "Meiko."

Fuck.

A tiny voice in the back of my head tells me to stop, that I shouldn't be doing this, but I snuff it out. I need this. I need him. I always have. My hand travels down, and when my fingers feather over his bare stomach, his hips punch forward as if he's aching to get his cock inside me.

"Fuck, Meiko, I've tried to ignore these feelings, but I want you so much. I didn't dare to hope, but please ... Please, please tell me you want me too."

My fingers explore his abs before teasing at the waist of his pants. "Yes. Yes, Sensei. Please."

He grips my chin, lifting my gaze to meet his. He stares at me with an intensity that makes me want to squirm out of his grip, but his fingers are like stone on my face. I can't move. I swallow and try to nod.

Slowly, he lowers his head and licks my bottom lip as he says, "You are infuriating." His lips press to the edge of my mouth. "You are stubborn." He presses a kiss to my cheek. "You are fierce." He kisses my brow. "You are strong." His lips brush my temple. "You are beautiful." When his mouth comes to my ear, I arch into him, fighting back tears as he whispers, "And right now, you are mine."

I gasp loudly as his teeth clamp onto my lobe before he sucks on it. My hands come to his face, and I pull him to me, slamming my lips to his with a groan. I open to him once more, letting my hand slide down, down, down his throat, his chest, his stomach, until my fingers pass over the fabric of his pants. I palm his cock, and he grunts, rubbing against my touch.

Fuck, he's big.

The room spins, and I find myself on my back, my teacher looming over me. My thighs part, allowing him to fit snugly between them. My body vibrates with growing pleasure as he looks down at me, along the column of my neck, over my small breasts, down my soft stomach ...

Why couldn't things have been different?

I can't seem to catch my breath, as if I've sprinted to our tree and back. His fingers wrap around my wrist, pulling it over my head, pinning my arm to the ground. This position forces my back to arch, and my necklace slides to the side. His lips press to the swell of my breast before he sucks my nipple into his mouth.

Bliss.

I buck under him, moaning, thrashing my head. The pleasure is too much and not nearly enough. I yelp as his teeth nip at my flesh, but at the same time, his hips roll against me, rubbing his cock against my clit through his pants, and the pain of his bite melts into pure pleasure.

"Sensei." My voice comes out breathy and needy, a tone I've never heard from myself before.

He kisses his way down my writhing body until he's between my thighs. He grips them, pushing them wide and starts to lean in. Self-consciousness pushes aside the pleasure for a moment. I know my cheeks are red, and I chew my bottom lip in embarrassment as I hold up a hand. "Don't. I haven't bathed since yesterday. I'm not—"

His voice comes out on a growl. "I don't care."

His mouth lands on me, and I release a high-pitched squeak as he licks me, flicking his tongue against my clit.

Oh, fuck. Yes!

My hand falls to his head, no longer trying to stop him, now pulling him closer. My fingers scrape his scalp before I grip his hair and grind against his mouth. He laps at me like I'm his last meal, like he's savoring me, and I lose myself.

Planting my feet, my toes dig into his futon as I lift my

hips and push down on his head. His tongue slides in and out of me before he wraps his lips around my clit and sucks.

"Yes, yes, yes. Oh, yes. Right there. Don't stop. Please. Oh, oh, oh ..."

I'm begging. I know I am. And I don't care. My sensei listens to my pleas, keeping a steady rhythm and maintaining the same pressure. I'm strung tight. I'm tingling. I'm so close.

He reaches down his body, and he grips his cock, stroking himself.

That undoes me, knowing how much he wants me but is making sure to give me pleasure first. I scream, my hoarse voice echoing around the cave as I come. My back arches completely off the ground, one hand cupping my breast, the other still gripping his hair. Electric shocks rock through me, pulsing from my clit and working their way outward. On and on, I come apart under my sensei, and he drinks me down eagerly.

The waves of pleasure fade, and my body melts to the futon. I focus to find my teacher staring at me, and I wonder if I'm wearing the same expression, because he's looking at me like he loves me.

Fuck. I shouldn't have done this. I should have stopped.

Because I love him too.

51

She's so beautiful. If only I could keep her. If only she would keep me. I would love her until the day she dies.

Meiko's hand slips out of my hair, falling limply to her side as she tries to catch her breath. I quickly sit up, shucking my pants. She's still so blissed out; she doesn't seem to notice. I grin as I work my way back up her body, pressing wet kisses against her skin. I've never done this with a woman before, but I seem to have pleased her, so I continue to let my instincts lead.

It's not that I don't know what women want. I've been inside pleasure houses. In theory, I know what to do. But experiencing it ... experiencing Meiko ... this is above and beyond anything I've ever known.

It's because you love her.

I do. She has soothed the cracks in my heart. They're still there, but the pain is less, it's distant ... because of her.

I kiss up her neck, fingering the small pendant I gave her, beyond pleased to see it still hanging around her neck.

Because she seemed to like it so much before, I bite her

earlobe again, sucking it into my mouth. She gasps, arching into me, and I chuckle into her ear, whispering, "Meiko." I love how her name feels on my lips and how she melts against me with a moan as I say it. The head of my cock nudges against her entrance and her eyes snap to mine. I grin against her mouth. "Want to know what you taste like on my tongue?"

I don't give her the chance to answer. My lips slam against hers, and I push my tongue into her mouth. She grunts, her hands coming to my shoulders. As I devour her, I slide into her.

Exquisite. Every inch is ecstasy. She's so hot, squeezing me with the flutters of another building orgasm. Her hand slaps at my shoulder, so I release her lips as I grind my pelvic bone against her clit. Her mouth falls open on a silent gasp before she says, "Wait. Wait. You're too big. Wait. I need ..."

I grin, circling my hips to hit her clit from a different angle. "What you *need* is to learn the shape of my cock, Meiko."

I pull out slowly, dropping my gaze to watch my wet length slide from her body until only my head remains inside her, her pussy spread wide around my girth. My voice comes out on a growl as I say, "That is the most beautiful fucking thing I've ever seen."

Meiko wraps her legs around mine, her feet digging into the backs of my thighs as she tries to pull me back inside her. But I want the full experience of what I'm about to do, so I sit on my heels. I grip her thighs, holding them wide, then I thrust as I yank her onto me. Our combined moans fill the cavern. Such a beautiful song. One I'll never forget.

I'm so close to coming. My balls are tight, and the snapping tingles of pleasure have spread from between my legs up into my core and all the way down to my toes. My fingers dig into Meiko's flesh as I slam her onto my cock over and over. The sight of my soaked length sliding in and out of her is a primal thing. I want ... so much. I want ... us.

Hope.

I want to stay with Meiko. Forever. I need her, and the thought of losing her one day feels worse than a sword to the heart.

Her body jerks with my thrusts, her small breasts swaying as I growl, "Meiko. *My* Meiko."

She arches, and I reach forward, placing my palm on her chest, holding her down, her pendant pressed between us. She bites her lip and squeezes her eyes closed, her expression caught somewhere between pleasure and pain.

Stunning. Perfect. And while it may only be in this one moment, she's mine.

My release erupts from me, and I roar to the ceiling, holding Meiko's hips flush with mine. On and on the pleasure rips through me as I jerk and twitch inside her, to the point where I can't breathe. But I don't care. I'd live in this moment for eternity. I'd die here ... if I could.

As I come back to myself, I look down at Meiko. She's breathing hard, the muscles of her legs still flexed, holding herself flush against me. Shit. I built her pleasure towards her second orgasm but didn't take her all the way before I came.

I reach between us, pressing my thumb to her clit, thoroughly enjoying the glazed look of ecstasy that falls over her eyes. I rub her side to side, then in small quick circles. My cock is only half hard, but I manage little thrusts as I work her clit. I pay attention to what she likes, and I build her back up quickly.

And now I'm almost fully hard again as I watch her pleasure peak then explode. She comes with a beautiful shout, her pussy squeezing me as she shatters and rides me through her orgasm. She's so glorious, and she's gripping me so tightly, my hips buck and my eyes go wide as another orgasm spills from me unexpectedly. I fall over her, catching my weight with my forearm. I groan as my balls empty and the last of my cum spills inside her. The tight flutters of her pussy fade, and we pant, catching our breath, our sweaty skin slick and pressed together perfectly.

Tell her.

I slide out of her and roll onto my side, pulling her with me so we lay facing each other. I stroke her hair and press a kiss to her forehead, whispering against her skin, "That was perfect. You are perfect."

She sighs, nuzzling into my chest, and I wrap my arm around her waist, stroking my fingers up and down her spine. We lay in contented silence for a while, the sweat on our bodies drying, the fire keeping us warm even with the freezing winds outside trying to push their way into the caves.

But of course, my mind can't help but be a dick. Questions and doubts start to creep in, and I tense. I don't want Meiko to notice. I don't want to bring down the mood of this amazing thing that just happened between us ... and hopefully happens again and again. I hold my tongue as I hold Meiko, stroking her skin. Her fingers trace little circles over my chest, her breaths hot against my collarbone.

Ask for her help. She's smart and resourceful. Maybe she can find a spell or something. Maybe there is a way ... Atagi will try to help if you ask.

Perhaps. But I won't bring it up right now. I don't want

what we just did to become transactional. One day, when the time is right, I'll ask.

I press another kiss to her forehead as I tug the futon over our bodies. There is a question that can't wait, so I whisper, "Meiko, tell me what happened. Why did you go out in that storm, nearly killing yourself to get here?"

52

MEIKO

My bottom lip worries between my teeth. I hate this habit, but I can't seem to stop myself from doing it whenever I'm stressed. Sensei watches me as he runs his fingers up my spine, over my shoulder and down my arm before tracing his way back up and down my back again. I know he's waiting, letting me gather my thoughts. He's always been like that, patient.

He's always been kind, and thoughtful, stern when he needed to be. He's always been here for me. Mentally, I snort, because now I know he physically couldn't leave, so of course he was always here, but that's not what I meant.

With a shaky breath, I blurt out, "My brother-in-law is dead."

My teacher's fingers stall for a long moment before continuing their stroking touch. I melt into him, my words coming a little easier. "For months, war has been brewing, but now it's here. The western feudal lord's army invaded. Reports say several of our cities have been lost, but we're only getting bits and pieces of information."

I take a slow inhale that pushes my breasts against his chest, and he presses a kiss to my temple as he continues to stroke my arm. I should pull away, physically and emotionally, but it's too late for that, so I give in and accept his comfort, allowing myself this moment.

Just a little while longer.

My voice is slightly muffled from where my head is ducked into his chest. "When my mother-in-law received the news that her second son had been killed in the fighting, she collapsed and hasn't woken up. She's dying. The house stinks of incense and death. The servants are scared, but they're loyal, and not only that, they're like family. They're looking to me to hold the household together. My sister-in-law is struggling with her new baby. She's scared, barely eating, and the baby wails all the time. My nieces and nephews cry where they think I can't hear them. The two-year-old doesn't really understand what's going on, but I know he feels the tension that's smothering our house. Yesterday ... I needed ..."

You. I need you.

He smooths his palm down my back, kissing my shoulder as he whispers, "I hate that you risked your life to come here, but I'm also very glad you did, Meiko. I want to be here for you. I ... I care for you ... deeply. I want to help."

"I know."

After a few moments of silence, I shift but stay close enough so that Sensei's hand doesn't leave my lower back. He traces small circles over my skin right above my ass, and I absently feather my fingers up and down his arm. I lean in, unable to resist, needing to kiss him, pressing my lips to the base of his throat. His cock hardens between us, and a gasp leaves my mouth. I could so easily take what he's offering, take another moment for me, for us. I could accept this distraction.

But I've stalled long enough ... too long.

We're out of time.

"This ..." My words catch in my throat as tears block their way. I blink and swallow, starting over. "This is good-bye, Sensei."

He goes deathly still, then his palm flattens on my back, pulling me closer as he whispers into my hair. "What do you mean?"

I pull out of his arms, feeling like I'm leaving a part of myself behind as I sit up, shifting to face the fire. Sensei pulls the futon around me, and he sits quietly at my back, his arm around my waist, his hand on my thigh over the blanket as the contents of that second letter flash through my mind.

I say, "Yesterday, word arrived that a neighboring village was burned to the ground. That village is a four-day's ride to our town. We are next. Hopefully the weather will give us more time, but ..."

"Meiko, does your town have a fighting force? Are there men with skill to protect you? Why are you here? Why haven't you gathered your family and run?"

I bristle at his words, but I also hear the fear behind them, and I know he's struggling with this news because he can't help.

"Run? With my dying mother-in-law, and my ailing sister-in-law with her newborn? With my young nieces and nephews, and my servants who all have families of their own? How? Where?"

"Here. I'll protect you. I'll protect your family, Meiko."

I shake my head. "No. Some of my family wouldn't survive the journey here, I can't—"

His body jerks, his fingers digging into my thigh. "Meiko. You can. You asked for my help. This is how I help. You're all that matters."

Wrapping my fingers around his muscled forearm, I shake my head. "I'm not. My family needs me. That place is not just a house, it's my home. I raised my sons there. I made a family there. I cried and struggled and endured. But I also laughed and grew and matured. I won't run."

"Meiko—"

I turn, cupping his face. There's sadness and desperation in his eyes, and I want to take it away, but I don't know how. "It's okay. You told me you have faith in my skills, and that I needed to find faith in myself. Well, now's my chance."

His fingers tremble as they caress my jaw. Tears shimmer in his dark eyes. "Gods, Meiko. Now's not the time to be stubborn. Just ... let me help you. I can't lose you. Please."

Leaning forward, I kiss him. Slowly, with a determination to memorize everything about this moment and about this man. I pull away, knowing if I don't, Sensei will keep me in his embrace and never let me go.

And I might let him.

My stomach churns as I wrap my hand around his. I don't know how he's going to react to my next question, but if there's a possibility that I might die tomorrow or the next day, I need to know ...

My fingers side down to his inner wrist, and he freezes, watching the path of my touch as I trace the scar on his wrist. The raised characters are rough, and I keep my gaze on them as I say, "I came here to say goodbye, just in case ... but ..."

The scars on his wrist scrape against the pad of my

finger as I say, "I've been searching for a way to help you." He jerks, but I don't let him pull away. I don't look at his face, because I don't want to be distracted by the emotions I'm sure are written there. "I've asked around, discreetly of course. I managed to locate a few descendants of your father's clients. I've sent letters asking about Guardian and any knowledge they might have of your village and what happened."

"Meiko—"

There's anger in his voice, but I shake my head, barreling on. "I have only received a handful of responses, most completely useless. I'm sorry, Sensei. I was sure I'd be able to find a way, some clue, something to free you. Maybe, after ... if I get more time ..."

I dare to look up into his eyes. His jaw is set, but there's such tenderness in his gaze, it's as if he's warring with himself. And I guess I can understand that.

I whisper, "I just needed you to know that if ... after ... I won't give up. I'll keep searching. I promise."

His next inhale stutters with emotion, and his palm comes to my face, holding me with a reverence that I'll cherish for however long I live. He says, "You are a gift. Thank you for thinking of me, even with everything else going on in your life."

I smile, my fingers still tracing his scar. After a moment, my lip pulls between my teeth, and I worry at it.

I shouldn't ask. Just leave it. It doesn't matter. Leave it!

My stupid mouth opens, and I ask, "Sensei, what is your real connection to Guardian?"

He frowns, his thumb rubbing back and forth across my jaw. "What do you mean?"

"You told me your father forged that blade. But no one recalls the master swordsmith having a son. He lived alone.

His apprentice, Motosue Saito died several years ago, and according to his grandson, the master swordsmith lived alone until the day he was killed."

Sensei drops his hand, his fist balling in his lap. Silence closes in around us, and it gets heavier with each breath. Suddenly, he stands. His bare ass flexes as he walks a few paces away from me, his fingers combing through his hair. He grips the dark strands and pulls, his head thrown back. The muscles of his back flex with tension.

I grip my Moon pendant as my heart sinks into my stomach.

With a sigh, he drops his arms, but holds his wrist before him, his back still to me as he looks down at his scar.

I prop myself on my forearm, daring to whisper, "Who are you?"

53

Meiko's question darkens the room. Storm clouds roll into my mind, my thoughts tumbling. This moment is too heavy. If only we had more time. I want to hope for the best, but I'm well aware of my fucking luck when it comes to hope. And if the worst should happen, I don't want this memory, this story, to be the final thing said between us.

But she deserves to know. I will give my Meiko my secrets.

I turn around, fingers still pressed to my scar. I meet her gaze, and we stare at each other. Meiko's hands tremble slightly where she's clutching the futon with one hand and her pendant with the other.

I drop my gaze to hide my shame. "I'm not sure where to start."

Her soft voice fills the cave. "Then I will." Lifting my head, I look at her beautiful face as she says, "When I came back and first saw you, I questioned my memories of this place, my memories of you. You looked the same, but I explained it away by telling myself I was remembering you through the lens of a child's perspective. Everyone looks grown up and adult when you're a child. But you really haven't changed, have you?"

Silence. It's so thick I'm choking on it. The words won't come. I can't take a full breath. It's hot. Too hot. My skin prickles and sweat slicks down my back. My tongue feels too big. The edges of my vision start to tunnel.

"Sensei?"

Her calm voice pulls me from my panic. As I lift my arm, I realize I'm shaking. My fingers trace the raised skin of my scar, the characters marking me with my name. When I look at Meiko, her eyes are on my scar as well, and my stomach tightens as she asks, "Why do you have Guardian carved into your skin?"

All those little fissures and cracks on my heart widen and expand, and the familiar ache in my chest returns. Because everything is about to change.

Meiko lifts her gaze, her full attention on my face. A tear drips down my cheek, quickly followed by another, and another. She doesn't move, she just watches me cry, she watches me fall apart. She watches me from my bed where I just gave her my heart.

I clear my throat, breaking eye contact while sniffing back my tears as best I can. Meiko's gaze sears me like a brand. Anger and sorrow fill me to the brim, and I turn, my gaze landing on my saya before unfocusing as I fall into my past.

My voice is hushed, as if the words themselves don't want to come out, but I manage to say, "My first memory is that of the last few words of a single-use spell, spoken by a master swordsmith ... my father ... my maker."

54

MEIKO

H is father, his *maker*.

No. Oh no! This isn't possible.

My heart breaks. I shouldn't have asked. I don't want to know this. But now that the first few words have passed his lips, the dam holding him back seems to have broken.

He says, "My magic wasn't meant to be red. I was created silver, bright and pure. As the hammer struck my heated steel, every move, every form of the katana blazed through me. I knew it all. It was who I was. It wasn't even thought. It was instinct.

No, my first *thought* was to protect. To protect my maker, my father. To make him proud. I needed to guard his home, his apprentice, his village, his neighbors ... If he cared about it, it was my duty to keep it safe. And as those thoughts solidified with each strike of his hammer, he marked me with my purpose. Every whorl in my steel existed to guard my father. And when he was finished, he smiled down at me, stamping my smooth edge. He named me as he completed the spell. I was his greatest work, forged in blazing flames, fortified and given purpose with magic, and named by my maker. Guardian."

No no no no. This can't be true. Please.

"Being Guardian was not just my purpose, it was who I was. It was all I *could* be. And for years, that was enough. I practiced with my father, my favorite times being when he'd take up my hilt in the evening, all his chores completed for the day, the village sleeping down the hill. That beautiful sound. Every time. *Snick*. And I'd be free of my saya. Those nights, it was just my father and me. The stars would watch as we danced in his yard, and I'd glint in the pale light as he smiled, moving through the samurai forms. I think I was happy."

I can't keep my tears from falling, but they're silent to allow my Sensei the space to finish his story.

"We traveled to far off villages and towns and cities, delivering his commissioned blades. He was so proud of his work, and each of his katanas was beautiful and unique, but none as special as me. Every time he gripped my hilt, I felt his pride. But over the years, as I watched, I also learned. My consciousness expanded. There were random moments when I found myself wanting more, but not knowing what that meant."

He pauses, breathing deeply, and I ache to rise and go to him. To press a kiss to his chest. I yearn to comfort him, but I don't. Because I can't. I don't know what to do. I shouldn't have sent out those letters. I shouldn't have pushed him. I don't want to know this. I love him. This hurts too much.

He quickly dashes away another tear as he continues. "I

was content. I was happy, as much as a magical object can be."

He chuckles softly, but I don't bother to give him a fake smile. This is all too awful.

"But with the passage of time, rumors spread. Rumblings passed between lips, dispersing like a disease. At the time, I didn't know where these rumors were coming from. My father was so careful. He knew how fearful people could be of the unknown. But of course, now I know ..."

His eyes, still unfocused, narrow slightly as he says, "People started avoiding eye contact. They'd huddle in the tea houses, whispering of magic and evil. Mothers would clutch their children to their skirts as if my father would hurt them. As if he was a danger to anyone. The absurdity of it all is astounding."

His fists clench at his sides, and he closes his eyes. I wonder if they are blazing red with his magic? Mine would be if they could. I'm so far removed from the experience of his story, but I'm still angry on his behalf.

His voice is gruff as he says, "And then one night, they came. I can still see every painful detail in my mind as if it happened yesterday. It was the middle of the night. If a sword can sleep, that is what I was doing, safe in my scabbard. I heard my father whispering to Saito. He was calm, but there was a tension to his voice I'd not heard before. The hand that wrapped around my hilt was not my father's, but that of his apprentice. My maker, my father, told Saito to take me and run."

He bows his head, as if the memory is too heavy to hold. I don't want to know the rest, but I don't stop him.

"I couldn't leave my father, but I didn't know what to do. At least Saito didn't want to leave him either. My magic felt his hesitance through our connection on my hilt. My father and Saito argued, wasting time. If only my father had taken me, things might have been different. But he shoved Saito towards the small exit in the back as the pounding on the front door echoed through our small house and workshop. The house where I was created. Where I was born." He pauses before a hint of smile tugs at the corner of his mouth. "No, not a house, a home. I do understand that, Meiko."

My lungs stutter with my next breath as I struggle to inhale around my silent tears.

He continues his story. "Calmly, with head held high, but hands empty where he should have been wielding me, my father strode out into the night. Saito followed. To this day, I'm not sure if Saito went out there of his own free will or if I shoved my magic into him, forcing him to go. I like to believe he did it on his own ..."

My sensei's hand rises to his face again, wiping away more tears. "There were so many people there that night. It felt like the entire village had come, holding torches, knives, katanas, hammers ... There were even children there, clinging to their parents' legs, staring wide-eyed with fear at my father ... A man who had never harmed any of them. A man who had shared meals with them. A man who created a magic sword to guard them and keep them safe. And there they were with violence in their minds and fear and anger in their hearts!"

His rising voice snaps with the rage held within it. His hair floats around his shoulders, and I can't help but marvel at him. He *is* magic. I grip the futon as waves of power crawl over my skin with growing intensity.

His voice gets deeper as he says, "It happened so fast. The crowd was yelling. Fear fed anger that fed fury that turned into madness. I couldn't figure out which threat was the most pressing. There was So. Much. Hate."

He finally looks at me, and I nearly gasp at the rage in his blazing red eyes as he scowls, "And I hated them back. Fully and completely, I *hated* them, Meiko."

His eyes burn brighter, reflecting off his skin. His hair blows in a non-existent wind, his magic beautiful and terrifying as he clenches his fists, and says, "My father raised his hands and tried to explain. Even then, with the yelling and the spitting and all the hate being aimed at him, my father was kind, he tried ... Someone lunged, and my father jerked."

The red in his eyes fades just a little, and my throat burns with my tears as his heartache bleeds into his words.

"The silence that closed in around me was deafening. I had never heard anything like it before or since. It was like the world stopped and held its breath. And then my father turned his head and looked at Saito. Blood trickled from the corner of his lips as his gaze slid down to me where Saito's grip tightened around my hilt. My father's eyes focused on me, and the last words he said were, 'Don't forget, you are Guardian. Don't forget.'"

Sensei presses a palm over his heart.

"My father collapsed, a kitchen knife sticking out of his chest. I watched the light in his eyes dim then die."

I choke on my tears, swallowing them down, trying to keep my sobs from bursting out, because he's not done.

His eyes blaze brighter again. "Rage. I was literally blinded by it. My magic bled with it, turning my silver a murderous red. As red as my father's blood." He waves a hand at his face, at his fierce eyes. "I no longer whispered to the one wielding me. I shouted. I screamed. I couldn't bear *just* being a sword any longer. I needed *real* freedom —the freedom to take my vengeance. I needed to be human. So, I shoved my red raging magic into Saito until there was very little of him left. I took over, and I used him."

He takes a deep breath, his red magic fading again with his slow exhale.

"I tore through the village, Meiko. I used an innocent man's hands to do unspeakable things. I drank their blood until it wasn't just my magic that had turned red, but the entire length of my blade as well the hard-packed dirt roads of my village—the village I was created to protect. But I wasn't sorry, in fact, I craved more. So, I kept going. Killing. All. Of. Them. And when there was no one else to kill, my control over Saito slipped away."

He glances over his shoulder towards the shiny black saya propped against the wall.

"But there was a yokai in our village. I didn't know, or I'd have found a way to kill her days, no weeks before. She was the one who did this. She whispered in people's ears. She fanned the flames of the rumors. And that night, she was there, green eyes laughing at me as blood soaked into my steel. Using my father's faithful apprentice, I slit her throat. It was most unsatisfying.

I felt Saito's absolute disgust with me as well as his crushing guilt towards himself. But the yokai's curse wrapped around me, and my father's apprentice finally managed to release his grip on my hilt. As I fell, the curse pulled me apart and remade me."

He sighs, dropping his head. "And then I was here, no longer a sword, but a man. My empty saya was with me, and it's been just us for over sixty years now."

55

MEIKO

S ilence.

I really shouldn't have asked.

But now I know. I know, and it hurts. It hurts because I love him, and I don't know what to do.

I swallow, picturing my dying mother-in-law, my newborn niece, my servants, my other nieces and nephews, my home where my dead son's ashes rest, where my other son will return to one day with a wife and family of his own ... My heart is split between two places and I'm slightly dizzy with the push and pull of my emotions.

I force strength into my voice as I say, "I'm sorry."

It's such a weak sentiment, but I don't have any other words. He shakes his head, his magic bleeding away. He looks tired. Empty. Alone. How lonely he must have been all this time, trapped in this place. I hate myself for keeping us apart for so many years, and over something that wasn't his fault.

My tears fall. I hold out a hand in silent invitation. I don't know what else to do. He lifts his head, sharp eyes landing on my face. He takes the three steps between us and grips my offered hand, kneeling and cupping my face as he says, "I'm sorry I didn't tell you sooner."

I allow myself another moment of weakness as I lean into his touch. A small smile plays at my lips, slowing my tears. "I wish you had, but thank you for sharing yourself with me now."

We fall back into silence, and I trace his name carved into his flesh as his thumb caresses my cheek. Some of the tension in my spine melts as I let myself just touch him ... and let him touch me.

How I wish ...

His voice draws my attention back to him as he says, "Meiko, you have made my existence here not just bearable, but enjoyable. You gave me something to look forward to. You gave me purpose all those years ago when you peeked around that tree and giggled at me. You have been the reason for my hope. Please. Please gather your family and come here."

I swallow, each time seemingly a little more difficult. Is it the heat of the fire, or is it actually getting harder to breathe? I watch my fingers trace over his name, and my tears start falling again. He tries to brush them away, but that only makes me cry harder. I don't know what to do. I'm desperate. We need more time! I love him, but my family needs me. My mind races as my heart breaks. Maybe I can bring my family here ... Would my mother-in-law survive the journey? Would the baby? How can I ask this man to not only protect us all, but to somehow provide for us for an undetermined amount of time? And if the invaders find us here ...?

The whirlwind of my thoughts stops, focusing on a possibility. It sits there in my mind like a single torch flickering on a moonless night.

"What if ..." I shake my head, biting my lip.

Sensei's hand on my face directs me to look at him. "What? What is it, Meiko?"

The way he says my name ... I want to melt into him and forget the outside world exists.

"Nothing. Probably nothing. I'm sure you've thought of everything at this point. I'm not going to come up with anything new."

A small smile pulls at his lips. "Surprise me."

I can't keep my own lips from lifting slightly as I say, "Well, have you tried to ... I don't know, turn back?"

Like a breeze blowing out a candle, his eyes darken and his hand slips from my cheek. "What?"

I swallow around my nerves, but excitement builds, because if he hasn't tried this, maybe it will work! It *could* work, and I could take him from this place, and he can help me protect my home. And after, I could find a way to change him back again. Right? Maybe?

The words tumble quickly as I ask, "Have you tried turning back into a sword? Maybe that will break the curse."

56

My heart splinters. She wants me to turn back into a sword?

Checkmate.

No. Wait. I need to let her explain. I shouldn't jump to conclusions.

Still, my voice falters as I ask, "You ... you want me to try and turn back into my blade form?"

Her hand darts out from under the futon, gripping mine. "Sensei, I don't *want* that. I only thought that perhaps it would break the curse. I'll be right here. I can take you away from this place. We can stay together."

I see the hope and the damned excitement in her eyes, and it guts me. Her fingers clutch at me tighter as she goes on. "It's not ideal, but as Guardian, you can help me protect my home, my family. You can *be* Guardian again, and then after, maybe I can find a way to change you back again! If—"

I stand up, pacing away from her as my rage builds, cutting off the rest of her words.

It might work.

I snarl at my saya, yelling at it in my head. 'Tell me this

hasn't been her plan all along!' My saya remains silent, and I grit my teeth as I beg, 'Tell me that she hasn't spent these past few months setting up her shogi pieces on the board of my heart, one careful move at a time. Tell me I haven't fallen into her trap.'

The silence in my head hurts. Everything hurts, and I feel myself cracking.

I wave a hand down my body as I spit the words at her. "If? Maybe? Possibly? Well, *Atagi*, I don't know how to give you what you want." She flinches at my tone, but I keep going, holding onto my anger. "I have no idea how to change back. So, I'm sorry, but I can't be your shining savior. You'll have to play hero all on your own."

"Sensei."

She snaps her mouth shut at my glare. I sneer at her. "You know what? I've lived in this place, paying my penance because I accept what I did. I always have. So, even *if* I knew how to turn back into a sword, and even *if* that were to break the curse, I wouldn't do it."

I grip my hair as I pace the room, uncaring of my nakedness ... or of hers under that futon. I still smell like her. We shared something beautiful. I love her. And it's killing me.

Another crack rips through me.

There's dejection in her voice as she whispers, "Please, just tell me what to do. Please, Guardia—"

I spin on her, pointing a finger down at her face, spit flying from my mouth as I shout. "No! Don't call me that!"

Her eyes are red from crying, and her face is puffy as she says, "Sense—"

"No! No more, Atagi." My voice breaks, and I realize I'm crying too. "Please. No more."

I sigh, letting my tears drip down my face, splattering on my chest. This is too much. All of this because of fucking hope. Haven't I learned my lesson by now? What the fuck is wrong with me?

This. After everything, *this* has broken me. I can't take any more. All those little cracks and fissures burst. I'm falling apart. It hurts. Please. Someone. Anyone. I can't go on. I can't bear this. Please.

Stop. Look.

Meiko's fingers curl into my tatami mat where she's hunched over. Tears splatter between her hands, and her body shakes with her sobs. Fuck.

She almost died just to come to say goodbye. There's a real possibility she could die in the next few days, but she's been searching for a way to help us. Quit being such a colossal ass and talk to her. Fix this! If this is the end, don't let it end like this!

I rush to her side, pulling her into my lap, stroking her hair. "Shh. I'm sorry. I didn't mean it. I'm sorry."

She hiccups, her hand coming to my chest as if she wants to climb inside. I hold her tight, smoothing her hair with my palm, calming both of us. Her tears slow then stop, as do mine. I rock us back and forth, kissing the top of her head.

I sigh. "I'm sorry. I ... I promised to help you. If you can't bring your family here, of course I'd go with you if there was a way. I just ... I'm scared. No, I'm terrified. Being confined in that steel ... I don't think I could bear it. Not anymore. Not after being truly alive."

And there it is.

"Even after all these years, after the torment, the loneliness, the pain, the suffering ... I don't want to go back to being a sword, even a magical one."

And I hate how selfish that makes me sound.

"I have felt—deep in my soul—all the human emotions." I chuckle softly before continuing. "I'm amazed at the breadth of the human experience. Being human is calm and beautiful like a springtime melody. It can be harsh and violent like a thunderstorm. It can be light and heavy. Uplifting and crushing."

I hold up a hand, wiggling my fingers. "Having a body ... I love the way my whole chest expands with my breaths. I love the feel of rain on my skin. I love the prickle of hot sunlight on my face. I've learned, I've created, I've survived. Even though I'm trapped in this place, I am in charge of what I do and how I do it. True freedom. Surely, *you* can understand that, Meiko?"

She nods her head against my chest. "I do. I just ... we're out of time, and I can't think of anything else. What if this is really goodbye? If there's a way to free you from this place, I can't leave you behind. I won't."

I rub her arm over the futon as I say, "I don't know how to turn myself back. But if I did, Meiko, I want to believe I'd be strong enough to take that chance on you ... to help you ... to stay with you. That's what I want."

The fear of being bound in steel once more threatens to crush my chest and close off my throat. A cold sweat breaks out on my forehead, and I clench my hands to try to hide slight trembling of my fingers.

"But?" The kind understanding in her voice makes my chest ache even more.

"But, even the thought of being back in my sword form is ..."

"Threatening to send you into a panic?"

My shoulders drop. I flex and relax my hands before resuming my gentle touch down her hair. "Yes. Being trapped in steel would be worse than being confined in these woods. I didn't realize it at the time, but that yokai granted my wish with my punishment. My desire for more had been building for years, but that night in my village, I needed to be real. I needed to be free. And for the first time, I had the ego to demand what I wanted. I wanted to be a man, so the yokai turned me into one."

Holding out both my hands, I turn them over. Meiko places her small hand in mine, her touch tracing the lines of my palms. I stare at my fingers with a sigh, "I love these hands." I run my fingertips up her arm, fascinated by the way her flesh pebbles, and I whisper, "The best thing by far that I've ever used these hands for is to touch you and bring you pleasure."

A sound between a sob and a moan punches from Meiko's lips, and I wrap my arms around her, resting my head on the top of her head. I breathe in our combined scents, and I say, "Being alive is a horrible, wondrous thing." A single tear slips down my cheek. "Though, I know life would lose its luster if I had to continue my existence as this man without you." Another crack splintering across my heart, my tear disappearing in Meiko's hair as I whisper, "But Meiko, the truth is, I'm ... I'm not a man. I'm a sword, and a broken one at that."

Truth

As the words leave my mouth, I gasp, trying to take them back.

No!

No! I didn't ... Wait! I take them back. I didn't mean to say that!

I jerk away from Meiko, her eyes wide with panic as I cry out. My magic scrapes across my body. Meiko crawls towards me, but I hold out a hand, stopping her. I scream as my skin cracks and red light leaks out, spearing around the room. I clutch my stomach, my howls of agony filling the cave.

I'm being torn apart.

No.

I'm being remade.

No. No. No.

As darkness creeps in at the edges of my red, I lift my head to look at my Meiko one last time. I love her so much. My magic rips at me, and I resist as the snug fit of my saya starts to form around me.

No. No. No. Please. No. I'm not ready.

I don't want to go.

Just a little more time. Please.

I hold Meiko's gaze for as long as I can. Her lips tremble, and I do my best to smile at her as I whisper, "I love you Atagi Meiko. Forever."

My saya snicks, securing me in its custom fitting. The warmth, the dark ... It's just as I remember within its embrace, but I also know my scabbard is the only thing holding me together right now, because what I told Meiko was the truth.

I'm broken.

57

MEIKO

He's gone. Oh gods, he's gone. But I have Guardian. I still have him ... he's still with me.

My heart feels like it's made of broken glass. I shouldn't have asked. I shouldn't have brought it up. This is my fault. I did this. I can undo this, right?

Hope and dread. I'm being choked by my warring emotions.

Oh, gods. What if I can't ...

All he wanted was to be alive, to be free.

With trembling hands, I reach for Guardian's hilt, praying, "Please let this have worked. Give us more time. Please."

As I wrap my fingers around the soft shark skin, a tingle shivers up my arm, and I nearly drop it. Magic. He's still here. I tighten my grip, holding Guardian before me, I whisper to the sword, "Sensei?"

A far away voice slides through my mind. *I'm here.*

My words rush out. "I'm sorry. I'll find a way to fix this, I promise." I look around the cave before quietly asking, "Is the curse broken? Can you tell?"

His voice seems a little farther away as he says, *Yes. Everything is as it should be.*

I frown, lowering the saya. I don't want to leave this place, my feet resistant to move, but I can't afford to linger. I need to get home. The town might already be under attack. Hopefully the weather bought me more time, but ...

Reluctantly peeling my fingers from around Guardian's hilt, I set him down and quickly dress, pulling on my kimono from where he must have set it up to dry near the fire. I don't bother wiping away my tears as I pull my sash tight. My gaze lands on the rumpled futon, and I lock my knees to keep from collapsing. I can't lose him. Not now. I'll find a way, no matter how far I have to go or how long it takes, I'll fix this.

I pick up Guardian, striding towards the exit. The only indication of his presence is a weak tingling against my palm. Sunlight spills inside the mouth of the cave casting a sharp, circular shadow. I glance at the wall of katanas as I pass, grabbing Moon and sliding her through my sash.

Together. We'll all leave here together. I'll take my Sensei home. I'll figure this out.

I stand at the entrance of the cave, looking out over the sunny clearing. At some point, my mare found her way back outside, and she flicks her tail as she munches on the small green shoots of grass poking through the melting ice. The clearing seems to shimmer and glitter with the new day, filling me with hope. As I look around the clearing, I smile. "So many happy memories here."

Guardian's distant voice spills through my head. *My best memories of this place are of you.*

I swallow the lump in my throat as I pat the black lacquer of Guardian's saya. "It may not be as a man, but I'm getting you out of here."

Clutching the hilt, I step out into the clearing, taking a deep breath of crisp, winter air. The clouds move quickly, hanging low in the sky. This is only a break in the weather. More ice and rain will move in tonight if not earlier.

Raising the saya before me, the black lacquer winks at me, and I say, "Are you ready to go home?"

I am home, Meiko. Thank you. For everything.

I frown, gripping the hilt. "We're far from finished, Sensei. You said I was your hope. Well, you're mine. I *will* find a way to hold you, the man, in my arms again, but right now, I'd love to see the blade your father was so proud of."

If it's possible to feel a smile, that's what tickles my palm where it grips his hilt. But something about it seems ... sad.

My thumb presses to the guard, and I flinch as a little whimper of pain accompanies the soft snick of the steel slipping free of its binding. My heart races as I slide the blade free, my palms sweating.

The first centimeter reveals a beautiful whorl of blue on silver.

My scream tears through the forest. Birds startle into flight. Guardian's cracked blade shines at me, refracting the weak sunlight for a single moment before the pieces fall apart and clatter to the ground. I collapse to my knees, scooping up the sharp metal, ignoring the slicing cuts digging into my hands.

"Oh, gods! No. No. No. This can't be happening. No. Please!" A thought races through my mind, and I shout, "Wait! I'll take you to town. No, to the city! I'll hunt down the best swordsmith in the entire country." A piece slips from my hands, and I rush to gather it back up. "I'll put you back together. I'll make you whole again!"

It ... it won't work. His pained voice fades more with each word, and panic steals my breath. *The magic is draining. The spell can't be recast. You ... you can have me remade, but ... I'd just be a ... regular blade. I'm sorry, Meiko. I'm sorry I can't stay.*

I weep, big sobbing wails tear from my chest as I clutch at the pieces of Guardian. The metal shines an unnatural silver, blazing with his magic, and I realize it's no longer red. "Please! Don't go. Please! I'm sorry. I'm sorry. I'm sorry. Not like this! Please!"

The silvery magic dims, and I sob my despair, rocking back and forth on my shins. As my tears soak the pieces of the blade, the light fades even more, his voice barely a whisper. *I love you. Thank you for the lessons.*

Guardian's silver light winks out.

I fall to my side, holding the broken pieces of the man I love. I hold him in my arms. The sharp edges cut into me, but I welcome the pain. I clutch him closer and I cry. I weep until my throat is raw, and my body aches.

I didn't tell him. I didn't say the words, and now he's gone. He'll never hear me say, I love you. Still, the words tear from my throat as I sob. "I love you. I love you. Please."

I hug the shards of Guardian even closer and curl into a tight ball, my sobs turning into whimpers. "I'm sorry. *Please.* I'm sorry, I'm sorry, I'm sorry ..."

58

ONE YEAR LATER
MEIKO

The owner of the teahouse sets my cup in front of me, giving me a little bow before scurrying off to see to her other patrons. The men at the table next to me huddle their heads together, whispering as they dart glances at the sword on my hip.

I smile, using my thumb to turn the silver ring around my finger. Let them gossip. Yes, I'm a woman with a sword. I protected my house from invasion and helped turn the tide of the fighting in my town. I proved my worth and my skill with a blade. And while there hadn't been time to have Guardian reforged before conflict descended upon my town, Moon served me well, singing her song as I wielded her to protect what was mine.

And I heard him. His voice was there in my head with the remnants of every lesson. My sensei was with me, almost as if he was holding my hand through the exhausting days and the terrifying nights of attacks ... of the fires and the screams ... of the pounding of horse's hooves and the thud of leather armor ... of the blood.

When our feudal lord's Samurai arrived, defeating the invaders, the dust had barely settled before I gathered the pieces of Guardian, embarking on the four-day trip to the nearest master swordsmith. Of course, being a woman kept me from darkening his doorway, but I managed to hire a young lad to pretend the commission was his. When the time finally came, and Guardian was back in my hands, I gripped the hilt so tightly, my knuckles turned white, and my arms shook. I strained, listening, praying ... even knowing my hope was folly.

He wasn't there.

I finish my tea, staring at the faint scars on my hands as I slip a few coins on the table before I stand. I nod with a smile at the scowling men, resting my hand on Guardian's hilt as I step out into the early afternoon sunlight. A grey cat crosses my path, and I pause. The small feline darts towards the shadows between two buildings, then stops. It looks back at me, its ears twitching, its bright green eyes blinking at me before it walks off with a flick of its tail. Watching it go, my eyes unfocus as I think of the latest letters I sent out in my search for something—anything, no matter how small or obscure—that might bring Guardian back to me.

No matter how well I tend it, the shark skin of his hilt is now faded and starting to peel. I'll need to have it re-wrapped soon, but I'll hold on to the original binding as long as I can. Every time I draw the blade, I hear his gruff voice correcting my form. I see his smile as he praises me. I hear him telling me to tighten my core, to relax my shoulders, to make every move count.

Guardian is with me.

And so is the guilt. It's so deep and oppressive, I've forgotten what it feels like to live without the acidic pit of remorse and shame eating away at my stomach.

As I stride down the road, my fingers twirl the wood pendant of Moon around my neck and my thumb caresses the ring I had made from a piece of Guardian's original blade. I've never taken it off, and I never will. Guardian is mine, and I'm his ... forever, until I find a way to bring him back or until I die.

And until then ...

A smile lifts my cheeks as the red banner comes into view, the slightly faded crest of my late husband's family proudly centered. The excited chatter of young girls spills out of the small building.

I duck into the modest space, and eight pairs of eager eyes stare at me before the girls bow, all chiming, "Hello, Sensei."

I bow to them, hiding the tears that well in my eyes until I can blink them away. I stand, my smile firmly in place as I say, "Hello, students. Everyone grab your bokken and let's begin."

The End

Reviews are so so so important, especially for smaller authors like myself. Please leave a review. It doesn't have to be detailed ... even a simple star rating helps.

ALSO BY T. B. WIESE

Scan the code below for links to my Amazon author page where you'll find the next book in this series as well as all my other books.

You'll also find a link to my website for signed books and swag.

ACKNOWLEDGMENTS

A huge thank you to my readers. Without you, this crazy dream of being an author would not be possible.

To all my sensitivity, beta & ARC readers, thank you! You had a big hand in making this novel what it is today.

Thank you to 小林 ナギ. Your insightful editing took this story to a whole other level!

And lastly, I want to thank all my friends and family for cheering me on and being as excited about my characters as I am—I love my tribe.

ABOUT THE AUTHOR

T. B. Wiese is a military spouse, dog mom, photographer, Disney nerd, and lover of spicy fantasy. She loves animals (She grew up with dogs and working with horses, including working at the Tri-Circle D Ranch at Disney World), so don't be surprised when you find yourself reading lovable animal characters in her novels.

If you'd like to keep up to date with future releases as well as new swag and sales, sign up for her newsletter via link in code below.

SCAN THE CODE WITH YOUR CAMERA APP FOR HER SOCIAL LINKS